Praise for

# ENORMITY

"Full of playful ideas leavened with lots of sex, *Enormity* is a witty excursion into male fantasy that will appeal to readers who enjoy authors such as Max Barry or James Hawes. Milligan writes with ease and exuberance and this fun novel is ideal for a rainy day in bed."
*The Australian*

"Raunchy and rowdy, poetic and perplexing, Milligan's *Enormity* is aptly named. Much like another favorite Aussie export, Nick Cave, Milligan doesn't shy away from the grotesque and the absurd as he shines his light on the terrible beauty of the human condition. This is compelling fiction that leaves you wanting more..."
*Jace Everett, American songwriter,* True Blood *theme 'Bad Things'*

"A satisfyingly gritty novel which maintains its integrity and keeps you picking it back up immediately after you put it down. One of those special reads that gets stuck in your head long after you have devoured the last page."
*Melody Pool, Australian songwriter*

"*Enormity* is genuinely hilarious, often scary, bizarre, consistently moving, sexy as hell, and packs one hell of a soundtrack. For those who like fiction drawn outside the box, this genre-bending read is highly recommended."
*Aaron Dries, author of* House of Sighs, The Fallen Boys *and* A Place for Sinners

"This book has it all. Intense imagery. Brilliant insights into the darker aspects of the male psyche. Not to mention sex, drugs and giant alien spiders! Milligan has delivered a vivid sci-fi epic with the greatest subliminal soundtrack since Nick Hornby's *High Fidelity*. I hope it's the first book in a new genre: neon-sci-fi."
*Dr Mitchell Hobbs, Lecturer in Media and Public Relations, University of Sydney*

Happy
Birthday
Grandma
I love you
and I hope yo
enjoy this book
~ Princess ♡
:)

HAPPY HAPPY
Birthday MOM
I thought you
Might ENJOY
this BOOK with
A glass of wine
I glass of wine
LOL with love
FROM LISA
Its FROM
The movie
Yesterday

# ENORMITY

NICK MILLIGAN

Second Print Edition, October 2014
© Copyright 2013 by Nicholas Milligan

For more information on the author visit
www.nicholasmilligan.com

ISBN-10:
0-9922724-4-0
ISBN-13:
978-0-9922724-4-9

*First and foremost I need to thank my beautiful Amanda for her constant love and support. You are an everlasting source of inspiration and the centre of my universe.*
*I also need to thank my friends and family members who have shown an interest in* Enormity *– your frequent inquiries about my progress have fuelled me during this four-year labour of love.*
*Thank you to Joe and Miriam for reading the first draft of* Enormity *and providing positive feedback. Both of you gave me extra faith that there was a method to my madness.*

enormity

*noun*

1. outrageous or heinous character; atrociousness; an outrageous or heinous act; evil: *the enormity of war crimes.*

2. greatness of size, scope, extent, or influence; immensity: *the enormity of the situation dawned on them.*

# CHAPTER ONE

Norman is a mobile phone. The name was Dylan's idea. I suppose he felt it was an unassuming title. Dylan's humour not only extends to naming communicative devices, but also to the idea of having our very own sex line. 'Why not give the fans access?' That's a justification Dylan frequents. Give the fans access. Why not?

The band has dropped by my apartment for what was promised to be a "quick visit". Good thing I didn't have plans.

Dylan, our lead guitarist, turns on Norman. "Four hundred and eighty-seven," he smiles. That's about the average. Dylan cycles through the text messages, occasionally stopping to read one. "There's a few from that Emily chick. Remember the one from Estoria? There's three from that girl that does marketing for Piper Dawn whiskey."

While some bands covet privacy, we have Norman. When the mood takes us we can turn on the tap and let groupies trickle forth. Sometimes they gush. Even the world's biggest rock band needs to socialise.

"Is there a message from those girls at the Waverley gig last month?" asks Emerson from the balcony door. Emerson is our bass player. He draws on the joint in his hand.

"Not sure," says Dylan. "I think this message might be. Was one of them called Suzanne?"

"I think so," says Emerson. "Someone put on some music."

Our drummer, Cohen, walks over to the stereo and puts on a

1

mixtape. Emerson nods and smiles as he draws on the joint again. The song is interrupted as Norman starts ringing. The ring tone reminds me of a Kinks song.

Dylan grins and answers. "You've called the Big Bang Theory love line. How may we be of service?"

I can hear a girl's laughter buzz in the phone, before I join Emerson out on the balcony.

"Big Bang Theory love line," chuckles Emerson. He hands me the spliff. "We're going to Hell."

I take a draw. "Yep," I agree. "There's definitely four beds waiting."

I peer out across the harbour and the neighbouring city. It's certainly a beautiful part of the universe that I've found myself in. This is a vibrant metropolis with a thriving underground culture. There's some artists with integrity and some without. Some people are cool because they're fucking cool, not because of the brand of sweater they wear. You just have to navigate your way through society. The girls in this town are crazy. Good crazy, not bad crazy. They're all beautiful and dangerous. Sometimes I get scared even dipping my toe in the water. It reminds me of the time I went fishing on a trout farm. I caught my weight in fish, but it was a hollow victory.

The city echoes and blinks in this midnight hour, bodies swarming between shadows and streetlights. The water in the harbour looks like oil, black and deep. My mobile phone rings. I pull it from the pocket of my jeans. It's our manager. I don't answer.

"Was that Amelia?" asks Emerson.

"Yeah."

"Probably calling about the meeting she's been trying to organise."

"Yeah," I reply again. "Pointless though."

"I suppose we need to get our story straight," says Emerson, as he finishes the joint and flicks the butt over the balcony railing. From this height it could land four blocks away.

"We don't need a story," I say. "It has nothing to do with us. The clowns in the media can keep their trapeze to themselves."

Emerson smiles. "You know what? We need to get fucked up."

"There's spirits in the freezer."

A comedy show plays on the TV and the sound is turned down.

2

It reminds me of an old British sketch show. *Monty Python* or the like. *The Mighty Boosh* even.

Dylan passes around a small bag of pills. They're fairly popular at the moment. Very similar to ecstasy. Barely any come down. We decide to double dunk rather than have just one. It tends to get the ball rolling slightly faster. Cohen racks up a pill and a few lines of gas. That can get the ball rolling too.

I feel the energy begin to well inside me. It's like ascending a rollercoaster, with pressure building in your chest. Soon the pipe will burst and I'll saturate the room with love and seemingly logical enthusiasm. The lyrics of the music that hums in the air will take on new meaning. They will transcend the embrace of sound waves and become something spiritual. I close my eyes. One of Big Bang Theory's songs has come over the speakers. Out loud I'm singing words that I didn't write, but released as my own. They're the lyrics of David McComb. They reply to me from somewhere in my childhood. The grass growing, the sun burning, the rain falling and sin leaving fiery little holes.

When I open my eyes again I've returned to the balcony. There's a girl smiling at me from across the table. She's one of three girls that Dylan has invited over. They were "in the area". Thanks, Norman. The girl keeps staring at me. She's clearly taken pills too, as her pupils are non-existent. Black fiery holes. Her friend is over by the balcony's railing, showing Dylan her breasts. Apparently they're fake. Dylan squeezes one of them inquisitively. He smiles and says, "They're fucking amazing. How much did they cost again?"

Emerson and Cohen are sitting next to me chatting to the third girl, who sits at the opposite end of my outdoor dining setting. Things seem cosy between the three. I smile and nod at the girl staring at me, and then push my chair away and walk inside to the stereo and put on some electronica. It adds to the experience. Always seems apt during the witching hour.

The two pills I've ingested begin to take full effect and I feel it displace all inhibition. I go to the kitchen and pour myself a rum and cola. Stepping out onto the balcony Dylan rushes to my side, throwing his arm around my shoulder. He's shirtless, sweating, wearing his skinny black jeans. He gestures toward the girl whose chest he has been assessing.

"Jack, this is Ebony. You've got to see her chest. They're not real, but you really can't tell. They cost her fifteen thousand!" He leads me, with a sense of urgency, to the balcony railing to meet Ebony's chest. She smiles at me, her pupils as big as dinner plates. Straight, blonde hair falls down her thin back.

"So," I say, dryly. "Dylan tells me you've had some work done."

"Yes," says Ebony. Slowly lifting her singlet top she reveals two perfectly shaped, yet surprisingly natural looking, breasts. She takes one of my hands and places it on the left one. I feel her nipple press into the palm of my hand as I study her with my fingers. They do feel incredible. Ebony moves my hand to where I should be able to feel the edge of the implant. It's definable, but not obvious.

Dylan shakes his head, giving me his 'Can-you-fucking-believe-this?' stare. He gives that a lot. He has no pupils either. He swiftly shoves a cigarette in my mouth and lights it. "Dude," he says.

"Dude," I respond. Dude is a word I brought with me.

Ebony pulls down her top and says to me, "Have you guys got any pills? I peaked, like, an hour ago."

"With a chest like that, you're always peaking," smiles Dylan. He reaches into his back pocket and pulls out a small bag. "You can have one of mine, but you have to come get it." He sticks out his tongue and places a pill on its tip.

Ebony smiles as she leans in to place her mouth over his. The encounter goes beyond the simple exchanging of a pill. They continue to kiss each other in a way that only fucked up people can. I turn and walk over to the outdoor setting, where both of the other girls are still sitting. Emerson and Cohen share a joint.

Cohen introduces me to the girls. I don't retain names very well when I'm this messy. But one is a tall, slender redhead with milky white skin. Possibly eighteen, but she could be any age you want her to be. The other is also a redhead, whose long straight hair and fringe are obviously dyed. But it looks good. She has a petite, lean body and a thin silver ring piercing the left side of her nose.

Cohen tells me they're both models. They giggle when he reveals this. Embarrassed, perhaps. I say hello to them. Introduce myself. It's nice to meet me, they say. "Pleasure," I say. I ask them if they like Big Bang Theory, which I'll later remember and feel disgusted about. They laugh and say "of course". I ask them what sort of modeling they do. They do all sorts of modeling. Mostly magazine stuff. Adverts and fashion shoots.

My mind darts backward in time. Once when we were on tour

4

we convinced two female catwalk models to have sex with each other in my hotel room. Cohen and I watched. It was one of the most primal moments of my life. I was quite sober while it was happening so I have a clear memory of it. Cohen was quite drunk, but his eyes were wide. Focused. I suppose it reminded me that civilisation is a facade. At the end of the day, we're still living in caves and walking on all fours. That's why dogs are a man's best friend. They say diamonds are a girl's best friend. Perhaps that's what separates the sexes. Men think like werewolves and women hunger for security.

The redhead laughs and points to Ebony and Dylan, who are still kissing. "Oh my god, she's such a trashbag," says the redhead.

"Aren't you girls trashbags?" I ask.

"No!" says the short redhead, pretending to be offended.

"I hope you don't mind me saying, but you both seem a little trashy," I say. They will agree with everything I say.

Cohen laughs. Emerson grins as he draws on the last of a joint. The girls pretend to be shocked, but they're not offended. In this city, the term 'trashbag' is a badge of honour.

As the drugs inside me reach another peak, the rush forces me to excuse myself from the table and walk briskly inside. I step down the hallway and into my bedroom, where I close the door behind me. Two of the walls of my bedroom are mirrored. There's wardrobes behind them. I look at myself. I'm sweating. Eyes are massive. Skin decidedly pale. More so than usual. I close my eyes and I can almost feel the blood rushing through my veins and arteries.

As I sat talking to the girls on the balcony, a song entered my head. I don't know why. I haven't heard it in years. But it's suddenly taken a hold of me and I'm overwhelmed by it.

I pick up the acoustic guitar that sits in the corner of the room and perch on the end of my bed. I stare at a point on the wall, trying to remember the chords. All I have is the melody.

I begin to sing at the bottom of my register, my voice guttural and deep. I croon the words of a man who has seen the future and where it ends. Drenched in his hedonistic pastimes he watches the fabric of society fray with the smug, fatalistic glee of the Devil. As I sing the words I realise that I can see the future, a growing, black shape in the mist. It approaches and it comes for only me. No one is spared. It finds me here veiled in vapour, across an expanse that has no time or volume that I can measure. I have brought it here and no one will be spared.

My mind begins to whirl with surprising clarity. A revelation. Something that had been lost in the past is uncovered. Like all things. I continue to play with light, picking fingers. The words are in my brain and I remember them. Fists rising up through the dirt. A face that's aged but I'll always recognise. A Leonard Cohen song.

Then another melody enters my mind and I use it like a crowbar to open the box. My fingers stop playing and I sing lyrics. It's another song by Leonard. The story of a man held prisoner by his music, tied down and trapped by the angels that whisper his inspiration. But it's also a man who finds refuge in music. It both protects and ensnares. The gift and curse of music. A man condemned somewhere in a tower.

I stare into the mirror across from the bed, wondering why a Cohen song appeared in my mind. My drummer's name is also Cohen. What does that mean? Does it mean nothing? Does it mean everything?

A knock at my bedroom door breaks the spell. I put my guitar down. "Who is it?"

The door opens. It's the two redheads. They've clearly lost interest in the balcony.

"I'm so sorry, we didn't mean to interrupt you," says the tall redhead.

"That's okay," I reply. "Come in."

I'm not sure how long I was asleep. Can't have been more than three hours. I'm still buzzing way too much. On either side of me sleeps a naked girl. Their long hair spreads across the pillows and on to my shoulders. I sit up slightly. There are thin beams of light coming through the window. My guitar lies on its back in the middle of the bedroom floor. I'm grinding my jaw. Clenching.

The shorter redhead, on my left, has a tattoo on her lower back. Just above the cleft of her buttocks. It's of a bird. Its feathers are dark, and as I lean closer I deduce that they're also ruffled. I lightly trace my finger across the tattoo and it stirs its owner. I roll on top of her body, as she lies on her stomach. Her eyelids part. She is looking back at me, smiling. I smell her hair and lightly bite the back of her neck.

The mattress rocks slightly as I penetrate her. She pushes her

6

face into the pillow, in a vain attempt to stifle her moans. The taller redhead wakes up and still drowsy, lies on her back and watches us. Taking a cigarette from the packet on the bedside table, she lights it and rolls on her side, propping her head on her hand, long red hair cascading down her naked chest. She drags on the cigarette, studying us, before finally saying in a soft voice, "You both look so beautiful."

Two suns burn somewhere beyond the shade umbrella. I can feel the heat of the day radiating through my aviator sunglasses. It's only two hours into the afternoon but I've decided to take a pill. I can feel it kick in as the waitress approaches my table.

I'm a regular here at Zunge Bohne. It's walking distance from my building. I feel a slight pang of guilt because I slept with this waitress a few months ago and I've completely forgotten her name. Total mind blank.

"How are you, Jack?" asks the waitress, her blonde hair up in a ponytail.

"I'm very well, gorgeous. How are you?"

"I'm fine," she replies. "I've had a lot of assignments."

"How have they turned out?" I ask. I believe her name is Rose.

"I think they've gone fine. So are you staying out of trouble?"

"I'm trying... but it's not staying out of me."

The waitress, whose name I decide *is* Rose, rolls her eyes.

"Just a black coffee," I add.

"Anything to eat?"

"No, not at the moment."

Rose smiles. "I've never seen you eat."

That is technically not true. "I don't have much of an appetite."

"Depends what you're offered?" she asks, wryly.

I smile. "So how's that coffee coming along?"

Rose turns on her heel and walks away. Not entirely professional table service banter, but she knows I won't complain to her manager. Like most people who aren't from my rock band world, she has been raised to distance herself from drugs and those that digest them. I was pretty fucked up when I met her. I suspect she feels I used her for sex. I got what I wanted.

Rose is nineteen. I remember that. I think. I remember her naked body. The shape of her breasts. Her hips. Her thighs. She told me I didn't have to wear a condom so, of course, I didn't. Like

7

so many girls I sleep with, I felt some small connection with her. But any emotions are lost in the whirlwind blur of my drug use. I imagine things that didn't happen and forget things that did. Looking at her now I'm reminded how stunning she is. I took that for granted.

I reach for the newspaper that's been left at my table. Despite my lowered ability to concentrate, I scan what's making news. The lead story on page two is about a man, a wannabe militant, who booby-trapped his front door with a homemade explosive because he was suspicious that his elderly landlady was sneaking into his home when he wasn't there. They only found parts of his landlady, who was mostly disintegrated in the explosion. She *had* been entering his home. I guess he wasn't crazy after all. The substance that the tenant used to create the explosion was not illegal and his landlady had been trespassing. It's believed he won't face any charges. Loopholes, baby. They're a very popular hole.

The front page is equally gruesome. Five catwalk models were in an elevator when a malfunction caused it to free-fall over forty storeys. Three of the models lived, but they were each paralysed from the neck down. One of them lost an arm. From looking at the photo of her she already didn't weigh much. One was killed on impact. The other was launched through the roof of the elevator and decapitated by a flailing cable. 'Model Carnage' reads the headline.

Deeper in the newspaper there's a few stories about missing girls. Smiling faces whose parents want them back. Young women often take off into the world, but the newspaper thinks it has found a suspicious pattern. I don't read on. A few pages further I come across an article about a new government campaign. Very thin, attractive people will be used in a series of billboards that will read 'You could look like this'. The initiative will attempt to curve the obesity epidemic. The only obese people I know personally are either fans or lighting technicians.

Rose returns with my coffee.

"Thank you," I say.

"Pleasure," says Rose, before turning back to the counter.

"Hold for a moment," I say.

Rose stops. "Yes?"

"Do you want to go for a drink some time?"

Rose glares. "Are you asking me if I want another night with

8

you?"

"No," I reply, firmly. "Just a drink. If you're worried, we can meet in a public place. In the daylight. Similar to this."

Rose leans close to my face and says in a low voice. "You think you can treat women any way you want, don't you Jack?"

I pick up my spoon and put it in my coffee. I don't respond.

"When I slept with you," continues Rose, "I was not only drunk, but I had you on a pedestal. You are no longer on that pedestal. You think I'm going to offer myself to you the second you give me the green light?"

"What colour would you prefer?" I ask, pulling a small bag of cane from my pocket and tipping it into my coffee. Rose looks appalled and walks away. I stir in the white powder and sip slowly on the black, boiling liquid. She's either a very good actress or she doesn't like me.


It's nearly seven hours into the afternoon and the suns are ducking behind the horizon. The children of the night are getting dressed, applying make-up and staring at themselves in the mirror. If they're anything like me, they'll be getting their drugs in order.

I'm sitting on my balcony table, looking at my supplies. Twelve pills. Two points of gas. Two grams of cane. I pour a glass of red wine from the bottle in front of me.

I stare at the horizon, which I've been doing a lot of lately. Both suns sit on the city's skyline. Two orange semi-circles. This planet has a strange axis and the suns move on a steeped angle across the sky, never quite appearing directly overhead. This is a city of long shadows, even in the middle of the day. Some of the planet's areas are almost completely in darkness for every hour. The nightclubs in those places are amazing.

Across from my balcony on the side of a towering skyscraper is a billboard. The image, which is nine storeys high, features a slim, athletic female model. Her coquettish expression stares at me. Below her read the words, 'You could look like this'. Below that is the number for a weight loss hotline. Food for thought.

When I'm as pensive as I am now, I often sing to myself. I get emotional sometimes. I remember the lyrics to a song that's stranded on Earth. If only I'd brought my records with me. Big Bang Theory is a way to keep that music in my life. Recording the past. Trapping ghosts.

I light a cigarette and sing 'How To Make Gravy' by Paul Kelly. Nothing but the cooling evening air to hear me. Then I wash down a pill with my wine and sing 'Kissing The Lipless' by The Shins. Then I rack a line of cane and sing 'The End' by Ryan Adams. As the drugs numb everything but my burgeoning euphoria, I almost feel at peace.

I lift the bottle of red wine again to fill my glass. It's only a quarter of its original weight. My leg bounces as I tap my feet. I think about our record label and their recent inquiries into my songwriting. They're hoping for another album soon. They've become accustomed to my prolific output. It's only been six months since our last release, but I feel a need to slow down. I don't know where my memory ends and when my recollections of songs will wither. Fountains surely don't last an eternity. The blurring of the weeks erases my sense of time and there are so many genres I want to explore. I'm either off my face or I'm recovering long enough to be off my face again.

My mobile phone rings. It's Dylan.

"Are you going tonight?" he asks.

"I'm undecided."

"Be reasonable. We should be seen at this thing."

"Wouldn't it be cooler if we *didn't* go?"

"Fuck that. I need something to do before I head to Lycan. I'm meeting some girls there at the second hour."

What Dylan doesn't realise is that I'm already going to the book launch. The author, a young gay guy called Mason Wagner, is hot shit at the moment. His new book is called *Misspent Youth*. Apparently he's the voice of a generation, capturing the mindset of disenchanted teenagers. The souls who only value a lack of values. Drugs, sex and socialising are the only currencies in their gritty underbelly and mummies and daddies everywhere are wondering where they went wrong as moral guides. Big Bang Theory provides much of the soundtrack to this sordid world.

Wagner is an uninspiring writer, but a former liaison of mine, Jemima, is his publicist and she will be there. This will mean that I'm not invited but I've lost all sense of boundaries and barricades. Doors open for Jack. Legs, too.

"Okay, I'll go," I reply.

"You sick fucker," says Dylan. "How many pills have you got?"

"Six," I reply, bending the truth.

"I'm low too," says Dylan. "Someone there will have some anyway."

"Just ask Wagner. Apparently he practices what he preaches."

"Fuck, I hope not. Depraved lunatic," responds Dylan, who doesn't seem entirely lucid. "Is Jemima still his publicist?"

"Not sure."

Dylan's limousine picks me up outside my apartment building. The record label pays for all of our travel. They claim it's because they want us to be comfortable and looked after, but it's really because they think we'll kill ourselves. They know better than to let their cash cows get behind a wheel.

The book launch is at a place called Pier Five. It's a rustic establishment. Imagine having a cocktail on a dilapidated jetty. It's beyond exclusive, with dank décor and masturbatory fashion and clientele. I take another pill before exiting the limousine. Dylan passes me the final sip of his sparkling wine and I finish it.

Pier Five is down an alleyway that opens off one of the main streets of Easton. It's an expensive area to live. Tonight a red carpet runs the length of the alley, ending at the entrance to Pier Five. As we step on to it, banks of photographers spot us and in a second we're blinded by exploding light. Dylan smiles at me. He loves the attention. It seems to make him more powerful. I, on the other hand, am feeling way too hectic to enjoy myself.

We get to the end of the carpet where Jemima stands, wearing a headset and holding a clipboard. She's not impressed to see me.

"Names?" she asks, incredulously.

Dylan laughs. "How cute! Well, my name is Mason Wagner and this is my gay lover, Jack."

"You two are not on the list."

"But it's my fucking book launch!" says Dylan, with mock camp.

As Jemima looks set to dig her heels in, a young man in a vibrant orange suit appears in Pier Five's doorway.

"Jack! Dylan!" exclaims Mason Wagner.

"Mr Wagner," smiles Dylan, and casually gives him a kiss on the cheek.

"You two look incredible," says Mason, who throws his arms around me in an exaggerated embrace. "I didn't even know you were coming!"

"Well," I say, "we wanted to show our support for the voice of a generation."

"You're such a sweetheart, Jack. But I think you'll find that *you're* the voice of a generation," says Mason, giving me a playful slap on the shoulder.

"Well, maybe there's two voices!" says Dylan. "You're a duo." His drugs have definitely kicked in.

Jemima gives me a subtle death stare. She knows I hate Mason's books.

"Enough chat!" says Mason. "You two need to get in there and start drinking all of that disgustingly expensive alcohol."

"If you insist," smiles Dylan.

I feel compelled to talk to Jemima, but there's a growing queue of people on the red carpet behind us and she may need to calm down.

As we step into Pier Five, I'm reminded that the most satisfying aspect of being a celebrity is walking into a room. I rarely like what's in the room, but walking in is always moreish.

The bar in Pier Five is made from wood panelling, as are the walls. The bar staff, both male and female, wear pseudo sailor outfits. I order a rum and cola. Dylan orders a sparkling wine. The best quality sparklings are incredibly expensive and source their flavour from a small flowering fruit tree called an astoria. The fruit are small and round, not dissimilar from grapes. Dylan has been known to take baths in sparkling wine. Because he can.

There's a woman standing beside us in the queue who has unspeakably large breasts. I glance at Dylan and see that she's already on his radar.

"What's your name?" I ask her.

"Ariana," says the girl, as I shake her hand.

"I'm Jack and this is Dylan," I reply.

"Yes, I know," smiles Ariana.

"That's an incredible outfit," says Dylan, who lightly touches her shoulder, near the left strap of her dress.

"Oh... thank you," blushes Ariana. "I really like your band," she says, loudly, to be heard over the DJ.

"Why, thank you," I say.

"I saw you guys at The Exile. I thought it was a really amazing show."

"That was a lot of fun," says Dylan. "Good energy."

"Definitely!" says Ariana. "So what are you guys up to this

evening?"

"Nothing too hectic," I reply. "Just here to support Mason."

"Isn't his book *so* amazing?" gushes Ariana.

Dylan nods. "He's the voice of a generation," he says, with a shrug.

Our drinks arrive and I can sense the queue behind us growing restless. "It was nice to meet you, Ariana, but we should let you get back to your boyfriend," I say.

"Oh, no," giggles Ariana, "I'm single actually. I'm just here with some girlfriends."

"Well, then," says Dylan, "lead the way."

Once Ariana has received a drink, we follow her through the crowd towards a booth where her friends are sitting. A social pages photographer appears and fires off a few shots at Dylan and I. Dylan sticks his tongue out at the camera.

In the booth we join Ariana's two friends, who seem to recognise us, but their pupils are wide and dark and I wonder how much cognition they're capable of. There's an air of frivolity around our new friends, and as my drugs suddenly peak I feel adrift and almost removed from myself. A world where anything is possible.

Dylan starts chatting to our two new friends, while I make some casual conversation with Ariana, who sits on my left. She's clearly drunk and her cheeks are flushed a rose pink. She lightly touches one of her giant silver hoop earrings and twirls some of her long brown hair. Dylan says something loudly to Ariana's friends, whose names I've already forgotten, and they both look at me and laugh wildly. I blow Dylan a kiss and he throws a small paper umbrella at me.

"It's okay," says one of the girls, who sits to my right, as she leans into me. "Dylan is being obnoxious."

"Really?" I say, then my mind goes blank and I have nothing else to say. My attempt at speech is interrupted when I feel Ariana's right hand place itself on my left thigh.

Her friend notices and says, "Ariana, are you being dirty?" with mock disgust.

Ariana says nothing and smiles, her eyes only partly open. "What if I am, Bree?"

Bree then puts her arm around my shoulder and whispers in my ear, "Let me know if you want me to protect you from Ariana. She can be a little forward." Bree places her hand on my right thigh, her manicured fingernails lightly grazing the crotch of my jeans.

"I'm not a fan of protection," I say, glancing at Bree's cleavage, which is now in close proximity. I'm suddenly aware of Bree's perfume as she leans further into me, her red lips lightly touching my neck.

I notice that Dylan has started kissing the second of Ariana's friends, leaving me to negotiate Ariana and Bree, who are becoming increasingly direct with their hands.

"So," I say loudly, the sounds of the DJ booth pumping a sonic heartbeat through the club, "what brings you girls to the party?"

Ariana looks a little too messy to answer. She doesn't. Bree smiles. "My cousin works for the publishing company. She got us in."

"Have you read Mason's book?" I ask.

"Not yet," says Bree. "I usually wait for the movie."

"The book's sometimes better," says Ariana, who rests her head on my shoulder, lips smiling, eyes shut. Her hand finds the zipper of my jeans and slowly pulls it down. My head is spinning from the drugs and I do nothing to stop her. Bree then turns my face towards her and starts kissing me. As my tongue pushes against hers, I feel as though I've left my body. I'm hovering somewhere above the booth, watching myself be devoured. No boundaries. No barricades.

Ariana then pulls me from Bree and pushes her mouth against mine. While I kiss Ariana, Bree slides her hand into my jeans and wraps her fingers around my growing erection. Instinctively, I glance sideways at the room as Ariana is pushing her tongue into my mouth. Few people in the crowd are watching us. But I see a pair of bedroom blue eyes staring from across the room. Jemima. We make eye contact and she turns and quickly disappears further into the club.

I unlock my mouth from Ariana's and gently put a stop to Bree's fervent stroking. "I've got to get some fresh air," I say, the room spinning. "To be continued." I climb on to the booth's table and escape. I scan the room for Jemima, almost forgetting to zip my jeans. I head for the entrance and find that Jemima is no longer on the door. Another publicist has replaced her. When I turn to head back inside, I'm face to face with my target.

"Hi," I say, my mouth numb. "I was looking for you."

"Don't," says Jemima.

"I have to. It's a compulsion. Irrational."

14

"You shouldn't be here. You weren't invited."

"I'm always invited," I reply, putting my hand against the wall of Pier Five's entry to steady myself. "I'm never *on* the list, I *am* the list."

"Tonight is a big night for me and it's incredibly unfair for you to show up," she says, scowling.

"And it's fair for you to ignore me for four months?"

"No, it's not fair. Fair would be to have you castrated."

"Let's not forget which one of us is married," I say.

"Fuck you," says Jemima, quietly. "I was one week away from leaving him. One fucking week..."

"So you told me," I reply. "You were always a week away."

Jemima throws her hands up. "This is why I've ignored you for four months! I don't want to have this conversation. I want you as far out of my life as possible." She pushes past me, up the red carpet and into the rows of human traffic that flood the streets of Easton.

Back inside the club, Dylan is entertaining Ariana, Bree and their friend. I rejoin them in the booth and Dylan exclaims, "Jack's back!" He extends his hand and I see he's holding a pill. I let him drop it in my mouth and then he offers his sparkling wine for me to wash it down.

"Let's get the fuck out of here," I say.

"Yeah, absolutely," says Dylan, rubbing his hands together. "Let's get somewhere a bit more primitive."

"Vial," I say.

"Vial, alright," smiles Dylan. "We can head there before Lycan."

"Vial? We've never been able to get in there! There's always a massive line and you have to know someone," says Bree.

I lean in close to Bree. "Guess what?"

"What?" she replies.

"We know someone."

A limousine drives the five of us across town. I learn that the third girl in our party is called Vivienne. She's strawberry blonde, tanned and athletically built. Dylan's type. Anyone's type.

We arrive at Vial, an incredibly exclusive nightclub where they serve mixed shots in test tubes. Potent elixirs, but when you're buzzing out of your brain like we are, you need a strong hit to feel anything.

As always there's a long queue to get into Vial. In reality, very few of these people will actually make it inside tonight. But they're happy to stand, smoke, take drugs and try their luck. Some of them are purely interested in seeing which celebrities might turn up. It's no surprise that when Dylan and I exit the limousine with our three companions, the queue erupts in high-pitched squealing and camera flashes. Dylan and I walk briskly toward the entrance, motion to the four giant security guards that we're a party of five, and then we all step inside.

Vial isn't over crowded, which is nice. There's a good vibe. Lots of familiar faces from television and film. As we head toward the bar, I feel someone grab my arm. It's a guy called Conway. He's the host of a morning children's program. He looks badly caned. There's even some blood dripping from his nose.

"Jack! Baby! How are you?" yells Conway, and hugs me. I recoil slightly to avoid his weeping nostril.

"Conway, I'm grand. You look like you're having fun." I raise a hand to my own nostril to indicate that he should check his.

Conway lifts a finger and dabs the blood on his top lip. Upon seeing the crimson smear on his fingertip, he smiles, awkwardly. "Wow. Looks like mischief. I wonder how that happened...?"

Dylan leans in and says to Conway, "Go hard or go home! That's my motto. At least you didn't bleed on one of your furry co-hosts."

Conway smiles, meekly, and makes a dash for the men's room.

"Loose bastard," says Dylan, watching him scamper. Then he suggests to our three new friends, "Let's get some more fluid. My charity."

The rest of the night slips into a blur and passes me by. I was there the whole time, but in some ways I wasn't. I just watched it all happen in fast forward, picking up plot points without sound. This person took that drug. This person kissed that person. At some point the suns rise and we're out on my balcony. Soon after, in my bedroom, the curtains are closed and a woman is doing things to me. Then a second woman takes her place. But it could be the same woman. Then once the narrative has resolved itself, the story ends and I press stop.

# CHAPTER TWO

When I wake up, the suns have set. There's a moment of confusion as I ascertain where I am. I'm on my sofa. There's a faint glow outside, but only enough to create dark shapes. No texture or colour. I reach out for the wine bottle on the coffee table and then remember it's empty. I'm shirtless, wearing only a pair of unbuttoned black jeans. My skull feels like it's packed with ice. The come down. I don't normally have a come down from pills, but I had been awake for forty hours, unable to sleep. I check my phone. I've been passed out for over ten hours.

In the near distance is the sound of music. Droning bass. Electronic samples. The machine-gun jackhammering of dance beats. Deep, throbbing bass grinding back and forth like numb teeth. The music could be a ringing in my ears. I did pass through many nightclubs.

I step across to the balcony and slide open the glass doors. On the outdoor table are a packet of cigarettes and a lighter. I inhale wistfully on a dart, slowly releasing the smoke through my nostrils. I put my feet on the table, reclining, unable to focus on anything. My thoughts chatter to me like a room full of people. I then stand and approach the balcony's railing. Dozens of storeys are crammed below me, each with their own tale to tell. I glance around the neighbouring skyscrapers looking for something interesting. An open window. Couples making love. A glimpse of glistening nudity, fresh from a shower's steam. Nothing. Darkened windows everywhere. A city with nothing to offer unless you forcefully take it. To my right is a new billboard that takes up almost the entire east-facing wall of an office block, lit-up with wide plumes of white spotlight. It features a young actress called Jennifer Fox. Barely nineteen. She's the face of a brand of lingerie. Not that her face is really the focus of the billboard. But she stares at me and I stare back, her giant blue eyes the size of Cadillacs. Her long, teased hair erupts around her seductive face like black magma. Jennifer's wearing black lace and as I study her breasts, wondering if they've been digitally enhanced, I remember that she emailed me last week and that I really should reply. I then work out that the billboard is approximately one hundred and five metres high. That's in Earth measurement.

I decide that I'd like to come down some more and try to sleep, so I venture to the kitchen to look for some painkillers. I have a box of super strength downers that fell off the back of an ambulance. I rifle through my kitchen, but I can't find them. The box isn't in the bedroom or the bathroom either. My frustration simmers beneath the surface, but never amounts to anything. Caring would require too much exertion. I find a bag of pills in my kitchen and take one. Not that it will do much. My body has just about given everything it can, so the entactogen will have little effect.

I wander to my door and put my ear against it. The music is coming from my floor. Hard and fast. There's only four penthouses, so it's not hard to narrow down where it's coming from. When I pull my apartment door ajar, I deduce that there's a party taking place directly across the foyer from me, in apartment 3801. I can hear the occasional excited scream. Female voices yelling. Lying in front of the door is a single tattered streamer, like a long yellow snake on the tiles. Apartment 3801 belongs to a middle-aged couple with a teenage daughter. Her name's Laurie. She knocked on my door one day to get a photo with me and to sign a poster. That was about three years ago, not long after I moved into my penthouse. Every so often I bump into her in the building. We sometimes ride the elevator together. She's an attractive young thing. Laurie often gives me a cheeky grin and suggests that we hang out more often. Like, "properly hang out", as she puts it.

On one occasion, I found a note slipped under my door. I'd just gotten home from tour. It read, "Hey Jack, it's Laurie. My parents have gone away for a week. Got the place to myself. Please come visit

18

*when you're back in town. xx."* Dylan would later curse me for not accepting the invitation.

Before I close the door, I hear the tap of footsteps. I spot one of my neighbours, Mr Roeg, marching across the foyer toward the party. He has an incredibly stern look on his face. Mr Roeg is a midget and besides his small stature, he has a rather unsettling appearance. Not only is he vertically challenged, but he also suffers from a form of alopecia. He has no eyelashes, eyebrows or cranial hair of any kind. He is the sort of fellow that people joke about when his miniscule back is turned, but I get along with him quite well. He can be a little intense. Mr Roeg is independently very wealthy, though he rarely speaks about his profession. He's away a lot on business. Someone once told me he has something to do with art. An art dealer perhaps? I'm also not aware of his first name. He's never offered it. Mr Roeg is also a fan of my band, which is nice.

Mr Roeg spots me peering from behind my apartment door. "Jack!" he says, in his small, nasal voice.

"Hi, Mr Roeg," I reply, warmly.

"Can you believe how loud this music is? I can't hear myself think. The walls of my apartment are shaking!"

"Yeah, they've got some serious equipment in there."

"Well, I've had enough. Just because her parents are away doesn't mean she can disrupt the peace."

"Well, that's what you kids do, isn't it?" I ask. "Have a giant party when you've got the place to yourself?"

I've inadvertently said that Mr Roeg is a child but he doesn't seem to notice.

"Laurie's parents told me she was going to have a small get-together for her twentieth birthday. But they didn't warn me that all hell was going to break loose."

Mr Roeg marches up to the door of Laurie's apartment and pounds his small, pale fist on its surface. He generates a remarkable volume for a small man. I push my door till it's almost shut, peering from the darkness. Mr Roeg knocks a second time. After a small pause the door is flung open. Two girls, both young, caked in make-up and wearing short party dresses, scream when they see Mr Roeg and immediately slam the door. He turns and looks in my direction, embarrassment and disgust already formed on his small, pointy features. He knocks again. This time a third girl opens the door and squeals.

"Oh my god," she yells, drunkenly. "What are you? Go away!"

"Turn that music down!" Mr Roeg yells, in his high nasal tone. "I will call the police!"

The girl stares at him for a moment and then slams the door.

Mr Roeg turns to me again, his pale features now stained pink with anger. He storms across the foyer to my door, which I open.

"Can you believe that?" he asks, puffing.

"Rude little bitches," I say. "They're just drunk."

"I just don't expect to be treated like that in my own building."

"No," I reply. "It's... uncalled for."

"Would you go and speak to them?" he asks, softening his tone. It's a plea for help, rather than a demand. "They'll listen to you."

"That's not necessarily a good thing," I say, unsure of whether I want to be dragged into a penthouse party of drunken, young girls. It would be a very hectic situation for me in my current mental state.

"Well, if they don't listen to you, I'm going to have the whole family evicted."

I know that Mr Roeg is somehow involved with body corporate. He has friends in high places. Well, most of his friends are in a higher place than him. I don't doubt that there is weight to his threat.

"Leave it with me," I say.

Mr Roeg smiles, relieved. "Thank you, Jack. I won't forget it."

"That's fine," I reply. "You just enjoy the rest of your evening. Fix yourself a stiff drink."

Mr Roeg sighs and returns across the wide foyer to his apartment.

I find a t-shirt and a jacket in my bedroom. I then grab the cigarettes and lighter from the balcony. Barefooted, I walk quietly across the foyer, as if in danger of being caught. The bass of the party's music is making the door shake. I can feel it buzz and vibrate beneath my knuckles as I knock loudly on apartment 3801. From within, melted against the sound of the music, are excited female voices. Then the door swings open.

Laurie yells, "Listen you little sh-" Surprise transforms her face as she sees me. "Oh... Jack," she hesitates, drunkenly. "I thought you were Mr..."

"That's okay," I smile. "Mr Roeg sent me about the noise. A few of your guests were rude to him."

"Oh... yeah," says Laurie, slightly embarrassed. She's wearing a short black dress. Her dark brown hair is up in a ponytail, allowing her cute round face enough room to be assessed on its own merits. Her figure is accentuated with rather attractive regions of puppy fat. Laurie's very pretty and obviously intoxicated. She's the kind of girl I would have gazed at in university lectures, undoubtedly the subject of one of my insufferable crushes. I would never have told her she's gorgeous, despite spending much time thinking about it. Right now, Earth Jack would politely ask for the music to be turned down, offer her a small amount of charm and then promptly return to the cold, dark solitude of his apartment. But Earth Jack died somewhere in space.

Over Laurie's shoulder I can see a number of girls, staring at me with shocked expressions. As if I'm not real.

"They were a bit freaked out," says Laurie. "It's a bit to take in if you haven't met him before. My parents told him that I was having my birthday party."

"Sounds like you've got a serious sound-system in there," I say.

"Yeah, my friend's boyfriend brought it over for me and set it up. He's in a band..." she says.

"Cool," I say.

"But they're not very well known. Not like you guys."

"I see."

Laurie is turning pink. "Sorry, I'm a bit drunk," she says.

"That's fine," I smile. "You're the birthday girl. You're allowed to be drunk."

Laurie sees that her friends are staring at us, so she steps outside the door and pulls it shut behind her. Now she's much closer.

"When are you going to invite me over to your apartment?" asks Laurie. "I know you got my note."

Her breath smells like butterscotch liqueur. It's a fragrance that immediately takes me to a barbeque seventeen years ago. In a suburban backyard. The first and last time I drank butterscotch anything. Underneath I can smell perfume. Hints of either citrus or mango.

"I've been real busy."

"Yeah, I'll bet," says Laurie. Her lips look incredibly soft.

"I haven't been home much."

"You were home last night. This morning I saw girls leave your

21

apartment."

"Have you been watching me?"

"I heard girls' voices," shrugs Laurie. "So I opened the door and two redheads were waiting for the elevator."

"Well... I suppose it's quicker than the stairs."

Laurie smiles. "I'm only telling you this because I'm really drunk," she says, gazing up at me. Her face is now dangerously close to my own. "But... I am madly in love with you."

"Is that right?" I reply, lost for words. My frail state of mind offers me very little. "But you don't know me, Laurie. I'm just your neighbour that is way too old for you."

"Age is a state of mind."

"Well then, my current age is *seriously cloudy*. I was up for two days."

"Maybe you shouldn't have redheads over."

"Should I stick to brunettes?"

Laurie pushes her face into mine and for a moment I kiss her back.

"Hang on a second," I say, after my delayed withdrawal. "Ah... I should let you get back to your guests."

Laurie's holding her arms around my waist and is reluctant to let go. "Jack, I think about you. I think about you visiting me." For the second time in the conversation, words are my enemy. They elude me. "I imagine you coming to visit me when I'm home alone," she adds, her voice now twisted with calculated innocence. Deliberate coquettishness. She pushes herself against me and the sensation of her soft flesh and the cocktail of aromas that pour from her arouse me. I'm betrayed by the release of dopamine in my brain.

"That's... nice of you to say."

Laurie tries to kiss me again and I pull away. "I should let you get back to your party."

"Aren't you coming in for a drink?" she asks.

"No," I say. "I shouldn't..."

"But it's my birthday," she probes. "I promise I'll protect you from my friends."

I pause. She takes me by the hands. "One drink," she says.

"Alright," I say. "But only if you turn the damn music down."

Laurie looks at me with quiet triumph. She opens the door and leads me inside. Around the apartment girls are chatting and dancing, squealing and spilling drinks. They're in party dresses.

Laurie introduces me to three girls in the kitchen who are shocked to meet me. Girls dancing in the living room all stop and stare at me. Laurie leaves to turn the music down. Groans erupt from the adjoining room and I hear Laurie say there have been noise complaints. The music then drops to a merciful volume.

"Laurie said you lived across the hall, but we didn't believe her," says one of the girls in the kitchen with me.

"She speaks the truth," I smile.

"We went with Laurie to see you guys at Bradfield Arena," says another girl. "You were really awesome."

"Thank you."

"What was that song you played where you howled like a wolf?" asks the first girl.

"That's a new song," I reply. "It's called 'Fresh Blood'."

"Wow," says the third girl. "It was pretty sexy."

"That's the idea," I chuckle. "Glad you like it."

"Isn't *Fresh Blood* the name of that Mercy Beau Coup record?" asks the first girl.

I think for a moment, slightly panicked. "I'm not sure. Is it?"

"Yeah, it's got a blonde woman on the cover. Dressed in red."

"Oh," I say.

"I really liked that first song you played for the encore," says the third girl. "Was it a new one as well?"

"Yes," I say, trying to remember. "I think so..."

"It had a man's name in it," she says.

"Oh, yeah," I say, remembering. "That was 'Kevin Carter'."

"Who's that?" asks the second girl.

"Uh... just a guy I know. No one in particular," I reply, unable to give any explanation of who the photographer Kevin Carter is, or who the Manic Street Preachers are.

From behind me I hear a girl yell, "Oh my god, is this the stripper?"

I spin around, a little jumpy. The girl recognises me. "Oh... I didn't..."

"Sarah!" yells Laurie at the girl, appearing behind her in the kitchen's doorway. "Leave him alone! He's just visiting. You're going to scare him away."

Laurie brushes past Sarah into the room. "Do you want a drink?" she offers. "Wine?"

"Sure," I say.

Laurie opens the fridge and pours me a glass of Cristalli sparkling wine, her back turned to me. The fridge is overflowing with expensive alcohol. Laurie turns around with an unreadable smile, handing me the beverage. She then leads me from the kitchen, through the candlelit living room to the balcony. Despite the music's lowered volume, girls continue to dance and laugh. They stare at me intently as I step past, transfixed. Glancing around the apartment, I surmise that this residence is the same size as my own. In fact, its layout is identical. Except it's all in reverse. It's an exact mirror image of my home.

The girls on the balcony are equally amazed by my appearance. One girl, without saying anything, rushes and throws her arms around me. Laurie gently tries to pry her away. The girl reluctantly lets go, almost in tears.

"It's cool," I say to Laurie. I extend my hand to the girl. "Hi, I'm Jack."

She shakes my hand, "Maddy," she says softly, her eyes glazed with intoxication. "I love you. I love your music..."

"Thank you. Pleasure." I pull a cigarette from my shirt pocket and light it.

Laurie introduces the half dozen girls in front of me, but I don't remember their names. I raise a polite hand in greeting. I lean on the rail and glance out at the city skyline. It's the reverse view of my own balcony, but it's much of the same. Just more skyscrapers shooting out of streams of neon signage and headlights. You can't see the harbour very well from this side. I conclude that I have a superior view.

"If this music's bothering you, we could put on something else?" offers one girl.

"No, that's fine. I like it."

"You like synthetic music?" asks the girl.

"Yeah, sure."

"So what are you guys doing at the moment?" asks another girl. "When are you going to play live again?"

"We're planning another tour," I say. "Just doing some recording at the moment. Once that's out of the way we'll get back on the road."

"Is it true that you guys are fighting with the Known Associates?" asks another girl.

"Clair!" spits Laurie. "Don't ask him personal questions like that."

"We're not fighting," I say, with a smile. "That's just some media bullshit."

"I also heard you were hooking up with Jennifer Fox?" asks Clair, with a sly grin.

Laurie doesn't cut her off this time. Instead she waits for my answer.

"We're just friends." I say, dragging on my cigarette.

"So where's the rest of the band tonight?" asks another girl.

"Don't know," I shrug. "Don't want to know."

"You should invite Dylan over," says Clair. A few of the other girls nod in agreement. "We'd love to party with Dylan," she adds.

I chuckle. "I'm not sure that would be a good idea."

"Why not?" asks Clair.

"Well... Dylan doesn't party with people. He parties *at* them."

The girls all chirp and flutter at my comment. I've only made him sound more appealing.

One of the girls that was dancing in the living room appears at the balcony door and steps up to me.

"Jack, this is Carrie," says Laurie, introducing her.

"Pleasure," I say, shaking her hand.

"Pleasure," smiles Carrie. "I really love your music."

"Thanks."

Carrie then says to Laurie, "Hey, come inside for a moment. I need to tell you something."

Laurie glances at me, then replies to her, "In a minute. I can't leave Jack here."

"He'll be alright!" says Clair. "We're not going to bite." A few of the other girls laugh.

"I don't trust you, Clair!" smiles Laurie.

"Hey, I'll be fine," I say to Laurie. "What's the worst that can happen?"

Laurie looks uncertain.

"C'mon," says Carrie. "It'll take a minute."

"Okay," says Laurie, reaching out and squeezing my hand. "I'll be right back." Laurie follows Carrie into the apartment.

Laurie's gone for a few minutes. I take a seat amongst the girls on the balcony and chat to them. I take a long sip of my wine and light another cigarette. Many of them go to the same exclusive university as Laurie. Rich girls. Or at least girls with rich parents.

When Laurie returns, she makes an announcement. "Sorry,

everyone. I need to borrow Jack. I promise I'll bring him back."

A few of the girls groan. "Laurie, he's okay here."

"I'll bring him back!" says Laurie, again. She gives me an awkward look and takes my hand, pulling me from my chair and leading me back inside.

"Where are we going?" I ask, as I follow Laurie through the apartment, down the hall.

"I don't want to share you anymore," says Laurie, holding my hand tightly.

We arrive at a door and Laurie pushes it open. It's a bedroom and clearly hers. It's coloured in shades of pink, culminating in a large four-poster bed that is draped with pieces of rose-coloured, sheer material. If this room were any more effeminate, it would have a vagina.

On the bed are two girls, sitting cross-legged. One of them is Carrie.

"This is Taylor," says Laurie, gesturing to the girl I haven't met.

"Pleasure," I say, wandering to the side of the bed. In a rush of delirium I lie next to them, stretching out face down into the mattress.

Carrie says to Taylor, "Time to shoo now."

"Aww, c'mon," groans Taylor. "I'm not going to tell anyone."

"No," says Laurie. "One other person's enough. I'll show it to you after."

"I want to watch!" whispers Taylor, before threatening, "I'll tell everyone."

Laurie huffs, relenting. "Fine. If you're going to stay, then go and lock the door and sit over there," whispers Laurie.

Taylor locks the bedroom door and then sits in a small, ornate seat that's opposite the bed. On the back of the door is a tall poster of me. Almost to scale. It's grainy black and white. My dark leather jacket hangs open to reveal my chiseled abdominal muscles and the sparse, inoffensive hair that spreads across my pectorals and descends in a thin line down my stomach. My jeans are dangerously low. I look sexual. There's a dilapidated brick wall behind me. Industrial chic. I remember being quite hazy when the picture was taken and I think that comes across. I stare through the camera's lens and down at myself lying on Laurie's bed.

Turning my head, I see Laurie eye me with an unreadable expression, as if it's a struggle for her to make eye contact. From beyond the door, someone returns the party's music to a deafening level. I hear screams and cheers. The walls of the bedroom shake and hum.

"Wait," I say, a little groggy. "Tell them to turn the music down..."

"It's alright," says Laurie, with a reassuring smile. "Don't worry about that now."

I sit up, propping myself against Laurie's large, pink pillows like a rag doll, arms draped by my side. I don't have much strength left. My brain buzzes and when I close my eyes for a moment I feel a sensuous burn radiate along my limbs. It feels different to the pill I swallowed in my apartment. When I open my eyes, Laurie is standing by the bed to my left. She lifts up the edges of her dress, finding the waistband of her underwear. She then slides the cotton panties down her creamy thighs and I notice that they have small love-hearts on them. On the right side of the bed Carrie is down on her knees, a digital camera aimed at Laurie and I. I try not to acknowledge that Carrie's filming. Laurie is lightly biting her lower lip as she gazes down at me. When she has stepped out of her underwear, she lowers herself on to the bed and slowly unzips the fly of my jeans. Across the room, Taylor is sitting up in her chair, watching Laurie's hands.

As Laurie strokes me with one hand and lightly grazes my testes with the fingernails of her other, I lean my head back and close my eyes. I feel Laurie's warm tongue begin to knead the tip and then her mouth closes over me, forming suction. I slightly open my eyes and see that Carrie is now kneeling next to us on the bed, the digital camera much closer to my abdomen. Taylor has left her chair and is leaning on the end of the bed, her chin resting in her hands. She watches intently, her eyes shifting between Laurie's head and my face. Although my mind is spinning, it doesn't take long for me to be fully erect. Laurie strokes me slowly, admiring her handiwork.

Taylor is obscured from my vision when Laurie swings a leg over my pelvis and straddles me. She positions herself accordingly and slowly lowers herself on to my cock. Despite the relative tightness of her opening, she takes me in rather easily. Once she has descended to its base, she holds my face in her hands and kisses me on the mouth, forcing her tongue between my lips and against my teeth. Drunken and fervent. From the corner of my eye I see

27

Carrie's camera hovering, capturing the fumbling of our mouths. My arms remain draped by my side as Laurie begins to move herself on me. Her grinding motions search for the correct rotation of my fixed axis. Behind my eyelids I watch circles of colour dance and spin like rainbow constellations.

I hear Laurie say to Carrie, "Are you getting everything?"

"Yes," says Carrie. "It looks so hot."

"Is there still enough battery?" replies Laurie.

"One bar," says Carrie.

"It should be enough," whispers Laurie, as I feel her vagina contract around me. The mattress begins to vibrate beneath us, as if the music has swelled in volume. She slides her arms around my neck in an embrace and rests her cheek against mine.

"It's alright, Jack," she whispers in my ear, her voice now strained with heavy breathing. "You can come inside me. I want you to."

I open my eyes and glance at Carrie. Her eyes are fixed intently on the camera's view screen. Her lips part in concentration. She then moves behind Laurie toward the end of the bed, aiming the lens and focusing on the penetration.

My eyes fix on a toy that stands low against the wall. It's slightly obscured by the bedside dresser. It's a plush animal that sits on its hind legs and is striped black and orange like a tiger. The shape of its snout is more like a dog's than a cat's, but what I find the most disconcerting are its plastic eyes. They're human-like, as if transplanted from a doll. Behind their lifeless translucency I feel like there is some cognition there. It knows who I am and what I am. I force myself to look away.

Laurie starts bouncing on me with more force. This vigorous rhythm begins to build an orgasm in me. I close my eyes and focus as Laurie pushes her cheek harder against my own.

The dance music stops. Instantly. A residual ringing continues in my ears, but I know someone has turned the music off completely. I give it no more thought, because I feel myself climax. For the first time during our intercourse my hands move to Laurie's body, grasping her soft buttocks. I come inside her, barely making any noise. She runs her hands through my hair, which is now matted and sweaty.

"Did he come?" I hear Taylor whisper.

"I think so," replies Carrie.

My arms return to the mattress as Laurie continues to move on top of me, searching for her own orgasm. She cranes back, her hands holding on to my neck for support. I watch her face strain with pleasure and concentration. A strap of her dress has slipped from the shoulder, revealing a small white breast with an equally small, crimson-coloured areola. I cup it with my right hand, mindlessly studying it. Besides my ejaculate, it's the most interest I've shown Laurie since she brought me to her room. A second later she collapses on me, releasing a moan into my neck.

I hear music again, though it's much softer than before. So quiet I can't make out the melody. Laurie kisses me again and I kiss her back. Past her ear the poster of Jack looks down at me and I notice the corners of my mouth in the image are threatening to smile.

"I've wanted that for so long," she whispers.

I don't reply.

Laurie's hips rise and I slide out of her. She gets off the bed and pulls some tissues from a box on the bedside table, wiping between her legs.

"Did you get all of that?" Laurie asks Carrie. "Did the battery last?"

"Yeah, I got it all. It looked so great," replies Carrie.

"Yeah, really hot," adds Taylor.

"Did it feel really big?" asks Carrie.

Laurie nods. "Yeah. Massive." She then smiles at me. "Thanks for the birthday present."

I tuck my penis, which is in a flaccid, post-coital state of exhaustion, back into my jeans and zip them up. "Does it seem quiet out there to you?" I ask, realising I can't hear any voices outside.

The girls all look at the door.

"I suppose it's a bit quiet," says Taylor. She reaches for the lock.

"Hang on a second," says Laurie, as she pulls her underwear back on.

Taylor waits a moment and then opens the door. Looking past her, I can't see anything beyond the bedroom. The apartment is in darkness.

"Hello?" calls Taylor. "Where is everyone?"

I get up from the bed and join Taylor in the doorway, peering into the hallway. A song drifts towards us, creeping from the sound-system. It's Blue Oyster Cult's 'Don't Fear The Reaper'. But it's not their version. It's the recording I released with Big Bang

29

Theory. I can hear my voice echo throughout the blackened apartment, dripping with the effects that our producer used on my voice.

I turn to Laurie. "Everyone is gone," I say.

"They must have hit the town," she shrugs. "I thought they were going to leave later. Or at least wait for us."

I notice Carrie putting the digital camera in her purse. I look past her to the corner of the room where the bizarre tiger toy sat and it's not there.

"Where did that big toy go?" I ask.

"What toy?" asks Laurie.

I point to the corner where I saw the striped, plush object with the unsettling eyes. "There was a toy... thing... sitting there."

"Do you mean my teddy?" asks Laurie, pointing at a stuffed bear on a dresser on the other side of the room. "That's Rufus."

I pause, not answering. Carrie and Taylor give me an odd look. I then leave the bedroom, finding a light switch in the hallway. Being in a flipped version of my apartment makes me giddy. Everything is in reverse.

My voice croons from the speakers with husky resonance, singing a song about eternal love. A romance that transcends the physical existence of its owners. I wander towards the living room, in the direction of the music, finding light switches. They're placed in the opposite position to where they are in my own apartment. The backing vocal sings and my voice echoes all around me.

As I get to the end of the hallway, I peer into the living room. The candles are nearly burnt out, but provide enough glow for me to see the shapes on the floor. Shapes everywhere. I squint, my eyes adjusting. They look like dresses. Scattered party dresses. One for every reveler who was here.

Laurie walks up behind me, peering over my shoulder into the living room.

"Why are everyone's clothes still here?" I ask.

"They must have all gotten changed before they left," replies Laurie, as if it's not unusual that clothing litters her apartment.

"Or they evaporated," I say, more to myself than Laurie.

Laurie wraps her arms around my waist and kisses my back. "I think you're a little delirious, honey."

"I'm going to head home," I say. "I need to try and get some sleep. Do you have any pain killers?"

"Um, yeah, I think so."

Laurie leads me into the darkened kitchen. Without switching the light on, she pushes me against the counter and kisses me again. I don't fight her advance. She runs her hands beneath the back of my shirt, dragging her fingernails down my skin.

"Can I have you again?" she whispers.

"Not right now," I say. "I... need to recharge."

Laurie makes a huffing sound, like a child that's been denied something it desires. She then releases me from her embrace and rifles through a cupboard above my right shoulder. She finds a box and switches on the kitchen light.

"Pain killers," Laurie says, holding them out to me. She looks stern.

I smile, taking them from her. "You're a life saver."

She shrugs. I lean in and kiss her on the cheek, lingering for a moment on the scent of her hair. Then I kiss her earlobe.

"Don't be a stranger," she says, softly, as I close her apartment door behind me. The lights in the foyer are all turned off, except for one that flickers. It needs to be replaced. It lights my surroundings like a yellow strobe. Glancing to my left, my heart stops. I see Mr Roeg standing outside his apartment door, staring intently at me, his eyes unusually wide.

"Mr Roeg?" I call, hesitantly, squinting. In the dancing light I see he's not there. I'm alone in the foyer. I really need some sleep.

After I swallow a bunch of painkillers I can feel myself slow down. I stretch out on the mattress, naked, limbs outstretched. I'm sweating a lot. For a second I wonder if I should invite Laurie over. Maybe her friends. My mind calms and my eyelids shut. Then my phone rings. It's buried in the pile of clothes next to the bed. I ignore it and the ringing stops. I close my eyes. But the peace is broken by my phone again, chiming and buzzing. I groan loudly and roll to the edge of the mattress, reaching down to find it.

I answer. "Yeah?"

"Jack, sweetheart. It's Amelia. Just checking on my favourite rock star."

"I'm fine. Just... umm... you know."

"You boys have been partying, I hear."

"Sort of. A few quiet drinks. Nothing too hectic."

"Right," says our manager. "Well, Dylan had to have his stomach pumped last night."

"Oh," I say. "Well, you know Dylan. Crazy kid."

"Yes, indeed," says Amelia. "They wanted him to spend the night in hospital, but he checked himself out. He still wants to record tomorrow."

"Well, Dylan would know if he's okay. He gets his stomach pumped like most people use stationary. For... taking notes and stuff. Rough sketches..."

There's a pause. "You sure you're okay, Jack?"

"I'm fine," I say, realising I just lost my shit for a second. "Just a little tired." I'm falling asleep.

"Will you be fine to record tomorrow? It would cost us a large amount of money if we had to cancel the studio, not to mention the orchestra."

"No, I'll be fine. Sleep will do me good."

"A car will be outside your place at nine in the morning."

"I'll be in it."

"And we also need to have that meeting about the news story. I'm handling everything with the record label, but I really need to brief all of you on what's happening. I've spoken to Cohen and Emerson."

"Well, it's all nonsense. Kids run away from home all the time. Let them roam where they want to."

"Okay, Jack. Well, I'll see you tomorrow."

"Bon voyage," I say, dropping the phone.

While I'm asleep I dream about everything in my life. Vivid situations and relationships formulate and crush me with biblical importance. I'm always accused of something horrific. There's always an accusation and inside the dream I know that I am to blame. I am certain punishment will find me. My back is to the wall and my accusers circle. But when I wake up I remember nothing. The details vanish. Perhaps one small moment remains, but it has no context. I have nothing to tie it to. No explanation. The one thing I always wonder is if my dreams are taking place on Earth or here. Does it even make a difference?

I sit on my balcony and watch the suns rise, two orbs appearing behind the city's skyline. I light a cigarette and sip on a black coffee that I've made. Next to it is a rum and cola that I'll knock back after the coffee. I don't have an appetite for any solid food. My hands shake and I still feel scattered from the drugs. The top joints of my jaw, just next to my ears, ache with varying levels of pain when I open my mouth. My lips are lacerated from my constant biting and licking and there's an ulcer on the inner wall of my cheek that I tongue every so often. For a while, I sing to myself. I keep singing an Ocean Colour Scene song called 'The Circle'.

Then I suddenly have an urge to call Jemima, so I pick up my phone and speed dial her.

She answers. "I don't want you to call me," says Jemima.

"You don't have to answer. You could block my number."

Jemima pauses, before saying. "What do you want?"

"I've written a song about you. It's going to be on our next record. I just wanted you to know."

"I'd prefer it if you didn't," says Jemima.

"I think about you a lot. Come back to me. Skip work and come over."

"It's the weekend."

"Oh," I say. "Perfect."

"It's before breakfast and you're drunk."

"I'm not drunk," I reply.

"I'm sure that's only temporary."

"Come back to me. I want you, Jemima."

"Really? How many women have you slept with in the past twenty-six hours?"

I think for a moment, counting. "Um, give me a second..."

"You're such an arsehole."

"I'm not an arsehole, I'm just fragile. Lonely."

"No, you're just an arsehole."

"I'm filling the void you've left in my life. You could destroy the void."

"You're just an arsehole."

"I don't think that's fair."

"Jack," sighs Jemima. "At some point, you have to at least entertain the idea that you're an arsehole."

"I'm not," I say, softly. "Though entertaining, it seems, is something I am very good at..."

Jemima groans.

"It's just that..." I continue, "I'm from another planet. I'm lost here. I'm..." I hear a beeping tone on the other end of the line and

33

realise Jemima has already hung up on me.

I put my mobile on the table next to me and light another cigarette, singing a different Ocean Colour Scene song, deciding which one I should take to the band first. This one is 'The Day We Caught The Train'. When I sing the lyrics the band will ask me, "Who's Groucho?" and I'm not sure I will know what to say.

A luxury vehicle picks me up and drives me half an hour to the edge of the city. Amelia meets me in the circular driveway outside of NorthWest Studios, inspecting me for a moment before leading me inside. She's a striking woman. Mid-forties. Brownish, blonde hair that she often has up in a bun. Fair complexion and finely shaped eyebrows. Perfect teeth. She regularly files her painted fingernails, always with the same calm care. Just as a chef sharpens their knives. Amelia almost always wears figure-hugging shirts and fitted pinstripe suit pants. She's also a gym junkie, though she would tell you otherwise.

"How are you feeling, Jack? Ready to record some music?" she asks, a little uncertain.

"Sure, I'm ready."

"How's your voice?"

"Good. I've been warming it up this morning. Got some new songs."

Amelia smiles. "Fantastic. That's great. Well, follow me."

NorthWest Studios is unassuming from the outside. Its derelict brick is surrounded by dense, tall gardens. But once you follow the path through the two glass doors, you step into a world of decadence. The inside walls are golden oak, the colour of honey. In fact, most of the surfaces are wooden, with each studio designed by the top sound engineers in the world. It's expensive to record here, but those artists with money behind them book rooms here without giving it a second thought. Out in the city there are aspiring musicians working their skin to the bone to afford a single day at NorthWest. Or perhaps just long enough to record some drum tracks.

As Amelia and I pass through the waiting room and by the front counter, she asks that a pot of tea and some organic honey be brought to the recording booth for me. A young male employee, with glasses and a moustache, nods and says he'll get it "right away". Once we head down the corridor, we arrive at the main studio where the orchestra is setting up. Dylan is lying on his back against one wall, reading a newspaper. He's wearing dark sunglasses, even though it's not too bright in here. Emerson and Cohen are beyond a glass window, in the mixing booth. I can see our producer, Joseph, standing over the wide mixing desk, adjusting bells and whistles.

Big Bang Theory is working on a symphonic album. Some songs are new, most are old, but they're each backed by a twelve-piece orchestra. I question whether this is a truly important and creative exercise. One could argue that this release is another way to wring some more coinage from our fanbase. But, so far, the songs sound good.

I record vocals for one of the "new" tracks. Nobody except me knows that the song was originally written by an Australian band called Birds Of Tokyo. I lay down my vocals for 'Wayside'. Then we record 'Off Kilter', another Birds Of Tokyo song. When I finish singing my vocal part, Joseph nods enthusiastically at me through the window of the mixing booth. I hear his voice through my headphones.

"You might have nailed it on the first take, Jack. Do you want to lay down another one for safety?"

I shake my head. "Nah, I was happy with that."


Once I finish some of my vocals, I head into NorthWest's kitchen to get some more tea and honey. Amelia follows me in, closing the kitchen door behind her.

"Sorry, Jack. I know you're trying to stay focused, so I'll be quick," she says.

"Focusing is overrated," I mumble, studying the kettle to find its on switch.

"I'm not going to lie to you. We could have a situation on our hands."

"Then get a hand towel," I reply, nonchalantly, switching the kettle on. "Wipe it off."

"That's very funny," says Amelia, who often substitutes that phrase for actual laughter. "But the media are really sinking their teeth into this story."

"I think you'll find that our involvement in this is circumstantial."

"Absolutely," says Amelia, nodding adamantly. "Of course."

"Can't we just point that out to people when we do our next round of interviews?"

"Yes, but we have to show some concern. These missing girls are all fans of the band and some of them even have professional connections with us."

"I *am* concerned," I say, squeezing a sachet of honey into my mug. "The situation is totally fucked. But I don't want to talk to any newspapers or TV stations if they're all trying to imply that any of this is our fault. We didn't choose our demographic."

"Well..." says Amelia, delicately, "some of the outlets are saying that Big Bang Theory are encouraging reckless behaviour in teenagers..."

I smile at Amelia. "I see... were you reckless as a teenager?"

Amelia looks slightly taken aback. "Um, well... yes. I mean, not really. Maybe."

"I wasn't reckless as a teenager," I say. "I was boring."

"Well, you couldn't afford to be reckless. You were a survivor," says Amelia, softly, referring to my fabricated history as a homeless person. A wild man living beyond society's nurturing embrace.

I smile again. I often forget that I have a secret story to maintain. No one, including Amelia, knows the truth. "That's right. It wasn't easy living out there. But... teenagers do reckless things without any prompting. That's my point."

The real reason I wasn't reckless is because I sat indoors throughout my teenage years reading astronomy books and teaching myself the guitar. I was quite fond of Black Sabbath records. I picked up calculus very quickly at high school. While people my age were stepping out into the world with a university degree and getting married, I was spinning around and around in human centrifuge training, learning to maintain focus while g-forces moved the blood away from my brain and eyes. At those speeds, your vision begins to tint a grey colour, as if you're looking through sunglasses. Some guys went to football matches. Some guys impregnated their girlfriends and negotiated mortgages. I did High-G training, defended freedom in foreign countries, flew fighter jets and was later launched into space. It was all at the expense of a traditional life containing a house and children. It also seemed like it would be the death of my dream to become a successful musician.

Emerson comes back to my apartment after the recording session, to hang out. Dylan and Cohen have gone for coffee with two of the violinists. Or maybe they were the cellists. The luxury car drops us off outside my building and we cross the footpath. The doorman lets us into the foyer. Emerson waits while I go into the postal room and check my mailbox. There's a wad of letters, which I flick through while Emerson and I ascend in the elevator to the top level. Level 38.

Most of the envelopes are uninteresting, except for one. It's brown and looks a little tattered. Aged. It has ornate trimmings, possibly gold plated. In calligraphic handwriting it says on its front, "Join us."

"Looks a little ominous," says Emerson, glancing at the envelope.

I turn it over and open it, tearing off the chunk of red wax that's been used to seal it. Inside is an equally stylised piece of paper. On quick inspection I read that it's an invitation to the opening of an art exhibition. Something called the Marioneta de Carne.

"You heard of this?" I ask Emerson, handing him the invitation as the elevator opens at our floor.

"Maybe," he says, reading as we walk toward my apartment. "I think this is that thing they're talking about on the news."

"Yeah?"

"It's a bunch of sculptures that are made from people. Like, body parts and stuff."

"Wow. That doesn't really sound like something I'd want to go to."

Emerson shrugs. "Could be kinda interesting. It's been a big controversy."

"Sounds gruesome," I say, letting us into my apartment. I throw the mail, including the invitation, on my kitchen counter, then head for the living room. "Help yourself to the liquor," I tell Emerson, who peruses the bottles in my kitchen.

Emerson joins me in the living room with two glasses in his hand. He places one on the coffee table in front of me. "One limonata on ice."

"Winning," I say, leaning forward in the sofa to reach the glass.

We watch a music channel for a while, commenting occasionally on particular songs or music videos. Then one of our own videos comes on. It's for a song we released called 'The Thief & The Heartbreaker'. It was originally recorded by a band from Earth

37

called Alberta Cross. I was a fan.

In the video, which is mostly animated, a black stick-figure is running through desert-like landscapes. Just running and running, its featureless body bounding over red, arid terrain as two suns set behind it.

"What's this video about again?" asks Emerson.

"Not sure. Don't you remember?"

"I don't think it was explained," says Emerson, shrugging.

"The director told me, I think. I don't know. Something about a dream?"

Emerson shrugs again and sips on his drink. Then a buzzing emanates from his pocket and he answers his mobile phone. "Yuh," he says. "Oh, hey man... not a lot, just at Jack's... um, yeah we could probably use something.... cool, well head on over.... you know the place, yeah? Nice one."

"Who was that?" I ask, sipping my drink.

"Roy."

"What's he bringing?"

"Not sure. Depends what he's got at the moment, I guess."

Fifteen minutes later Roy knocks on the door and Emerson lets him in. Roy has an olive complexion, a week's stubble and a greasy ponytail. He's wearing a tattered t-shirt, ripped jeans and slip-on shoes.

"Jack, what's shaking? You look well, my friend," says Roy, wandering through the apartment into the living room and dropping on to the single sofa adjacent to me. Emerson joins me on the large sofa.

"Thank you, Roy," I reply, cycling through channels on the television. "How's business?"

"Great," says Roy, who looks a little spaced. His eyes watch the television as programs flicker and disappear. "Things are great. Demand is getting bigger. Good times."

"So those anti-drug campaigns on TV aren't working then?" says Emerson, with a grin.

"No, not at all. They've improved business. Helped spread the word. People want to try out some gear. They find people like me to hook 'em up."

"Well if someone is speaking out against drugs, that just means they haven't tried them yet," says Emerson, sipping his drink.

"You ain't lyin'," says Roy.

"So what's been happening?" I ask him.

"Nothing much. I was pretty drunk this morning and it was raining so I went to the beach. Went for a surf. Good times, man," says Roy, who starts pulling small bags from his pockets and placing them on the coffee table. Plastic pouches of powder, clear gels and pills.

I look at Roy's assortment. It's all the usual suspects. The bread and milk items of the drug user. Staples that you always have at home. Cane. Pills. Gas. Grass. Lysergide. Uppers. But what goes up must come down.

"We'll take it all," says Emerson, casually. He looks at me and shrugs.

"Sure," I add.

"Cool," says Roy, who looks happy. "Because you guys are my best customers, I'll do you a good price. Cost price."

"Thanks for looking after us," smiles Emerson.

Roy then stands up and starts digging into his back pocket, looking for something. "I've got something else for you guys. I don't want you to freak out though."

This peaks our interest. Roy produces a small metal tin, no bigger than a matchbox. It's a metallic green colour, old and chipped. He places it on the table and, pausing for dramatic effect, pulls the lid. Emerson and I both lean forward to see inside. There's four capsules in there. Two green, two white. Emerson and I exchange a glance, each guessing what the drug might be.

"Is that...?" asks Emerson.

"Yes," says Roy. "A pretty good find, yes? A friend of mine encountered these. They are only small hits, but you'll get the idea."

"Fuck," I say. "That's hectic, Roy. That's really hectic."

"How long do they last?" asks Emerson.

"About six or seven hours," replies Roy. He picks up one of the green capsules. "You take the green one, then half an hour later you take the white one. Then lie down somewhere and get ready. You can't forget to take the white one, because it brings you out of the coma."

This drug that Roy is offering us isn't supposed to exist. I've never seen it before. Only heard about it from people. Junkies boasting in nightclubs. There's rumours that there are dens where people go to take it. Underground labs. A drug that sends you into a weeklong hyper reality. A playground in your mind that is real, as believable and tangible as anything else you've ever experienced. A mental wonderland without rules or consequences.

"So Narc dens are real then?" asks Emerson.

"Fuck yeah," says Roy. "I've seen one, man. Had a look around. Fucked up."

"Were there many people?" I ask.

Roy just smiles. "Hundreds." Roy likes to tweak a fair bit. He's partial to a good hallucinogen. I don't know whether to believe him. Then he continues. "They're all hooked up to tubes, man. They get fed slowly. Lasts a week. A week in paradise. Medical students are wandering around checking people's vital signs. Emptying their shit bags. Wild stuff."

"Wild," I say, sipping my drink. "Well, we'll take them then. How much?"

"Five grand each," says Roy.

Emerson shrugs. "Done."

"What happens if you don't take the white one? Does the dream last forever?" I ask.

"Pretty much," says Roy. "But you'll die eventually. That's why in the dens they have you hooked up to the tubes. Keep you from starvin'."

"How real is the dream?" asks Emerson.

"As real as you and I sittin' here now."

A minute barely passes after I've farewelled Emerson and Roy before there's a quiet knock at my door. I reluctantly get back up from the sofa and wander to the peephole. Laurie is standing outside with an anxious expression on her face. I open the door and she looks relieved. She's wearing a white singlet top and grey trackpants. Her hair is up in a ponytail and though she's only used minimal make-up, I can see foundation on her face.

"Hi," she says, hesitantly.

"Hey, how are you?"

"I feel a bit run down," she says, sheepishly.

"Yeah. I can imagine."

"How are you feeling?"

"Good, I suppose. Still need some more sleep, I think. Been a big day. Recording and stuff."

"Oh, cool," says Laurie.

There's a pause. It's remotely awkward.

"So, what's up?" I ask.

"Nothing much. I've got the place to myself. I was wondering if you wanted to hang out or something."

I feel a small knot in my stomach. It's an ambiguous sensation. I can't tell if it's guilt or nerves. Or whether I'm turned on by Laurie and what transpired between us. I don't know whether to be concerned that there is currently a sex tape of me and Laurie together. But the more I consider it, the less I care.

"Umm," is all I say, my brain analysing a long list of potential scenarios.

Laurie appears upset that I haven't immediately accepted her invitation. "It's okay," she says. "You've probably got to sleep or practice or something. I won't bother you."

I feel myself relent. "No, it's cool... what's the point of us sitting on our own in separate apartments, right?"

Laurie smiles. "I know. I'd rather hang out with you than be by myself."

I stand aside, motioning for Laurie to enter. "It's my turn to be host."

I allow Laurie control of the television. She aims the remote at my broad flatscreen TV, flicking through channels. She's curled up on the opposite end of the sofa, with no more than half a foot of space between us. I watch her face as she concentrates on each programme long enough to decide whether it's interesting. My heart feels like it's beating faster, straining slightly against my ribs.

Laurie notices that I'm watching her. "What?" she says, turning pink.

"You're being too indecisive," I say, with a smile.

"Well, I can't decide! Everything is boring."

"Fine."

Laurie goes back to changing channels as I continue to watch her. Now she's aware of my gaze. Her face remains flushed with colour. "Stop looking at me!" she says.

I sigh and slide down on to the floor, stretching my legs out and leaning back on the sofa. "Just put it on a music channel. You can't go wrong with MV2. They play cool stuff."

We watch a few music videos in silence. I occasionally look at Laurie. Her feet are tucked underneath her and her face is propped in a hand. She doesn't look particularly interested in the television.

"I'm going out for a smoke," I say, gesturing at the balcony.

"Okay," says Laurie. When I reach for my cigarettes on the coffee table, she asks, "Can I have one too?"

"Sure."

Outside, Laurie puts a cigarette between her rose-coloured lips and I light it for her. Then I light my own. A wind picks up and Laurie tries to cover her bare arms, leaning into me.

"I didn't realise how cold it was outside," she says, goosebumps rising on her pale skin.

I turn Laurie around and wrap an arm across her collarbones, holding her against me. She rests the back of her head on my shoulder, as I smell her hair. She relaxes, leaning back against me. We stand like this until we've finished our cigarettes. I put my butt in an empty wine bottle and Laurie does the same.

"We should get you back inside," I say, sliding open the door into the living room. But rather than follow my suggestion, Laurie hurriedly takes my face in her hands and kisses me.

Because the temperature in the apartment dropped, I had to turn on the central heating. On the sofa, Laurie sits on my lap, curled against me while we continue to kiss each other. When my hand begins to roam underneath her singlet, Laurie takes it off. Every so often I focus on her neck and ears, sometimes her shoulders, teasing her with small bites. At one point, our attention is drawn to the television when a Big Bang Theory song comes on MV2. It's our cover of 'Atlanta', which was originally a Stone Temple Pilots song. My face stares out at me as I sing into the camera, filmed in grainy black and white. I look sad, my eyes projecting sorrow. That was an instruction from the video's director, but perhaps I didn't have to act.

"Will you sing it to me?" asks Laurie.

"Do I have to?" I ask.

"No, you don't," she replies, adding coquettishly, "but I'd love it if you did."

I relent, singing in a deep, crooning tone. It's my impressive impersonation of Stone Temple Pilots singer Scott Weiland, who in turn was impressively paying homage to the voice of Jim Morrison. But no one on this planet knows that. They haven't heard this love song, full of lament. How "Mexican Princess" heroin entwined his life with roses and thorns. To me it's also about losing a lover.

While I sing the song, Laurie rests her head just under my own and I hold her tightly.

In my bed, Laurie lies next to me under the blanket. She's completely naked now and while we kiss, I touch her. But lying here, with the warmth and comfort of her soft body, I feel exhaustion catch up with me and I begin to fall asleep. I sense that Laurie is falling asleep too.

Minutes pass and we lie still. I'm not sure if Laurie's asleep, but I ask her a question. "Why did you let your friends film us making love?"

"I was drunk," says Laurie, softly, "and I'd had a pill. I get pretty... crazy... don't you do wild things like that all the time? I've heard about the parties you go to..."

"I suppose so."

"I promise I'll keep it a secret. I won't show anyone. Neither will Carrie or Taylor."

"Okay," I reply. "I trust you..."

A small span of silence lies between us. Then Laurie says, "I think... I was worried that one day I would wonder whether it really even happened..."

# CHAPTER THREE

I was terrified when I arrived on this planet, a simple fear of the unknown. But I was also relieved to have reached the surface. The thought of drowning in outer space scared me even more. Slowly starving of my resources.

There was a moment when I realised I would not be returning home. I was surprised by how calm I felt. Any potential outbursts of panic remained deeply buried. I decided that I would endure and I would not concede to the vastness of space.

I think less and less about the Planet Earth, but when I do it hurts. The faces of my family and my girlfriend return to me when I sleep, but I don't know if they look the same. Time blurs their appearance in my memory. I am mourning them. I tell myself they're alive and well, bounding through life somewhere in the distant cosmos. Just like the fool that thinks of the great beyond. I hope that my girlfriend has moved on and managed to reassemble her life, closing the chapter of our relationship.

I often forget where I am. In quiet minutes I remember. The realisation that I am a great distance from home appears in the ether. An alien ingratiated in a society that must never know my secret. Of course, I question my decision to pursue this music career, but I suppose I would rather hide myself in broad daylight. The spotlight can darken as much as it illuminates.

Back home I always loved introducing my friends to new artists and now I gain enormous pride when another one of my releases touches a universal nerve. Imagine a world without Neil Young, The Beatles, Queen, Led Zeppelin, Leonard Cohen, Jimi Hendrix, Ryan Adams or The Beach Boys. It seems so unthinkable. Those songs that transcend sound waves and become something spiritual. I wish I could play them all. Right now. But what race of people is ready for the back catalogue of Earth to be dropped on them all at once?

I wonder which songs they played at my funeral. I assume they must have had one for me. I try to see my girlfriend's face as she flips through my record collection, deciding which tracks touched me more. Which songs portray my life with dignity? I hope to Christ there weren't some fucking cheesy astronaut references creeping from the church speakers. 'Starman' by David Bowie? Good song. Just not sure I want it to accompany my eulogy. 'A Spaceman Came Travelling' by Chris De Burgh? Good song. Given my current situation, its subject matter is very appropriate. But NASA's space programme didn't summarise me as a human. Maybe they played 'Spaceman' by Babylon Zoo?

I picture an American and an Australian flag draped over an empty coffin and my loved ones, despite themselves, imagine my corpse floating throughout the nether regions of the universe, rotting in my space suit. They think about eternity and my journey into it. But my death is no different to any other. If you are a believer in Christianity, then perhaps my journey to another world is one intended for all of us. Here on this planet, with this other race of humans, I've been reborn. To survive death in the way that I have leaves me with a sense of power. I'm indestructible. I'm not just a small stroke in NASA's death tally. I have survived another accident in space that shouldn't have happened.

The limousine slithers through the torrential traffic. A slick eel in the city's streets winding towards the giant spotlights that cross like swords in the star-spangled night sky. The awards ceremony is at a place called The Imperial Theatre. It's a grand building, historic by anyone's standards. Another limousine cruises along next to us. Their windows are tinted like ours, declining either vehicle a glance at the other's passengers.

The McCarthy Awards are a big deal. Big money, big media coverage. It leaves the Grammys for dead. Glitz, glamour, and masturbatory acceptance speeches. Backs raw from the slapping. Big Bang Theory are nominated for five awards that cover everything from our music videos to our most recent album, *The Dawn Of Man*. It's an epic title, sure. It was well received. I focused mostly on British rock and early punk. 'Ever Fallen In Love?' by the Buzzcocks is on there too. One critic said that we'd refined our sound and were closer to realising our full potential as artists. Right on.

The band sits in the limo with me. We've been drinking for a few hours now. Nothing too hectic, mind you. We're performing tonight. Our new single is called 'Black Dog'. It's a rampaging rock song with some insanely excellent shifting tempos. We're going to unleash it on the sweethearts of the music industry, who by now will be trickling into the Imperial. I can picture them. Dresses and suits whose cost could feed a starving family for a year. Noses in the air, accidentally bumping into each other. Smiles and mild apologies. Vacuous people in a vacuum. Glittering jewellery. One's retinas need to adjust in the buzzing chaos of it all.

"Do you think that Jennifer Fox will be here?" asks Dylan, before taking a heavy sip on his scotch and ice.

"I'm pretty sure she's presenting an award," replies Cohen.

The limo that was content to cruise along next to us slows down as we approach the theatre. It then moves in behind us. I suppose they're hoping to arrive last. It's fashionable to be late, but ultimately the coolest people don't even show up. Punctuality is a state of mind.

A man in a tuxedo and headset waves us into a parking space along the footpath. Beyond our windows is a sea of photographers divided by a red carpet. Our driver steps out and briskly stands next to the passenger door. The photographers raise their cameras, like an impatient firing squad. A few premature shots go off. I reach into my inner jacket pocket and find a pill, which I promptly swallow and knock back with a shot of something that tastes like tequila. God knows I'm going to need it. Men can fake enthusiasm as convincingly as an orgasm. Tonight I'll fake neither.

The ceremony itself is nauseating. I can never understand how plastic people don't melt under such intense lighting. Smiling down the barrel of that autocue. The corridors of the backstage areas are like a termite's nest in full flight. Lots of hurried gnawing. The four of us are draped around our dressing room, waiting for our call up. We're going on after another popular rock group called the Known Associates. We'll be given a ten-minute warning, then a five-minute warning. Then it's show time.

I go over the lyrics in my head. Led Zeppelin. I love this song. Tonight we're going to make them sweat and groove. The song has an amazing time signature. Big Bang Theory was quite impressed when I brought it to practice. 'Hey guys, look what I wrote. The greatest blues-rock song of all time. Cool, huh?' Of course, I don't have the whimsical vocals of Robert Plant, but I do the song some justice.

A curtain is lifted and the crowd roars as we appear on stage. It sounds genuine. I've clearly managed to gain the respect of the music industry. My mind briefly concentrates on the lyrics of 'Black Dog', a song I listened to as an eight-year-old on my father's record player. Headphones that were too big for me. I often wish that I could go back and listen to *Led Zeppelin IV* for the first time. Even when placed next to all the amazing music that humans have produced, it's in a universe of its own. Melodic nirvana. 'The Battle Of Evermore', with its penetrating harmonies, pastoral imagery and parochial sensibility. I lie awake at night and hear it over and over again. Echoes of a world lost.

Dressed in disheveled designer suits, we perform with measured enthusiasm. Nothing over the top. I don't look at anyone in the crowd. Behind my dark sunglasses I just sing to the back wall. To no one in particular. I hold on tight now to nothing at all.

After our set we're led through a back exit and into an alley where our limousine waits. At one end fans scream from behind a tall, wire fence. They're begging me to walk towards them. To acknowledge them for the smallest moment. To make me real. I briefly consider going over there to say pleasure, but I don't. I just wave and force a smile. I sometimes endeavour to build a relationship with the loyal folk out there, but now I feel slightly empty. I'm not up to it. I hope my spirits lift by the time I arrive at the after party. I reach into my pocket, take another pill and jump into the limousine with my band mates.

There's a number of after parties to choose from. It's amazing how many people give a fuck about who is where. We've been invited to all sorts tonight. A perfume company. Yeah, right. A prominent music magazine called *Proverb*. Fairly tabloid. We've decided to attend a private party that the head of our record label, Endurance, is throwing. A gregarious, silver-haired old codger, Martin Brannagh sure knows how to host a shin-dig. It's difficult to pass up one of his get-togethers.

Brannagh's apartment, a penthouse in the upper hills of East Terragon, is incredibly monotone but somehow alluring. Like passionless sex. And a little like Brannagh himself. His apartment is all sleek, white surfaces and bright lighting. A metallic, open kitchen. Cubic furniture. Glass tables. Icy marble floor. The odd runner and rug to keep the decor slightly textured and organic. Semi-surrealist artworks hang around the wide, open-plan entertaining area. A projector screen throws music videos by Endurance artists on to one of the bare walls. Waitresses in short black skirts and white, tight buttoned shirts tray champagne and canapés.

The apartment is already quite full. You can be fashionably late to one of Brannagh's parties but it will mean missing something outrageous. At least the drugs and drinks never run out. We step into the small foyer and a number of people spot us. Quick whispers. More eyes turn. I glance around the room, recognising some faces. Members of the Known Associates. A model that's on the cover of one of the women's magazines that's on the news stands at the moment. I know this because the cover is on a billboard opposite my apartment balcony.

In the kitchen is Jennifer Fox, the film industry's darling. Dylan intends to pursue her but she has continued making advances at me. I still haven't returned her email. She's talking to a slender brunette girl whom is facing away from me. But I immediately recognise her. I've probably seen the back of that girl's head more than the front. Make of that what you will, but I've just never given her much reason to walk towards me.

I catch Jennifer's eye and I see her mouth something to the brunette girl. The girl then turns and glances at me with two vivid, sky blue irises. It's Jemima. I haven't had much luck with her. It's hard to make someone think you're a nice guy when you're unquestionably a womaniser and drug addict. But I could love Jemima. I sometimes think about her. Maybe I'm just desperate and adrift, looking for someone to anchor me. Men often put women on a pedestal and there's no doubting that Jemima teeters somewhere above me. A height I'll never reach. I wonder if I'll ever persuade her to forgive me. If not, I'll move on. There's no better way to get over a girl than to get under another.

Jemima makes eye contact for a fraction of a second, before

calmly walking from the kitchen and disappearing into the party. I imagine she's heading for the balcony. I could follow her, attempt feeble conversation and fail. Alternatively, I could head to one of the bathrooms where lines of speed and cane will be on offer. Perhaps I could strike up a torrid sexual encounter with two lingerie models in one of the many bedrooms. Important decisions like these require a much clearer mind than my current fog can offer.

Cohen has seen Jemima too. "Wow, fancy seeing her here," he says, smugly.

"I was positive she wouldn't be here," I say.

"Yeah, right," says Cohen.

"Maybe I should go talk to her."

Cohen smiles. "That would be bad."

"She's had time to calm down since the book launch."

"Is she ever calm?"

"What are you talking about?"

"Well," says Cohen, choosing his words. "She can be a little tight."

"You're munted."

"Doesn't matter. Just leave her alone. Why break a sweat chasing her? Did you see how many women went to powder their noses when we got here? You've got to get some control back."

"I am in control."

Cohen chuckles. "She's cigarette smoke. A little puff and you'll be back to a pack a day."

"Well the patches aren't working."

Cohen shrugs. "Your call. I'm heading to the bathroom." He gives a knowing grin. Emerson and Dylan follow him.

"Nice one," I reply, and head toward the balcony, passing through the kitchen.

"Jack!" squeals Jennifer Fox.

"Jen, how are you? You look breathtaking."

Jennifer grins with her white, immaculate teeth and perfect skin. She has bedroom features, all sultry and seductive. She leans in to kiss me on the cheek, but her lips move to graze the edge of my own. "You guys were amazing tonight. That new song was so sexy. What's it called again?" she asks, running a hand through her long dark hair.

"'Black Dog'," I reply. A waitress walks through the kitchen with a tray of blood-red cocktails.

"What are these?" asks Jennifer.

"They're called a screaming orgasm," smiles the cute waitress.

"Well, how can I refuse?" asks Jennifer, slipping me a glance as she takes a glass from the tray.

I take one also. "I've never passed up an orgasm," I say.

"What man does?" asks Jennifer, before imbibing a sip of her beverage.

I smile, feeling another sudden rush. I'm very hectic. "How's your new movie progressing?" I ask.

Jennifer shrugs. "Fine. I'm looking forward to wrapping it up." She makes a few more comments that don't register because my mind is moving too quickly.

"Not enjoying it?" I ask.

Jennifer shrugs again, and takes another drink from her glass. There's a pause before her face lights up again. She asks, "So, tell me Jack, who in your band is single? Because you are a gorgeous group of men."

"Cohen, Dylan and Emerson are all single. But please don't tell them you think they're gorgeous. You'd be throwing petrol on a house fire."

Jennifer chuckles. "Well I wouldn't want that. But you didn't include yourself in that list, Jack."

"I see lots of people. Can't really get away from them."

"I bet you can't," says Jennifer, with a grin. "I've also heard a rumour about you."

"Oh? That sounds ominous," I smile.

"I've met a few of the women you've slept with and they tell me that you're quite... endowed."

"Well Jennifer, you are in a position to accurately clarify that rumour."

"If I remember correctly, it was more than one position."

I smile and sip my beverage. "So what are these rumours exactly? What have you heard?"

"One girl told me that you're practically a conjoined twin."

A laugh escapes my throat and I glance around the room again for Jemima. "I hate to be rude, but I need to find someone. I swear I'll return..."

Jennifer just smiles. "You're a busy man."

"To be continued?"

"To be continued," smiles Jennifer. "Do you promise to find me later, when you're leaving?"

"Of course," I smile.

Jennifer leans in and gives me another kiss on the cheek. Again her lips land dangerously close to my own.

I return the smile and push past her, drinking my orgasm in a quick gulp as I leave the kitchen. If my conversation with Jemima doesn't go well, then I could do a lot worse than having Jennifer as backup. 'Auxiliary tail', as Dylan would call it.

When I get to the balcony, where I anticipate Jemima might be, I can't find her. There's at least one hundred people outside, smoking, laughing, gazing across the city below, but no sign of the one woman I want to see. They all turn and look at me, whispering, laughing. A few people wave, who I vaguely recognise from other parties. The record label. Possibly my bedroom.

I walk back inside and scan the entertaining area. Nothing. I push through the chatter and chinking of glassware towards the hallway. Three of the bedrooms are locked. I put my ear to one and can hear the muffled sound of a female crying. Nothing hysterical. Just tears. I listen to another door. Definite moans. Also female. Not Jemima's.

As I follow the hallway and take a sharp turn to the right, I find her. She's banging on a bathroom door, demanding to be let in. In the dim lights of the corridor, I can tell my ex-lover is not happy to see me. She lights a cigarette as I approach.

"Want a lighter?" I ask.

Jemima huffs. "Only if you're flammable."

"Wow, sparks are flying already. I better watch out."

Jemima produces her own lighter and puts the tip of a cigarette to the small orange tongue of flame. "Jack, just because we're surrounded by important people doesn't mean I won't harm you."

"This is my record label's after party. I'm celebrating several music awards. You knew I would be attending."

"With all those trashbags at the ceremony, I honestly thought you wouldn't make it back here."

"We followed them here."

"Don't waste your precious time on me. There's plenty of women here that will actually go home with you."

"Maybe I should send them over to you for a character reference."

"Ha," says Jemima. "You'd be a very lonely man if I was your only advocate."

I smile. Jemima doesn't. She used to enjoy our verbal jousts, but now it feels like something between us is broken. I'm not going to have any success. Forgiveness won't blossom in arid soil. It doesn't matter how much glitter I sprinkle on the shit I've caused, it's still going to stink. I give her this round.

"Sorry I bothered you," I say, before walking away.

I push through the crowded living room, my mind rushing from the pills. One of Big Bang Theory's songs comes over the stereo. I hear my voice permeate the room. People turn and smile at me. I give an embarrassed shrug. It's one of my favourite songs. The lyrics tell the story of a man trying to shed the emotional burden of a broken relationship. He drags himself back out into the world and is greeted by apathy. A world where caring is creepy and everything around him is all surface and no feeling.

My band and I have done a decent job of recreating the magic of a few Shins songs, like this one, but I desperately miss hearing the originals. The drugs in my veins give me a sudden rush of euphoria as Dylan walks over to me. He holds out a glass of sparkling wine, laughing.

"Who put *this* shit on?" he jokes, putting his arm around me.

"Someone with popular taste," I smile, before singing the next line out loud for the room to hear.

A photographer from *Souljacker*, a monthly magazine, appears on his knees in front of us, snapping off a number of shots with an overly exaggerated flash. Looks like we'll be in print again. Dylan roars at him like an animal and more photos are taken. This is how rock stars behave.

"Come over here and meet my new friends," says Dylan, leading me out of the room.

"Fuck yes," I say, with an overwhelming, drug-fuelled rush of enthusiasm.

Back in the hallway, I'm introduced to three women. Dylan tells me they're models and articulates their recent achievements in the hope of contextualising them for me. One is the face of a fairly extravagant brand of perfume. Another, Jessica, is on the album cover of a well-received new release called *Fresh Blood*, by a group called Mercy Beau Coup. They're an electro, new wave sort of thing.

Very stylish, but as deep and meaningful as a bowl of porridge. The third woman, who's introduced as Cherie or Cherry, is in a children's pop group called Spangle Road. I vaguely recognise her from morning television. Usually in the early hours of sunsrise when I'm trying to get to sleep.

I take each of their finely manicured hands and lightly kiss them just below the wrist. This old-fashioned form of greeting was uncommon on this planet, so it's become my unique trademark. Another idiosyncrasy. But I perform this greeting on most of the girls I meet, so its stocks have slowly declined in value. "Pleasure," I say to each of them. Somewhere in the background, I hear my voice singing 'Novocaine For The Soul'.

Jessica is strawberry blonde and curvaceous. Two unavoidable breasts peer out from the V-shaped neckline of her red dress. In my addled state, I probably look at them for too long.

"You might know my boyfriend," says Jessica.

"Really? Who's that?" asks Dylan.

The perfume model giggles. "She's dating Chris from the Known Associates."

The plot thickens. "Wow, cool," I say, grinding my back teeth and tapping my right foot.

"Yeah, we know Chris!" says Dylan. "He's a sweetheart."

"I know," says Jessica. "He's adorable."

Another new Big Bang Theory track blasts over the sound-system and I hear my voice sing prophetic words that I've stolen from Mark Oliver Everett of the band Eels. I sing something along the lines of: "It is hard to recognise where I end and what they are making me begins."

"So do you guys have a new record coming out soon?" asks Jessica, with genuine interest.

"We're doing a symphonic record at the moment," says Dylan, leaning towards Jessica flirtatiously.

"Wow, like, with an orchestra?" asks Jessica.

"Yes!" says Dylan, putting an arm around her waist. "See, I like talking to someone who actually *knows* something about music. I'm sick of all these *poseurs*."

Jessica giggles. She seems a little awkward in regard to Dylan's advances, but she makes no effort to push him away.

"Then we're making a new studio album," I add.

"Yes!" says Dylan again, suddenly releasing Jessica and grabbing my arm. "I forgot to tell you, I have a name for it."

"Tell me," I say.

Dylan holds up his hands, as if moulding each word individually in the air. Hanging the title in invisible neon. "*Up Skirts On The Outskirts*," he says. I think for a moment, while Dylan studies me for a reaction. The three women look at Dylan, trying to determine if he's joking. He's not.

"Good," I say, finally. "I like it. Yes."

"Nice," smiles Dylan. "I've got the cover all worked out. It's a hot, brutal desert and we're standing out in the distance, almost a mirage. As if, maybe, we're not even there."

"I'm listening," I say, craving a cigarette.

"In the foreground, like right in front of the camera, is standing a girl. The hot desert wind is blowing her skirt up and you can see a portion of her ass," adds Dylan, weaving his visual poetry. "She's facing us. And we're standing there, looking at her, as if to say 'Come with us. Come with us and you will never need a skirt again'."

"Wow," I say. "That's powerful."

"I know," says Dylan, happy with himself.

"I'm going to leave you here with these lovely ladies," I say. I need some fresh air and a change of scenery. I push through the room to the stairwell that leads to the roof. I can hear partying up there.

I squeeze past revelers on my way through the small, shadowed stairwell and then up the narrow stairs. There's hundreds of party-goers up here, smoking and drinking. A few particularly loose people are dancing to the minimal beats of a DJ who's set up in one corner, between two large ferns. I'm spotted by people. A few shake my hand and congratulate me on our awards. I smile and thank them politely. A well-dressed couple gets their photo taken with me.

Out of the gawking crowd appears a girl. She approaches me and instantly everyone else disappears. It's just her and I, alone on a rooftop, surrounded by a fleshy, sweating haze that leaves our focus and never returns. This girl has a brown, bob cut that stops at her chin. Flawless caramel skin. Full bodied lips and dark green, seductive eyes. She's wearing a short black dress with an over-sized, white man's shirt over it, which hangs open. The plunging neckline of her dress warrants a criminal investigation. It's an inadequate refuge for her large, seemingly natural breasts. She is a perfect and ideal specimen.

"Hi, Jack. I'm Natalie," says the girl. She extends a hand, and I notice that she's wearing fingerless black lace gloves.

"Pleasure," I say, lightly kissing the fabric on the back of her right hand.

"We met once before, but you probably don't remember."

"You look familiar," I say. "Was it another of Brannagh's gatherings?"

"Yes, I believe it was," she smiles, before adding, "I just wanted to say that you guys were awesome tonight."

"It sounded okay?"

"Of course! That new song was so sexy. I just wanted to get up and dance in the aisle."

Can't go wrong with Zeppelin. "Yeah, the band's really happy with it. You should have gotten up on stage with us."

"Yeah, right," she says, "and get molested by some security guard? No thank you."

"So what are your plans for the rest of the evening?" I ask.

"Probably some mischief," she says, smiling.

I take two glasses of sparkling wine from a passing waitress and offer one to Natalie.

"Thank you," she says.

"Pleasure."

We make our way to the edge of the rooftop and lean on the railing. The city stretches out below us, blinking and flickering with electric light and humming with traffic and street noise.

"You're a very mysterious man," says Natalie, sipping her sparkling.

I shrug. "I don't know about that. I'm sure you're equally mysterious."

Natalie smiles and shakes her head. "No, not me. I'm an open book."

"I bet you're a real page-turner."

"Well, put it this way," says Natalie, leaning closer. "You wouldn't put me down until the climax."

I almost choke on my drink, but quickly regain my composure. "How about we play a little game?" I ask.

"Sure, I'm in the mood for a game," responds Natalie.

"I ask a question of you, then you get to ask a question of me."

"Alright."

"So what do you do with yourself?"

"I... work for an agency, mostly," smiles Natalie.

"Modelling?"

"I do some modelling," she replies, elusively, before adding, "that was two questions. Now I get two questions."

"Fire away."

"What's your earliest memory?"

This takes me by surprise. My earliest memory. I remember a Christmas present. I was given packets of glow-in-the-dark galaxy stickers to put up around my bedroom. Hundreds of stars, comets, and planets that would glow brightly straight after the light was switched off, then slowly fade away after I fell asleep. My father helped me arrange the stars in the formations of actual constellations. I remember the half-man, half-horse creature, Centaurus, with Alpha Centauri burning as its brightest star. I was a young boy with a clear sky above him every night. Long before the clouds rolled in and hung there forever.

"My earliest memory..." I say, pausing for dramatic effect, "is sleeping under a rail bridge in Lower Easton. Trains rumbling overhead. Freezing cold."

"You were a little street urchin," says Natalie, sympathetically.

"That's a nice way of putting it."

"How did you learn to play the guitar and sing?"

"Well, singing... I'm not sure. I suppose I had a lot of spare time to practice. To make music. When I was young I found an old guitar behind a block of apartments, in their garbage. I taught myself to play it and it became like a third arm."

"That's an amazing story," says Natalie, gazing at me. One of her delicately gloved hands reaches out and touches my arm. Another drug rush comes over me and I realise I'm completely at this woman's mercy. "Your turn to ask me a question." Natalie smiles with her full, mesmerising lips. I suddenly have the urge to bite them from her face.

Glancing around the party, I can see people looking at Natalie and I. I can't tell if any of them know her or whether they're wondering who this devil is that's holding my attention. Having me to herself. Across the rooftop I see Jennifer Fox. She's talking to a few girls I don't recognise and she's laughing mildly, playing with her hair and watching me out of the corner of her blue eyes.

Jennifer never breaks character, but I can see her inspecting Natalie, assessing this rival. This competitor. As beautiful, wealthy and famous as Jennifer is, Natalie is unequalled. Natalie is sex personified. Natalie takes what she wants. Natalie doesn't like to share.

"Um," I stammer, trying to think of a question. All I want to do is disappear from this party with Natalie and do unspeakable things to her. Abhorrent, profane things. I don't know where this lust is coming from, but I can't control it. Its tendril fingers are in my body, in my blood, and I'm utterly helpless. I'm at the bottom of a very dark pit, gazing up at a pinprick of sunlight.

I feel a tap on my shoulder and turn to see Martin Brannagh grinning at me. He opens his arms and gives me a hug.

"Jack, my favourite rock star. Are you having a good time?" he asks, with genuine interest. Brannagh looks like a veteran actor of daytime soap operas. He's had a number of facelifts, but wrinkles still form in his tanned, leathering skin. His hair is white as snow, slicked back to his head. A wide, equally pale moustache balances confidently on his top lip. His pupils betray his real age, now a soft faded grey, but they are no less intense. Brannagh's eyes are always studying and evaluating you.

"Marty, you needn't ask," I chuckle, slapping him on the arm.

Brannagh returns my smile, glances at my companion, then back to me. "I see Natalie has found you," he says.

"Yes," I reply, as Natalie wraps an arm around my waist. She gives Brannagh a knowing smile.

"I asked Martin to introduce me to you again," says Natalie, feigning embarrassment. "But I found the courage to introduce myself."

Brannagh laughs. "Natalie, I told you, Jack doesn't bite." Then, to me, he asks, "Isn't that right?"

"Yes, of course," I nod, before adding, "Not unless you put something near my mouth."

Brannagh puts a hand on my shoulder and laughs heartily. He then says, "Natalie's a lovely girl. You'd fail to find more charming company."

"Marty, stop it," says Natalie, giving him a light, playful shove. Mischief gleams in her emerald eyes.

"Jack, I'd love to catch up with you soon," says Brannagh. "Will you come over for dinner this week? If you're not too tired from recording the new album."

"Sure, that'd be great," I reply. "I'll get Amelia to arrange something."

"Excellent. We'll chat when things are a little less..." says Brannagh, waving a casual finger at the crowd around us, searching for a word.

"Hectic?" I offer.

"Yes. Exactly," says Brannagh. Turning to Natalie he adds, "Look after Jack. He's very precious to me."

"Don't worry, I'll leave him in one piece," promises Natalie, though I don't believe her.

Brannagh is absorbed back into the party, as everyone bides for a moment of his attention.

"So where were we?" asks Natalie.

"I was about to ask you a question," I respond. "But that was your second question, so now I get two more." Natalie huffs, knowing I've caught her out. "So what do you do for fun?"

"I love art. I work with an art group. Curating exhibitions, organizing openings, that sort of thing."

Exhibitions and openings. I let that one slide. I would ask her to elaborate, but every question is precious. "Alright, second question," I say, pulling her closer to me. My interior is electrified, tingling, buzzing and pulsing. My exterior is in control. Focused. Like stone. My hand slides down the small of her back, feeling skin through the fabric of her dress. My fingers find the top of her g-string. Natalie takes an audible breath when I whisper my question in her ear. "What colour is your underwear?"

My new acquaintance looks as if she may blush. For the first time in our encounter, she's not in total control. "You might get to find out," she says, softly.

"I will find out," I reply.

Natalie smiles, coquettishly. "You seem very sure of yourself."

I position myself between Natalie and the raging crowd of party guests behind us. Instinctively, she moves back slightly, leaning against the white rendered wall that fences the rooftop. I lean in and smell the skin near her ear, then lightly run my tongue across her earlobe and upper neck. I sense her body buckling from the sensation and a soft gasp escapes those delicious lips. If she really wants to enter Jack's world, then she will pay a toll.

"Give them to me," I whisper.

"What?" asks Natalie, glancing into my eyes, then over my shoulder at the party.

My hand reaches down and takes her right buttock in my hand, squeezing it tightly. The flesh is so firm it resists my fingers. "Take off your panties. Give them to me," I say in a low voice. My mouth is now dangerously close to hers. Her body is tense, as if she's bracing for me to take her. To defile her. Natalie's eyes are looking into my own, but her lust for me glazes them and it's as if she's looking inside me, seeing places the suns don't reach.

"Now?" she asks, barely audible.

"Yes," I reply, still clenching her buttock.

Natalie looks over my shoulder at the partygoers. Though I'm not facing the crowd, I know it's likely someone is watching us. But my body mostly blocks their view of her, affording limited privacy. Natalie looks me in the eyes again, our faces close and I feel her subtly reach beneath her dress and slide her g-string down, letting it fall to the ground. I kneel down and help her step out of the underwear, pulling the tiny black lace over her high heels. I fold them once and place them in my inner jacket pocket. When I stand up again, Natalie gently pushes her mouth against mine. Barely a kiss. More a rush of lust that has bubbled to the surface.

"Take me somewhere," she says, quietly.

"You lead and I'll follow."

Natalie smiles, the wicked glint returning to her eyes. I imagine it's similar to the final glance that sirens gave sailors before they tore the flesh from their bones. We begin to weave through the party, towards the stairs that lead back down to Brannagh's apartment. We pass Jennifer Fox and she doesn't look impressed, her eyes looking at Natalie's hand grasping my own. A few people say hello to me as I pass, but I can only nod. My focus is completely on Natalie and my overwhelming hunger.

On the footpath below, Natalie and I try to catch the attention of a passing taxi. It rolls past in the thick, balmy night air without seeing us.

"Where are we going?" I ask, still holding Natalie's hand. "Your place?"

I'm not allowed to take women back to my own apartment anymore, even though it still happens. I do try to discourage it and avoid it. For the first two years after my discovery I had to move home six times, because the world kept finding out where I lived. The footpaths on my block turned into an endless candlelight vigil, where thousands of teenagers sat and waited for me to appear. It was tranquil, flattering and a little disturbing. I don't have many possessions, so changing residence wasn't unbearable. I've been in my current apartment for nearly two years because the place is a fortress and the PR team at the record label do a darn fine job of spreading rumours that I live in Lower Easton, but spend most of my time on an island in the middle of the ocean. Of course, parties still happen. Girls still come and go. Fame keeps me reclusive, but only slightly exclusive.

Natalie turns and takes me by the collar of my shirt, pulling my body against hers, kissing me. As her tongue pushes against mine, I can feel blood turn on its heel and start advancing toward my groin.

Sensing my burgeoning excitement, Natalie pulls away. "No," she says, her eyes gleaming. "I'm going to make you wait."

The lights of another taxi pull into our block and Natalie quickly steps out into the road, the vehicle screeching to a halt in front of her. In the headlights she beckons me over with a finger. Once we're in the backseat, the driver asks us where we're going.

"Durté," says Natalie, squeezing my hand. The driver nods and takes off.

"Durté?" I whisper. "It's going to be a bit wild if I get recognised there. Shouldn't we head back to yours?"

"No," says Natalie, "we'll go to the new VIP room. We'll be safe in there."

"Sure," I shrug, feeling adventurous. "I'm putting my safety in your hands."

"Such a bad idea," says Natalie, before running one of her delicate, gloved hands through my hair and pulling my mouth against hers. Knowing she's not wearing a bra, my hand dives into the front of her dress, finding two breasts that make the concept of Heaven seem a little bit overrated.

Aesthetically, Durté is no different to any other seedy establishment, but the tastemakers decided it was cool. So now it's a choice locale to hang and you can barely get inside the place. Me and the other guys from the band used to go there because it was low profile. You could chill out. Now there's a perpetually long queue to get in. Overpriced drinks. Various famous faces and generally attractive clientele.

The cab pulls up outside the bar and there's a large crowd of people on the footpath. The neon Durté sign flickers above the tattered red awning that hangs uselessly over the entrance. A lot of people that went to the McCarthy Awards have come back to Durté to party on. Giant security guards in black uniform and radio headsets try to herd the human flock into a line.

We exit the cab after I pay the driver. Natalie leads me across the footpath towards the bustle of the doorway. Almost instantly the flash of cameras lights up the dim footpath. Natalie gets the attention of a security guard. Recognising me, he unfastens the velvet red rope and swiftly gestures for my companion and I to enter.

The air is thick with cigarette smoke and heavy metal music. Natalie and I push our way through the crowded room, with its sweaty bodies and raw brickwork. Most of the walls are covered with fading rock posters. Bands I've never heard of, most of which probably haven't even played this venue. Hanging behind the bar, above the rows of brightly coloured spirits, is a framed, autographed Big Bang Theory photograph. My serious expression looks down at me from across the room. I recognise my signature, though I don't remember writing it. If my eyesight serves me correctly, Dylan has drawn a penis rather than sign his name. That seems appropriate for so many reasons.

A random woman grabs my arm. She looks a similar age to myself and has bleached blonde hair and a lot of black eyeliner. Looks kind of punk. She yells over the music, "I love you, I love you!" She's sweating, as if she's on a lot of gear. Her eyes are wide and she's staring so close to my face that it makes me slightly uncomfortable.

"Pleasure," I say, trying to shake her hand. I don't kiss it. But she's squeezing my upper arm with both hands. She just stares at me, as if I'm not real. Then a friend of hers appears behind me and grabs my other arm.

"Stay and party with us. Please, just party with us," says the second woman.

"We love you," says the first woman. "Stay with us."

"I have to... go," I say. "But I'll come back."

Natalie has moved ahead without realising I'm not behind her. She turns to see the two women accosting me and quickly darts towards us, a fist raised.

"Get your fucking hands off him," she yells. The two women, despite their desperation, quickly release me. Natalie grabs the front of my jacket and starts pulling me through the room. I hear the women crying out behind me. This alerts more people around us who turn and recognise Jack. Bodies move towards me, shuffling like a room full of zombies who have caught a whiff of living meat. We quickly reach the far side of this main bar area, arriving at a red, velvet curtain that seems to glisten, as if made of flesh. A security guard, broad and tall, moves to block our path. Natalie motions toward me with an impatient hand and the security guard's face widens with surprise and recognition. He hurriedly pulls the curtain back for us to enter the VIP area.

It's not as crowded in here. Luxurious antique furniture is arranged around the spacious room, dark and leather upholstered. Dim lampshades. The people in the room all look up from their lounge chairs as I enter, recognising me. A few smile. A few wave. I vaguely recognise people. A swimsuit model. A television actress. A fashion designer. A record producer. Natalie seems to know most of them, greeting people as we float through the room, bending down to kiss them on the cheek. Natalie introduces me to a young man who is apparently a film producer and director. He says I should call him because he's got some "really fresh music video ideas that would really work for our songs". He hands me a card, which I put in my back pocket.

As we make our way toward the bar I catch three striking girls sitting at some lounges over in the corner. One of them is turning around, craning her neck to see me. I stare at them blankly. Then Natalie taps my arm.

"Jack, this is Lucius and Lyone," says Natalie, introducing me to two similarly dressed young men. Lucius has tight black jeans, buckled shoes, a loose fitting tee and a blonde quiff. There's a thin blonde moustache on his top lip and he's quite tan. Lyone has a black, military-style cap and a thicker, dark moustache. They both look vaguely familiar.

"Pleasure," says Lucius. "We actually met a few months back. At Brannagh's fashion fundraiser."

"Lucius owns Jest Station at the top of town," explains Natalie.

"Oh yeah, Jest Station. I've... worn stuff from there, I think," I say.

"That's one of our jackets," smiles Lucius, pointing at me. "Lyone actually designed it."

Lyone smiles. "It looks good on you."

"Lyone's clothing is fucking gorgeous," says Natalie, admiring the jacket. Then she asks me, "Did you know that Lucius and Lyone have a band now?"

"No, I didn't know that. I'm out of the circle," I say. "What are you called?"

"We're calling ourselves Gash," says Lucius.

"Gash? Nice," I say.

"Yeah, we're happy with the name," replies Lucius. "I think it sums up what we're all about."

"Party," I say.

"Oh, and congratulations on the awards tonight. Nice new song. Very buoyant... and kinetic," offers Lucius.

"Apreciativo," I smile.

The three girls from the corner of the room appear, sidling up to our conversation. Lucius smiles as he recognises them. "Jack, these are my friends Juniper, Anais and Mirabelle. They do a lot of modelling for the store," says Lucius.

"Pleasure," they all say, almost in unison.

"Pleasure," I say, lightly kissing the back of each of their hands.

"Actually, it's perfect timing that you're here," says Lucius. "The girls were just saying to me the other day how amazing it would be to get you in our next fashion shoot. The girls would love to work with you. What would it take to get you to come in for a fitting?"

I ponder for a moment before Natalie squeezes my hand and whispers in my ear very softly, "Those girls are total mechs." A term that's short for mechanics. Car mechanics. They do most of their work on their back.

Despite Natalie's petulant jealousy, I smile and reply, "I'll think about it."

The girls pout at my non-committal answer.

"It'll be tasty," says Lucius. "Nothing sour. Something with impact. With a serrated edge."

"Sounds intriguing," I reply. "Maybe. I'm just not sure, man."

"Okay," says Lucius. "To sweeten the deal I'll give you a lifetime's supply of new outfits. You'll never have to go naked."

"Well, my lifetime's almost over," I reply, with a sly grin.

"Oh, don't be so silly," says one of the models, whose name

might be Juniper. She has long limbs and is almost taller than me. Her face has a radiant allure, framed by long, straight black hair and a low fringe. On one of her bare shoulders is a colourful flower tattoo. "It'll be lots of fun."

"Fun, huh? I can't argue with that," I smile. I tell Lucius to get in touch with my management and "we'll organise something". The models then all ask to get photos with me and after they've each given me their phone numbers and suggested that I call them sometime, they return to their corner of the room and Lucius and Lyone head back to their group.

As Natalie and I pull up a stool at the bar, she turns to me and says, "A shoot for Jest Station? That's so under you."

"I thought you liked Jest Station?" I ask.

Natalie makes a disgusted sound. "It's cheap and boring."

"What about my jacket? It's a Jest Station special."

"It looks good on you," she smiles. "But everything does. I just think a shoot would be under you."

"When are *you* going to be under me?" I ask, before getting the bartender's attention.

Natalie smiles. "Are you being impatient?"

"Sort of. I keep remembering that you're not wearing any underwear."

"Well whose fault is that?"

"That you're not wearing underwear or that I keep remembering?"

I order two berry elixirs from the barman. He's a tall, muscular boy in a tight black tee, with a square jaw and a closely shaved head. As he begins mixing the drinks on the bar in front of us, Natalie studies him. Despite his obvious bartending experience, he seems slightly nervous to be serving me. Natalie keeps staring at him until he notices and glances back. He gives a meek smile and I can tell Natalie is satisfied that she's making him awkward. Her hand squeezes my upper thigh as she watches him.

"So," I ask Natalie. "Am I meeting your expectations?"

"What do you mean?" she asks, returning her attention to me.

"You must have had a perception of me before tonight."

Natalie ponders for a moment. "I think you've exceeded expectations."

"Cool," I say.

"I thought you'd be a bit more shy. You've been very forward. I like that."

"You've caught me in a weird mood."

"Weird? Is that your word for being really fucked up?"

"Maybe."

"Your pupils are massive and you're sweating," says Natalie, wiping my brow.

The barman finishes our elixirs and places them down in front of us. Natalie gives him an appreciative wink. As we both pick up our glasses, I propose a toast. "To new friends," I say. Natalie smiles and lightly chinks her glass on my own.

As I take a sip on my elixir, I feel a tap on my shoulder. I turn around to see two young women. One girl, who has an amazingly beautiful face and straight blonde hair, looks instantly familiar. She's a young actress by the name of Zara. I can't quite remember her last name. But she's in this film at the moment that's making huge amounts at the box office. It's about a girl that befriends a talking alien. I've only seen the poster, but to me the alien looks like a cross between a ferret and a spring roll. Children seem to find the alien's droll wit amusing and have been scooping up as much merchandise as their tiny arms can carry.

Zara seems excited to see me. "Hi Jack, it's pleasure to meet you. I love your music."

"Pleasure," I say, shaking her hand and lightly kissing the back of it.

"This is my friend Beattie," says Zara, motioning towards her friend, a petite brunette girl.

"Pleasure," I say, kissing Beattie's hand.

I can barely recognise Zara from what I've seen of her in film. Her characters are always conservative. Polite, dainty and well spoken. This is a slightly older version of her that is wearing a thinly strapped pink dress, which stops high above her knees. Her blonde hair is tussled, her face reinvented with make-up. Reimagined with drugs and dim lighting. I pull out a cigarette and light it.

"Did you win any awards tonight? Beattie and I were invited, but we couldn't make it," says Zara.

"Yeah, a few," I say.

"Congratulations!" says Zara, drunkenly, reaching out and putting her hand on my arm for balance.

"Gracias," I reply. I glance over my shoulder at Natalie and I can see her eyeing Zara and Beattie warily.

"I've just signed on to do a movie with Jennifer Fox," says Zara, now quite near my face. "You're *friends* with her, aren't you?"

I acknowledge how loaded her question is. "Yeah, we're friends," I reply.

"Right," says Zara, sipping more of her elixir. She stares at me as she puts the glass to her lips, as if I'll give something away at any moment. Then after she swallows, she asks, "So you're just friends?"

"Zara," says Beattie, embarrassed. "Leave Jack alone. Stop being such a trashbag."

"I'm not offending you, am I Jack?" asks Zara, mischievously, as she puts an arm around my shoulder.

"No, not at all," I reply, casually. "How's that alien movie going? I hear it's doing very well."

Zara shrugs, leaning into me. "Yeah, it's going well. Who knows? I shot it eighteen months ago."

"Well, you're great in it," I say.

"You saw it?" asks Zara, incredulously.

"Sure," I say. "But you look quite different in it. You look different now."

"Well, it was eighteen months ago," smiles Zara. "I look like an idiot in that movie."

"I really liked the alien," I continue. "But he looks kind of edible. He always looks really edible."

Zara pulls a weird face and Beattie laughs at my comment.

"They want to make it a quadrilogy," reveals Zara. "Three more movies."

"Will you and the alien marry?" I ask.

Zara and Beattie laugh.

"You know, Jack, you're as different as everyone says you are," says Zara, with a smile. "And that alien was made out of some weird rubber that gave me a rash. I hated the little bastard."

"Well, most wives find their husbands irritating," I say, dragging on my cigarette. "Just give it some time."

A socials photographer appears and asks all of us to get together for a photo. Although Natalie hasn't joined in the conversation, and has been quite territorial, she enters the photo, leaning into the left side of my body. Zara remains on the right and Beattie stands next to her. We all smile. All good friends. Another wave of euphoria washes over me and every sensation in my near vicinity becomes a beacon of boundless joy.

Once the photographer moves away, I introduce Natalie to Zara and Beattie. She shakes their hand politely.

"Do you girls come here often?" asks Natalie.

They both shrug, nonchalantly. "Maybe. If it's pumping. Depends on the crowd."

"We were about to leave, but then we saw that Jack was here," says Beattie.

"Well, gracias for coming over," I say, chinking my glass with Zara and Beattie. I feel immensely good right now.

"Do you come in here often?" Beattie asks me. "We've never seen you here."

"Yeah, I heard you don't even go out in public," adds Zara.

"I do," I say. "But I try to keep a low profile."

"I suppose it must be tough," says Zara, with a sympathetic expression. "I mean, I get recognised a lot, but it must be so much worse for you."

"You get used to it," I shrug.

At this moment a security guard steps in from behind the curtain to the VIP area and weaves his way around the room, whispering to the groups of people around us. As he murmurs his message, their facial expressions fill with concern. They stand and begin making their way toward the bar.

"What's going on?" I ask Natalie, pointing at the guard.

"I bet it's a raid," she says, reaching for her handbag. She rummages for a second and then hands me something small. I feel its diminutive weight drop into the palm of my hand, but don't look down. "Take this. It's the last of my drugs," whispers Natalie.

"What is it?" I ask.

"It's an anti-inhibitant."

"You don't say," I reply, slipping it into my mouth, swallowing with a sip of my cocktail.

Zara taps me on the shoulder. "Why is everyone... panicking?" she slurs.

"Drug officers," I say.

"Oh," says Zara. "Well, I don't have any left."

"Then you'll be fine," I smile.

Patrons arrive at the bar and hand the bartender small bags, which he places in what looks like a leather-bound book. But it's not. It's a safety deposit box that's been made to look like a book.

Once everyone has handed their drugs over, he approaches me.

"Is there anything you'd like me to look after, Jack?" he asks.

"No, I'm fine. Thank you though."

He looks slightly concerned. "Are you absolutely sure?"

Natalie takes my arm, seeing that I'm deep in a drug haze. "Jack, are you sure you have nothing on you?"

"They've brought porcines with them," adds the bartender. "They'll definitely sniff you out if you're carrying."

"Pigs?" says Natalie, with disgust. "They can't be fucking serious. They're going to bring pigs into Durté?"

The bartender shakes his head, mirroring Natalie's disdain, and walks away, sealing the security box. I stand up from my barstool.

"Where are you going?" asks Natalie.

"Just heading to the bathroom," I mumble, and walk towards the back of the VIP area.

Natalie calls something out, but I can't hear her. The room is spinning and I feel like I will collapse unless I get to the bathroom very soon. In some rudimentary way I know where I am, but my body and mind begin to draw apart. People are probably looking at me, but just like the DNA in the dank carpet and the smells soldered into each piece of furniture, they all disappear. Everything ends and I don't even realise.

The banging wakes me up. There's a voice somewhere in front of me. It occurs to my regained consciousness that my eyes haven't been shut. I'm sitting on a closed toilet, slumped back against the wall. Wide eyes staring blankly, rolling back in my skull. The loud thumping begins again, shaking the cubicle door on its hinges. I glance up and see a small mirror hovering above the door, an eye reflected in it.

"Sir, open this door now," yells the man.

I groan a response and sit up, preparing myself to stand. The officer bangs again.

"This seat's taken," I say in a low voice.

"Open this door now," says the officer again, more agitated.

I get to my feet and straighten my jacket, sparing a remote thought for the five pills and gram of cane in its inner pocket.

I unlock the door and pull it open. In front of me is a young drug enforcer. His black, collared uniform is crisp and ironed. Boots all shiny. Paraphernalia hangs from his belt. A neat haircut. Clean shaven. A rather forgettable individual. As his eyes widen, I can tell he has recognised me. His assertive tone suddenly escapes him.

"Uh, could you please step... outside the cubicle," says the young officer.

"Sure," I smile, then extend my hand. "Pleasure."

"I'm sorry, sir. I can't make contact until our porcines have inspected you."

"No problem," I reply, feeling more than a little groggy. I step out into the wide, dark bathroom. The lights in the ceiling have failed. The only illumination is the dull glow of long fluorescents that run across the top of the mirrors above the sinks. All the walls are covered in layers of ripped rock posters and calculated graffiti that are designed to look authentic. The white tiles below are stained like a chain smoker's teeth. "So we'll have contact after I'm inspected?" I ask.

The officer glances at me awkwardly. "Uh, that... depends on the results of the inspection."

"Can't you just inspect me yourself?" I ask, taking a step back and leaning against the rear wall of the bathroom. "Do you really need an animal to do your job for you?"

The officer doesn't reply. He shifts his weight from foot to foot. Another ten seconds of silence pass between us and he quickly steps to the bathroom's door, looking for his colleagues. He hurriedly motions at someone and says, "Bring them in here. All three."

"Are you sure you don't want to inspect me yourself?" I ask again, my voice reverberating around the room. "You never know what you'll find." I reach into my inner jacket pocket, locate Natalie's underwear and then hold them out for the officer to see. He nervously looks at me from the doorway, eyeing the small piece of fabric I dangle in the air. He looks away. I shrug and then hold the panties to my nose for a second before putting them away.

The officer returns to the centre of the room. "Please remain very still, sir. And do not touch the porcines. They can be very aggressive."

I smile, continuing to lean back against the wall. I'm feeling good again, as if the buzz has reached its plateau and I can just sit back and enjoy it.

I hear a series of deep grunts and snorts from outside. Then, as if some long, muscular blob of ink is pouring into my field of vision, the first of the giant porcines lumbers into the room. Its hooves hit the tiles and it stops for a second, almost recoiling, before it puts its snout to the tiles and snorts again. Regaining its confidence, it turns into the bathroom and inquisitively wanders in my direction. Another drug enforcer follows it in, holding a leash that's attached to a neck collar around the porcines broad, sinewy throat.

Porcines essentially look like giant pigs. Their broad bully heads give them the appearance of mutant heifers, pointed with a snout-like appendage. When fully grown, the concave curve of their backs is usually above the height of a man's waist. They're potentially very dangerous and if you encountered one in the wild you would run. Their rows of teeth are like that of a shark, jagged and unforgiving. In nature, they grow two sharp, straight tusks that jut from their drippings maws towards the ground. These marrowed implements effectively bust open live prey or carrion like a surgically-tuned boning knife. Although these professionally bred sniffers, which are currently honing in on me, have their tusks removed and are trained not to bite, they are still intimidating. They wear electrified collars that are used by their handlers to keep them in line, plugging them with a voltage if they follow their natural instincts.

The porcines' sense of smell is unparalleled. When trained to smell narcotics, they can detect them from anywhere. It doesn't matter where you're hiding them, whether its behind layers of clothing or in a bodily orifice, the snout seeks it out. The only thing that can fool them is airtight containers of a non-porous material. Something like the bartender's mystery tin, which at this moment is providing asylum for the VIP room's stash.

The first of the porcines clops toward me. Its handler's facial expression confirms that he too has recognised me.

"Be very still," says the first officer. "If the porcine senses something, it will raise its head and growl. It will not attack, but we will have to search you."

"So I shouldn't pat it?" I ask.

"Pat?" asks the man. "I, uh, don't know what that is."

"It's when I reach out a hand and gently stroke it," I reply.

The officer shakes his head. "No, no, definitely do not touch the animal."

The giant black pig tweaks its ears slightly and shudders, the dense muscles of its shoulders vibrating for a moment. It then slowly raises its head and the two black orbs in its eye sockets lock with my dilated pupils. It remains silent. I'm wary of it, as these animals have been known to shred a man's arm to the bone.

Then, led by their handlers, two more porcines idle into the bathroom. Now three pigs stand in front of me, forming a semi-circle, their intimidating presence a sight to behold. In my addled state, the grandeur of the situation is quite overwhelming. The two new porcines snort around my ankles, heaving air into their lungs. Then, almost simultaneously, they raise their bulbous heads and stare at me with empty, colourless eyes. A clear film of mucus moistens their kidney-shaped nostrils. All three stare. All three are silent. The ends of their snouts are dangerously close to my face. The four officers look puzzled, waiting for them to respond. To confirm my guilt.

"Remain still, sir," says one of the handlers. "If they growl, we are legally obliged to search you."

"They're... not growling," I say, smugly. "It seems they just want to be friends."

The three impressive creatures stare at me silently, not uttering so much as a sniffle. Their expression, though difficult to decipher in its livestockian vagueness, could almost be likened to genuine puzzlement. As if some aspect of me is elusive. They stare blankly. Intrigued.

The four officers look at each other for direction, before one says, "I think we'll have to assume this is a positive response," he says.

The other three seem uncertain. They don't know what to do. I'm clearly twisted beyond belief. Five minutes ago I was unconscious in a nightclub toilet cubicle. The only way I could be more obviously under the influence of drugs was if I was laughing maniacally and lobbing fistfuls of pills at them like confetti.

"They normally growl," shrugs one officer. "We can't search if they haven't identified him properly."

"I tell you what guys," I say. "Why don't we pass on this whole inspection thing. I'll sort you with some backstage passes to one of our shows. Bring the pigs. We'll have some fun."

"Sir, please be quiet for a moment. If those pigs make just the slightest noise, we're searching you," says the first officer.

The four of them all step away, forming a small huddle and discussing their next move. While they're distracted, I lightly pat the porcine to my right. As my hand strokes the rough, leathery hind on the back of its head, it gently faces downward, allowing my touch. No animosity or fear. Just some sort of mutual adoration or respect. Like a domesticated dog that just wants attention. Human contact. My hand moves down to its snout and it slithers a long, serpentine tongue from between its drooling lips, which falls across the back of my hand. I see glimpses of its jagged teeth, which remain tucked away and unbrandished.

At this point the other two porcines move in and try to nuzzle my hand also. All of them gentle and unthreatening, despite their unsettling appearance. In my warm chemical glow, I never feel fear. Just amazement at these giant, pig-like alien creatures that I've crossed paths with in my new life.

"Hey!" exclaims one of the officers. He wrenches a pistol from a holster on his belt and aims it at me. "Get your hands away from them!"

"Calm it down," I smile back. "They're licking me. That's a big emotional commitment for anyone. You'll embarrass them."

All four officers gape at the animals, their eyes wide in disbelief.

"They've never done that before," says one of the handlers. "They don't normally..."

The officer lowers his gun, as his colleagues stare at me. Returning the pistol to his holster, he looks at me and says, "They don't normally behave like that... toward people."

"They clearly recognise a fellow swine," I smile, suddenly feeling like a cigarette. "Gentleman, I need to find my companion. In the absence of a genuine ID, am I free to leave?"

The officers all look at each other, realising they're in unchartered territory. They've found themself somewhere that isn't on the map. After another quick group huddle, they let me go. This is extraordinary luck. If I had been apprehended and blood tested in my current state, the list of results would resemble the periodic table.

I'm in the side alley of Durté, kissing Natalie against the weathered brick wall. We're in darkness, unnoticed by the people that scurry past on the sidewalk a few metres away.

"So, Natalie," I say, between drawn-out, torrid tongue exchanges, "is it time we go to yours?"

Natalie shakes her head. "Not yet. I'm going to make you wait."

"No," I say, also shaking my head. "I can't." I put my hand up her skirt and push it against the smooth opening between her legs.

She gasps, grasping my wrist to push me away. "Ok, ok," she says. "One more club. One more club and you can take me."

"Where?" I ask, becoming agitated. My mental state means that patience is a virtual impossibility.

"A special place. It's so good, I promise you won't want to leave."

I hold my hand between her legs, pushing her against the wall. Trapping her. "I already know where I want to go and I *know* I won't want to leave."

"Jack," she says, quickly kissing me again. "One more club and I'm yours."

I should be suspicious when Natalie leans forward and seductively writes the name of our destination on the back of the taxi driver's hand, rather than simply telling him where we want to go. The lack of verbalisation should be a big hint. If you're going to the supermarket, then you generally feel comfortable just saying to the driver, "I'm going to the supermarket. Thanks buddy." It would be unusual to retrieve a pen from your handbag, give the driver a "come hither" smile and then make sure the cleft of your ample bosom is clearly visible as you lean forward into the front of the vehicle and scrawl something slowly across his hairy knuckles. But that's what Natalie is doing and I don't really quiz it. Natalie is unusual and a little scary. She just does things like that. It's in her *nature*.

I'm not even paying proper attention when the driver reads his hand and then turns to Natalie with a shocked expression. She just vampishly reclines into the rear seat of the taxi. "C'mon Mr. Driver. We don't have all night." She then lifts her left calf and drapes it over my right leg, slightly parting her magnificent thighs. The driver glances hesitantly in the rearview mirror and then drops his foot on the accelerator.

Natalie and I kiss in the backseat. She takes my hand and moves it between her legs, my fingers assessing the area and sending visual descriptions to the rest of my body. It's clear that the feedback is well received. I'm so preoccupied that I don't notice that our vehicle has left the main arteries of city traffic and begun winding through the outskirts of the central business district. My peripheral vision senses the lack of neon lighting outside our car, which is now weaving through side alleys, following two wide cones of headlight.

"Are we...?" I try to ask, before Natalie pushes her tongue back into my mouth. Another turn and we're at our destination.

I can see neon again. There's a glowing sign, with groups of shadows loitering near the entrance that it marks. I can hear the distant sound of hard electronica. Like cannon fire rolling beyond nearby hills. But we're in the industrial district and all around us, everywhere you look, is decrepit brick and decaying masonry. Concrete central.

The neon sign says Membrané. I've only been here once, but I didn't stay long. The very mention of this place makes even porn stars raise their eyebrows and say, "That place is fucked up."

Natalie hands a note to the driver and tells him to keep the change. He nods meekly, almost too nervous to turn and look at the venue he's dropping us off at. Natalie takes my hand and swiftly pulls me from the cab. The doormen immediately recognise me and the entrance is pushed open.

The dank smell of sweat hits me like a tissue soaked in chloroform, giving me a heady, spinning sensation. All the lights are red. Bright red. Dark red. Blood red. There's no other colour besides scarlet, crimson and various black shadows. This is where the depraved come. Though some would argue that they're quite normal. In tune with their prehistoric disposition. Perhaps it's the faux mask of civilisation that is too perverse to be allowed through these doors. Those fragile pillars of decorum are not welcome.

As we make our way through the seated area near the entrance, where people sit around low tables, I get a hazy sense that there are people engaging in sexual activity. Not blatantly. People are laughing and chinking glasses in a display you might see in any nightspot. But their hands are under the tables. Stroking. Squeezing. This is where the exhibitionists come to be a part of the throbbing exhibit. Many of the punters are too drug-fucked and preoccupied to notice my arrival, but a few catch my eye and stare, summing me up. Figuring out if that's Jack they see or some apparition.

Natalie orders two drinks at the bar. The barmaid, a tattooed, busty girl with facial piercings, dark spiky hair and a black singlet, glances at me and smiles. When she puts the two drinks on the bar, which are served in test tubes that dangle in a rack, Natalie leans over the bar, asking her a question. The barmaid leans in to hear her and then points toward the back of the club to our right.

Natalie lifts each of the tubes from their holder and hands me one.

"Ready?" she asks, yelling in my ear so I can hear her over the throb of the music.

"Sure," I say, lifting the tube to my mouth before asking, "what is this?"

"A night to remember," smiles Natalie, and pours the elixir down her throat.

I do the same. It burns slightly, but as it slides down my chest it feels extremely good. My skin feels as though it may rise in goosebumps. I feel charged and content, ready to do anything. Natalie is too tantalising and my layers of decency and self-control can no longer protect her.

Still at the bar, I pull Natalie against me and put my mouth next to her ear. "I can't wait," I say. "Let's do it now, or I'm going."

Natalie kisses me. "Are you sure? You're ready to go?"

"I was born ready," I reply.

"Ok," shrugs Natalie, cheekily. She takes me by the hand and leads me to a corridor that feeds off the back of the dance area. People gyrate around us to the DJ's selections. Even in the disorientating flash of the strobe I can see that people on the dance floor are having sex, grinding against each other.

As we walk up the corridor, the music shifts from its relentless hum to a slow-building release. Halfway up the narrow path begins a series of red curtains, like a laneway of dressing rooms. Most are closed. As the music becomes more distant I hear muffled groans from behind the sheets of draped material.

Halfway down the row, we arrive at an open curtain. It exposes an empty booth. Natalie leads me inside and closes the red velvet. The booth is only a few metres wide, with a bench seat running around its inner perimeter. On one corner of the bench are a bottle of lubricant and a box of tissues. The walls are slick and black, immaculately polished and our reflections stare back at us, as if etched in the surface of obsidian.

Natalie takes off her white shirt. I pull the thin straps of her dress from her shoulders and it falls down, revealing her large, caramel breasts. I take each of them into my mouth, gorging on her flesh. Natalie runs her sharp, taloned fingers through my hair, pulling me against her.

My jeans are unzipped and Natalie reaches in, taking a firm grip on my quickening erection. Pulling it out she leans down and takes me in her mouth. I savour the sensation of her lush, soft lips and her darting tongue. She strokes me with one of her thinly gloved hands as she moves her mouth on me.

Natalie lifts her head and I lean down to kiss her, our tongues pushing against each other. She puts her hands on my cheeks and looks me square in the eyes. "I want you inside me," she says. Reaching for the lubricant, Natalie screws off the lid and starts to squeeze the thick, clear contents over my fully hardened shaft. She then pulls off one of her gloves and uses her bare hand to spread the lubricant over the length and tip. Taking a tissue, she daintily wipes her hand and then turns away from me, lifting her skirt. Her smooth, perfect buttocks appear and my eyes descend down the muscular curves of her thighs and calves. Natalie's naked rear is pointed at me, awaiting entry.

"I want you to fuck my ass," she says, looking back at me with unleashed intensity. "Use me..."

Natalie relaxes her rear opening as I push against it, and I'm allowed inside. While at first I treat her gently, thinking that I may cause her discomfort, it is apparent that she wants me to take her with a higher degree of animalistic savagery. Natalie forces herself back against me, pushing her hands against the wall in front of her for leverage. I watch the entire length of my erection disappear inside her firm backside.

As we build into a consistent rhythm, Natalie starts to squeeze her rectal muscles around me. In response, I hold her firmly by the hips and begin to fuck her as she requested. She throws her head back, resting it against my shoulder, grunting with abandon. I bite down on her neck, sinking in my teeth as far as I can without drawing blood.

"Yes!" she howls. "Bite me. Bite me... fuck me harder. Don't stop fucking my ass."

The semi-human traits Natalie and I had before entering this booth have surely left us. We rut like two fallen angels, tangled in a knotted ball of sweat and interlocked biology. Completely alone with our most carnal desires. With every thrust, I bury myself as deep in Natalie as our mechanics will allow, seemingly bringing her greater pleasure. She takes one of my hands, bringing it in front of her, and I find her pussy with my fingers. She grips my wrist tightly, forcing me to stimulate her.

I light a cigarette. The combination of tobacco and the chemicals my brain has released post-orgasm, trigger another high and the drugs in my system kick into another gear. I pull a pill from my wallet and chew it, my mouth filling with the dirty, medicine taste.

"That was so fucking hot," says Natalie, as she reclines on the bench across from me. Her eyes are closed and she drags on a cigarette of her own. "I wonder if *they* enjoyed it," she adds, motioning towards the wall next to us.

"They?" I ask, despite immediately comprehending her revelation. We're in a booth. Not a private booth.

"Our audience," smiles Natalie, finally opening her eyes and gazing at me. Her pupils are wide and dark and she's clearly peaking.

I drag on my cigarette and the pills in my system cloud my emotions. My reaction to this voyeuristic twist is dulled. I don't feel anything.

"I've wanted to fuck you since the moment I first heard you sing," coos Natalie, closing her eyes again, submitting to the pills. She rests her head against the black reflective wall. "I first saw you play at the Ellis Theatre. I knew one day I'd have you inside me."

"That's very nice of you to say."

"One night I met you at the Walkley Gallery," she adds.

"I remember."

Natalie smiles. "You want to keep partying with me?" she asks. "Now that you've had me?"

"Why not?" I reply. "I may as well see where the train terminates."

"It doesn't," says Natalie. She opens her eyes and stares for a moment, exhaling a plume of smoke from her nostrils. Then she leans in and whispers. "Did you know that this club has a Narc den?"

"The wonder drug?" I ask, with a hint of sarcasm.

Natalie huffs and leans back again. "Don't joke," she says. "I tried it a month ago. It's everything people say it is."

I don't respond, my eyes wandering across the skin of Natalie's legs. My mind is bouncing around a series of thoughts, like a fly navigating a glass room, looking for the exit.

"Words can't describe it," says Natalie, closing her eyes. "It's like walking with God."

"I don't think I have a spare week," I say.

"Spare a week. Trust me. A week is just a period of time. Narc is bigger than time. It controls time."

Natalie finishes her cigarette and redresses. She then takes me by the hand, leading me from the booth. We descend deeper into the club. Passing the rest of the booths, many of them with their curtains closed, I squint in the darkness to get a bearing on my surroundings. The blackness is lit by strobing lights of red above us that blink rapidly, setting all movement in slow motion. The corridor opens up and we step into another dance floor area and I can see and feel bodies moving all around us. Swaying to the music. Natalie stops for a moment and turns to kiss me. She bites on my lower lip but I'm too drug-addled to feel any pain. The pulsing, electronic music wraps us in its cocoon.

Natalie leads me across the rest of the dance floor to a dimly lit staircase. As we descend, we squeeze past a couple having sex against the wall. At the base of the stairs, a man performs fellatio on another man. We step into a foyer-like room with a low ceiling. The walls are dark concrete, like a bunker. Across the foyer stand two heavily-built security guards dressed in black uniforms, who are positioned either side of a reinforced steel door.

Natalie approaches one of the guards and leans up on her toes to kiss him on the cheek.

"Mind letting us in?" she asks, coquettishly.

"You've been here before, haven't you?" asks the guard.

"Yes, I have," she smiles. "But this time I've brought a friend."

The guards turn their eyes on me. Both of them nod in respectable greeting, recognising me. The silent guard pulls a small card from his pocket and swipes it across a panel to the right of the doors. The doors then make a muted, echoed growl, like a piece of metal retracting, and slowly swing open.

"Thank you for visiting us," says the first guard, and nods at me again. Natalie takes my hand and excitedly leads me through the door.

More stairs. This time I can't see the bottom. The narrow tunnel's roof has lights sporadically placed every few metres, just enough to see the stairs directly below them.

"You ready to go deeper with me?" asks Natalie, turning to kiss me again.

"Yes," I say, when she pulls away. "I've no reason not to."

This makes Natalie smile. She takes my hand and we begin our descent. The heavy door is closed behind us and the throbbing music of the club is almost silenced. Its lingering echoes may only be in my ears. My hand runs along the ancient grey brick around us, as I attempt to balance on my shaky feet.

The stairs arrive at a silver elevator door. Natalie pushes a small button and the door parts for us.

"Someone told me that this place is an abandoned military facility," says Natalie, as we step inside. I look at the elevator's control panel. There's no other option than a single button with an arrow on it. The arrow points down.

"Hectic," I say, more to myself than Natalie.

Natalie wraps her arms around my neck in an embrace. "I'm so glad you're here with me." She rests her head on my shoulder and I take a moment to smell her hair. With a loud, locking sound, the elevator's movement slows and we are again stationary.

The elevator doors open and we step out. We're in a giant room that's as big as an airplane hangar. It's so long I can barely see its end. Running throughout much of its length are beds. Hospital beds. Next to each of them stands a drip with a bag of clear liquid. There's over a dozen rows and they stretch as far as the distant wall. On all of the beds around us are people, who lie in an assortment of outfits, many of them uniforms. Most have their eyes closed, others do not. They lie with their arms folded across their chest, as if arranged for an open coffin. In their mouths they have a piece of plastic, like a horse's chomping bit. The air is filled with the sound of quiet moaning.

Between the rows wander male and female attendants in hospital garb, who stop at each bed and make notes on a clipboard. To our immediate right is a small reception desk. Behind it sits a young, blonde girl. She has a computer in front of her, chews on gum and is twirling her long ponytail. She's wearing a telecommunication headset. Her eyes fix on us as we approach and she smiles.

"You're back again, Natalie," says the girl, grinning widely.

"Yes," says Natalie, nodding enthusiastically. "And I've brought a friend."

"I can see you have," says the girl. "A very famous friend, by the looks of it."

"Pleasure," I say.

The phone on the girl's desk rings. "Excuse me for a moment," she says, and answers. "M and L Accounting, how may I be of service?" she asks into the mouthpiece of her headset and listens to the person on the line. "Mr McCarthy, how are you? ... Yes, we are close to capacity... I have some new clients about to check in, but I will call you straight back. Thank you." She hangs up.

"I'm sorry I don't have an appointment," says Natalie to the receptionist, "but you mentioned that sometimes it was worth coming down here anyway. Just to check."

"Yes, of course," says the receptionist. "You happen to be in luck. We have some beds that just became available. Will you both be staying with us?"

Natalie looks at me. I don't say anything.

"You're staying, aren't you Jack?" asks Natalie. She whispers, "I want you in the bed next to me."

"I don't think I can," I say.

Disappointment crosses Natalie's face. I put my hands on her waist as reassurance. "I have to do interviews tomorrow, plus a photo shoot. If I don't turn up, it will arouse a lot of suspicion."

Natalie pushes my hands away. "Fine. You go on playing their little games." She turns to the receptionist. "Just one bed."

"Excellent," smiles the receptionist. Turning to me she says, "Of course, there is no pressure. But you will enjoy yourself here, Jack."

"I don't doubt it," I say. "But this isn't a good week for me."

I hear Natalie huff, petulantly. A young woman in a nurse's uniform and nametag approaches us.

"This is Anjelika," says the receptionist. "She'll show you to your bed, Natalie."

Natalie follows Anjelika into the maze of beds, never turning to say goodbye. She walks solemnly, her disappointment with me still evident.

"So the drug lasts a week?" I ask the receptionist.

"Approximately," she replies.

"And the reality starts instantaneously?"

"Yes. Some people describe that they don't even feel like they've gone to sleep. They lie on the bed, then stand up and leave here. Their dream starts in a way that's entirely normal or believable to them. Something familiar. Then within a few hours they become more imaginative. That's when the fun really starts."

"Why are they all moaning?" I ask.

"Well," says the receptionist, "it's a completely realistic sensory experience and you're in total control. It doesn't take men very long to figure out that in their Narc sleep, they can have anything they want."

"You're one of the last women that these men see before they go under," I say, smiling. "So you'll be fresh in their mind."

She shrugs. "They're not hurting anyone."

"What makes the women moan?"

"Although we can't know for sure, my guess would be that their inner desires aren't all that different from the men."

"Is it addictive?" I ask.

"The drug's not. But the sensation of having no boundaries is."

I stand on the footpath outside Membrané and glance back for a brief moment before calling a taxi. I don't remember much of the ride home. Just streaks of neon reflected in the vehicle's windows. I pull Natalie's g-string from my inner jacket pocket, smelling it for a moment before returning it to its resting place.

When I wake up, I'm ablaze with sunlight. My bedroom curtains are drawn back and I'm lying naked on my bed. My head throbs. Lying against my ribs is an empty bottle of Vodkai, which I don't remember drinking.

I roll on to my stomach and drag myself to the top draw of my bedside dresser. I find a bottle of painkillers. Taking an unopened beer that I've left next to the bed, I wash down four tablets.

I lie on my back and wait for the imminent calm to lift me. I close my eyes and watch shifting shapes of colour dance and then devour each other. I try to focus my thoughts and stop myself from drifting off into darkness, but I can hear voices pushing me. Whispers of paranoia. Pixels of light scattering across the universe. Somewhere in the expanse there's a flash of orange and two voices scream. Two screams I never heard.

I really hate bad comedowns.

# CHAPTER FOUR

"I just consider myself a songwriter. I'm not a rock writer or a punk writer or a pop writer. A good song transcends genres. You should be able to convert it to any style and still have it retain its emotional impact."

I'm generous with my time when it comes to the media. We share a relationship. I find that the more I give them, the less they want to make up or invent about me. It also takes the novelty away from unauthorized images of me. I have nothing to protect or to lose.

The interviewer, a young punk chick with a sleeve of tattoos on her right arm and black, thick-rimmed glasses smiles and glances down at the questions on her notepad. Our chat will be turned into a cover story for a national magazine called *Distortion*.

"Do you ever feel at odds with your fame?" she asks.

I pause, before finally answering, "Yes, I suppose. I sometimes wonder whether I deserve attention. Am I diverting coverage away from people that really matter? But then I remind myself that I love sharing my music. It's like giving a mixtape to a new girlfriend. It's a unifying experience."

"What can you tell me about your next record?" she asks.

"It's just another collection of songs," I shrug. "There's no over-arching aim beyond releasing another bunch of music. We're really happy with it. It's a diverse record, but it's also consistent and cohesive. I think that's been the key to our success. We're able to try new things without alienating our fans."

We're in the Evelyn, a hotel only five blocks from my apartment. It sets a high benchmark for decadence. Endurance Records often books rooms here to conduct media days with its artists.

I'm feeling particularly lucid, which is unusual considering the pills I've dropped, so I take a long sip from my rum and cola. I feel a deep, comforting burn slide down my throat and into my stomach. It's strong. The dash of cola I added was only a token gesture.

"Will it be a happy album?" asks the girl.

"I think so," I reply. "It won't be an *un*happy album. We're very aware of our live shows and what feels good on stage, so I think we've focused on writing songs that really move an audience. Like, 'Black Dog' is a real party-starter. We've got another new song that's coming together called 'Seven Nation Army'. I'm looking forward to getting that one out there for people to hear."

"Any slow songs?" she asks.

"Yeah, there's a couple. There's one called 'Winter Coat' which is this wistful tune about a guy who owns this old coat that one of his ex-girlfriends bought for him. They're long broken up, but every time he wears it he remembers her," I say.

"That's sweet," says my interviewer. "That's why whenever I break up with someone I get rid of everything that reminds me of them and burn it. It's easier that way."

"I suppose everyone's different," I smile, and for a moment wish that I had something tangible from one of the people from my past life. Some artifact to remember them by.

The girl asks me a few more questions, one of which is about my love life. "Equal parts treacherous and depraved," is my answer.

Once all the questions are asked, a publicist from the record label leads me into an adjacent bedroom, which has been decked with studio lights. A camera on a tripod is pointed at the wide, elaborate bed. I'm shown to a stool that sits in front of a table that is covered in various kinds of make-up and a free-standing mirror. A young, attractive woman in tight jeans and a singlet then hovers around me, teasing my hair and dabbing products on my face. Foundation. Eye liner. Then lots of hair spray. When once I was retardant, now I am flammable.

I'm introduced to the photographer, Marcelo. He says he's delighted to meet me and shakes my hand effeminately. He and the stylist stand back, analyse my appearance and share quiet remarks.

The stylist makes slight alterations to my hair. Once they're both satisfied, Marcelo shows me to the bed. Shirtless, I recline into the bank of extravagant pillows and cushions. I lie back, my hands draped by my side. Marcelo repositions a few of the lights and then approaches me, holding out a light meter and taking readings in the space around my face. He then stands back and assesses me, rubbing his chin.

"I think we need to sex this up a little bit more," he says, with a hint of an accent. "You should unbutton your jeans. We need to tease."

"Not a big scandal, just a hint of scandal," agrees the stylist.

Marcelo firmly suggests that I undo the top two buttons of my jeans. It's a cover shot, so a line must be drawn somewhere. Marcelo peers through the camera and starts snapping. Then he tells the stylist to hand me an acoustic guitar, which is then propped next to me on the bed.

"Give me more from your eyes, Jack," says Marcelo, as he takes the camera from the tripod and begins to bob and weave, shooting from various angles. "Pretend I'm your next conquest. Seduce me. Make me want to come on to the bed with you."

"That would be easier if you gave her the camera," I say, motioning to the stylist. She blushes.

I give Marcelo a burning stare and my audience seems to love it. I should feel more uncomfortable, but I have so many pills circumnavigating my bloodstream that I feel peaceful, almost removed from the situation.

I pick up the guitar and Marcelo continues to take photos as I strum the strings, gazing out the open doors on to the balcony and at the city beyond. I play the melody of 'It Ain't Me Babe'.

My mind wanders as I gaze at the skyline of mammoth skyscrapers, like grey columns coated in reflective glass. Marcelo continues to dance around the room, creating the magic that has made him hot property in the world of fashion photography. It was his idea to have me draped, half-naked, on a bed holding an acoustic guitar. Genius. The editor of *Distortion* felt that it would "depict me in my natural state". The planned headline for the cover story is 'Sheets Music'. It's telling when your libido draws more attention than your songs.

Once Marcelo is satisfied, the shoot is a wrap. I step out to the balcony and light a cigarette. Marcelo's assistant brings me a cold beer. I use it to wash down another pill. She offers me some food, but I politely decline. I haven't had an appetite for a few days now.

I think about Natalie and leaving her down there somewhere in the ground. A dark place beyond most people's imagination. I wonder if I'll see her again.

The magazine has provided me with a driver, who is supposed to take me home. Instead, I ask him to take me to the beach, which is only a ten-minute walk from my apartment. A minor deviation. He drops me off across the street from the sand and I hand him a random note from my wallet. He thanks me and drives away.

Dusk is approaching, but the beach is still covered with bathers who either frolic, play games, or lie on their towels with a book or magazine. Soaking the final rays of the descending suns. Casting twin shadows. I walk down the warm concrete steps towards the beach, which is mostly covered with the elongated silhouettes of the tall buildings towering above.

I sit away from the crowd, down the far end of the beach. I pull off my shoes and lie down, stretching out into the cooling sand. A group of young, bronzed bodies play a game of football about fifty metres away and out on the ocean surfers lie on their boards, waiting for the next set of waves.

Luckily, no one has noticed me. My mind is too empty to make conversation. When I step out in public like this, I'm invariably hounded by fans or attention seekers. It can get ugly. Sometimes I'm reminded that it would be so much easier to be in a coma. Or better yet, a Narc coma where anything I want will morph before my eyelids. But this is the reality I've created.

Of course, a world without physical boundaries, like a Narc reality, could go either way. I might engage in even more sexual activity than I do now. A waiting room and a turnstile on my bedroom door. A river of flesh that washes me downstream. I could drown in carnal sensations and blooms of serotonin.

The calming sand drifts me away. I close my eyes and from somewhere in a past life I watch an explosion. I press my face against a reinforced window and see a hollow expanse of darkness flicker with sparks and debris. Desperate silence. Pieces of twisted metal and personal belongings from our living quarters are sucked into cold eternity. I don't know where my crew is but they are definitely not on my side of the airlock, which I closed behind me.

It would have meant joining them in their fate.

My section of the spacecraft, now completely broken away from its lower half, swings around, giving me a view of the wreckage. The lower half of the Endeavour has almost completely disintegrated. If I stay where I am, I risk my section ripping apart also. I can't see them. I turn and head for the escape pod.

Flecks of sand land on my face. I open my eyes behind my sunglasses and see a ball resting next to my head. Bounding after it is a short, blonde girl with breasts that are disproportionately large compared to the rest of her body. Maybe only sixteen. A honeyed complexion and a tiny, two-piece bikini. She picks up the ball and smiles down at me, staring for a moment with big blue eyes.

"Are you... in a band?" she asks.

"Which band?" I reply.

"Big... Bang Theory?" she guesses, hesitantly.

"Yes, that's me."

"That's so loose. Hang on a second!" The girl runs back across the sand, returning the ball to her friends. She then comes back on her own.

"My name's Britney," she says, extending a hand as she sits next to where I'm lying.

No shit. That's the first time I've heard that name on this planet. "Nice name," I say. "Sounds exotic."

Britney looks a little embarrassed. "Yeah, my mother sort of... invented it."

It could be the drugs in my system, but I suddenly have a small existential panic attack. "Nice one," I smile.

"This is so crazy, my friends would die if they realised who you were."

"Is that right. Why didn't you tell them?"

"Have you ever seen gulls fighting over scraps?"

I give a small chuckle. "So you're a smart gull."

"Yep," grins Britney, with her cherub-like features. "So how come you're on your own?"

"Circumstance. I just did this photo shoot and I was pretty bored, so I came here."

"Who was the photo shoot for?"

"*Distortion.*"

"I love that magazine!" gushes Britney. "Are you on the cover?"

"Yes, I believe so."

"Crazy," says my new friend, who begins to play with her short ponytail, which is matted with sea salt. "You must have an amazing life."

"I get by."

The shadows of the city's skyscrapers have now covered the sand and the increasing breeze blows gusts of cold air from the ocean, extinguishing the humidity.

"Does your band have any new music coming out soon?"

"We're working on something."

"Hectic," says Britney. "That's really hectic."

"Yes." Despite my better judgment, I'm examining Britney's body from behind my sunglasses. She's a compact collection of firm curves that never cross paths with each other.

"You seem to bring out a lot more music than other bands," says Britney. "And everything you write is so good!"

"That's very nice of you to say."

"Is it true that you were homeless?"

"It wasn't that I didn't have a home. My home was everywhere."

I ask Britney about herself. She's seventeen. Last year of high school. Loves music and going to concerts. Wants to be an astronomer, of all things. She speaks enthusiastically and candidly about her plans, without the pretentious chest-beating that I often wade through in my social circle.

As the suns approach the horizon somewhere behind us, Britney's friends call out and tell her they're leaving. "I'm staying here!" she calls back. Her friends all shrug and walk up the beach toward their cars. Britney then turns to me and asks randomly, "How old are you?"

I contemplate lying, which I do. "Thirty-four."

"Twice my age," smiles Britney. "You're an old man."

"I feel old," I say, finally sitting upright.

"So, what are you doing now?" asks Britney. Her question is loaded. It should be owned by the military.

"Nothing really. Probably just heading home."

"Cool, well we should keep hanging out. You're really nice."

"I'm not just some creepy old guy?" I say, getting to my feet and brushing the sand off my jeans and shirt.

"You're famous, old and creepy," she says with a cheeky grin, still sitting.

"Well, you want to hang out with me, so I can't be *that* creepy."

Another cold wind sweeps up from the waves and Britney lifts her arms to cover her bare shoulders. It pushes her breasts together and the sight is regrettably magnificent.

"My ball landed next to you," says Britney, who also stands. "It could have landed next to anyone. But it landed right next to my favourite singer."

Another cold wind envelops us and Britney starts to shiver, her flesh rising in goosebumps.

"You should get your things," I say.

"Yeah, everything's over there," she says, pointing. We start walking over to where Britney has left her belongings. A small tote bag and a towel. No clothing. We walk up to where the sand meets the footpath, and stand in the declining light.

"You don't have to be somewhere?" I ask.

Britney shakes her head, wrapping the towel around her small waist. A jogger runs past with a dog in tow, his eyes inspecting Britney and I. A paparazzi appears across the road, squatting behind a parked car, and I realise I can't be here any more. A hire car turns into our street and I step out, flagging it down. I open the back door for Britney and she steps inside.


Britney is standing in my kitchen. She removed the towel from her waist as we entered my apartment. There's very little fabric to protect her modesty. I pull a pill from a small jar in the cupboard and put it in my mouth, discreetly. I offer Britney a drink.

"What have you got?" she asks.

"Everything."

"I'll have something mixed with juice, if you have it."

"I do." I make two mixers, putting twice as much vodka in my own as I do hers. I hope it blocks the softly spoken voice of my conscience. I then take a sip to wash down the pill that waits patiently in my mouth.

Britney sips her drink. "Your apartment is amazing," she smiles.

"You should see the view," I offer.

"I'd love to, but I feel pretty gross," she says, motioning toward her exposed body.

"Of course," I say. "You can have a shower, if you like."

I find Britney a towel in my bedroom closet, as well as a suitcase of women's clothing I've accumulated. Britney stands in my living room and I hand her the towel. Setting the suitcase down, I explain, "This is a bunch of clothes that you can try on if you want." I click it open and lift the lid. Britney's eyes widen and she kneels down next to it, rummaging through.

"Who owns all of this?" she asks.

"Lots of people. Clothing gets left here sometimes." Few come back to claim their forgotten items. It's a suitcase of cotton memories.

Britney occasionally lifts a garment up to examine it, holding some against her body to see if the size is right. She lifts up a simple, but expensive looking singlet top. "This is a Magasin de Sueur," she says, reading the label. "This brand is really expensive."

"Have it," I say. "It won't fit me anyway."

Britney chooses the top and a small pair of denim shorts, and heads for the bathroom, the towel tucked under her arm. I adjourn to the balcony for a cigarette. When I finish it, I pack up the suitcase and return it to my room. As I walk up the hallway I can see light pouring from the bathroom, which has been left wide open. I hear the sound of running water. I walk to the bathroom door, leaning against the frame. Britney is standing naked in the open shower, rinsing her hair under the jet of water. She sees me and smiles.

# CHAPTER FIVE

I'm not sure how long I've been out. There's a thick burning smell around me. Pain is shooting through my shoulders and up the back of my neck. Everything is silent and for a minute I panic that I've lost my hearing. But when I move my arms I can just make out the ruffled sound of my space suit. I sit in darkness except for a red, blinking light above me.

I take a deep breath. There's an aching near my ribs, but I'm alive.

I don't know how long I lie here for. Perhaps half an hour. My pod is rocking slightly. It feels like I'm on water. Floating. It must be water.

I unclasp the harness that holds me down and attempt to stand up. My right ankle feels tender when I put weight on it, but I can reach the escape hatch in the top of the pod. I rummage and find the oxygen tanks and face mask that are secured under a panel in the floor.

When I open the hatch, I find the world outside in near blackness. A faint, distant glow on the horizon provides little light, but I'm on an ocean. Through my mask I can smell salt. The dark liquid around me stretches to every corner of the horizon, where it meets the thin red line of an apparent sunset. Black, yellow and red congealing in the distance.

I breathe oxygen from the two small tanks on my back. I'm hesitant to inhale the air around me, but I know my supply will eventually empty and I'll have no choice. I take deep breaths to calm myself, but my heart continues to race.

I locate an emergency flotation device and then delicately climb down the pod's exterior. The metal beneath me makes sporadic squeals as it cools. Plumes of smoke erupt near the edge of the liquid, which is only inches from my toes. I deploy the flotation device and it self-inflates. It's designed to carry three adults, so I'll have legroom. One lonely, silent passenger. It bobs gently as it floats on the liquid. I inspect it for signs of corrosion. There's no hissing. No steam. Just the faint smell of salt. I attach a small outboard motor to the back of the life raft. It's only the size of a wall clock, but it can really fly. I then locate a travel pack in the pod, which has minimal rations, a thermal blanket and a flare gun. It also contains a universal phone. We use them to communicate in space. If someone comes to rescue me, they'll make contact via this small black device. I place the travel pack in the raft.

Safe in the knowledge that I will die of starvation if I stay with the pod I lower myself into the raft, start the motor and set off into the disappearing light. I can't say I'm not scared but if death is my fate on this planet, then there's no point in milking the suspense.

Once I'm about five hundred metres away, I slow the motor until it rolls to a halt. I can still make out the triangular shape of the pod on the ocean. I reach into a side pocket on my pack and remove a small rectangular box. It's a detonator. I peel a sticker off the back of the palm-sized device and find a twelve-digit number. I then enter the code on the keypad on the front of the detonator, watching the numbers appear in the small digital display. I click a confirmation button five times in one second intervals. A red light appears above the display. I kick the motor into life and take off, speeding away.

After twenty seconds I glance back to see the pod erupt into a ball of fire, a thousand shades of yellow and orange twisting and twirling before turning into black smoke. Small pieces of debris shoot through the darkening night like flaming arrows. I pull the back of the detonator away from the front to ensure it's no longer airtight and then throw its parts into the ocean.

Set in the front of the raft is a small compass. It appears to be working, but I can't trust it. I have no point of reference. Nevertheless, it may help me avoid travelling in a circle.

Hours pass and I start to shake uncontrollably. I can't stop my body from convulsing. But I'm not cold. I'm just frightened. The raft is skimming the surface of the liquid at a rapid pace. The thin glow on the horizon has died, leaving me to charge into nothingness. I have turned on a small light on the front of the raft, which carves through the night and exposes the metres in front of me. At this speed, if an obstacle appeared in my path I wouldn't have time to avoid it. I'm as good as blind. But I need to keep moving.

The surface of the liquid becomes choppy and the raft is suddenly dipping up and over waves. I hold on tightly, slowing the motor down to a canter. The sudden roughness of the liquid indicates that I've entered shallow water. There's possibly land ahead. Waves spray over me, exploding on the front of the raft, and the smell of salt is stronger than before. I lick my chaffed lips and I can taste it.

A minute passes and the glow of the light catches something. Land. I lift the motor, so as not to damage it and the blades chop at the surface, carrying me the final twenty feet until I'm beached. The material beneath my raft looks like sand. I gently lean over the edge and run a gloved index finger through it. Then I pick some up and let it fall through my hands. Sand. Or something that feels a hell of a lot like it. I marvel at it as if I was discovering the granular substance for the very first time.

I roll over and lie for a few minutes, assessing my situation, still breathing on the oxygen. My heart pounds. My body aches all over. All that's visible in the raft's spotlight is more sand, stretching into the darkness. There's a very slight slope. Ocean. Salt water. Beach. It's all familiar. Eerily familiar.

With adrenaline still pumping through me I get to my feet, take the travel pack from the raft and step, delicately, on to the beach. I pull the light and compass from the front of the raft and I also bring the small motor, which I could use as a weapon. I'm going to head up the sand, away from the water. I should destroy the raft, but right now it is my only transport should I need to escape to the safety of the open ocean. I start my journey, leaving the raft to the sound of crashing waves.

After fifty metres the sand becomes riddled with small grass shoots. Vegetation bursts beneath my boots. I squat down, running my glove across the tops of the grass stems, inspecting the flora. Some have small black flowers. Despite their colour they appear radiant and healthy. As I continue onward, the grass thickens and soon the sand is barely evident. I wave the light around me, feeling more scared with every step. A few more metres reveal a line of trees. Trunks erupt from the earth in large numbers, thick like a forest. I shine the light upward, amazed that I can't see the top of the foliage.

I feel like I'm on Earth and the sensation lulls me into a sense of security. For a moment I question whether I haven't, somehow, found my way home. Through some improbable series of events, I've defied time and space and returned to my corner of the universe. But I know that's not the case.

I approach the treeline, peering into the darkness. It's ominous. I stand, staring and listening. There's no other sound besides the surf behind me and an occasional insect-like chirp.

I could wait to see if the dim light returns, but I don't know exactly how long it might take. I step slowly into the forest, staying alert. My muscles and bones ache. I'm sure I've cracked or fractured some of my ribs, as my chest throbs more painfully with each breath. Adrenaline sends electricity through my body and it crackles in my ears.

Putting one foot in front of the other I move through the trees, which are thick and close together. I'm knee deep in swaying undergrowth that brushes against me, almost weightless. Grass and weeds. I hear a squeaking sound somewhere to my right, like the noise a rodent might make. Pointing my torch toward the disturbance, I see nothing. Just the floor of a forest flowing between tree trunks.

I stop to touch the bark of the tree to my right. It's hard and rough. Very normal. Very familiar. It crumbles against my glove, which is covered in small shards when I pull it away.

I feel something brush against my foot. Jumping, I reel my leg away. I frantically wave my torch. But there's nothing there. I breathe deeply on my oxygen, locked to the ground beneath me. If I don't move, I'm invisible. But I doubt that. I don't know this place. The very air around me could harbour an unseen threat. The trees themselves could be allowing me to idle by before they reshape and come alive. Before they take me by each limb and ease me into pieces like freshly baked bread.

I take a deep breath and continue, this time with more urgency. I hear more squeaks, shrill and sharp as I proceed. But I ignore them, brushing past tree trunks, and my torch peels back the intense darkness with each painful step.

The trees part and I step into a clearing. I stay very still, examining the wash of torchlight in front of me. I'm a quivering lighthouse in a space suit. In front of me stands a giant gate. A high fence on either shoulder stretches into the distance. The gate itself appears to be made of iron and is three times my height. Maybe even twenty feet high. Beyond it is an assortment of upright slabs and metallic fencing. Small, rectangular pillars of concrete. It's a graveyard. Just as it would look on Earth.

I gently push on the gate and it moves. Unlocked. I hesitantly point the torch, peering through the bars to see if anything is hiding behind the wall. But there's only grass and a field of headstones. The night around me is enveloped in silence. All I can hear are my long, deep breaths on the oxygen tank.

The stone blocks that sit next to each other are a variety of shapes and sizes, each of them chipped and cracked, like rows of gnarled teeth. Weeds, moss and grass have invaded their faded skins. The rusted, skeletal remains of metal fencing shoot from the ground. I step forward into the rows, inspecting the worn stones.

The first stone says, 'Richard Edwards 2156-2185. Dearly missed and always loved.' English. Remarkable. I stare at the numbers for a long time. Four-digit years. If this seemingly ancient, decaying headstone was erected in the year 2185, then I'm far beyond that date. Many hours have ticked over this grave.

The next headstone in the row is covered in a climbing vine. I pull back the leaves to expose the inscription. The name is mostly worn away, but the numbers are '2156-2195'. I breathe deeply on my oxygen.

From somewhere to my right I hear a noise that pierces straight through me. It's a twisted scream. A howl projected from the lungs. Anguished and desperate. The sound turns into a strangled moan, deep and guttural. The death cry of some lost soul, alone in the endless dark.

Too frightened to move, I turn my head just enough to see something standing near me. Perhaps only ten feet away. The humanoid shape has wide yellow eyes that reflect the feeble glow of my torch. The presence of this creature paralyses me. It howls again, glaring at me and trembling. Maybe it's excited. I look at it, hoping it can be placated. My eyes traverse its height. It's more than a foot taller than me. The long, spindly limbs and torso are covered in black fur. When it howls a third time, black lips peel back to expose rows of jagged teeth. Then it salivates, its wide, yellow eyeballs locked on me in anticipation. The boat motor hangs from the back of my pack, but I won't have time to use it.

As the creature hesitates for another moment, waiting for me to move, I decide that I have no choice. I break into a run, darting between the rows of gravestones. Immediately I sense it move to chase me. I wave the torch about in front of me, weaving my way through the closest gaps. Behind me the night becomes the sound of claws on stone. Its enraged growls feel so close that I prepare for its sting.

In front of me appears a large shape. Something the size of a small house or shed. As I race between gravestones, I see that it has a broad wooden door. I charge, lower my shoulder and hit it with the full weight of my body. It crashes open and in a second I have thrown it shut behind me. I catch a wooden slat on the back of the door with my bobbing flashlight and pull it across. My pursuer crashes into the door, but the slat keeps it outside. It claws and wails in anger, throwing itself against the entrance. I stand back, grabbing the motor and pulling the ripcord. It springs to life, whirring and buzzing. Almost instantly the attacking sounds cease. I listen intently, but hear nothing. Just the sound of the motor sawing through the deathly silence. After a minute I turn it off. The quiet continues.

Still drawing on my oxygen, I collapse to the ground. Like a goldfish next to its tank. Exhaustion tightens around me like a fist. Miscellaneous pain spreads throughout my torso. Rolling on to my back, I point the torch around the inside of my fortress. It's tiny. Some sort of workshop. Tools hang from the walls, all of them familiar. Shovels. Pitchforks. Saws. Mallets. Wrenches. Next to me is a bench that's covered in a white sheet. The roof and walls appear to be made of wood. The floor is dusty and hard, grey like concrete.

Many hours pass as I lie on the cold floor. I fall in and out of sleep, barely able to move. I don't hear the creature again, hoping the sound of the motor scared it far away. I draw deeply on the oxygen. Once. Twice. Something doesn't feel right. Inspecting the gauge, I feel a pang of panic. The tanks are empty. I draw deeply on the mask again, but it offers nothing. Calming myself, I acknowledge that I can still breathe. That I'm ok. I pull the mask from my face.

I sit up. Mottled light creeps through the room's only window, which is encrusted with an incoherent layer of grime and dust. I get to my feet and inspect the tools that line the walls, each hanging in their delegated positions. An array of aged, well worn utensils. All familiar in shape. All recognisable.

I turn to face the workbench in the middle of the room. Underneath the sheet are various unintelligible lumps. I gently lift one side of the stained, yellowish cloth and peer underneath. There's a bone. Unmistakable. I drop the sheet back and step away, feeling my heart race again. I now have a desire to get out of here. The growing daylight outside will make the wilderness safer.

But curiosity becomes me and I pull back the entire sheet, letting it fall to the floor. A skeleton. Femur, carpals, ribs, spinal column, shoulder blades. A skull. A very human skull. It sits on its jaw, straight up, facing the shed's entrance. I notice a hand is missing, as well as parts of the left arm. It's as if someone's piecing together a jigsaw, with sections missing. A shed project. But whose shed?

I return the sheet and venture to the caked window. Around its edge are what appear to be spider webs. Which means spiders. But I can't see any. With my gloved hand I wipe at one of the panes, the muck smearing but thinning enough to create some transparency. Placing my face near the glass I can see the graveyard continues into the distance. Beyond it is more dense forest. In the cemetery's centre, perhaps only one hundred metres away, is a building. Its high, pointed roof is scaled with weathering tiles. A church.

# CHAPTER SIX

Today's newspaper says that an abnormally large shark was seen at the beach near my house. It cleared the water pretty damn quick. Guards closed off the waves to swimmers. Another girl has gone missing and it's believed she was last seen at the beach. Authorities refuse to comment on whether she was taken by the shark.

Another story says that severed limbs were found in a motel bathtub on the other side of town. They belong to an adolescent female. Fingerprints have not determined who the limbs belong to. It's harder to blame that one on the shark. If the shark even exists.

On page six is a story about a giant pharmaceutical company that has recalled their entire line of popular sunscreen. It's been discovered that long-term use of the product is carcinogenic.

Laurie is over. Her parents have gone away for the weekend. Apparently her friends have been pestering her to throw another party. They want to hang out with me some more.

"If too many people know you live here, would you have to move again?" asks Laurie, who is sitting on the opposite lounge, mucking about with one of my acoustic guitars. She's wearing a simple white singlet top and a pair of small denim shorts.

I glance up from the paper and shrug. "Don't know. Maybe not. I can't be bothered moving again."

"There's lots of security here," says Laurie, as she strums a chord. It clangs in disharmony and she grunts softly in frustration.

"There is," I reply. "And if someone scales the outside of the building, they're welcome to come in for a drink."

"Someone would!" says Laurie. "My friends are nearly considering it."

"Send them up," I shrug. "Your friends seem nice."

"Really?" asks Laurie, incredulously.

"Yes, they seem... observant."

"How come you never reply to my phone messages?"

"What do you mean?"

"I send you messages and you never reply."

I think for a moment, then quickly realise that Laurie probably has Norman's number. Norman isn't turned on all that often. I should probably give her my new number.

"I got a new number," I say. "The other one leaked online."

"That's unfortunate," says Laurie. "Must happen a lot."

"Yeah, you should delete my old number." I pull out my mobile phone and tell her my actual digits. "Of course, you have to keep that a secret."

"I didn't give your old number to anyone," she replies.

"No, of course. I trust you implicitly," I smile.

On the next page of the newspaper is a picture of a girl. She's gone missing. Lower down is a grid of small images, each the size of a postage stamp. All photos of missing girls.

In an eerie coincidence, Laurie asks, "It says in the newspaper today that you and your band know the girls that are missing."

"It says lots of things in the newspaper," I reply.

"They've all been to your concerts," adds Laurie, focusing on the arrangement of her dainty fingers on the guitar neck. "Apparently some of them work for your record label?"

"Lots of people have been to our concerts and many women work at the record label."

Laurie stops and looks up at me, smiling. "You sound so guilty."

"What do you mean?" I scoff. "I don't sound like anything."

"Aren't you worried about them?"

I fold the newspaper and throw it on the floor at my feet. "What would your parents think of you visiting me?"

"Well, let's see," smiles Laurie. "I'm an impressionable twenty-year-old girl. I'm their darling daughter. Their only child. And, for all they know, I'm a virgin."

"A predatory virgin," I say, slightly under my breath, leaning toward the coffee table to pour myself a scotch.

Laurie rolls her eyes and continues, ignoring me. "You're a 35-year-old rock star. A renowned bedder of the opposite sex. I still have a poster of you on my wall."

"For dart-throwing," I say, reaching for the ice bucket.

"It faces my bed," says Laurie, strumming the open strings on the guitar.

"I'm aware," I say, dropping three ice cubes into the golden elixir. "But if they knew the Laurie I know, they'd be damn more worried about me."

Laurie strums the guitar again, as if to mock me. She pulls a face that I sometimes make on stage when I'm improvising a solo. Somewhere between concentration and ecstasy.

"Wow, you really know how to handle that thing," I say, pointing at the instrument.

Laurie strums a random chord and it clangs. "Teach me how to play something."

"Like what?" I say.

"I don't know! Anything."

I laugh to myself. "Ok, bring it over here then."

I lie back on the couch and open my legs so that Laurie can sit between them. She perches on the edge of the sofa and leans back into my body. I show her some chords, moving her fingers to the correct strings. Once we repeat the sequence of chords a number of times, I show Laurie the rhythm she needs to strum with her right hand. Within five minutes she's playing something that resembles 'It Ain't Me Babe'.

My cheek is close to hers. I watch her face, masked in concentration, her eyes moving from hand to hand, sliding with her fingers up the neck. I kiss the bare skin on her shoulder.

When Dylan knocks on my apartment door, Laurie and I are still on the couch.

"Who's that?" asks Laurie, panicking. "It might be my parents."

"Aren't they away?" I ask.

"They're supposed to be," she replies.

"Go hide in my bedroom," I say, and Laurie dashes down the corridor.

I swing open the door and am greeted by an unexpected guest. "Random visits," I say to Dylan. "This is one of your best."

"Do I need an excuse to see you?" he asks, with a big grin. He seems under the influence of something. Booze. Drugs. Society.

"Early afternoon drinks?" I inquire, as he pushes past me into the apartment.

"I just felt like being..." he says, trailing off. He starts opening cupboards in the kitchen, probably looking for my drugs.

"Now's a bad time, Dylan," I say.

"Really?" he asks, opening more cupboards. His t-shirt is matted to his back from sweat. He's wearing faded jeans and his feet are bare and dirty. Dylan's short blonde hair is pushed down on his head, sticking to his scalp.

"Really," I say. "I wouldn't lie to you, sweetheart. Come back later. Stick to the booze. Pass out somewhere."

He grabs an unopened bottle of scotch from my kitchen counter, twists it open and takes a long swig.

"Did you see the paper today?" he asks.

"Yes," I say.

"Can you fucking believe it?"

"Well, remember," I say, walking over and taking the scotch from him. "When you swim in the ocean, you're entering a shark's home. You take that risk."

"What?" asks Dylan, reluctantly giving up the bottle. "No, I mean the girls. The missing girls. They think we're responsible? They think we're killing girls, man."

"No, they don't," I say. "They're just pointing out that many of the girls were last seen at our concerts."

"Girls all go to our concerts," says Dylan, wiping his forehead. I sip on the scotch and give him back the bottle. "Girls fucking love us, Jack. They fucking love you."

"They love you too," I say.

Dylan laughs, loudly. "They love me Jack, because they love you. They *worship* you," he adds.

"They worship the music," I say. "It's all about the music."

Dylan shakes his head, grinning, acting like I'm a real laugh riot. "You just don't know," he says, still shaking his head.

"Dylan, take a fistful of painkillers and mellow the fuck out," I say. "I have company. You are currently embezzling my fucking company. We'll spend some quality time soon."

"Your company," scoffs Dylan. "You have no idea who your fucking company is."

"Is that right?" I say, smiling. "Enlighten me."

"The company you keep," he says, grabbing the back of my head and pulling my face close to his. "They're a very big company."

"Good," I say. "That's always a good sign."

Dylan smiles, then notices something to his right. We both turn to see Laurie standing in the living room. Dylan yells, as if he's seen a giant spider. Laurie jumps, taking a step back.

"Laurie, this is Dylan," I say, calmly, trying to reassure her. "He plays guitar in my band. His hobbies are drug-taking and random visits. He sometimes reads the newspaper."

"Hi," says Laurie, meekly.

Dylan's persona softens and he takes a deep breath. "Hi, I'm Dylan. You must be Jack's company."

"We're neighbours," smiles Laurie.

Dylan gives me a knowing glance. "Well it's very nice to meet you," he says.

"I was just teaching Laurie how to play 'It Ain't Me Babe'," I say.

Dylan visibly stiffens, his tentatively poised mask of charm slipping. "Teaching her how to... play?" he asks.

"Yeah, just a few chords."

Dylan leans close to my face and whispers. "So this is who takes the reins, huh? Guitar duties? My replacement is a fucking teenager?"

"She's actually twenty," I smile.

Dylan's face turns red. "Is that right?" he asks me. Then he turns to Laurie, asking with more aggression, "Is that right?"

I wink reassuringly at Laurie.

"Yes," says Laurie. "Jack's been showing me all your songs so I can join the band."

Dylan gives a nod of acceptance, as if he's been expecting this revelation for some time. He keeps nodding as he heads for the apartment door, still holding my scotch.

"Goodbye, Dylan," I say, as he opens the door.

He turns to me, with hurt in his eyes. "I loved you, man. We really had something. We had chemistry."

"I know, I know," I say, with mock guilt. "But Laurie has prettier eyes than you."

Dylan looks over at Laurie, who just smirks. Dylan nods again and keeps nodding. "Well, I hope her fucking *eyes* can play the five-minute guitar solo in 'Nantucket Sleighride', because that little devil looks like she'd struggle with her times tables."

"You don't mean that, Dylan, you're just being bitter," I say, waving him out the door.

He looks at me for a moment, his eyeballs bloodshot and bleary. "Well," he replies, as if his next comment will bring him some form of triumph, "at least I don't have a midget in my elevator." He slams the door.

I walk over and hug Laurie, to make sure she's ok.

"Dylan seemed a little loose," she smiles.

"He has episodes," I shrug. "A whole extended series of episodes. Too much money, too much spare time. He sits around while I write the songs. He doesn't know what to do with himself."

"You need a haircut," says Laurie, changing the subject. She grabs the end of my hair, which is now down near my shoulder. Dark and greasy. I don't wash it enough.

"Am I looking a little ragged?"

"Just a little," she says. "And your stubble scratches my face."

"Stop kissing me then."


A luxury car picks me up from inside my building's underground carpark and drives across town to Martin Brannagh's place. It's been less than a week since the McCarthy Awards after party. By now Brannagh's various staff will have returned his apartment to the comfort of its sterility, disinfecting every surface.

My chauffeur drops me outside Brannagh's building. I walk quickly across the footpath and a doorman allows me into the vast foyer. A security officer then escorts me in the elevator to the top floor. When the doors open into Brannagh's apartment he is standing, waiting for me.

Dressed in a crisp, white suit over a collared, blue pinstripe shirt, Brannagh's tanned, ancient face lights up in welcome. He opens his arms.

"My favourite rock star," he smiles, pulling me into a hug.

"Marty, how the hell are ya?" I say, my question partly muffled by his shoulder.

He pulls away and looks into my face, keeping his hands on my shoulders. "I'm good, kiddo. How are you? You ok? You been getting enough sleep?"

"Sure," I reply. "Plenty."

Brannagh starts leading me across his apartment, towards his grand dining table. He keeps an arm around my shoulder.

"That's good to hear, Jack. Very good to hear," says Brannagh, before adding, "but I bet you didn't get much sleep after my party the other night." He fixes me a grin.

"Oh, um, yeah. That was a big one," I reply.

"You left here with Natalie, didn't you?" he probes.

"Yes, I did. We moved on to a nightclub. You know, a change of scene."

"Sure, sure," says Brannagh, nodding. "Somewhere with a bit of privacy, eh?"

"I suppose. She's a very nice girl," I say, diplomatically.

"Oh, she's a real treasure," says Brannagh, as we reach the table. He pulls out one of the heavy, metallic chairs and I sit down. He reaches for the adjacent chair and takes his seat at the head of the table.

Over in the kitchen a male chef is preparing food. Tall, young and tanned. A brunette waitress with olive skin and dark eyes stands, smiling patiently with an empty bar tray balanced on one hand.

"Two elixirs," calls Brannagh to the waitress, with a casual wave of his hand. Then to me he says, "I heard officers went through a nightclub while you were there. They had porcines?"

"Three of them," I reply. "Or maybe just one. My vision was a little blurry."

Brannagh nods. "Did they search you?"

"No, I wasn't searched. The porcines bailed me up in the bathroom."

"But you... would have been carrying something, yes?"

I pause for a moment, not sure what to say. I hadn't spared much thought for how unusual the porcines' behaviour was in the Durté bathroom. "I think so."

The waitress puts our drinks down in front of us. Brannagh smiles and thanks her.

"Well, Jack. I've never come face to face with one of these sniffer pigs, but from what I hear they're pretty accurate. Unfairly so."

"Yeah, normally. Maybe they were sick. Blocked nose. Pigs must get sick too."

"Seems miraculous," says Brannagh. He then lifts his drink in toast. "Thank you for coming over this evening. To your continued success. Salut."

"Salut," I reply.

We lightly chink glasses and take a sip of our respective beverages.

"There's a few things I wanted to talk to you about tonight," says Brannagh.

"Shoot," I say.

"Firstly, I wanted to have a quick discussion about this horrible situation with the missing girls."

"Ah," I reply, nodding. "Horrible."

"As you probably know, I've demanded that the promoter increase security at every show. Not just inside the venues but around them too. Near bus stops, train stations. We're creating parking areas specifically for parents to pick up their children."

"Sounds good," I say. "An increased presence is important."

"Definitely," replies Brannagh. "Also, without encroaching on your onstage mood, it might be good for you to start mentioning at the concerts that everyone needs to keep an eye on their friends. An eye on each other. Promote awareness of the situation."

"We haven't publicly acknowledged that there is a situation here," I say. "The link with Big Bang Theory is purely circumstantial."

"But public pressure is building. We need to look like we care. We do care. Don't we?"

"Yes," I say. "We care. I care."

Brannagh nods in agreement and sips his elixir.

"Until the situation is sorted, the responsible thing to do might be to stop playing shows altogether," I say.

Brannagh swallows a little too quickly and coughs. "Let's not go too far," he says, clearing his throat. "People should be allowed the opportunity to hear your music in a live setting."

"Sure," I say.

"After all, we're not certain there's any link between the missing girls and your concerts."

"No," I agree. "We shouldn't be too hasty."

"But we should acknowledge the situation," nods Brannagh, before adding, "have you seen the pictures of the missing girls?"

"A few," I reply. "In the paper."

"None of them are familiar to you?"

"No, not really," I lie.

"I see," says Brannagh, still nodding. He's studying me with his eyes and it makes me uncomfortable.

"If I do recognise one of them, you'll be the first know," I say with a reassuring smile.

"Excellent," replies Brannagh.

"Doesn't one of the missing women work at our record label?" I inquire.

"Yes, but the woman they're talking about is not missing. She's simply on holiday. I've explained to the authorities that she's on a remote safari. Uncontactable by phone but certain to return," says Brannagh.

"Well, there's really nothing to worry about. Girls run away sometimes. All coincidence," I say.

"I couldn't agree more," says Brannagh. "My main concern is that all this will distract you from your music. I wouldn't deem that acceptable."

"Thank you."

"The second thing I want to discuss is one of the newer groups on our label. More recent members of the family."

"Yeah?" I say, guessing to whom he is referring.

"The Known Associates," says Brannagh, delicately. "Have you heard their music yet?"

"Bits and pieces."

"They've got something special. Great sound. An amazing look. Big Bang Theory has been a big influence on them."

"Really? That's grand," I say.

"Definitely," agrees Brannagh, adding, "they're working on their second record at the moment."

"Nice," I say.

"The boys are in the studio, writing and recording."

I nod and sip on my elixir.

"I wanted to ask, how would you feel about joining them in the studio and doing some work with them?"

"What did you have in mind?"

"Well, perhaps you could collaborate? Work on their production. Give them some direction with their songwriting."

I'm not sure whether to tell Brannagh how much I dislike The Known Associates. They're blatantly ripping off Big Bang Theory's sound and image. Riding our coattails. Brannagh certainly encourages them to do so. Since I'm already riding the coattails of other songwriters, The Known Associates adds even more dead weight to a weighty situation. I can't show them how to write songs. I don't know how.

Endurance was a big record label before I came along, but my band has become the biggest meal ticket of Brannagh's career. He'd love to have a second Big Bang Theory in his stable. Two horses drawing the carriage.

"Can I think about it?" I ask.

"Sure," he replies, "of course. I don't want it to impede on your own music. I just thought I should bring it up with you. To gauge your reaction."

"Well, I apologise if my response is hard to gauge."

"It's fine, really. Take your time. Talk about it with your other band members."

"Sure. I will."

"I also wanted to sound out the possibility of The Known Associates perhaps opening for you guys on your next tour. They're the perfect support band for Big Bang Theory."

"Yeah," I shrug. "No problem. Why not. They'd be perfect."

"Grand," says Brannagh.

We both sip our elixirs, before he calls to the kitchen, "Could you bring out the first course soon? Something to build the appetite?"

The chef nods and smiles, continuing to chop and stir the various pots and coloured lumps of food in front of him.

"And two more of these drinks!" says Brannagh, swallowing the last mouthful from his glass.

I pick up my glass and quickly gulp it down, so as to keep up with him. Two more drinks are brought to us by the waitress. She spares me the hint of a smile as she makes eye contact.

"So, I have two more things I want to talk to you about and then we can get on with our evening," says Brannagh.

"No problem," I say, lifting my new glass. "I'm all ears."

"All ears. That's funny," smiles Brannagh. "You have some odd expressions."

"I like to innovate," I reply.

Brannagh chuckles, then continues. "I know you've been under a lot of stress lately, particularly with this whole missing girls thing."

"Well, yeah, maybe," I shrug.

"I wanted to offer you Godiva for a couple of weeks. There's nothing like it. Breathing the fresh air up there. It's the perfect getaway. It'd be just you and the forest. No traffic noise. You could really focus on some new music and unwind."

"Wow, that's a cool idea. That could be really... good," I reply.

"You'd be very isolated, but it would be great for you. I go up there to settle myself when things are too hectic and it always puts me back on course."

I don't mind Brannagh's suggestion. Godiva is a spectacular residence and it's at a high altitude and surrounded by nature. Spending some time there might be a good way to lay low and extricate myself from society for a little while. With no parties to go to, it might allow me to detox too.

"Marty, I'd love to. It's a seriously tempting suggestion."

"The studio is just as you left it, so you could throw down some recordings and work on new material," says Brannagh. He gives me an encouraging expression, lifting his tone slightly. He wants me to write more chart-topping, million-selling records for him.

"You know me, Marty. Rubber arms. Easy to twist."

"Good," he smiles, then reaches into his inner jacket pocket and produces two thick, dark brown cigars.

"Cigarro?" he offers. "We should head outside before the first course."

"Sure."

On the balcony, the city stretches out below us. I twist the end from my cigar and Brannagh lights it for me.

"They want to write a biography of you," says Brannagh, putting a flame to his own cigar.

"They?" I ask.

"A publisher. A big one. They want it to be an official biography. Something that will once and for all explain who you are."

"Does Amelia know about this? I haven't heard anything from her."

"No, she doesn't know. I'm friends with one of the leaders at the publisher. He has asked me directly. I'd really prefer it if no one else knows about this."

"Marty, I don't know if I can keep it from Amelia. She's my confidant. In making a decision, I'd want to hear her advice."

"Of course," smiles Brannagh, tapping me reassuringly on the shoulder. "But it might be best not to say anything until an official offer comes through. This is all just a hypothetical right now."

"Of course," I smile, and puff on the cigar.

"A lot of people out there would like to know more about you."

"I'm sure," I reply.

"You know that a lot of my friends in the cinematic business ask me to convince you to get into acting. Amelia gets sent quite a few scripts."

"Yes, she tells me."

"Nothing has been of interest?"

"I don't have an interest in acting right now," I reply. "I'm not a good actor."

Marty chuckles. "Well, you wouldn't have to be. We can get something written for you. Something that suits you and your personality."

"I'll think about it, but I'd rather focus on my music. I need to be unoccupied when a song comes to me. I need to be able to write it down straight away."

"Yes, yes, of course," Brannagh says.

There's a pause while we both take a puff on our cigars, the rich smoke filling my mouth before I shoot a grey plume into the night air.

"What's your earliest memory, Jack? Do you remember being a child?"

"Bits and pieces," I say. "It's a blur."

"So you can't remember who your father is?"

"No, I don't," I say. "I believe I was abandoned."

"So who raised you? Someone must have fed you and taken care of you until you could be independent."

I stop and puff on the cigar again, looking out at the city. There are neon grids of lights far below. I wonder whether it's easier to jump. The questions will never end. The more vague I am, the more people think I'm hiding something.

"I just don't remember," I shrug. "I have a memory of a presence standing over me. Some kind of protective entity. Someone taking care of me. But in my mind's eye they don't have a face. Or a sex. The only thing I'm certain of is that I've been alone most of my life, right up until I taught myself to play music."

"Yes," nods Brannagh, "yours is truly an amazing story."

"Well, you do what you can. You know... to survive."

"It's almost as if someone brought you to us," says Brannagh.

"Someone?" I ask.

Brannagh smiles and I'm unable to read his expression. It's a pained smile.

"Jack, I'm afraid I've been deceitful," says Brannagh, hesitantly.

"Oh?" I ask.

He reaches into his inner jacket pocket and pulls out a piece of paper. "I did some investigating recently," he says, still choosing his words with delicacy.

"What kind?"

"Genetic."

A familiar weight appears in the pit of my stomach. I stay silent, taking a long drag on my cigar.

"I acquired some of your DNA last week. I thought maybe I could help provide you with some answers about your past."

"Right," I say. "That's very... nice of you?" I offer. I consider lifting Brannagh and dropping him over the balcony. I could tell his chef and waitress that he threw himself.

"I know it's incredibly invasive of me, and I've betrayed your trust, but I have a lot of connections and I thought I could help find your biological parents."

"How did you get my DNA?" I ask, and then the answer pops into my head before Brannagh tells me. An escort. An irresistible accomplice.

"Natalie was able to ... help me out," says Brannagh. "Again, I apologise for this deception. Natalie didn't feel comfortable betraying your trust either, but she couldn't refuse the opportunity to gain access to you. To spend an evening with you."

"She's only human."

Brannagh lets out a nervous laugh. "Yes, she is. Very human."

"Ok, so let's cut to the chase," I say. "You've sneaked off with my DNA and had some lab people take a look at it. Is there some kind of revelation I should know about?"

I could push the burning stub of my cigar into Brannagh's face and, as he's reeling, flip him swiftly over the balcony's rail. But the burn would be evident on the body. No, I need to push him cleanly and without a struggle. I'm capable of this, but the implications of doing so are not good. Two potential witnesses in Brannagh's kitchen. Possibly a league of assistants at the record label who know I was coming here to meet their boss tonight. This isn't a man you can kill quietly.

"The people in the laboratory unfortunately were not able to match your DNA to anyone on the government's register," says Brannagh.

"Oh well," I shrug. "Nothing gained, nothing lost."

"Everyone that's born is on the register, except for backyard births. Unregistered," he says.

"I see."

"But there's something else," adds Brannagh, a little hesitantly. "They weren't able to match your DNA to ... any other human being."

"What do you mean?" I ask. Half of me is interested to find out what Brannagh knows, and the other half is readying to grab his ankles and launch him into oblivion.

Brannagh looks at the paper in his hands and says, "There's a lot of science speak in the report, but basically what it says is that the scientists couldn't identify your twenty-third chromosome."

"Go on," I say.

"The first twenty-two of your chromosomes are perfectly normal, but your last chromosome, which is the one that decides whether you're male or female, is different."

"How different?"

"It just says that the chromosome is 'unidentified'."

"But what does that mean? What does my chromosome look like? How different is it?"

"It's just unidentified," replies Brannagh.

"But what does that mean, Marty? Does it look like a chromosome, but it's slightly different? Or does it look like a fucking salad sandwich?" I question, taking a final puff on the cigar and tossing it over the balcony.

Brannagh quickly folds the paper, puts it away and attempts to calm me. "I'm sorry, Jack. Just stay cool, ok? I don't mean to upset you. It's just that the results are ... intriguing. Wouldn't you agree?"

"Maybe they got it wrong."

"I don't think so," says Brannagh. "The people I know are the best."

"Who are they?"

Brannagh smiles and shakes his head. "I really can't say."

"So your mystery lab says my DNA is a mystery. I'm a mystery."

"They'd very much like to run some more tests, if that was an avenue you wanted to go down. To find answers."

"If there's one thing I've learned in life, Marty, it's that the only thing available to you is the future. The past is set in stone."

"But don't you want to know who you are?"

My blood boils. "*I* know who I am," I say, emphasising each word carefully and with brooding menace. "And I'd like to keep it that way."

Brannagh stares at me, entranced by my sudden change in disposition. It sounds like I'm threatening him and in many ways I am. He's a shrewd individual and he knows better than anyone that if you bite the hand that feeds you, its owner may retaliate.

"Ok, Jack. Ok. I won't bring this up again."

I take a deep breath and construct a reassuring smile. "Don't sweat, my friend. I appreciate your help. Now where's this first course?"

The van, with its tinted windows and silver, streamlined body, slides around the curved driveway, like a shark through shallow water. It parks in front of the grandiose, double doors that open into the foyer of Godiva. We're in the building's vast shadow as I step onto the driveway's terracotta tiles. The driver retrieves my bags from the rear of the vehicle. No doorman, so I assume I'll have to open them myself. The chauffeur places my luggage next to me as I stand, gazing back and forth along the wall of the grand mansion. Godiva towers above me, extending a great distance on my left before stretching off a great deal to my right. In the latter direction the building ends with a tall spire, like a protruding gun tower from its roof. This is the observatory.

Aesthetically, Godiva has a wooden, naturalistic feel. Like someone has kept a log cabin in a cage and riddled it with growth hormones, mutating it until it's disfigured and unrecognisable. As far as dwellings go, Godiva seems rather egotistical and opinionated, secretly disliked by other buildings. But nothing could deflate it. It's sturdy and self-assured. Deep red brick, chocolate finishes. Earthy. Rustic. Bombastic.

Nestled in the middle of nowhere, in this persistent, enthusiastic wilderness, in this expanse of nature, the air around Godiva is fresh and crisp. I'm at a high altitude. The breeze is spiced with floral aromas. Birds and insects argue in shrill, sporadic bursts of singsong gunfire.

At the front doors I swipe a card that Brannagh gave me. The security panel ponders it for a moment before accepting. Then it asks me to stare into a small lens while it scans my retina. This form of security check isn't uncommon on this planet. Every eye is a unique fingerprint of capillaries and microscopic arrangements. Once the intense red light has assessed the inside of my eyeball, I pull back, blinking, before glancing through the glass of the front doors. Unlit furniture creates odd shadows. Difficult to decipher.

Suddenly I hear Brannagh's voice, emanating from the security panel next to these double doors. "Security approved. Welcome... Jack."

"Thanks Marty," I say, despite knowing the voice is pre-recorded.

Stepping inside, I drop my two bags on the white expanse of marble floor. When I take another step forward I trigger a sensor and a light blinks on above me, illuminating the foyer. I hear Godiva's voice, sultry and feminine, appear over hidden speakers.

"One guest," she says.

"Am I the one guest?" I ask to the room.

"Yes, Jack," replies Godiva, warm and inviting, echoed all around me.

"Do you remember me?" I ask Godiva.

"Yes," replies the voice.

Godiva's advanced security system includes motion sensors and weighted panels in the floor. She knows how many people are inside her at any one time. One guest. I have the place to myself.

I explore the building, familiarising myself with the layout. Every room in Godiva has these screens. Next to every door is an LCD panel, mounted at head height, which displays information on interior temperature, incoming phone calls, closed-circuit cameras and outside weather conditions. Invariably each room I step into has a wide, sleek television on the wall, mounted opposite beds and lounge chairs.

There's a clean smell, denoting the recent use of scented chemicals. The products of the faceless employees who venture out here to maintain Godiva in her extended absences of company. To sterilise her. She opens occasionally when Brannagh decides he needs a break. Or to throw an exclusive party.

Once I've wandered for a few minutes, I return to my bags in the foyer. One of the numerous living areas stretches out in front of me, full of furnishings both antique and modern. To my left is the well-applianced kitchen and entertaining area. To my right is the mouth of the wide staircase that curls up to the top level, like an eager tongue. Behind the staircase is the entry to a corridor, which ends in a second staircase that descends to the basement level.

Down there is an underground maze of more bedrooms, bathrooms and an impressive, fully stocked wine cellar.

I've been here a few times, but never on my own. It's strange to see Godiva so dormant and at peace. I associate these rooms with frivolity and music. Dropped drinks. Attractive people sprawled over the historic artifacts that Brannagh purchases as lounges and futons.

On one occasion, Big Bang Theory came up here to record an album. Brannagh trusted us with his holiday house. Four guys, two engineers and a producer. What could go wrong? Nothing went *wrong*, as such. Depends on your definition of the term. Some people would say it was very wrong. We invited a number of girls up here. About twelve of them. It was all rather civilised until we started offering them drugs and then taking drugs ourselves. Part of the week was taken up with what could only be described as an orgy. It was rather prolonged. Almost casual. Perfectly normal. My memory of it is mostly of the overall act. Not individual females. I remember the young women who were here more as a collective. Their faces, personalities and voices detached from the parts of them that were entered into the deal. A blurred miasma of parted thighs and glazed eyes.

I look back on it and wonder if I was there. Who was there in my place if it wasn't me? Who is Jack if he's not the man that died in space?

With the suns slowly fading, I remove all my clothing and walk naked out to the long in-ground pool that's cut cleanly into Godiva's immaculately manicured lawn. The view stretches from the surrounding garden and rolls across the top of ancient trees to a thin blue line of ocean on the horizon. The dots of ships hang in the canvas as tiny flecks of black paint.

I float on the surface of the pool, my eyes closed, weightless. Absorbing the suns' final rays. Then I wade in the shallow end, looking across at the sparse cloud of insects that hovers above the gardens that rim the yard. The shadow of Godiva grows long and overwhelming as the suns shift in their slanted arc.

People ask me a lot if I can tell them where I came from. About my past. They don't ask out of suspicion, but general interest. A homeless drifter who is a gifted songwriter? Where was I born? Where did I grow? To them I must seem monumental. A poet of unsurpassed prophecy and a distiller of the human condition. My words speak to them. The lyrical ruminations of another planet, which they believe to be the crystallisation of their own.

As the suns fade, I pull myself from the water and walk across the lawn. The air remains warm and with no one around I think nothing of modesty. There's a statue protruding above one of the trimmed hedges. Fading, weathered stone that has survived a thousand seasons. Despite my intergalactic journey, this man-made sculpture of a female, with its curved figure, robust breasts and flowing cloth, has seen more than me. It has existed for longer.

Standing here before it, the statue now only a silhouette before the burning candlelight glow of the horizon, I remember that I once gazed here during a previous gathering, airborne on hallucinatory drugs. I asked this statue, "What is evolution?" The statue didn't reply at the time and I accepted this, because there were a lot of people around. We weren't exactly in private. But I felt quite strongly that someday this statue would divulge the answer. "What is evolution if two worlds evolve in parallel? Is everything preordained?" This time I don't verbalise the question, mainly because I observe the lady statue's lack of functioning ears. If it has the answer, it will tell me either way. I feel affinity, as we are both created. Carved from something much bigger. We are both unreal and I sympathise with this statue's eternal predicament.

Somewhere to my right, beyond the hedged edges of the garden, I hear bleating. An animal. Many animals. I'm reminded of Brannagh's pets, which he keeps in an enclosure. His herd of labbia. Tall, majestic creatures, statuesque and imposing. Smooth, soft white skin covers a body that stands above a man, like a fully-grown llama. A sleek, giraffe-like mammal. They're the rare endangered species that every human-inhabited planet has in some form. Too beautiful to co-exist with people, hunted for what they offer the makers of cosmetic possessions.

I push open a small, rickety gate and follow a winding, narrow path that divides Godiva's outer gardens. The sound of the bleating labbia increases, deeper than that of a sheep or goat. When the path opens out into a small clearing, the entrance to the labbia's enclosure is in front of me. A tall mesh fence, about twenty feet high, shoots up from the ground, before turning into a mesh roof. It looks simple, but it's a high-tech security system that registers any weight that pushes against it. Try to climb it and it will shoot enough electricity through you to turn you to charcoal. There is a door-sized entry into the enclosure, which is locked. There's a security panel next to it, with a set of numbered buttons. A pin code would open it, but I don't know the combination. I glance up one side of the enclosure and it stretches off into the undergrowth. The labbia sanctuary is many thousand square metres.

Peering through the mesh, careful not to touch it, I can only see shrubbery and trees. The suns are now completely gone and very little is apparent. A faint glow comes from small white lights embedded in the surrounding gardens. Then I hear a snorting sound and the bushes beyond the fence move. A labbia, which is at least two feet taller than me, strides from the plantation, lowering its neck to inspect me through the wire. It smells the air, assessing me. Sizing me up. In the very dim light I can see its large, piercing blue eyes.

Labbia are ancient creatures. Some scientists believe they may be psychic, communicating with others in their herd via radiated energy. Heat signals that are reinterpreted as data. Messages. In turn, they can surmise a human being. They know if you're a threat. Labbia can be the most placid creatures in the universe, but if you're evil they will bite your skull in two.

"Hi," I say to the labbia.

It snorts again.

"It's ok," I say in a gentle voice. "You've got nothing to be afraid of."

It raises its neck, standing at full height. It's looking up toward Godiva. It bleats loudly, splitting the humid evening with its sharp call.

"What are you bleating at?" I ask.

It ignores me and continues to stare up at Godiva, which is partly obscured from view by the tall foliage of the surrounding gardens. Just a distant mass of outdoor lighting.

The labbia bleats again. It seems distracted, so I bid it farewell and start back up the path to Godiva. As I walk away it bleats even louder, as if warning me of something. I stand in silence, looking back at the lean, impressive creature behind the mesh of its sanctuary.

A second and then a third labbia appear. The two new animals stare at me for a moment and then also turn their round blue orb-eyes to Godiva, which stares down at us from atop the hill. The labbia bleat, as if agitated that I'm leaving.

"It's cool, guys," I call to them. "I'll come back tomorrow and visit."

Their bleating continues and is barely audible as I pass the pool and walk around the far side of Godiva, looking for the walkway that leads to the small outdoor music studio.

Lights dot the edges of the path, bringing me to a small house. It's built in the image of Godiva, as if the mansion gave birth to this miniature version. Next to the door is a panel. I stare into the small lens and the computer identifies me.

"Welcome to the studio, Jack," says Godiva's inviting bedroom coo.

"Thanks," I say, pushing through the door. The ceiling light turns on, revealing a room full of instruments and recording gear. There's mixing desks, microphones and black leads that snake across the floor like ropes of licorice. Drum kits sit under white sheets and guitars rest on small tripod stands. Other guitars lie in cases around the edges of the room.

I pick-up an electric guitar and pluck a few notes. I then plug it into an amplifier and begin tuning it with my ear. Once I've twisted a few pegs and strummed my finger across the six strings, sublime musical notes fall through the air.

Grabbing power cables and leads, I throw them over one shoulder and carry the guitar and amplifier back to Godiva. I make my way through the house and find the door that leads out to the giant deck that looks down from the mansion's second storey, over the gardens and pool. I think I can faintly hear the sounds of bleating labbia, but when I pause to listen for a moment I can only hear the buzzing sounds of the night.

I run the power cable to an electrical outlet then aim the amplifier outward from the deck. Standing next to it, I put the electric guitar's strap over my shoulder and plug the lead into the amp. A song has been knocking around my head, drifting back on the neurons from another part of the galaxy.

I play the opening notes and they are chill-inducing. Beneath their aching cry I sing, wondering if someone on a distant lump of rock can hear me. The words were written by Neil Young and are full of longing and starstruck reverence for a woman.

'Like A Hurricane' blasts out into the landscape, scattered across this distant patch, soaking into the leaves and soil. Forgotten and absorbed. Each note disappears once its echo dissipates, replaced by another in the barrage. Something invisible and undetectable that will be there forever.

I put down the guitar and walk inside to one of the bars, where I pour myself a strong spirit on ice. I return to the vast balcony, placing the beverage beside me and picking up the guitar again. The suns are long gone, vanquishing my view of the distance. The ocean is now lost in black. The dotted lights of ships leave pinprick traces.

Godiva's exterior lights illuminate most of the garden below me, except for its fringes. I riff on 'No Surface All Feeling' for about ten minutes, before I begin to work out the intro to 'Under The Bridge', trying to remember the chords from when I played it as a teenager. Each intricacy explodes from the shaking amplifier, firing out into the night. An evening that is so bloated with possibility.

As I sing the lyrics, I randomly remember a documentary I saw on Earth. It was discussing how scientists were unable to prove why cigarettes caused cancer. The exact explanation remained an acute medical mystery. But the undeniable statistical data had made the idea a known fact. Nicotine will kill you. But no one ever demanded categorical proof. This seems unusual to me, especially now that I'm living on another planet that shares that same belief in regard to the dangers of smoking. But I realise that I never believed in God because I never saw any evidence of it. No damn evidence at all. So I've remained an atheist based on my own statistical data.

I wake up early in the morning. The clock next to the bed tells me it's two hours past midnight. I'm sweating profusely and I kick the blanket off. I hear something. There is a scratching sound somewhere beyond the bedroom door. Like soft, fast footsteps. Scurrying. I stop breathing for a second, my head against the pillow. Muscles locked. Listening. The sound is gone. Minutes pass as I lie in this hollow darkness. I must have woken from a nightmare. My mind grasps at elusive images, but they slip through my fingers. I fall asleep again.

I sit at the white, immaculate grand piano which stands in a corner of the main entrance way. Dressed in a pair of cotton shorts I run my fingers over the keys. I've never had professional piano lessons, but my ear for music generally allows me to sit down and work out songs. Right now I'm tinkering, trying to recall 'Counting

On You' by Chris de Burgh. I just worked out 'Heaven and Earth' by Blitzen Trapper, which I think could work well as a Big Bang Theory song. Then I muck about with 'In Other Words' by Ben Kweller and another Chris de Burgh song, 'Borderline'.

Over near Godiva's front doors I notice that I've left muddied shoe marks on the marble. I didn't realise my boots had been so dirty when I arrived.

After a few hours of playing I feel a little sleepy, so I rack a line of cane off the smooth surface of the grand piano. My nose goes numb and the familiar taste begins to slide down the back of my throat. I then walk down to the wine cellar, browsing the many aisles of bottles. This place is as big as a rural town's public library. It's carved into the earth, floored with radiant, polished wood. Lights are set in the floor, beaming upward. After pulling about twelve bottles from the racks to inspect their labels, I choose a red wine. The regions mean very little to me, so the design of the label becomes a deciding factor.

I head back to the pool and stay mostly in the shallow end, smoking cigarettes, swigging on the red wine bottle and leaning on the edge. I smoke a lot of cigarettes as I stand there, staring off into the gardens. I wonder whether I should eat anything, but I don't have an appetite. My stomach, despite my tranquil locale, is permanently knotted. I wonder whether I've ever been completely relaxed while sober since I landed here. Whether I've had a calm, lucid moment. Drugs help you forget, but they also keep your guard down. The subconscious mind rears its ugly head and bubbles upward. The canary goes to sleep on its perch and things creep up on you. But I mostly drink and self-medicate because if I truly acknowledged the weight of my guilt, it would crush me.

I think about the missing girls. Those bright naïve faces arranged like a yearbook in each newspaper and in the online galleries. Their frantic parents are sick with worry. As every new face is added to the growing list, the walls around me inch a little closer. Do I really believe that no one will ever find out? It doesn't matter. I'll just keep playing the part while I still can. I'll continue to be the almighty hedonist.

I'm not sure what to make of Brannagh's little DNA science experiment. The thought that I'm not human makes me feel even more alone. Of course, I know I am human, but not on this planet. Not here. I'm different. I'm also acutely aware that Brannagh is becoming a tanned, leathery thorn in my side.

Before going to bed for the night, having done little work on my music today, I head to the observatory. The spire is Godiva's highest point, shooting high from one end of the building. Looking out through one of the windows across the black shapes of the surrounding forest, I feel a little like Rapunzel. A cool wind hits my face.

I take a seat in front of the giant telescope that sits in the centre of the observatory and look through the eyepiece. If I had to guess, I'd say this is a catadioptric telescope, which uses a combination of both mirrors and lenses. Thanks a lot, Galileo Galilei. You're part of the reason why I'm in this mess. Was the world such a dim place without modern science? Humans still fed heartily and fucked with sufficient regularity. Doomsday was only penciled in the calendar after humans acquired a hunger for knowledge. We're insignificant and incapable of controlling our universe. We'll all die before we understand it. Every larger capacity hard drive and smarter phone is bringing us one step closer to oblivion.

Part of me regrets not paying more attention in biology. There are so many interesting samples on this planet. So much life. I'm just an astronaut. I have experience testing aircraft. Great at mathematics and physics. Twenty-twenty vision. An acceptable blood pressure when sitting down. But none of that really matters.

Through the eyepiece, I scan the heavens. The bottomless abyss that we float in. There's not much to see. Constellations all take shape if you try hard enough. A few tiny streaks of colour. Billions of stars blink at me, even though I'm seeing light that was generated a millennia ago. I'm drunk and burned out.

I wake up, groggy with sleep. I glance at the bedside clock and it says three hours past midnight. I've woken from a nightmare where I've been running from unseen danger, fleeing through streets and in and out of suburban homes. I feel fatigued. My body relaxes as reality spreads through me. But then I hear a voice. Godiva, ringing clearly throughout her walls. "Two guests."

As her voice echoes, hanging in the pitch darkness, I assume I'm hearing things. I remain very still, waiting to see if Godiva will speak again. She says nothing. I sit up slightly, looking around the room. Nothing's visible. No moonlight creeps through the curtains. I step out of bed and walk towards the monitor next to the door.

When I touch the screen with my index finger, the display turns on. In the bottom right corner it says 'two guests'.

I rub my eyes and attempt to wake up. Two guests. Me and someone else. Behind me I hear rapid taps on the bedroom windows. Rain. It falls harder. The monitor still says two guests. I open the closed circuit camera menu, picking full screen mode. A camera's view fills the panel. It's in night vision and is looking at the foyer. I can't see anything. Just furniture and the grand piano. Everything is as it was before I went to bed. I can see the white marble floor. The footprints I assumed I had made, which I noticed while sitting at the piano, are still visible. But there are more of them.

I start hitting the 'next' button, cycling through the cameras. Different rooms appear. Everything is deathly still. I can't see this supposed guest anywhere. I scan through what feels like a hundred cameras and nothing reveals itself to me. Maybe it's a glitch in the system. Maybe a piece of furniture fell over and triggered one of the weight panels.

I tell myself to go back to bed. I've been doing large amounts of narcotics. But to ease my mind I decide to flip through the cameras one last time. To be certain. I begin the camera cycle again. All I see are empty rooms, tinged with green. Whites appear in bright lime. The night vision picks up nothing of interest. I'm flicking faster now, the images almost a blur. But a jolt hits me as I see something. I'm tapping so fast on the panel that I've gone straight past it. I slowly move backwards in the camera order. A living area. Empty. The games parlour. Empty. The kitchen. There's someone in the kitchen.

I recoil from the screen. My heart nearly bursts through my ribs. A figure stands deathly still, hands by its side, looking up at the camera. It's wearing what looks like a pale, protective suit. I can't see its face because it's beneath a helmet. An astronaut helmet. It's someone in an astronaut's suit.

I'm unable to move. I must be dreaming. This is the deep sleep. The rapid eye movement phase. But with my own eyes, I'm staring at a security panel and there is someone wearing a NASA space suit staring back at me. The person lifts one of their hands and slowly waves. How does it know I'm even looking at it?

My body shakes with fear. My guest waves for a few more seconds and then returns their hand to their side.

Then I hear Godiva's voice. "Three guests."

Staring at the screen, I can see a shape moving behind the astronaut. Someone else is standing just out of the camera's focus. A white shape looming in the background. A third guest.

"Jesus," I spit out. As I take another step back, my foot hits something on the floor. I spin around and in the glow of the security panel I can see the electric guitar lying on the thin carpet. I wield it by the neck and point it at the door. My eyes are fixed on the monitor. The astronaut stares back from behind the reflective visor of his space helmet. I can still make out the silhouette of a second figure in the background, but it never steps into focus.

I move around the bed and sit in the corner of the room, looking over at the screen, my knees tucked against my chest. I continue to hold the guitar out in front of me. The sound of rain is heavy in the bedroom. The first astronaut turns and walks off screen and from what I can tell, the second astronaut follows. They've moved to the right, which means they're heading in the direction of the stairs. Up the stairs toward me.

"W-who are they?" I stammer.

Godiva hears me. "They're your guests," she replies.

I remain tucked between the wall and the nightstand, curled up, strangling the guitar's neck with white knuckles. I snatch my phone from the nightstand and call Brannagh. It rings out. No reply. I should call the police. I should definitely make an emergency phone call of some kind. But what do I tell them? I put the phone down on the carpet and listen intently, waiting to hear footsteps in the hallway. The sound of torrential rain outside throws a blanket of noise over everything.

I wait and seconds tick in slow torture. I've always considered myself a brave man and I've certainly done brave things. I'm an expert martial artist, even though I'm a little out of shape these days. I'm a fucking jetfighter pilot. But here I am, cowering in a corner, waiting for phantom spacemen. I close my eyes, rest my head on my knees and listen. Waiting to hear anything at all. Then Godiva speaks.

"One guest."

I lift my head and look across the room at the security panel. One guest. I push the guitar away and stand up, crossing the floor. In the bottom right corner of the screen it says one guest.

"How many guests, Godiva?" I ask.

"One guest, Jack."

I make the executive decision to invite people over. Actual guests. I can't be alone here anymore. On the lounge opposite the bed is my luggage. In the glow of the security panel I rummage through one of the pockets and find a small, familiar shape. Norman.

I switch Norman on and he begins to load up. But just as the menu screen appears, he gives me a battery warning and shuts down. Fumbling in the darkness, I find Norman's power pack and plug it into a socket next to the nightstand. Once Norman is finally switched on, I can see that there's 218 unread messages. Girls are persistent, there's no doubting that.

Without opening any texts, I open a new message template and begin composing an open invitation to anyone that's interested. Party at Godiva. Right now. I include the basic co-ordinates, as most watches and phones include a global positioning system. I then compile a recipient list, adding girls' names. Faceless fans. I cycle through the long database that Big Bang Theory have amassed. Willing recipients of our social outpourings.

I stop. I can't do this. I can't randomly message these girls because it means confronting my denial. Not all of these young women are unknown to me. While their names mean very little, deep down I know that there's phone contacts in Norman that correspond with those of the missing girls. I need to face this fact. That collection of smiling faces in the newspaper. I do know their faces because I'm certain I've slept with all of them. I've been telling myself I'm mistaken. Wishing and hoping that I could be wrong. After all, a lot of girls come backstage at our concerts.

I keep scrolling down the list, my mind ticking over. Norman is my contactable resume of conquests. The band's portfolio of carnality. The ladies that each member of Big Bang Theory takes to bed use this number to reach us. To thank us for a wonderful evening. Even though this very precious phone never leaves my side, the other members of my band use it when they're with me. Every girl gets the same number. If someone wanted to kidnap girls that I've slept with, they need only search the contents of Norman.

I scan through the list of unread messages, opening a few. They're so honest and sweet, sincerely trying to engage the band and thank us for hanging out with them. For bringing joy into their lives with our music and company. For making them feel privileged and special. Part or an exclusive group. A select few.

When we don't reply, and we very rarely do, the messages become agitated and distressed. I keep flicking through the lengthy list of texts, each from random names whose faces I can't place.

"*Hey, I know I must seem crazy for messaging so often, but I really want to see you again.*"

"*Jack, I really need to see you again. It's important.*"

"*Hi gorgeous. Just heard your new song on radio. So so good. Can't stop thinking about you.*"

I find one from Laurie. Then I find two more from Laurie. One of them has been opened and read, but not by me.

It says, "*Getting naked with you was a dream come true.*"

I immediately call Laurie's mobile, but she doesn't answer.

# CHAPTER SEVEN

I lift the wooden plank from its mooring and the door creaks ajar, sunlight slicing through. I stand and listen. The demonic scurry of last night's creature has left. Instead there are sounds that chirp and buzz.

Peering out, I can see that the graveyard is not as foreboding during the day. Like most cemeteries, I suppose. The temperature has risen, so I strip out of my pressure suit and fold it up. I keep my boots on and roll up the sleeves of my one-piece, which is made of a protective material but it breathes.

Underneath the bench in the middle of the room, beneath the bones and sheet, I find two doors which hide a small storage space. I hide my suit and the outboard motor inside and pull the sheet back down.

With my pack strapped firmly over my shoulders, I step into the sunlight, looking around to the edges of the clearing. Just trees and green-flecked gravestones. Climber vines. Metal fencing. Two bright suns. I push the shed door closed and notice broad, savage scratch-marks in its surface. Marks that most certainly would have been in my hide had I not found sanctuary.

I walk through the rows of gravestones, heading toward the church-like building. Squinting, I marvel up at the two suns burning over me. The air remains scented with wild, floral smells and the calls of birds and insects never make way for the animal howls that bore down on me the previous evening.

The steeped building is only fifty metres away. I continue towards it, scanning the tree line for signs of movement. Then something in my periphery makes me stop. Flapping to my right, hovering on the light breeze, is a butterfly. It's quite large. Perhaps a hand span in diameter. Its wings are mottled orange and yellow with black, messy cross-hatching. I freeze and watch it move about, determining if it poses a threat. But then it flutters away, as if its interest in me dissipated.

I stand in front of the church, looking at the crucifix atop its spire. The building looks old, but well kept. Broad, mighty beams of wood make up its walls. A deep brown timber. The steep roof is lined with chocolate tiles, slate-like and covered in small flourishes of moss. Little aquamarine dots across the grid of rectangles.

Stone steps lead to the church's entrance. Two large oak doors. They're wide open. It's dark inside but I can see the faint glow of stained glass. I adjust the pack on my back and ascend the stairs.

My eyes adapt to the dim lighting. I can smell scented oils. A rich red, patterned runner lies through the centre of the giant room, dividing two long rows of pews. The aisle ends with steps at the foot of an alter. Above it, bursting out of flower arrangements, is another towering crucifix. A massive cross that shoots towards the church's ceiling. Hanging from this cross is the statue of a bearded man, naked except for a small loincloth. He's nailed to it, a crown of thorns on his head. He has a forlorn expression. Perhaps a look of disappointment.

There's movement in the corner of the room. A figure pottering at a bookshelf and a table. He or she is about the same height as me and is wearing a black hooded cloak that prevents me from seeing their face. It's too short to be the creature that chased me through the graveyard.

I step back towards the entrance and a sharp creak in the floorboards betrays me. The figure spins around, revealing a grey, wispy beard and thin bony face beneath the drape of the hood. It's an old, human face. It tilts its head back and I can see two grey eyes staring at me.

I refrain from sudden movement. This creature seems human, but I shouldn't take his withered frame for granted. He is an alien. He could have immense physical strength, the power of telekinesis or know any number of martial arts.

"Can I help you, young man?" he asks.

English. Clear and distinct. Just like on the gravestones outside. I comprehend every word.

"Uh, yes," I say. "I'm... lost."

The man remains still. Then says, "Lost?"

I panic that I've used a word he doesn't understand. "Um, yes. Lost."

"Well you have come to the right place," he replies, his voice like bark peeling from a trunk. He walks towards me, pulling back his hood. He has white hair, cut short on his ancient skull. "This is where the lost are always welcome."

I wonder how I must appear to this priest-like individual. I haven't shaved in over twelve months and a thick, brown beard wraps around my face. My hair is matted and down past my shoulder.

The man shuffles up the aisle, moving towards me. He stops a metre away, studying me with his clouded eyes. I wonder if he's blind.

"I'm sorry," he says, taking a step closer. "My eyes are failing me."

"That's... fine," I say. "I think mine are too."

"Where are you from?" he asks.

"Where am I from?" I ask back, flicking through my brain for an effective answer. "Not really... anywhere. I'm a traveler."

"A traveler?" queries the priest. He takes another step closer, squinting. "And you've lost your way?"

"Yes," I reply.

"Where are you trying to get to?"

"Not sure. Nowhere. I'm not really... going anywhere."

The priest pauses, his eyes trying to focus on me. "Well I'm not sure that you could be lost then." He looks at me blankly. "How did you get here?"

"I just walked," I say.

"Walked?"

"Yes," I say.

The priest looks at me. "Oh," he says, finally. "Yes. Of course. Of course you walked."

"I'm not familiar with this part of the...world."

He nods slightly. "You don't know where you are?"

"Not exactly."

The priest steps into the pew next to where I stand and sits down. I take a seat in the pew directly across the aisle, sitting my pack beside me on the polished wood.

"This is The Everlasting," says the priest.

"The... what?"

"This is The Everlasting. We're on an island."

"Oh," I say. "An island..."

"Your accent is unusual," says the priest. He faces forward as he says it, looking up in the direction of the statue and the crucifix.

At the mention of my accent, I acknowledge the priest's. It's familiar, but difficult to define. Perhaps somewhere between American and British. Or maybe there is a Scandinavian lilt to it. I can't align it with anything specific from Earth. It's deep and husky, but just a voice. Generic as it is wise.

I don't know why I ask my next question. Perhaps it's to alleviate any lingering irrational paranoia I have about travelling through wormholes. "Am I on Earth?" I ask.

This question prompts the priest to turn and look at me. He seems perplexed. "No, of course not. Why would you think that?"

I don't answer. I don't know what to say.

The corners of the priest's mouth turn, threatening to smile beneath his thinning beard. "You seem delirious," he says. "Would you like some water?"

"Water?"

"Yes, it's all I have I'm afraid."

"Water would be perfect."

# CHAPTER EIGHT

My conscience told me to speak to the police when the first girl went missing. I spent a week weighing up my pros and cons. The risks involved. So far I've managed to evade prosecution on any personal misdemeanor and I feel I have to keep it that way. If you're charged with something, then serious questions are asked. "So where are you really from? Where were you born? How old are you?" What makes me mysterious can in turn make me a prime suspect.

Once the second girl went missing, and then the third, I was concerned. But I only truly recognised the first. There was absolutely no mistaking her, but the other two I couldn't be certain of. The fourth looked familiar. The fifth looked familiar too. Then the next two I couldn't honestly say I recognised. The eighth girl though, I knew her. She was this work experience lass. About twenty-six years old. An intern at Endurance Records. We attended a party at the top of town and then decided to go to another party. On the way there, things got a little heated between this girl and me. We wandered into a park and in the shadows a sexual liaison took place. There's a reason why parks attract that kind of behaviour. They're an oasis of nature in the middle of man-made construction. A beacon of honesty amid the faux walls of common decency. A window to the past. If you want to relax, then you swim in the ocean. If you want to fuck like a chimpanzee, then you go to a park.

I've fed hungrily on naïve denial, but Norman must be the link. However, taking this to the police could prove monumental. A gigantic investigation of devastating proportions would take place, almost certainly knocking my brazen mask from its already tentative position. I'd blow my cover. There would be blood tests. Further DNA tests. The fantastical story that I've spent my life living in the wild isn't going to cut the mustard in court. The blind eye suddenly regains its vision.

Only four people get to read Norman's contents. Big Bang Theory. Which means that one of them might know something. But none of them have mentioned that they recognise any of the girls. While the link between Norman and the girls is compelling, is it not circumstantial? It is perhaps suspicious that my fellow band members have never said anything, but these trysts are so often a rapid blur where faces are rarely in focus. But the phone is a clue. Despite my need to keep a low profile, I feel subtle investigation is warranted.

The driver drops me off inside the safety of my building's carpark. I thank him, grab my bags from the back seat and jump in the elevator. Once inside my apartment, I drop my luggage and head into my music room, looking through the drawers of the computer desk. I find a data stick and put it in my pocket.

I knock on the door of Laurie's apartment. There's a faint noise emanating from inside. Heavy breathing. Many voices. Some kind of commentary. It sounds like a sports broadcast on television. I knock and no one answers. I knock a second time.

The door opens and Laurie's mother appears, surprise sweeping her face. She's wearing black leggings, a pink over-sized t-shirt and her hair is pulled back with a sweatband. She's an attractive woman. An older version of Laurie's cute, elfin features. She's not a lot older than I am.

"My apologies," I smile, "I hope I'm not interrupting your workout."

I can hear music and more heavy breathing wafting from somewhere over Laurie's mother's shoulder.

"No, that's fine," she smiles. "I was just doing some aerobics. I prefer to do it when I have the place to myself."

"Privacy is a valuable commodity."

"Yes," she says, "I'm not used to people knocking randomly on my door. No one can get up here."

I nod and smile. "I won't bother you any further, I was just wondering if Laurie might be home?"

"No, she's away at the moment. She went north with some friends. There's a place they go to on the beach called The Nautilus."

"The Nautilus, right," I say.

"What did you need to see her about?"

"Oh, just a song she wanted to hear. We've just recorded a demo and I thought I'd play it for her." I hold up the data stick.

I can hear the television continue in the background, though I think I can distinguish the sound of a woman moaning. Must be a thorough workout.

"Well you're welcome to come inside and play it for me, if you like," smiles Laurie's mother.

"Um, you know what. I just remembered I've got to do an interview. I'd better get home."

I turn to walk away.

"With the police?" she asks.

"Sorry?"

"On the news earlier, it said that the police are questioning you. You know one of the girls that went missing? Terrible thing."

"I know lots of girls," I say. "Yes, I spoke to the police but I couldn't be much help."

As I go to close my apartment door, Laurie's mother calls out, "I saw you on television last night."

"Yeah?" I reply.

"It was the music video for 'Sound Of Silence'."

"Excellent," I smile.

"Such an amazing song," she says.

"It's not bad."

"I can't believe you wrote it."

"Neither can I."

"Your voice was in my head as I went to sleep."


I'm standing in front of my bathroom mirror, wearing only my jeans. My cheekbones are particularly prominent these days and my eyes appear sunken compared to what they once were. I just don't eat food very much. No appetite. Constant anxiety.

I plug the hair clippers into a power socket next to the mirror.

They buzz to life with shrill vibration. With one hand I grasp a fistful of hair above my face and with the other I begin moving the clippers into the dense, matted thicket that has adorned my head for almost two years. When I pull the clippers away, hair cascades into the basin and on my scalp is a long white stripe, finally given a peek at the outside world. The image reminds me of my father mowing the lawn. How it looked as the rotors stripped it bare.

In a surprisingly short amount of time my hair is gone, shaved close to my skull. My scalp is rough when I run my hand across it. The naked sensation almost gives me palpitations.

Wearing my wide, dark sunglasses, I sneak out a rear emergency exit of my building and head towards my regular café, Zunge Bohne. I keep my head down when I pass people and manage to make it there without anyone accosting me with hyperactive excitement.

The suns are reaching their peak heat for the day and the footpath surrounding the café is crowded with bronzed beach goers, heading back and forth to the sand and waves across the road. The surf looks good and I can see a large number of surfers out on the water, which is bursting with the violent white reflection of sunlight. It's almost too much to look at. I squeeze past a few people, who smell of sweat, salt and sunscreen, and sneak inside.

I step up to the counter and Rose is facing away, making some sort of milkshake. Another waitress notices me and when she serves me, confused recognition crosses her face.

"Hi there, Jack," says the girl.

Rose immediately spins around and looks me up and down with an indiscernible expression. "Nice haircut."

"Thanks, I did it myself."

She huffs and turns back to the milkshake maker. The other girl smiles.

"Would you like me to find you a seat?"

"I actually need to speak with Rose very briefly," I reply. "Then I'd love a table with a view of the ocean."

"I'm busy," says Rose, over her shoulder.

"I know," I reply, trying to keep my voice low, "but this is really important. Seriously."

"Kate, could you please find a table for Jack. I'll talk to him later," says Rose to the other girl. She's seizing this opportunity to stay annoyed.

Kate looks at me awkwardly. "Would you like to follow me?"

"Sure."

I leave my sunglasses on as Kate leads me through the café. A few people look at me but glance away just as quickly, fooled by my haircut.

"Can I bring you anything?" asks Kate as I sit at a small two-seater table. I'm next to the short, thin hedge that surrounds the café's courtyard, giving me a clear view of the beach.

"I'll have one of those new Eiskaffee drinks. It's too hot today for a regular coffee."

"Certainly," says Kate. "Can I bring you anything else?"

"Today's newspaper, thanks."

I probably shouldn't be out here, but I have always hidden in public. It's been my refuge. I pull out my mobile phone and try to call Laurie. It rings and rings, then the dial tone stops. I press redial. The tone continues, then just before I'm about to hang up I hear a voice.

"Hello? Jack?"

"Laurie?"

"Hey, what's up?" she says, seemingly excited to hear from me.

"Nothing much," I say, casually.

"Why are you calling me? Do you miss me?"

"Sure I do."

"I heard the police have been speaking to you about the missing girls. You're on the news a lot."

"Yeah, sort of," I reply, wondering where all these false news reports are stemming from. "How's your holiday?"

"Good. The weather is amazing." I can hear noise behind Laurie's voice.

"I didn't know you were going away."

"Well you didn't tell me you were going away either."

"Well, do we have to tell each other these things?"

"I don't know. Maybe," says Laurie.

"How long are you gone for?"

"About a week."

"Who are you with?"

"A few friends. We're at a funpark at the moment."

"You're staying at the Nautilus, yeah?"

"Yes. How did you know that?"

132

"Your mum told me."

"You were talking to my mum? That's weird."

"Is it?"

"Yes."

"Why?"

"Because she's older than you."

"Are you safe?"

"Yes. Why wouldn't I be?"

I search for an answer. "Um, because... I don't know."

"You don't know?"

"I just want you to be safe. You know, don't take any risks."

"Sounds boring."

"I know, but it's for the best."

"Why do you care?"

"Because... I care?"

"You like me."

"Yeah, of course I do."

I hear a female voice call out her name.

"I've got to go," she says. "We're about to go on the Skytrain."

"Cool," I say. "Well, good luck."

"I'll see you when I get home, yeah?"

"For sure."

She hangs up. I'm not sure my warning against kidnappers had the potency I was aiming for. The waitress brings me over my drink, a spoon and today's newspaper.

People walk up and down the beach. Some lie on their backs. A few young teenagers throw a Frisbee-like object. All of them seeking improvement. Staining the whiteness from their skin. If I pretend, I could be back on Earth looking across at the beach where I spent holidays with my family.

Amidst the shifting sea of flesh that enjoys the sand's warmth and the water's cool embrace, I notice someone. A figure standing very still. A woman who is smiling at me. My stomach surges when I recognise her. A curvaceous brunette watches from the sand. She's waiting for me to notice her, dressed in a tiny white two-piece bikini. A sheer, mango sarong is tied around her waist, brushed aside by the gentle breeze. There's a pair of sunglasses on her face.

Natalie keeps smiling at me, waiting for me to respond. To wave. Is she stalking me? I lower my sunglasses, fixing my eyes on her. She knows I've seen her and approaches.

Natalie stands on the footpath across the road, waiting for a break in traffic. Then she sidles between the expensive convertibles that roll down Easton Boulevard and walks around to the front of the café. Natalie passes the counter as all eyes turn on her. Her mesmerising form winds through the tables of the courtyard, where she slides into the seat opposite me. Natalie is not ideal company for someone trying to keep a low profile. The small fabric triangles of her bikini provide limited modesty.

"The Devil hath power to assume a pleasing shape," I say, sipping my iced coffee.

Natalie smiles, wryly. "I suppose I must seem like a devil," she replies.

"You're dangerous," I say. "No good can come of you."

"I deserve that," she nods. "I also owe you an explanation. Nice haircut, by the way. I like it."

Kate walks over to our table. "Can I bring you something to drink?" she asks Natalie.

"I'll have a lime miasma," replies Natalie, barely looking at our waitress.

"Sure," smiles Kate and bounds away.

"So are you here for another sample?" I ask.

"I hope so," says Natalie.

I don't respond.

"I'm just kidding," she says.

I'm wary of her sheepish behaviour. One pout and I'm gone for. I stir my iced coffee and then take another sip.

"I know I betrayed you," she says.

"That's a start," I say.

"You must be angry at me."

"I feel a little...betrayed. Giving Brannagh a DNA sample was a little... perverse. Under-handed."

"Well you never said I *couldn't* have a sample."

"So it's an assumed agreement?"

"You were very forthcoming."

I shake my head. "How did the conversation go exactly? Did Brannagh call you up and say, 'Hey Natalie, you're irresistible. You like fucking people. How about you get a sperm sample from Jack for me?'"

"He didn't specify."

"Didn't specify what?"

"That it had to be sperm. That was my choice."

"Jesus."

Natalie grins and reclines in her seat. Beads of perspiration roll down the flawless cliff face that starts at her neck and descends her chest and stomach. The rays of the suns seem to sneak under our umbrella to find her skin.

"I like you, Jack," she says.

"Tell me why I should continue this conversation. Why shouldn't I call someone and tell them you're stalking me?"

"Because you're wanted for questioning by the police. You're a flüchtling," she smiles. Her drink arrives in a tall cocktail glass, a mix of cream and lime liqueur that swirls in clouds. "I see you as a flesh and blood person, Jack. I see you differently to everyone else."

"No, you see me as a challenge. A little game. How much did Brannagh pay you?"

"Nothing. He said he was trying to help you, so I agreed."

"Trying to help me?"

"He wanted to help find out more about your past. He didn't think you'd want his help, but he had to try anyway."

"Because he has a stake in some book about me. He's sourcing information for an unauthorised biography."

"Oh," says Natalie, seeming genuinely surprised. "He didn't mention that." I don't reply. "Brannagh offered me the opportunity to meet you," she continues. "He gave me access to you. That was my motivation."

"Did you even stay in the Narc den?"

"No."

"You left after I left?"

"Yes."

"Wow, you're good."

"So what was the result of the DNA test?"

"What?"

"What were the results of the test? Did it shed any light on where you came from? Your parents?"

"It seems I don't have any."

Natalie raises an eyebrow. "Immaculate conception?"

"Immaculate deception."

"Ah," says Natalie, "nice answer." She takes the straw of her cocktail and places it between her full, red lips.

"I'm good," I shrug. I open the newspaper to page three. I see something that makes me freeze.

"Look, I'm sorry I betrayed you," says Natalie. "It seems awful. But I wasn't acting. I had an amazing time with you."

Rose is waiting a nearby table and I spot her eyeing Natalie, then glancing back at me. I look at page three again. I can't believe my eyes. I have to get out of here.

"Are you ok?" asks Natalie.

"I have to go," I say, quietly.

"What's the matter?"

"Nothing," I say, closing the newspaper. "I just don't feel too well." My body starts to tighten with panic. "Call me," I add. "Don't be a stranger."

"Why don't you come over for a swim in the ocean with me? That will calm you down. You need to relax."

"I can't."

"Why not?"

"Uh... sharks. There's sharks."

"Oh well," shrugs Natalie, before adding suggestively, "...I'm not afraid of being eaten."

"Dear god."

Natalie studies me for a moment. "You've seen something in the newspaper... do you know that girl on page three?"

"No, stop being heinous," I reply, getting to my feet, folding the newspaper under my arm.

Natalie puts her straw to her mouth and takes a long drink, nearly emptying the glass. "I'm coming with you," she says.

My phone starts to vibrate on the table's surface. It's Amelia. I don't answer and shove it in my pocket.

"Who was that?" asks Natalie.

"Unknown number." I walk towards the counter and Natalie follows. I throw a random note from my wallet next to the cash register. Kate picks up the note as I say with a calm smile, "Keep the change."

Outside I'm on the footpath, trying to find a taxi. Natalie's by my side. I step to the edge of the road and she follows.

"You're coming home with me, aren't you," I say.

"Yes, I think it's for the best."

A convertible rolls past, four tanned guys turn to look at her. "Need a ride?" one of them calls out.

Natalie just smiles back and shakes her head. The four men

continue on their way.

"Well at least no one is going to notice me while you're by my side."

"See, I'm helping already."

I wave at a taxi that cruises past, but it has passengers.

"You know what the really fucked thing is?" I ask. "I wouldn't be talking to you right now if you were unattractive. Isn't that... gravely unfortunate?"

"Not for me," she shrugs.

"Maybe not, but it's depressing. Genuinely depressing."

Another taxi approaches, its light on. Before I have lifted my hand to wave it down, Natalie steps out into the road. The vehicle screeches to a halt.

"Ah, so *that's* how you stop traffic," I remark, following Natalie into the backseat.

The driver drops us off in the rear lane of my building, which is deserted. I pass him a random note and he then eyes Natalie as she exits the car. I unlock a rear fire exit of my building and we step through a back entrance to the main foyer and into one of the empty elevators.

Halfway to the top floor, Natalie pushes me against the wall and kisses me. Pulling away for a moment she asks, "You know the missing girls, don't you?"

"I think so, yes," I say, completely at her mercy.

"How do I know I'm not next then? How do I know you're not going to kill me as soon as we get inside your apartment."

"I suppose you don't. But what difference does it make? You're already a target."

"And whoever is kidnapping them has a pretty good record so far," she says.

"Well, I must always get my girl," I smile.

"So there's no point trying to resist you? I should just accept my fate."

"I could ask you the same question."

Natalie smiles with her luscious mouth. She reaches out and pushes the emergency stop button. The elevator grinds to a halt.

"I always get my guy," she says.

"Turn the elevator back on."

"Why?"

"Because I need to get to my apartment."

"You'll get there," smiles Natalie. "Eventually." She gives a short tug at the knot of her sarong and it falls to the ground.

The mirrored walls of the elevator surround us. I have a hazy flashback to being with Natalie at Membrané. A fly in a web.

"You like mirrors, don't you."

"I don't *dislike* them," she smiles.

"This isn't fair."

"Jack, you're a free man. If you want to go to your apartment, just turn the elevator on."

Natalie moves her sunglasses from her face and puts them up on her head. Seeing her eyes again reminds me of the manipulative intensity she held over me after Brannagh's party.

"I will," I say, but I don't move. I could take her right now and she'd let me do anything to her.

Natalie reaches an arm behind her back and unties the knot of her bikini top. The fabric falls loose at the front. The reptilian part of my brain grins smugly at my moral conscience.

"I promise I won't keep a sample this time," says Natalie.

"How would I know?"

"Because you can watch me swallow it."

My heart stops beating for about three seconds. But somewhere in my blossoming lust I find a shred of self-control. "I can't do this..." I sigh and lean past her to restart the elevator. It surges to life.

"Impressive," she says, retying her bikini top. "That took some will power."

I lean against the wall of the elevator, unable to look at her. "It's just the distractions," I sigh. "It's the distractions that kill you in the end."

While Natalie is showering in my bathroom, I start filling a small suitcase with things I'll need. I need to disappear for a while. I'll work out what is going on and put things right. But I don't know where to go. Where to start. I don't even know why I'm packing, but it feels pro-active.

Natalie walks into my bedroom. Her hair hangs limp and moist. The towel I gave her is tied across her chest. I gave her my smallest towel.

"This isn't a very big towel," says Natalie.

"Uh, yeah. All my bigger towels are... unavailable."

"Is that right?"

"Sure, why not."

"I don't suppose you have any clothes I could put on? In the interests of modesty."

"I didn't think you had much interest in that."

She gives me a sarcastic smile and walks towards the bed. "Don't think I'm on offer all the time. Your windows of opportunity aren't open as often as you think."

"Yes, but some windows take longer to close than others." Pointing to the closet, I say, "I've got a suitcase full of women's clothing if you want to have a look."

"Very funny."

"I'm serious."

"Why would you have a suitcase full of women's clothing?"

"Left overs."

"Well I'm sure the police wouldn't find that suspicious at all."

"I think a portion of them might belong to the missing girls."

"Seriously?"

"Yes, I think so."

"Show me."

"Look in the bottom of the far cupboard."

Natalie crosses the room, slides the built-in robe open and pulls out the black suitcase. She wheels it into the centre of the room and unzips. Kneeling down, she sifts through the items.

"Wow, this is quite a collection."

"Expensive tastes," I say, lying back on the bed with the newspaper next to me.

"So this is like your trophy cabinet?"

"It's just a lost and found."

"If the police found this, it would look bad."

"I think they'd be secretly impressed."

"Or they'd think you're a cross-dresser."

"I've tried, but most of those are too big for me."

Natalie holds up a black lace negligee. "Does anyone know about this suitcase?"

I take a deep breath. "Britney does."

"Britney is the name of the girl in today's newspaper. On page three."

"Yes."

"Fuck," says Natalie.

"And when she left my apartment she was wearing clothing from this suitcase."

"So... Britney was wearing something that might belong to one of the missing girls?"

"Yes."

"And now she's missing?"

"Only if you believe the newspapers."

Natalie picks up a short, white summer dress that has a pink rose-flower pattern. "Who did this belong to?" she asks.

I'm starting to stress. My mind's racing. I lean over to my bedside dresser and rummage through the top drawer. "That dress belonged to a girl called Stephanie." I find some pills in a small plastic bag and pull one out, swallowing it with some water from a plastic bottle next to the bed.

Natalie stands up and drops the towel from her body. She then pulls the dress over her head and eases it down over her perfect, naked figure. She doesn't button the front, leaving the garment to hang open from her navel upward.

"Did Stephanie throw herself at you?"

"I wouldn't say that."

"So you seduced her?"

"I don't know."

"Why is her dress here? Did she leave in her underwear?"

"No, she stayed for a few nights. She brought clothing with her. She spilled red wine on the dress and I put it in the washing machine and she left without getting it."

"She didn't come back for it?"

"No."

"Why?"

"It had something to do with obscene substance abuse, mood swings, weird, unintelligible ramblings and bizarre bursts of midnight affection."

"Sounds like she was a handful."

"I was talking about me."

"But women worship you. It must take more than that to scare them away."

"They don't see me as a suitor. I'm more of an other-worldly experience."

"And now Stephanie is dead?"

"You're not exactly a vessel of optimism, are you?"

"What was the sex like with her?"

"Good."

"Did you fuck her with passion?"

"Those words are mutually exclusive."

Natalie looks at the dress, running her hands down her torso, feeling the material. Trying to extract its memories. "Did Stephanie wear this dress while you fucked her?"

"Yes," I reply.

"So she didn't even get to take it off?"

"No."

"Why?" asks Natalie.

"Because the dress turned me on," I reply. "Because I was more aroused when she was wearing it."

"Did she like that?"

"I believe so, yes."

"What look did she have in her eyes?"

"Pain. Pleasure and pain."

"And she liked that?"

"She didn't ask me to be rough with her, but she never stopped me. She stayed for three days."

"You didn't try to romance her? To love her?"

"I thought we were talking about sex."

Natalie picks up the newspaper from the bed, still open on the page of photos. She points to the picture of Stephanie, her voice still calm. "So when you saw this photo of her in the paper, you didn't know immediately that you were somehow connected?"

"She works at the record label that my band are signed with. So, yes. I was aware of a connection."

"Why wouldn't you go to the police?"

I stand up and take a step toward Natalie. She stands her ground. When I take another step toward her, she moves away slightly. Back towards her reflection in the wardrobe's doors.

"What would I tell them? 'Hi guys, just wanted to let you know that I've had sex with this missing girl. She stayed at my apartment not long before she disappeared. If it's any help, I've still got her dress. It's in a suitcase along with many other items of clothing, which probably belong to other missing girls that you're looking for. I can't give you any information that would lead to her whereabouts, but I thought I should just come forward and suggest that you look at me as a suspect.'"

141

Natalie smiles. "But you're innocent, so you should have nothing to fear. You've become a suspect anyway."

"Joke's on me, huh?"

"You're not hiding something?"

I take another step toward her. Natalie steps away. Her fist that holds the newspaper tenses, crumpling the pages.

"Nothing to hide," I say. I step forward again and Natalie leans back against the glass surface of the built-ins, unable to move any further. I'm almost pressed against her.

"What did the DNA test really say?" asks Natalie, probing me. Pushing me.

"It said that I can't trust you."

Natalie looks away. Something crosses her face and I wonder if it's fear. She remains defiant.

"I betrayed your trust," says Natalie, taking a deep breath. There's a heavy silence between us, before I push my hand underneath the dress, between her legs.

Natalie drops the newspaper and for the next half an hour I'm anything but gentle with her.

# CHAPTER NINE

I dream that my escape pod is visible from Earth, as I move further away. I'm a prick in the solar system. The black eternal darkness is the only constant. The light of stars appears and fades away. But the black will never be extinguished. If the stars live forever, infinitely hanging in time, then every line of sight would contain one. If their light travelled forever, then the night sky would glow brighter than the sun. A star everywhere you look. But here, in my place among the stars, I take comfort that I am not the only one that is going to die. We all will.

I will ultimately share the fate of my two crew mates. The span of time in which it matters whether I made the right decision will cease. It has an end point.

# CHAPTER TEN

I haven't slept soundly. I've been lying in that scattered, half-awake delirious state, where my thoughts bounce back and forth like a bird in a cage. No exit. When I reach out an arm, I already know Natalie isn't there. I think I remember her leaving. Maybe I don't. But now my bed is large and empty again. Night has barely fallen.

I lean over and switch on my bedside lamp. The suitcase of clothing, which had been left near the foot of the bed, has vanished. It seems Natalie has taken my trinkets. It's a fairly damning piece of evidence to lose. However, when I sit up further, I notice a colourful item draped over the end of the bed. It's the patterned dress. Stephanie's dress. Natalie has left it. It is almost certainly riddled with Natalie's DNA, and some of mine too. She's left it deliberately. Perhaps as a sign of good faith? It links her to me and perhaps any wrong doing on my behalf. Not that I've done anything wrong. This is Natalie's token gesture.

I'm not sure when I'll see Natalie again. I expect she's someone that comes and goes as she pleases. Nobody owns her and nobody tells her what to do. Her role in my life has the potential to become like a twenty-four hour virus. She'll appear when I least expect it and probably at the most inconvenient time. Nevertheless, I am very taken by her. She's devastatingly attractive and far more mysterious than what I am typically comfortable with. I wish she was still here and I hope she returns.

I get out of bed and take a shower. The steam envelops me and for a minute I feel better. But my head is still buzzing from the drugs and my stomach is beginning to turn on me. My thoughts return to the missing girls. I'm so scattered that they had actually skipped my mind. But my concern has reached a level that I can no longer ignore. So I need to devise a plan of action that is both proactive and won't risk my persona.

Something tells me that Rose is next. If the girls were disappearing in chronological order she would already be gone. If there are sinister hands snatching my liaisons, then girls have been taken for far less than what Rose has done. She must be in danger. A small voice whispers it and once the thought announces itself, it doesn't go away. It echoes around the yellowed walls of my skull. Whether I should trust it or not is a different question. Not all of my inner thinkings lead me in the right direction.

If I am to investigate, I need to avoid the police. Let my management take care of them. They get a percentage of everything, so I feel it's their duty to buy me some time. I'll hide up here in my tower, like a herd of cattle crammed in the shadow of a lone tree. I need to steer clear of that boiling paddock and wait until things cool down.

I go to the kitchen and start washing down painkillers. A few downers should slow my mind. But then I hear a knock. Someone at the door. I step very quietly over to the peephole and peer through. There's nobody there. This can only mean one thing. I open the door.

"Mr Roeg," I say. "Hi."

"Jack, how are you?" he smiles, his small pointed teeth spread in greeting.

"A little tired," I reply. "Stressed even."

"Oh," says Mr Roeg. "Well, I don't mean to stress you further... but there's some policemen downstairs that are asking about you."

"Really?"

"Yes, I passed them on my way up just now."

"I see. Is security letting them up here?"

"I'm not sure. But they were waving a piece of paper and seemed quite agitated."

"How rude."

"Jack, I know the security guards here. I'm sure they'll take care of this. You're a part of our community and we all need to look out for each other. Especially for you."

"That's very kind," I say.

"Why don't you come over to my apartment, in case they access our floor?"

"Um," I say, considering the offer. I'm not ready to speak with the police. I do need time. "Sure. That would be good."

"Excellent," says Mr Roeg. "I'd like to help you. We all know you have done nothing wrong and we can't have the authorities impeding your work."

"The world needs music."

I quickly grab my apartment keys from the kitchen counter, lock the door behind me and follow Mr Roeg across our foyer. He unlocks and opens his apartment door. The handle has been lowered for him.

I step past Mr Roeg and he then closes the door behind us. A moment later I hear the elevator door open outside and voices emerge. Kneeling down, I look through Mr Roeg's spyhole. There's two policemen in jet-black uniforms. They have shiny badges and emblems on their shirts, and belts of varied paraphernalia. With their hats pulled down, they march toward my apartment. One of the big security guards from my building steps closely behind them.

"I don't think he's in there," says the guard, in an innocently dissuading tone. "We saw him leave a few hours ago."

One of the officers knocks loudly on my door which, of course, I don't answer. He knocks loudly a second time, then turns to the guard. "Open this door." He holds up a piece of paper.

Sheepish, the guard pulls a set of keys from his belt and unlocks my apartment door.

"Shit," I whisper to Mr Roeg, who is pottering about somewhere behind me. "They've gone inside."

"They're inside now?" I hear Mr Roeg ask.

"Yes, right now."

When I turn around I see Mr Roeg has picked up his mobile phone. He speaks into it. "They've entered." He hangs up and puts the phone in the pocket of his tiny pants.

"Who's that?" I ask.

"Just the building's security. Nothing to worry about. I'm keeping them in the loop."

"Isn't there a camera in our foyer? Why would they need you to call them?"

Something flashes in Mr Roeg's tiny, dark beady eyes and he

smiles, revealing his miniature, pointed teeth. "The cameras are being troublesome. Why don't you make yourself comfortable until the officers leave?" He motions to his modern living room, which sits by dim lamplight. To the right is a custom-built kitchen, which opens into the wide living area. His apartment's layout appears to resemble my own, but the dwarf furniture makes his dwelling seem far bigger. As you would expect of someone of Mr Roeg's miniscule stature, all of his furnishings are shrunken. Everything is in proportion to his toddler's frame, except for his flatscreen television, which is quite large. A low bookshelf. A coffee table. A few well groomed plants. To my left is a normal sized single-seater sofa, which I quietly sit in.

On the walls are three macabre artworks, penned in black ink. Vivid in detail. Illustrations of winged creatures and naked humans and flames.

"Interesting artworks," I say, pointing at one.

"I dabble in sketching," says Mr Roeg.

I hear the elevator door open outside and the sound of more footsteps. Sharp, heavy shoes echo off the tiles, striding with purpose.

"Can I get you something to drink? Would it be inappropriate for me to offer you some red wine?"

"Far from it," I smile.

Mr Roeg pulls two wine glasses from a low cupboard and then retrieves a bottle of wine from his pantry.

"I must say," says Mr Roeg when he hands me my glass, "it's quite an honour to have you here in my apartment. Drinking red wine."

"Don't be silly," I say, dismissively. "Pleasure is all mine."

Mr Roeg looks as though he may blush, then fetches his own glass. He sits in a small armchair across from me and a reflective moment passes as we both sip our beverage. On the wall behind my host, perhaps seven feet from the ground, is a medium-sized wooden crucifix.

"So when is your band performing again?" asks Mr Roeg.

"Soon, I hope. We'll probably announce some dates in the next few months. But nothing's confirmed."

"Would it be a long tour?"

"Possibly. We might go around the world again."

"So you'd be leaving us?"

"Temporarily. But nothing's confirmed. A lot of promoters harass us, so I'd say we'll have a festival headline spot locked in somewhere."

"Excellent," nods Mr Roeg. "I can't say I've been to a festival, but I might come along to your next one. Stranger things have happened."

"Yes, I think that is a fair observation."

Mr Roeg chuckles lightly, with his odd, high voice. Like air escaping a balloon. He composes himself and asks, "So, with your songs, how do you think of them? How do you keep writing such amazing music?"

"Uh, they just come to me I guess. I hear a melody in my head and I start fooling on the guitar. It's difficult to explain."

"Do songs appear to you anywhere?"

"Yes, they can. If I'm not near my guitar I might sing a tune into my mobile phone and record it until I can get home."

"So this inspiration follows you? It's all around you?"

"Yeah," I shrug.

"Like direct gifts," says Mr Roeg, and his eyes become distant, no longer looking at me but through me. I'd be more freaked out by him if I weren't capable of kicking him through a plate-glass window. He's just a little eccentric. "What you've given to the world is miraculous," he continues. "Music that's unlike anything that has been heard before... so deftly spiritual."

"Music is spiritual," I say, casually. "Or at least it should be."

We both sip our wine which, if my palate serves me, is an expensive drop. Then the phone, which sits low on the wall near the kitchen area, begins to ring. Mr Roeg drops from his small seat and waddles across the room, red wine in hand.

"Yes?" he says, then listens to the voice on the other end. "Oh, good. Excellent. Thank you for letting me know." He hangs up. "That was security downstairs. They say it's safe for you to go home now."

"Great," I say, and rise from my seat, taking a long gulp on my wine.

"Oh," says Mr Roeg. "There's no need to rush off. You're welcome to stay and talk."

"I'd love to," I say, "but I've got so much to do."

"Of course, of course," says Mr Roeg.

I finish my wine and place the glass on Mr Roeg's low kitchen counter. I then head for the door and Mr Roeg rushes to open it for me.

"It was an honour to have you here, Jack," he says.

"No, no, the honour was all mine. You've been a wonderful host."

"You're welcome to visit any time."

"That's very kind. I promise I will... when my life settles down a bit."

Standing inside my dimly lit kitchen, glancing across the uncluttered breakfast bar to the living areas beyond, I can't spot anything out of place. Everything is as I left it. But I can smell something strange. An odour from the tiles. I switch on the kitchen light and kneel down. The tickle in my nostrils takes me through space and time to hot summers in the public pool in the small rural town I grew up in. Memories that lose the three-dimensional clarity of video footage and become singular snap-shots. Then the colour fades from those images and they lose their detail. They fall from the photo album over time and you try to put them back in sequential order. But then you stop trying and decide that it doesn't matter.

I can definitely smell chlorine, or a similar cleaning chemical. I put my nose to the surface of the smooth tiles. Rocking back, I shift to my feet and squat down, continuing to glance around. Looking for a sign that someone was even here. I saw them walk inside. They must have looked around, opened a few cupboards or rifled through some papers. They've not even touched the mail on my breakfast bar. Some of it is still unopened. That might have given them a few useless clues.

When I look at the white cupboard directly in front of me, beneath the bar, my eyes fix on something. I lean forward and touch it lightly with the tip of my index finger. It's only small and so insignificant, but when I pull back and rub my index finger against the pad of my thumb, there's a smear of red. On the cupboard door, the dot I poked has spread out, admitting its vivid redness. A puny crimson stain that the word droplet would exaggerate.

I walk to the sink and rinse my hands. Checking the time on the oven, I determine that Rose finishes work in around an hour. Tonight might be the perfect time to strike.

I turn on my mobile phone, expecting there to be a trillion

missed calls and frantic messages. Mostly from my manager. I scroll down the list of texts, trying to avoid opening any from Amelia. Then, as if on cue, a call comes through. The tiny device vibrates and whirs in my hand. It's Brannagh.

"Marty," I say. "What's happening?"

"Jack!" he says, sounding incredibly relieved. "How are you?"

"Fine."

"Good, good," he says. "I heard that you're back in town. You didn't stay out at Godiva?"

"No."

"Oh... ok. Was there a problem?"

"The isolation was getting to me."

"Right," says Brannagh, maintaining his politeness. "After two nights?"

"Yes," I reply. "It's haunted."

"Haunted...? I'm not sure what you mean? Is it infested?"

"Sort of."

"That's terrible. That's totally unacceptable."

"Completely."

"Where are you now? Are you safe?"

"Yes."

"Excellent. That's excellent news. Well, I just want you to know that I am taking care of this situation. I've been in regular contact with the authorities and have made it clear to them that it is inappropriate for them to be pestering you about a random bunch of girls who have probably taken off with their friends, or run away from overbearing parents. Their reasons for wanting to speak to you are circumstantial, at best."

"I agree."

"Our desire is transparency. We have been sharing your work schedule with the investigators and I have been demonstrating to them that you have alibis for every single one of these supposed disappearances."

"They're more like... misplacings."

"Yes, absolutely," says Brannagh. "Even the girl that you were seen with. I've explained that that could have been anyone."

"Girl?"

"Yes, the witness. You haven't heard about it?"

"No, I haven't heard about it, Marty."

"A taxi driver came forward today and made a statement that he saw you with the girl in today's paper. He picked you up from the beach with a blonde girl and dropped you home."

"Outrageous," I say.

"The girl's friends have all said that they left her at the beach talking to a stranger."

"To me?"

"They couldn't be sure, but they said that it definitely could have been. Just guess work. All guess work."

"I get approached by lots of blonde girls, you know that. I barely have time to sleep with them all, let alone kidnap them."

"I know. You're in a precarious situation where a lot is expected of you."

"Too much. Too much, if you ask me."

"Well... I just wanted to assure you that I'm sorting everything for you."

"Much appreciated."

"We'll talk again soon, yes?"

"Sure." I hang up.

I slip on a pair of black jeans, a black tee and a black hooded jumper that I zip up to my chin. When I take the elevator to the foyer, I head out through a back door and into the garage. Rather than use my pin code to exit through the roller doors of the garage's street entrance, I hang out of sight behind a pillar, in the shadows, until a car exits. It only takes a few minutes before I'm given the opportunity to casually stroll outside and duck the automatic door before it closes on me.

With hands in pockets and hood over my face, I walk briskly across town towards my favourite café. Soon I smell the salt of the ocean, blown on the humid swirls of night breeze. The footpath is buzzing with revelers who fill tables outside restaurants and bars. Queues form in front of the nightclubs.

I turn a corner and I can see Zunge Bohne, lit from within and clearly busy with people seeking a light, but over-priced supper. The establishment's name glows in cursive neon on the roof. Beyond the outdoor lighting of the café's courtyard area, I can see crowds of people strolling along the beach side of the road, taking that romantic wander by the sand's edge, rolling down a well-trodden cliché that for most suitors still works.

The sound of the waves increases as I walk towards Zunge

151

Bohne. I stand directly across the street, the beach surging down to my left. Through the glass floor-to-ceiling windows of the café I try to spot Rose. She generally works the same section of tables. After thirty seconds my target appears, looking typically beautiful. Her blonde hair is in a neat ponytail. Dressed in a white blouse, black skirt and apron, she carries three plates of food to a trio sitting at a table against the glass.

Rose is beautiful, there's no questioning that. She has turned heads since puberty and short of disfiguring herself, there's not a damn thing she can do about it.

It's getting late and the kitchen will close soon. I'm hoping Rose isn't the last to sign off. I take a few deep breaths as the night drops in temperature. I lean against the brickwork of the shop-front behind me. It's a little boutique homeware place that is long closed. People walk past me as I stand there, hood pulled down. A few folk glance at me suspiciously, but most are too caught up in their proceedings. I mostly keep my eyes down, looking at the mottled, gritty concrete footpath beneath my feet.

The song 'Reckless' by Australian Crawl enters my head and I hum it to myself, trying to keep the memory afloat long enough to remember its every detail. When I'm not near my guitar or a recording device, I have to concentrate on songs I remember. Like balancing spinning plates in their precarious centrifuge. I pull my mobile phone from my pocket and when no one is near me, I sing quietly.

Putting my phone away, I steady my mind and refocus. I stare hard at everything around me, inspecting every detail of the surrounding block; how many people, what they're doing, how many cars are parked, what sort of cars.

It's natural to feel nerves before any kind of mission and as far as missions go, I've been on more than most humans. The unknown goes on forever, so there's no point taking it slowly. The speed doesn't matter. Although I stand here very still, I am really hurtling into a dark, sloping tunnel with no bottom. But I feel confident. Any sense of doubt that I will be successful tonight is elusive. Perhaps not even there at all. I am in complete and utter control. I can manipulate the environment around me and it bends when I flex it. I take what I want and give back what I want. Such is the life of the privileged.

Half an hour passes and I lean on this shopfront and remain a statue. I examine every vehicle that passes between the peripheries of my vision. Inside Zunge Bohne, trade is slowing. A number of tables in Rose's section have paid and left. Rose, being a diligent worker, has cleared the vacated tables and stripped their cloths. I watch her move about her work with a sense of urgency. Such is the behaviour of the hospitality worker. Sign-off can't arrive soon enough. Rose should have finished work by now.

Ten minutes later a group of men stand up from the final table in Rose's section. They're well-dressed, yuppie-types. Bobo larvae. Offspring hooked up intravenously to a trust fund until they're old enough to be self-sufficient and exorbitant on their own income.

They're clean cut, wearing jeans with vests and polo shirts. One even has a sweater tied around his neck. Handsome in a very uninteresting way. They belong in a retail window, rather than a café. They look primed and ready to join a college rowing team. Or the space program.

Rose is behind the cash register, scanning a credit card that one of them handed over. She's smiling that unassuming, slightly embarrassed flirty smirk that she constructs when she's a little smitten. I've seen that smile and some would accuse me of exploiting it.

The men turn for the door and she gives them a polite wave goodbye. When the group of five reaches the footpath, one of them, who has a square jaw and a no-nonsense haircut, turns back. He approaches Rose, who has already started clearing their table. She smiles when she sees him. His mouth moves as he asks her something. Rose beams for a moment. She then pulls a pen from her apron and scribbles something on an unused napkin. It is then handed to the man and he smiles and bids her farewell.

He rejoins his friends and they head in a group towards the beach-end of the block and then disappear around the corner. I think about the man with the square jaw. I know him. But I can't remember how.

Half an hour later I'm still standing in place, watching Zunge Bohne close for the evening. People still wander past, but it's too dark to recognise me. Rose waves goodbye to one of her fellow waitresses. Her apron is draped over her left shoulder. She pushes through the swing doors and into Zunge Bohne's kitchen and out of sight. I peel from my position and cross the road. To the right of the building is a narrow laneway. I unhinge a small gate and pull it quietly shut behind me. I then weave up the lane, stepping around unemptied bins of food scraps. Various smells, all of them noxious, reach out to grab me. Soon I'm at the end of the path and waiting in the dark.

Behind Zunge Bohne is a small carpark that's used by staff and deliverymen. I press against the wall, out of the single streetlight that illuminates the area. The entry to the carpark is off a small back road. It meets the beach at one end, to my left, and then travels up into the city connecting with a main road. The carpark has a high fence on each side, which meets the ground at a small flowerbed.

Rose exits the rear kitchen door and moves beneath the streetlight and over to a skip. Behind the large steel box she bends down to retrieve something that's between the skip and the small flowerbed. It looks like she's unwrapping something, but she's facing away from me.

When Rose stands up, she's carrying what looks like a bag. A double-handled travel bag. She glances around to see if anyone's watching. Rose looks directly at me for a few seconds and I wonder if she's seen me. I dare not breathe.

Then Rose takes off, stepping briskly towards the street, her flat work shoes slapping the cold concrete. I follow, stepping into the streetlight and over to the skip. Peering around, I see that Rose has turned right up the footpath and is walking towards the city. Giving her a small head start, I dash to the carpark's entrance and squat down next to the end of the flowerbed and security fence. I can see Rose walking up the footpath on her own. No one around. Not exactly a safe place, but she's moving quickly and with purpose.

To my left is the beach and the esplanade, groups of people wandering about, laughing. I look about for somewhere to move to, so I can follow Rose and stay out of sight. There's plenty of parked cars. A few closed stores and a number of apartments. In between are a few terrace homes, most of which will have security lights that are sure to turn on when I sneak past. But Rose is the only one that will see me. The street is completely deserted. Like a vacuum.

Rose doesn't drive, as far as I'm aware. Which explains why she's walking. Perhaps towards the major bus stop at the end of the block. But that doesn't explain the secretive travel bag. For someone like me, a stalker in the night, Rose is making herself an incredibly easy target.

I make a move. I decide to simply follow her on the footpath. If she sees me, I could be easily mistaken for a random pedestrian. As I stand up, a white van swings around the corner into the avenue, heading away from the beach. It's moving quickly. I freeze, avoiding the urge to duck down and look suspicious.

It's not a shiny new van, but it's been well looked after. I drop down after it passes, pretending to tie my shoe. On the side is the logo for a bakery. A company called Boddie Bread. I don't recognise it. The tag line, in small cursive, says *Still Feeding The Masses*.

It slows down when it catches up with Rose and she notices it and stops. She's perhaps one hundred metres away. I stand up and begin casually walking towards her. She hasn't looked back. She hasn't seen me. The back of the van opens and three men get out. They're wearing balaclavas and dark clothing.

Rose doesn't scream, but looks at them inquisitively. One of them looks like he's talking to her. Given their ominous appearance, I increase my pace. They're not wearing t-shirts that say '*Kidnapper. Beware.*', but they needn't be. These men are the cause of the severe pain in my ass.

I'm within fifty metres and Rose is walking towards the back of the van. They have her surrounded and she's not putting up a fight. When I'm within twenty metres, I've kicked into a run. "Hey!" I yell out. "You motherfuckers!"

The man closest to me turns to look, his eyes wide behind his balaclava. His hand drops to his pocket and in a second he's produced a flick-knife which, despite the dim light, gleams with inarguable savagery.

Rose screams and it's the first time she has seemed alarmed about this situation. The other two men spin around to face me and they both produce the same long, thin flick-knives. Adrenaline kicks in and when the first man swings his blade, I take his wrist, bending the knife from his grasp. Using his arm as leverage, I force a knee into his diaphragm and he silently wails as his ability to breathe leaves him. I scoop the knife from the ground and spin him in front of me, pushing it against his throat.

The other two men, clearly alarmed, look at each other as they delicately step towards me. The man I'm holding is basically immobilised, but he pushes back against me in terror, trying to wriggle free.

"I'll cut his fucking head off," I say in a low voice. "Put the knives down."

The two men look at each other, then both shake their heads. The man I'm holding thrashes again, pushing backward. The movement, which I manage to contain, makes my hood slip backwards. I draw the knife slightly and it cuts the man's throat. The slice is superficial, but enough to make my captive moan. The other two men freeze, staring at me. Inexplicably, they both drop down on one knee, as if bowing. Rose's face contorts in surprise. She drops her luggage by her side.

"I'm so sorry," says one of the men. "We didn't know it was you."

"Put your fucking knives down!" I yell.

The two men instantly toss their knives toward my feet. I shove the man I'm holding away and he leaps forward when he's released. I grab the two knives from the ground, holding them in my left hand. My right hand keeps its knife poised, ready to dice if required.

The man I've released spins around. His eyes widen and he also drops down to one knee.

"Jack," says Rose. "What's going on? I don't understand!"

Two more men, not wearing balaclavas, jump from the cabin of the van. "What the fuck is going on?" says the driver. They're the men that sat at the table in Rose's section tonight. The boringly attractive rich kids.

The van's passenger points at me, "It's him!"

They also drop to their knees.

"What the fuck is going on?" I yell. I turn to Rose. "What the fuck is going on?"

"They were just collecting me," says Rose, her voice wavering in the promise of tears. "I don't understand."

"No one is fucking *collecting* you," I say. To the men, I yell, "Who the fuck *are* you people and where are the girls? Tell me where the girls are!"

"We don't understand," says one of the men in balaclavas, his voice wavering also.

"Is that right?" I ask. I walk towards him where he kneels and swiftly lunge the tip of the knife into his back, just below the shoulder blade. He roars in pain and shock, clutching at the wound.

"One more vague response and I start slicing arteries," I growl.

"We'll answer anything," says the van's driver. "Anything!"

"Where are the girls? Where are the fucking girls that you've been taking?"

"They're safe!" says one of the balaclava wearers. "They're still where you wanted them."

"What?" I ask. "Where? I don't want them anywhere!"

None of the men speak. They remain kneeling on the road's surface.

"Rose," I say, and she just looks at me, shaking like a leaf. "What is going on? Do you know these guys?"

"They're just collecting me," she says again. "Like you wanted."

"I don't *want*," I say. "I don't fucking want. What the fuck are you talking about?"

"You don't want Rose?" asks one of the men.

"Shut your mouth or I'll cut your tongue out!" I yell at him. Then I say to all of them, "Let me make this very, very clear. Let go of the girls you've taken or I'll hunt you all down. I'll hunt you down one by one." I speak in my most menacing voice and it seems to work.

"We're sorry," says the passenger. "We didn't know there was a change of plans."

"Let the girls go," I say. "I've found you once and I'll find you again."

"Yes, yes, of course," says the man who was my captive, grasping at the bloody cut across his voicebox.

"Get in your van and get the fuck out of here," I say.

The five men stand up. Those wearing balaclavas jump in the back and slam the door shut. The passenger and driver return to the cabin and the vehicle speeds off.

I turn to Rose. "I'm going to go out on a limb here," I say, "and suggest that you have some explaining to do."

"I just don't understand," she says.

"Really?" I yell. "Well we have a lot in common!"

"Why didn't you let them collect me? I don't understand. I've done everything I was supposed to."

I take a deep breath. Looking down at the knife I'm holding, I flick it closed and put it in my pocket, then I close the other two and also push them the back waistband of my jeans. Rose tenses as I approach.

"Rose," I say, gently. "Calm down, everything's fine."

She continues to shake. "I did everything I was supposed to. Have I let you down?" she asks.

"No, no, you haven't let me down. You're... wonderful," I say.

"But... why? Why couldn't I go with them?"

I didn't expect Rose to be so disappointed with my bravery. "It's fine," I say. "You've done nothing wrong."

"Really?" she asks, her voice still shaky.

"Rose, sweetheart," I say. "There's clearly been a miscommunication."

"Oh," she says. "I'm sorry. I'm sorry if it's my fault."

"Rose," I say. "I'm going to ask you a serious question and I want you to think very carefully before you respond."

"Ok," she says.

"Have you gone mental?"

"What?" she asks, seemingly confused.

"You don't seem like yourself. You've given me very negative vibes since our one-night stand and now you're jumping into a strange van?"

"Yes, but that's what I was told to do. To be mean. That was our cover, wasn't it?"

Although it is abundantly clear that something quite odd was taking place in this quiet back street, it is dawning on me that something far stranger has been going on under my nose. I've just tripped over the tip of an iceberg.

"Rose, let's head back to my place," I say. "You're already packed. Let's just hang out and we can figure out exactly where and how this... miscommunication has happened."

"Alright," smiles Rose. "I'll go with you."

# CHAPTER ELEVEN

On the way to my apartment, I hold Rose's hand. Her other holds her luggage.

"So you don't hate me?" I ask.

"I don't hate you," she says, quietly.

"But you've been pretending to."

"I thought that's what you wanted."

"Who told you that?" I ask. "Who told you to pretend?"

"I don't understand," she says. "I thought I was doing what you wanted. If you're quizzing me to prove my faith, then I'm doing my best. But I only know what I know."

"Rose, I don't know what you've been told, but it has nothing to do with me."

"But it does! It has everything to do with you. It's all about you."

"But I know nothing about it."

Rose doesn't reply. She seems broken somehow. It's hard to digest. This strong-willed girl suddenly seems empty. I don't know her all that well. I had one night with her, she works at my caffeine hangout and she doesn't like me. That's our relationship. Our connection.

If she's been pretending to dislike me then I should put her in contact with a few casting directors. You are no longer on that pedestal, she said to me. You think you can treat women any way you want. That's old-school method.

I spare a thought for the fact that I'm leading Rose back to the place where I drunkenly brought her to have sex. It was questionable, definitely. We were both messy. I was messier. I think I avoided her afterwards out of shame.

Rose had come to one of our local concerts, and along with her friends, she appeared outside our dressing room. Girls seem to manage it all the time. Often members of our road crew venture into the audience after our set and invite females backstage. Other ladies talk their way past security guards. A man's basic philosophy is that you just don't use the word 'no' if there are breasts present. A girl's assets are easily offended by rejection, so you must keep them happy. Smile and nod. Award any desire. Security guards are susceptible to female persuasion, hence the scores of girls that find their way to our dressing rooms after shows. The French back on Earth called it a "buffet". All you can eat. Pile your plate.

So Rose, a sweet, shy and innocent thing, came back to my dressing room, astonished by my presence. Mesmerised by the sight of me in her vicinity. And I exploited it. Boy meets girl. Boy meats girl. It's such a time-worn, romantic cliché.

Though it's close to midnight, there's still security outside my building. One of the doormen opens the entrance for us and we step inside.

In my apartment, Rose places her bag on the breakfast bar and looks around the open-plan design.

"Do you remember this place?" I ask.

"Yes," she says. "I was drunk, but not that drunk."

"You seemed that drunk."

Rose just smiles. "I'm sorry I panicked before. I just didn't know what was going on."

"That's fine, don't apologise," I say. I change tactics, deciding I might leech more information from her if I play along. "Sorry I confused you on the walk here. I just didn't know who was listening. You should have been informed about the change in plans."

Rose turns to look at me. "That's ok. I'm not angry, I'm just very grateful to have been chosen." She smiles, with the threat of a blush.

"You're very special to me," I smile. "I hope you know that."

"Thank you," she says, and sits on my couch.

"Do you want something to drink?" I offer.

"Wine, if you have some."

"Maybe later. How about some water?"

"Sure, whatever you think is best."

I pour us each a glass from the fridge and sit on the couch next to Rose. I haven't slept well all week and I can feel my mind begin to hit a wall. But I need to tread carefully here. I require my faculties to function. To fire on all cylinders. I take Rose's hands in my own and we sit there for a moment. We occasionally escape each other's grasp to lift our water glass to our lips, but then we return our hands to their comforting union. The fingers she uses to lift the glass feel cold every time, but I warm them between my palms.

We both sip our water, contemplatively. Then Rose breaks the silence. "If you don't mind me asking, what are your plans for me?"

"Plans?" I ask.

"Yes, you didn't let them collect me. To join the others."

"Because you're special, Rose. I'd like you here with me."

"Oh," she says, definitely blushing. "Thank you."

"Where are the other girls?"

"The other girls? I'm not sure. They're at The Disciplinary, aren't they?"

"Good," I say. "Yes, they are. Do you know *who* they're with?"

Rose looks at me, a perplexed expression shaping her face. "Are you testing me?"

"Sort of," I reply.

"Oh," she says again. "They're with The Discipline."

"The Discipline in The Disciplinary. Makes perfect sense," I say.

"They worship you," adds Rose. "I worship you." I've heard that comment a few times lately. Worship. Dylan turned up at my apartment ranting about it. Everyone worships you, he said. Natalie made a point of saying she didn't.

"Have you met their... leader?" I probe.

"Leader?"

"Yes, the person looking after everything when I can't be there."

Rose shakes her head. "No, I'm sorry... I thought *you* were the leader." She smiles, sheepishly, as if worried she's answering incorrectly.

I try to gather my thoughts. It's like pulling twenty helium balloons into an airtight embrace. Big ideas cradled by inefficient arms. "Sorry about all of these questions," I say. "I just need to make sure there've been no more miscommunications."

Rose smiles and nods. Her mindless, agreeable expression makes me a little uncomfortable. I prefer scorned Rose. Hard-to-get Rose. The Rose I drunkenly tried to fertilize.

"I just want to say," she says, leaning towards me. "I think it's so amazing that you're here with us. Walking amongst us and giving us the gift of your music."

Religious rhetoric. Unmistakable. A horrid feeling creeps into my bones. I swallow the rest of my water. Putting the empty glass on the coffee table, I move closer to her.

"Rose," I say, choosing my words carefully. "I have to ask you an important question..."

"Yes?" she asks. "You can ask me anything."

"Who do you think I am?"

Rose leans into me, resting her head on my shoulder, her delicate hands still between my own. She whispers an answer that makes my chest tighten.

# CHAPTER TWELVE

I break into a sprint, hurdling the fence as if it's barely there. Across the clearing, with my heart racing, I move like a frantic streak of beige. A second later I've passed beneath the clothesline, snatching a pair of pants in my left hand and a shirt in the other. They pull from their pegs with little effort and the brisk bend and hum of the line is only a whisper by the time I'm gone.

I never turn to look at the mansion, terrified I might see something. Perhaps someone casually gazing out one of the many windows, not expecting to see a hairy, wild man wearing a pajama-like, off-white one-piece outfit, and a backpack, tearing across their yard like greasy lightning. Maybe there's a ferocious family pet sitting somewhere out of sight, whose day I've made by dragging my sorry carcass through its playpen.

I leap the fence on the opposite side, dash to the tree line and only stop when I feel I'm out of sight. I finally look back, my chest heaving with exertion. I see no one. No sign of alarm. The country estate stands as if deserted.

On the twiggy floor of this outcrop of trees and shrubs I quickly drop my pack, strip down from my one-piece, pulling it off over my boots, and change into my newly acquired attire. The shirt is a little big, but the pants are drawstring and I'm able to tighten them to an appropriate diameter.

I'm not an expert on the legal system of my new planet, but I'm fairly certain I've committed my first felony.

I choose a dark brown, unsealed road, not knowing where it leads. There are two suns in the sky and the exposure of broad daylight keeps me off the road's edge, sticking close to the trees. There are walls of pines on either side of me, which occasionally recede behind wide paddocks that stretch into the distance. Far away I can see what appear to be herds of animals, possibly cattle. They're the size of livestock, but just grey lumps in the distance. Every so often a bird flaps across the tops of the trees. A coloured dot with wings.

I cross a long bridge, walking on the outside pedestrian lane. The river beneath flows quickly, wide and blue-grey. I keep my eyes down, focusing on the cold concrete in front of me, as two cars pass. They casually roll by, heading in the same direction as me. Two simple, plain-looking four door vehicles. Identical to what you'd see patrolling the suburbs of my hometown. Affordable family cars. Not new, but miraculous and mind-blowing in their breathtaking mediocrity. They even have license plates. I'm gripped by a sense of wonder, as if I've laid eyes on a motor vehicle for the very first time. It's as if I'm an import from a bygone era seeing the science fictional innovations of the future.

The trees on either side of the road continue, but they thin out completely. Paddocks appear and then make way for occasional businesses. One small, wooden building sits in a gravel parking lot and looks like a fuel station. It has bowsers. I walk up to one and pull the nozzle from its holster. When I put it to my nose there's no mistaking the abrupt fumes of petrol. When I look over at the weathered building, which is draped in faded advertising, an old man stares at me suspiciously through a window, behind his counter. I smile, meekly, and replace the nozzle.

My stomach becomes restless, groaning in my abdomen. This was inevitable. I'm already out of rations. The suns are sliding toward the horizon and I've reached the outskirts of a city. There's a haze ahead of me, but with every step it peels back to reveal the skyline of a metropolis. A crooked set of teeth rising on an unseen jaw. I'm on a footpath now, passing small shopfronts. Awnings, tattered and decaying, form a canopy above me. The road has two lanes and is sealed with what looks like bitumen. Cars roll past at a higher frequency.

A lot of the businesses have "closed" signs hanging behind their glass. Their names are mostly familiar. Hairdressers. Bakeries. Newsagents. Second hand electrical. A fruit merchant. Any business names I don't immediately recognise can be deduced from their various logos and signage. One store has a picture of a spider-shaped creature with a large red cross through it. Perhaps some kind of exterminator.

More vehicles cruise past me and every so often I see another person, who strolls on their way. Dressed conventionally. Eerily normal. Eyes, ears, nose, mouth. Human beings, just like me. They don't give me a second's notice.

The city grows larger around me. The distant wall of skyscrapers approaches and the shopfronts become multi-storey office blocks and factories. The latter are broad and impressive, often surrounded by high razor wire trimmed fencing and large, deserted carparks. Their turrets don't emit anything. They just point upward, mammoth in height but seemingly useless. No plumes or billows. An industrial area that seems largely abandoned. The suns have set further, colliding with that jagged skyline.

I pass what looks like a take away shop on a busy corner. There's bright red, Perspex signage across its front, giving it that polished, chain-store sheen. The name of the business is Casa Bistecca, which flows in white, neon cursive.

Lots of cars pass through the intersection outside Casa Bistecca, and when I stop at the entrance and glance in most of the booths and tables are full of people pushing food into their mouths. None of them acknowledge me. I'm not unusual to them. I'm human like they are. Many of them use their hands to devour what appear to be burgers. Others saw with knives at slabs of meat, then stab a piece with a fork and angle it into their mouths.

I turn right at the intersection and walk up the footpath, heading towards the rear of the food outlet. I find a small carpark behind it with four dingy looking vehicles. One is tiny and red and has the Casa Bistecca logo on its sides.

There's a rear, fly screen door on the building and I can see into the kitchen. Young-looking people in uniforms move around broad hot plates, flipping meat. On the far side of the carpark is a large skip.

I watch silently for a few minutes. A young employee with pale white skin, shaggy red hair, a crimson shirt with a logo on the breast, black pants and a black cap, shoulders open the door. He holds a grayish green garbage bag with both hands. Rather than throw it in the skip, he just drops it against it. He brushes his hands together and steps briskly back inside the rear of the restaurant, never looking at me. It's as if I'm transparent.

Once he's gone I head for the skip. I walk with purpose, never looking up at the restaurant's rear door. I grasp the garbage bag, return across the carpark and head up the footpath. I keep walking until a few blocks pass beneath my feet. Between two dirty, tall brick buildings I find a lane and follow it, waiting till I get a reasonable distance from the road before stopping to inspect my find.

I kneel down and tear the bag open and the warm smell of fresh food scraps blooms upward. These are leftovers fresh from the tables, barely discarded for long enough to go cold. I sift through the garbage with two hands, finding a few half eaten burgers still folded in their wrappers. I lift one out and inspect it. There's circular bite marks. I lift off the top of the bun and see red sauce, something dark that appears to be a meat patty and a creamy coloured, cheese-like square, which is melted. I lean back and sit against the wall of the laneway. After a few sniffs of the scrap in my hand and some encouraging murmurs from my aching stomach, I bite into the half-eaten burger. I should be shocked when it tastes as I expect. I should reel from the numbing horror of a cheeseburger existing on two separate planets, but all I do is savour the sensation of sustenance descending my esophagus. I dip into the bag and pick out a few soggy yellow sticks that taste like potato fries. I'm exhausted and sweating from a day of walking, but I don't let fatigue upset me. Nor do I judge myself for eating from the garbage. Mentally, I'm in survival mode. I'm in the wild, boldly going further than any other Earthling. I'll observe the culture before I dissolve into it completely.

After picking through the unwanted morsels of the clientele at Casa Bistecca, I leave the bag and return to the footpath and follow the road I took from the intersection. The city and its skyscrapers create a backdrop to my left.

This factory area isn't as well kept as the previous one. On the corner of a block I find a building that is locked up and seems empty. It's not in as dismal condition as some of the surrounding structures. Everything in this district has been left to ruin. But this building looks like it may have been loved a little longer than these patchwork factories around me, which almost wobble in the wind like a morning's drunkard. This building, with its aqua paint job, garnered someone's respect for longer than the surrounding blocks of industrial detritus.

The awning of this building looks ragged, but the exterior paintwork isn't too bad. None of the windows are smashed either. There's a square sign jutting out from the third storey, but the lettering has been scraped off.

I round the side of the building and head up another lane, looking for a rear entrance. The windows on this side are high up, tiny and have steel security bars on them. I step around garbage bags, bins, a few old broken desktop computers, pieces of cardboard and wooden pallets. Parts of the concrete are slippery and seem coated in a thin layer of moss.

I find a door. There's two small concrete steps at its base and to the right of the frame, around chest height, is a small black box. It has a groove through it that looks designed for a swipe card. Which I don't have. Just below the small black box is a grey box with a keypad on it. Zero through to nine, with a hash button as an extra option. It looks designed for a key code or pin number. Which I don't have.

I look up at all the windows above me. Most have bars and they're all too high up. I suppose there's not much point having windows on this side of the building when your only view is the dank brick wall opposite.

I take a step back, feeling quite defeated. I'm disappointed, because I carefully selected this residence. It seemed appropriate to squat in. Four walls and a roof. Shelter from an alien planet. I inspect my surroundings. Maybe I'm aiming too high by picking such a plush hideaway. I should find some cardboard and just sleep in the alleyway. Many Earthlings do it.

I look around for cardboard and notice a box lying on its side about two metres further into the alley. On closer inspection, it's a box of papers. The lid has fallen off and folders have spilt onto the alley floor. I kneel down and take a handful, flipping through the pieces of paper that have been aging and abandoned. The words are in English. There are a lot of sheets that have the term "booking form" at the top. They're photocopied and various areas of the page are filled out with scribbled handwriting. Some have been stamped "Approved". Further forms have "Invoice" written at the top or "Remittance". In between these booking forms are photocopies of what look like print adverts. They're plugging various businesses. There's a lot that seem to be promoting "holiday activities", "cheap deals on cars" and "pest experts".

Amongst these fairly innocuous documents I find a small envelope and someone has written "Open" in blue pen and neat handwriting. I flip it over, following this direct instruction. Inside are a plastic card and a small, scribbled note. It says, "To whoever finds this, please enter *The Easton Inquiry* offices and enjoy yourself. Do as you see fit. If this includes burning its forsaken walls to the ground, then I encourage you to do so unhindered and uninhibited." There's no name. I hold up the plastic card. There's what looks like a black magnetic strip. Beneath are the word "Security" and a six-digit number.

On the top step, I swipe the card through the black box. I hear a beeping sound, then the lock on the door clicks. When I push against it, it swings open.

Once inside, my nostrils fill with the faint smell of cleaning agents and a musty, damp carpet odour. There's no light on this side of the building, so I step through the darkness, allowing my eyes to adjust. The ground beneath me feels carpeted and every so often my feet crunch something that's probably paper. My eyes become familiar with the low light and I can see the shapes of office desks and chairs. Most are empty and have had their drawers cleaned out. Others still have a computer monitor on top or an occasional keyboard and mouse. I run my hand along the top of one of the monitors, feeling dust gather on my fingers. I'm amazed by the technology.

The lifeless, scratchy fronds of a withered indoor plant brush against the back of my hand and I tense up. Moving slowly, keeping my eyes and ears alert, I arrive at a door and glance out into the corridor. It's long. Light creeps from open doorways, breaking the shadows. Both directions in the corridor seem equally ominous. All I can hear are car engines from the road outside. I detect something that sounds like a siren, but it's not nearby.

I remain still, unsure which way to go. Then I hear something. It's a sound so insignificant that it might not have happened at all. I hold my breath, waiting to see if it repeats itself. Silence. But then I hear it again. A drip. I move up the corridor to my right. I pass the doorways of two rooms that face each other. Looking in both, I can see that they're just more offices. Then another drip. I continue up the hallway, treading softly through the shadows.

At the end of the corridor is a door and a word is printed on its wooden surface. "Amenities". I push it open and step inside. My movement triggers a motion sensor and the roof's long fluorescent lights flicker into existence. I'm in a bathroom. There's a row of basins with soap dispensers drilled next to each. Off-white tiles cover the floor and travel up the wall to meet with the tops of mirrors. There are two long rows of toilet cubicles. I walk past them, inspecting each, pushing open the light brown doors. I find that the two on the far end of each row are not housing a toilet, but are showers. I step into one and angle the showerhead at the wall. I turn on the taps. Water jets and as it washes over my left hand I feel it become hot.

I strip down and stand under the water, savouring its sensation over my body. This is the first proper shower I've had since entering the escape pod. I had antiseptic wipes that I used to keep clean, but they don't really compare to hot, running water. I can feel the grime and sweat loosen its grip on my skin.

I sit on the floor of the shower for what feels like an hour. Eventually, and with some reluctance, I turn off the water. Sitting on a small bench just inside the door of the shower recess, I take slow breaths, feeling utterly rejuvenated.

Without a towel, I can only wipe excess droplets from my skin with my hands. Though not completely dry, I get dressed. I then step across the tiles to one of the basins and drink water until I'm bloated and satisfied. The plumbing behind the wall groans loudly then subsides when I turn off the taps.

In one of the smaller rooms off the corridor, I lock the door behind me and curl underneath one of the two desks. The weight of exhaustion drags me very quickly into a deep sleep.

I don't know what time it is when I wake up, but when I venture to a window that faces the street, the suns outside are low, rising with the morning. The interior of the building is more illuminated than it was at dusk. Exploring the downstairs level I find what appears to be a main foyer and push through swinging glass doors to a front administration room of some kind. There is a long L-shaped counter. There are desks behind it where receptionists may have worked. Most are stripped bare. Others still have in and out trays with a few papers left in them. Next to the doors are a series of freestanding metal racks that hold piles of newspapers. The masthead says *The Easton Inquiry*. I lift a copy from the top and skim through the cover story. It's about an economic crisis due to the closure of various polluting industries.

The décor of this building's interior seems old. It feels like a public high school. Fading carpet, kitchenettes with linoleum and wooden paneling on some of the walls. It doesn't seem modern, but I don't really know what modern looks like here.

I find a flight of stairs and ascend to the second storey. At the top of the stairs is a sign. It has the words "Advertising and Production" next to an arrow pointing right. Beneath that it says "Library and Human Resources", with a left arrow. I stare at the word "Human".

Following the corridor to the left, I arrive at a double door. Inside is a long room, divided down the centre. There are many computers on the right, each sitting at small booths. The left side of the room is made up of rows of shelves. They're about eight feet tall and full of books. I walk among them, reading the spines. Most are in English.

I spend the day pouring over books, sitting on the ground in the aisles. I spend a particularly long time reading medical texts, examining diagrams of human biology. As far as I can tell, it's identical to my own. The different systems are all there, from the respiratory to the circulatory, digestive, endocannabinoid, endocrine, immune, integumentary, lymphatic, musculoskeletal and the nervous system. I read a chapter on the ins and outs of the reproductive system, my heart aflutter at the sight of ovaries, testes, the uterus, the prostate and the almighty urethra. I laugh to myself when I read a Layman's explanation of the vestibular system and how it gives humans a sense of "spatial orientation". I hope mine is running smoothly.

My autodidactic afternoon is spent flipping through books on history. I read about a few great wars. Nations I've never heard of bickering about places and cities I've never heard of. There's one war that seems to have ended all conflict. A battle so terrible that this planet collectively refused to ever engage in that level of violence against each other again. A global peace treaty. One vision for a better future. Even weapons manufacturers closed down. Remarkable. So unlike my concept of humanity. It seems that governments still need to be overthrown and there are examples of coups and rebel militia ruling towns and cities, but they're few and always dealt with diplomatically or in as non-violent a means as possible.

I look for books on industry, particularly those that harvest and imbibe natural resources. I find a section that provides for this particular subject and read through books on iron ore, water desalination and something called "cray", which from what I can gather is a substance like coal. There is also a book about the history of "fuel" drilling, which seems to be their term for petroleum. One book confirms the planet's reliance on solar energy, which makes sense given its two suns. But wind turbines are also used. No sign of nuclear power. Very interesting indeed.

I'm hungry again but I try to ignore it. I check the index of every book and find nothing that relates to Earth or anything that suggests that they know of my planet.

Despite the peaceful modern era that this world finds itself in, the similarities to Earth are eerie. I ponder the idea that this is in fact Earth and it's been stumbled across through an anomaly in spacetime. It's not my area of expertise, but the evidence is compelling. I'm sure every chaos theorist on my home planet would probably explode if they knew I'd landed somewhere that is inhabited by humans who speak English and have seemingly evolved in some kind of parallel to Earthlings. They would drool at the prospect of analysing the dynamical systems that have made this world a reality.

There are things in space that we haven't discovered yet, of that I am certain, so I need to keep an open mind if I am to understand where I am. Only a fool would suggest that Earthlings are experts on the universe. I recall reading a book while at NASA on the science of black holes. A deformation in spacetime. Nothing escapes a black hole. It absorbs light and doesn't reflect it. It just hangs there, a mass with an undetectable surface that, once crossed, cannot be returned from. It's a one-way ride. The point of no return is called an event horizon. Around the black hole it is non-spherical and a person who crosses the event horizon does not know it has happened. They would never know that precise moment when it was too late to turn back.

Headaches are common when trying to get your head around the idea of a black hole or even a *supermassive* black hole, for that matter. There is actually a supermassive black hole located near the constellation Sagittarius A, which is in the Milky Way galaxy and just near my star sign, Sagittarius. That had to be a bad omen. I missed that one.

So what happens if you enter a black hole? Are you simply trapped inside, looking out as if you're in a giant bubble? No, that would just be an inconvenience. You could fold out a deckchair and watch the pretty lights of space blink at you. No, a human would fall into the black hole and be crushed to an infinite density, joining its region of gravitational singularity. That is a wonderful place where the spacetime curvature becomes infinite.

When you die, I wonder if you're granted an opportunity to look back and hypothesise where your own event horizon might have been. That invisible moment when you crossed a line from which you couldn't return. And if you do pinpoint it, are you free from the shackles of regret? This idea is something I've considered before and I'm sitting here considering it again. I consider it a third time when I find a section in this private library on religion and theology. I pick up a dusty, time-stained old book called *Believe It Or Not: The History of Religion*.

My interest is gripped rather savagely when I read the opening line. *"At no point will this book argue that the idea of Earth is not wonderful."*

# CHAPTER THIRTEEN

After I've paced back and forth across my living room for about ten minutes, Rose starts to stress.

"Is everything ok?" she asks. "Did I offend you somehow?"

"No, no, not at all. Don't be silly," I say.

"Ok," says Rose. She looks up at me with her lost eyes. I suddenly feel very cruel, as if it really is me that's responsible for these missing girls. They're out there somewhere under some false impression. A lie spun from my own web of deceit.

I return to the couch, sitting close to Rose. "I need to be honest with you," I say, "and I need you to accept everything I say as the truth. Ok?"

"Yes, of course," she says.

"Promise?"

"Yes, I promise. I swear," she says, solemnly.

A word is half way up my throat when something stops it. A sharp, earnest knock at my apartment door. Rose and I freeze, both turning to stare. We're silent. I don't dare move. Then we hear it again. This time it's a slow little rhythm, five knocks playing out in either jest or calculated menace.

I leave Rose's side and move across to the door. Peering through the spyhole, I see someone standing there that I completely did not expect to show up at such an inappropriate time.

"Don't pretend to be asleep, Jack," calls Jennifer Fox, in a singsong voice. "We both know you don't sleep."

I swing open the door, feigning casual surprise. "Jennifer, wow, what are you doing here? This is like... so... unexpected, but great."

"Nice haircut," she says. "You look hot."

"Thanks," I say, running a hand over my shaved head. "What brings you here?"

"I was in the neighbourhood," she smiles. Jennifer is wearing make-up, her hair hangs long and jet-black and her famous body, tacked to millions of teenager's walls around the world, is hidden beneath a pair of black, skin-tight leggings and an equally black, tattered rock t-shirt. I think it's a Known Associates design, but I try not to stare at her chest area. Her tanned midriff is showing too. Jennifer Fox. On my doorstep. In the flesh.

"In the neighbourhood?" I ask.

"Well, I was in the building. I was actually on the twenty-first floor. At a twenty-first birthday. How about that?"

"How about that," I reply.

"The party was kind of fun, but when I realised they weren't going to get all that drunk, I skipped out of there."

"What were you doing at a twenty-first?"

"She my publicist's sister."

"And she knows I live here?"

"My agent mentioned you live on the top floor of this building. It wouldn't let me come up in the elevator, so I politely asked one of the guards in the foyer to grant me access."

"Well... that was very polite of you."

Jennifer smiles and reveals her pearly whites. Her blue eyes glimmer. I realise at this point that I'm not going to be able to tell her she can't come in. I can smell an expensive perfume, but there's also the faint punch of spirits on her breath. Maybe vodkai. "Aren't you going to invite me in?" she asks.

"Sure..." I say, smiling. "It's just a little awkward."

"Really? Why's that?"

"I've actually got company."

"Oh, right. I see." Jennifer tries to glance over my shoulder. "Is she pretty?"

"Uh, yes. She's very pretty."

"Is she open-minded?"

The irony of the question moulds my cheeks into a smile. "You have no idea."

"Good," she smiles, and pushes past me into the apartment.

In the living room, Rose's eyes fall on Jennifer and they widen at the sight of my celebrity acquaintance.

"Hi, I'm Jen," says Jennifer. She offers a small wave.

"Yes, I know," smiles Rose.

"Jen, this is Rose," I say. "She works at a café I frequent."

"Nice," says Jennifer. To Rose she asks, "I bet he's your favourite customer."

"Very much," nods Rose, with a slight laugh.

I realise that this conversation could get very weird. It's been less than an hour since I saved Rose from the hands of what I can only assume is a cult. A cult that takes girls under pretense. It's not something you can explain in an off-the-cuff manner.

"Rose, could you excuse us for a moment? Sorry to leave you alone, but I have to show Jennifer something," I say. "Won't take more than a minute."

"Oh, ok," says Rose, with a smile.

Jennifer gives me an odd glance as I grab her hand and lead her up the hallway to my bedroom, closing the door behind us.

"So what's going on here, Jack? Is Rose, like, your next victim or something?"

"Not funny," I reply.

"Why haven't you kidnapped *me* yet? I'm a little offended."

"Listen, I'm going to try to make this quick, but I need you to believe every single word I say, without hesitation."

Jennifer nods. "I'm listening."

"Rose thinks I'm... the Messiah."

"What? What do you mean?"

"She literally thinks I'm the Messiah. She thinks I'm... the son of God. Well... I'm not sure if she thinks that, specifically. But, at the very least, Rose thinks I am a Messiah... of some description."

"Wow, that's quite a pedestal," smiles Jennifer. "So she's a groupie?"

"Not just a groupie, Jen. Someone has convinced her that I'm the freakin' Messiah. The same people that are taking these girls. I rescued Rose tonight from a group of men."

Jennifer's expression indicates that she believes me. "Serious?"

"Serious."

"If you're joking with me, Jack, I'm going to be very disappointed in you."

"I swear to... I swear I'm not joking."

"So men tried to kidnap Rose?"

"Yeah, but she was going willingly. She thought that I had sent someone to collect her."

"Jack, you have to go to the police."

"How can I? Rose thinks I'm the one that's choosing these girls. All the girls think that I'm somehow involved. It doesn't look very good."

"So what are you going to do?"

"I have to tell her the truth."

"That seems fair."

"I'm hoping she can tell me something that might explain where these disciples are."

"Disciples?" asks Jennifer. "Fuck, it's bad enough having fans."

"Whatever they've been telling Rose, it has brain-washed her. Maybe you can help me convince her that she's been tricked."

"Jack... seriously, I think you need to go to the police. When they hear her story, it might help them out. They might know stuff that you don't know."

"I've read the papers and they clearly have no idea what's going on."

Jennifer shakes her head. She seems a little worried. "We shouldn't fuck around with this poor girl."

"But if you're backing me up, she'll believe us. We're celebrities. People only listen to celebrities."

Jennifer rolls her eyes. "I've been hired to convince people to buy acne medication, cotton panties, soft drink and dietary supplements. I've never tried to tell someone to alter their spiritual beliefs."

"Think of it as your first serious acting role."

"Fuck off," says Jennifer, connecting her fist with my shoulder. "You can be such an arsehole."

"Seriously, Jen. Please do me this favour. I will owe you. I will owe you two favours."

Jennifer stares at me contemplatively, then says, "Five favours."

"*Five* favours? For *one* favour?"

"Yep, that seems fair to me."

I don't have much choice. "Deal. Five favours. No fine print."

Jennifer smiles with smug satisfaction. There are uglier people I could be indebted to. That is a small comfort. "I own you now, Jack."

"Only if you help me convince Rose."

"Trust me, I'll have no trouble convincing someone not to like you," she says. When I turn to open the bedroom doors, she adds, "This party is already much better than the twenty-first."

When we return to the living room, Rose is flicking through one of the magazines on my coffee table. It's an issue of *Infamy* with their fifty most attractive people of the year. I beat Jennifer Fox to the number one spot for a second consecutive year. Dylan was third, which he was not too happy about. It's a great position to get. Third place shouldn't be scoffed at. But the woman journalist did make the fairly backhanded remark, "*Dylan is an amazing guitarist, but he plays second fiddle when his lead singer is around. We'd still take him home in a heartbeat.*"

Jennifer sits next to Rose on the couch and I sit in an adjacent single-seater.

"Rose, there's something I need to tell you... what you've been told in regard to me being... the Messiah... it's not entirely true," I say.

"It's entirely untrue," adds Jennifer.

Rose looks at Jennifer, then back at me, then back to Jennifer again. She gives a nervous smile. "What do you mean?"

"Someone has been tricking you. It's the same people who have been taking the other girls."

"But..." says Rose, looking perplexed, "*you've* been choosing us... is this a test?"

"No," I reply. "It's not a test."

"Are you testing my faith?" she asks.

"No, definitely not. This is not a test, trust me," I say.

"Have you ever had direct contact with Jack? When receiving messages from these people?" asks Jennifer.

"No..." replies Rose, "just letters. Videos. Messages from some of the other girls."

"They weren't sent with my permission or knowledge," I say.

"But the men who were picking me up tonight knew you," says Rose, insistently. "They were scared of you. You stabbed one of them and they didn't even retaliate."

"They recognised me because I'm famous!" I say.

"You stabbed one of them?" Jennifer asks me.

I groan. "Barely. It was just in the back."

Jennifer raises her immaculately waxed eyebrows. "You stabbed someone in the *back*?"

"I didn't stab anyone! It was a jab. A light jab."

"What's the difference between a stab and a jab?" probes Jennifer.

"Fuck, I don't know. A few inches?" I reply. "I'm not a fucking forensic pathologist."

Jennifer looks at me with concern, then turns to Rose. "What videos are you talking about?"

"They sent me videos on discs. The first was the video of Jack bringing the girl back to life. That's what first made me realise his power."

"What's she talking about, Jack?" Jennifer asks.

"I have no idea," I reply, even though I kind of do.

"I have the video here, I can show you," says Rose. "Jack told me to bring everything with me. Everything I'd been sent."

"That wasn't me," I say, shaking my head.

"So you have the videos here?" asks Jennifer, her voice tinged with excitement.

"Yes, they're in my bag," says Rose, gesturing at the hand luggage sitting on my kitchen counter.

"This is heavy," says Jennifer. "We have to watch them."

"Not a good idea," I say.

"I thought we were figuring this out?" says Jennifer. "Investigating?"

"Sure... but..." I say. I don't have any reason against it. I just feel very uncomfortable.

"Rose, sweetie," says Jennifer, calmly. "Grab the videos and we'll watch them."

"We can't," I say. "My player is broken."

"We can watch them on your computer then," pushes Jennifer.

"Broken," I shrug.

"You fucking liar! What are you so worried about?"

"I don't know... the aging process, climate change, the stock market..."

"Fuck off," laughs Jennifer. "We're watching these damn videos."

"Yes," Rose chimes in. "I think it would demonstrate why I'm not wrong about Jack."

"See?" Jennifer says to me, smugly. "We will be able to see where Rose is coming from here."

"Jen," I reply, trying to stem my anger. "It doesn't matter what is on the damn video. I'm not a redeemer. I'm not anointed by God. Nor am I a saviour."

"Are you sure?" asks Rose.

"Yes," I nod, adamantly. "I haven't been chilling out at God's right hand, waiting to return. I've just been doing a lot of acid."

"But I've seen what you can do," says Rose, shaking her head. "You are here and your followers have been invited to spend eternity in your new world. The realm of your creation. You have descended in flesh and now dwell among us."

I let out a laugh, which sounds more mocking than I intend. "That's very flattering, but..."

"There's proof in my bag," adds Rose, defiantly.

"Let's see the proof," says Jennifer.

"You're meant to be helping," I say.

"I know, but I want to see what Rose is talking about. I might be making a fool of myself."

"But I'm not the Messiah!" I yell.

"Well maybe you are, Jack! Rose seems pretty normal," replies Jennifer.

"Yes, she *is* normal. She's also deluded."

Rose looks on edge, like a child in the same room as her parents' argument. She says softly, "Why don't I just go and get the evidence from my bag."

"Marvellous," I say, leaping from my chair and marching to the kitchen. I grab a bottle of scotch from the cupboard, open the lid and swig a mouthful. The burn descends my gullet and calms me slightly. I rest my hands on the counter and close my eyes, hanging my head. I take deep breaths. I'm not sure it's such a good idea that Jennifer sees Rose's evidence. It will thicken an already sludge-like plot.

"This is very exciting," I hear Jennifer say behind me. I hear Rose unzip and rummage through her bag on the breakfast bar. Then Jennifer adds, "Actually, I really need to be high before I see this. I'm way too clear-headed. Jack, have you got anything? Pills? Cane?"

Without opening my eyes or lifting my head, I raise an arm and point across the kitchen to three ceramic pots that sit on the counter next to the hotplates, pushed back against the wall. "Cane," I say. When I turn around Jennifer has already reached the pots. They have cork lids and are labelled "Salt", "Sugar" and "Flour".

Each has about a three-litre capacity.

"Which one?" asks Jennifer.

"Flour," I reply, looking up at her.

Jennifer picks up the ceramic receptacle and uses all her strength to pull the cork from its hole. She looks inside, confused. "There's just flour in here," she says. "Heaps of it."

"No there's not," I say.

"Is it... buried?" she asks.

"Is *what* buried?" I reply.

"The cane? Is it hidden?"

"No," I say. "You're looking at it."

Jennifer looks into the pot, her eyes widen. "Fuck off. Are you serious?" She reaches in a finger, dabs it in the white powder and licks it. She tastes for a moment. "Holy shit, my tongue just went numb. I've never seen so much cane in my life."

"You never know when you'll be in the mood to bake," I shrug and return to my single-seater with the scotch bottle held firmly in my fist.

Rose returns to the couch and sits down, a number of pieces of paper on her lap. I can see she's holding a few discs too. I swig the scotch, eyeing Rose's potentially damning possessions, listening to the sound of Jennifer snorting fingertips of cane up her perfect nostrils. When Jennifer returns to the sofa she's wiping her nose with the back of a finger. She then asks Rose to hand her the disc that she thinks we should watch first. When Jennifer ventures over to my entertainment unit, pushing the disc into the player, I'm almost too grumpy to inspect the toned curvature of her buttocks through the thin fabric of her leggings. Jennifer looks back at me with a wicked smile. She's not oblivious to the acuteness of her current stance and the view it provides me. She's also taking delight in making me squirm. Making us watch this damn video.

Once the disc is inserted, Jennifer grabs my television's remote control from the coffee table, switches it on and finds the disc player's channel. When she does, the screen is black. Nothing. We stare at ourselves in the inky reflection.

"Oh well," I say. "Looks like it doesn't work on my player."

"You just have to wait a minute," says Rose.

Jennifer has returned to her position beside Rose on the couch and is almost huddling against her. I ponder how much convincing it would take to get them to kiss each other. Then my mind snaps back to my incredibly awkward situation.

An image appears on my widescreen and the video begins.

# CHAPTER FOURTEEN

The yacht rounds the heads and we leave the bosom of the harbour. The vessel is only at a canter. The sails are down and a long, naked mast points skyward to the canopy of stars. The hum of the motor makes the deck vibrate beneath me as I sit on the farthest point of the opulent vessel's nose. A driver, a hired hand that I don't know, tall and lean, sits in front of a set of controls, positioned above the cabin. He eyes the ocean quietly, not responding to the activity around him. Invisible.

I'm on my own, watching the black ink water part for the yacht, rippling along the ribs of the hull. I try to enjoy this moment's peace, though it's hard to distinguish. My band are partying behind me, celebrating our freshly signed contract with Endurance Records. Our signatures are barely dry. There are about twenty people on the boat. Maybe thirty. They're strangers to me.

I'm having a hard time trying to relax. I'm with a group of musicians I haven't known that long. Only a few months. I have known Emerson a little longer. The band has been pieced together for me. Handpicked by the head of our label. From our extensive rehearsals and jam sessions, they seem to be remarkable musicians. No complaints here.

I've grown fond of Dylan rather quickly. He's wild and enthusiastic about everything he does. He's a freakish guitarist. His skill is matched only by his astoundingly short attention span. But not during songs. When he's playing the "compositions" I've brought to the group, he loses himself. During the throes of 'Achilles' Last Stand', 'Nantucket Sleighride' or 'South Side Of The Sky', Dylan closes his eyes and I can see him leave this world with me, floating upward towards Earth.

I feel a variation of a brotherly bond with Dylan. I'm watching him seize this opportunity that I should have created for myself when I was his age. Emerson told me that Dylan had been in two other bands on the Endurance roster but due to substance abuse he was asked to leave both groups. The owner of our label has granted him a final lifeline in allowing him to join Big Bang Theory.

Like Dylan, I could have floated through life and pursued art, indulging in life's distractions. I could have been adrift with no signs of shore. While he is more than ten years my junior, our lifestyles are inverted reflections of one another.

When I look back at Easton it's just dots of light, undulating in a wall behind us as this motoring spaceship cruises into the open ocean. It's a dark night and I'm reminded of my landing. How I tested the water to see if it was acid. How I landed and walked through those gates, greeted by the dead. If I could have seen myself now, I would have rushed up that beach like a soldier.

On the deck behind me, Dylan, Emerson and Cohen are all drinking and chatting loudly. They're accompanied by five girls. There's electronic music blasting from hidden speakers near the entrance to the downstairs floors. A few of them walk below deck to party in the extensive inner workings of the boat.

One of the girls that remain on deck, Jemima, is a publicist who is going to be working closely with Big Bang Theory. She's brought two friends on board with her. They're all about twenty-four or twenty-five, little darlings living the dream lifestyle that the music industry serves you on its silver platter. The fourth and fifth girls work for our record label too. One is an intern and the other is also a publicist, who works with a number of other bands on the roster. I had sex with the intern after a party downtown. Secluded, but in a public place. Her name is Stephanie. She told me that she's religious. She was raised in a religious family and went to religious schools. This is at odds with the overt way that she interacted with me. But who am I to judge or dictate? She said she'd be forgiven.

To complicate things further I have also been sleeping with Jemima, who will be our exclusive publicist at the label. That in itself is not a big deal, but she is married. She's hitched to an aspiring musician. But I feel a little helpless in this situation. Jemima has skin the colour of maple syrup and big, bedroom blue eyes. Add this to her soft brown hair and firm body, and you have a recipe for impure thoughts and uncontrollable urges. It doesn't matter who you are or your moral hygiene. You can smile in the skin of an absolute gentleman. But when a girl like Jemima is smiling back at you, your insides are shaped around a hard, twisted centre. The preening grace of the good guy is like the shimmering of peacock feathers. It's all for dramatic effect. Pure mating ritual.

My promiscuity is on a gradual increase, but I have the perfect justification. Research. Assimilation. No one would question my need to feed myself. To survive. So I don't question my own sexual requirements. To observe and engage. Total immersion. Why deny myself these encounters when they're thrust upon me? Especially when I'm already so familiar with the biology of these Heavenly creatures.

Jemima sees me looking at her. Her eyes meet mine, which I wasn't intending. But now it seems as though I've been gazing at her and she's caught me. Although she's clearly marinating in the euphoric glaze that all casual drug users enjoy, she responds to my eyes. I see her place some significance in them. Jemima is dancing with her friends. The rest of my band has scampered below deck to join the party down there.

After a few more twirls and giggles with her social sisters, Jemima walks up the boat towards me. She's wearing small white shorts and her blue denim shirt is unbuttoned, a mandarin coloured bikini top across her chest.

"Jesus, how amazing is this?" she says, gesturing to the black ocean that we're rolling into. A warm wind picks up, blowing her wavy hair from her shoulders and face. Jemima is backlit. Just a feminine outline traced by the downward floodlight that perches high on the mast. Despite the shadow, I can see her blues eyes look down at me, piercing like two precise javelins. "Mind if I join you?"

It's a question with no easy answer. "Sure," I smile, and tap the hull next to me.

"Isn't this boat amazing? I can't imagine having my very own yacht," says Jemima. She sits down, leaning against me.

I can hear her friends continue to frolic behind us, whooping when they hear a new song they recognise. Jemima puts her left hand on my knee and I see she isn't wearing her wedding ring.

"Everything fine?" I ask.

"Of course!" she responds, as if I've broken the record for silly questions.

"No ring."

Jemima pulls her hand away and her face adjusts slightly, betraying her hidden sorrow. But then her smile returns as if it never left.

"I'm having too much fun," she says, with a shake of her head.

"So no heavy stuff?"

"No heavy stuff."

"I like you," I say.

"Oh," says Jemima, and she looks away. Awkwardly. Maybe blushing. The music pounds behind us. The city's lights fade, joining together in a tapestry of artificial fluorescence. Then she says, "Congratulations on the deal."

"Thank you."

"You deserve it so much. You guys are going to be massive."

"It's exciting."

"You won't know yourself, Jack," she smiles, giving me a nudge with her elbow.

"I won't know myself," I echo.

We're silent as we watch the ocean roll toward us. In my mind, which is responding to the pills I've taken, I imagine that the yacht is completely still and it's the world that's moving.

Jemima closes her eyes and rests her head on my shoulder. I smell her hair. It occurs to me that I want Jemima in my life more often. On a regular basis.

"I like you too," whispers Jemima. I think she said it. Maybe she didn't.

I hear a wild holler behind me, which sounds like Dylan. Reluctant to shift Jemima's head from my shoulder, I don't turn around.

"What's going on over there?" calls Dylan, with mischief.

Jemima sits upright. I turn in time to see Dylan running across the deck towards me. He drops to his knees and throws his arms around my shoulders.

"This is the life, Jack," he says, clearly in a jubilant frame of mind. "In a month, everyone will know our fucking band." He throws his right arm around Jemima, including her in his embrace. "And we have the hottest publicist on the planet!" he adds. Jemima laughs and shakes her head. "How are you going to publicise us?" queries Dylan, as if it's a formal interview.

"Well, you're four hot guys who make amazing music. You've got a mysterious singer who has lived on the streets his whole life. You're a publicist's dream," says Jemima.

"A publicist's dream," repeats Dylan, as if the words taste good in his mouth. "With a mysterious singer." Then he asks me, "Jack, are you a publicist's dream or a publicist's reality?"

Jemima blushes and looks away.

"Dylan, you're being outrageous," I say.

He responds by kissing the back of my head. Then he says, "You are a musical genius, my friend. We're going to take over the world."

"It's all about the music," I say. "Not the take over."

Dylan slaps my back, and then says to Jemima and I. "C'mon children, time to get amongst the people. You're not behaving as star attractions should." I groan reluctantly. "Jack, there's a lot of people on this boat and they all want to party with you." Then he says to Jemima, "Don't be greedy. You need to share this man."

"You make me sound like a wheel of cheese," I say.

Dylan jumps to his feet, giving a tug on the back of my t-shirt. Jemima and I stand and follow him down to the main deck area, where some of the revelers have emerged and are now dancing, loitering and chatting. They don't stay in one place for very long, especially on this floating fun park. Now that my drugs have fully kicked in, I don't mind getting up and moving about. I suppose it's my duty to "get amongst it".

Martin Brannagh, the owner of our new record label and the man who will forever be attributed to my discovery, has emerged from below deck with the rest of the party. He's wearing white, loose-fitting clothing. An open shirt and long, square-cut fisherman's pants. His white hair is slicked back and his chin peppered with salt-coloured stubble. He exudes the mystique of a Zen guru, with the hedonistic undertones of a pagan philosopher. Life is here to be lived. You betray your soul when you don't indulge each desire. He seems harmless enough. I think he sincerely loves music and he is certainly a world-renowned tastemaker. Plus, he owns a spacious yacht. Many boxes ticked.

The air throbs with the swollen pounding of electronic music, surging and receding on the synapses. Brannagh walks through the crowd to me, throwing his arms around me in a warm hug.

"Jack. I am so glad I found you," he says.

"I was just over there," I say, pointing toward the nose of the vessel.

"That's not what I mean," he chuckles. "I'm glad I've brought you in from the cold."

"Right," I say.

"You, my friend, have a gift," he says, pressing a finger into my chest. "I don't know where your songs come from, but may your inspiration never run dry."

"Thank you," I reply. "And thank you for taking us out on your boat. It's sufficiently large."

"Don't be ludicrous!" he exclaims, slapping me on the shoulder. "This is why I have the damn thing. To get away from that city." He points back to the distant lights of Easton. "When you head out to the open ocean, you eliminate everything. You cancel out every element, except for the people that come with you. It's like a purging."

"So you just need to add water," I say, not exactly sure what I mean.

"Water or alcohol," he smiles, and then leads me over to a section of the surrounding bench seat, which hides a refrigeration unit. He lifts the seat. "What's your poison?"

"Whatever's good," I say.

Brannagh smiles and leans down, pulling out a bottle of what looks like beer. "This one's the best. Expensive, but also the best." He grabs a bottle for himself. We both twist off our respective lids. He then turns to the group of people around us and says loudly, over the thumping music, "Could I have everyone's attention for just a moment." Everyone stops what they're doing and turns to listen. "I don't want to delay anyone's immediate intentions. I would like to ask everyone to drink to the newest members of the Endurance family. Big Bang Theory."

Everyone cheers, claps and then drinks from their beverages and the party continues. I walk over to Cohen and Emerson who are sitting down, talking.

"Gentleman," I say, sitting next to Emerson. I chink my bottle against his, then lean across to chink Cohen's.

Emerson leans back and puts a hand on my shoulder. "Exciting times, my friend," he smiles, his weathered face wrinkles in a smile.

He's only a year or two older than me, but has worked outdoors for most of his life. His face is framed by long dark hair, similar to my own. We could both do with a shave.

"Can't argue with you there," I say.

"Where do you think you'd be tonight if you didn't have a record deal," asks Cohen, who is much younger than Emerson and I. His hair is shaved close to his head and as far as young men go, he's quite pretty looking. Olive skin. He rarely goes unnoticed.

I think about Cohen's question. "Probably just wandering somewhere, watching the world go past. I hopefully would have found a decent meal and be getting ready to find a place to sleep."

"That's wild," says Cohen, and takes a quick swig from his beer. "I can't imagine what it would be like to live that way. I've been so lucky."

"It's all relative," shrugs Emerson. "If Jack hadn't grown up the way he did, seeing the world, he wouldn't write the songs that he does."

I've seen two worlds. "That's a nice way of looking at it," I smile.

A shrill female scream from the dance floor next to us reminds me of our female company. The women are dancing in a group, drinking and laughing. Including Jemima. She's not looking at me.

"That girl is something else," says Cohen, quiet enough so only we can hear.

"Which one?" I ask.

"The blonde one dancing with Jemima."

He's referring to Stephanie.

"Well you should be over there dancing with her instead of sitting here, talking to our old carcasses," says Emerson, who then gives me a wink.

"Yeah, maybe," says Cohen, and I sense he's nervous.

"Cohen, you're a drummer in a band. Soon you might be the drummer in a famous band," I say.

Cohen smiles. "Yeah, so?"

"If you survey all women, most of them would pick the drummer over the singer," I add.

"No way," says Cohen, shaking his head.

"It's true," says Emerson. "Drumming is a very sexual activity. Sweat and muscles. Women find it hypnotic. Their rationale is this, 'if that guy can handle a drum kit like that, imagine how he could handle me'."

Cohen just smiles and swigs on his beer. The drugs in my system are messing with me. For some reason I feel compelled to tell Cohen that I've slept with Stephanie. But why? Why would I tell him that? It's not a competition. I manage to contain that piece of information.

Cohen watches Stephanie as she gyrates against Jemima. Two bright young things. Cohen looks like an innocent as he gazes across at Stephanie, though his pupils are a little too wide to be mistaken for a saint. But he's still so young. At least fourteen years my junior. He's still malleable. Not fully formed. Briefly an adult. Open to influence and void of the emotional soft tissue damage of middle age.

"Get over there and dance with her," says Emerson. "You won't have to vie for her attention."

Cohen looks at Emerson, then at me. I just nod. He accepts our encouragement and walks over to her.

"C'mon," says Emerson. "Let's find somewhere a bit more quiet. This music is going to give me an aneurysm."

We both retrieve an extra bottle of beer from the fridge seat and head toward the back of the yacht. I give a polite nod to the driver and he nods back. Emerson and I find another white leather bench, but this one faces off the back of the vessel. The lights of Easton are gone. I don't know how far into the ocean we're travelling, but the driver shows no intention of dropping anchor.

"So what do you think you'd be doing professionally, if you weren't a musician?" I ask Emerson.

"Not sure," says Emerson. He pulls a cigarette from a pack in his jeans pocket and lights it, contemplatively. "Probably still doing something with my hands. Hopefully still painting."

"Would you ever work an office job?"

Emerson chuckles. "I'd sooner perish."

"But someone has to do those jobs don't they? The boring shit?"

"I don't think so. We didn't need accountants and solicitors when we were roaming the landscape as primitives. We just shared everything equally. The idea of possession didn't even exist. Imagine that. Not knowing what it is to *own* anything. Ownership was not even an idea."

I pull a cigarette from my own pocket and light it. "But we have to evolve," I say, with a shrug. "Otherwise we don't have an expiry date. We'll be here forever if we don't move forward. Towards the end."

"That's grim," says Emerson.

"Everything gets bigger and bigger until it's too heavy."

"You know, sometimes I think there's a chemical in our brains that is an amnesiac. That makes us forget what we are, where we are and where we're heading. You only remember when you're reminded of it."

"Is that where the name of your old band came from?" I ask. Before joining Big Bang Theory, Emerson had once been in a group called The Blissfully Unaware. They achieved moderate success. Emerson, who was one of the principal songwriters in the group, still gets royalties from the few radio hits they had. Their "best of" compilation experiences moderate sales.

"Something like that," says Emerson.

"Do you miss being in your old band?"

"No, not really."

"Why?"

Emerson smiles. "Being in a band is like being married. But you can sleep with other people."

"I see."

"You've got to like the people you're working with," he continues. "Because you're in a room with them a lot. You need to get along. Even if it's a love hate relationship, the love needs to outweigh the hate."

"I once chose a career over music," I say, without considering the statement.

"Out in the jungle?" asks Emerson, with a knowing smile. "Out on the streets?"

"Yeah," I reply, smiling back. I think that Emerson knows there is more to my story than the drifting existence of an urchin. He can tell I'm educated, which is a bit of a giveaway. But he never brings it up directly. "Out there in the wilderness, there's all kinds of careers to be had."

"Wild," he says.

"Maybe I should have never stopped playing. Maybe being here is someone's twisted punishment."

"Here on the boat?" asks Emerson.

"Here... in general."

"Do you love music?"

"Yes."

"Then you're living the dream."

"Perhaps."

"Do you know how many people live the dream?"

"Not many?"

"It's a percentage so small you would round it to zero."

"And then double it," I say, dragging on my cigarette.

"Yeah?"

"Yeah, in case there's a second human race out there somewhere."

"Shit," says Emerson. "That's a scary thought. But why stop there? There's probably infinite planets out there coated in humans. It doesn't end. How do you ever visualise that? No exit. No end point."

"It's not easy," I say. "Maybe we should talk about something less gigantic."

"I like those new demos you did," says Emerson, in a swift change of subject. "They all have a really timeless quality to them. They already seem so fully formed too."

"Well, they're just me and a guitar. Wait till you hear them with the full band treatment."

"Have you already got the full arrangements in your head?"

"Sort of, but I'm happy for you guys to be involved. Everyone's allowed to have input. I'm just writing the tunes."

Emerson nods and drags on his cigarette. "I'm looking forward to our next session."

"Me too. We're pulling some really good sounds in the studio."

"I just hope we can keep it ragged," says Emerson. "I want it to sound unclean. Some of these bands are coming out with these albums and you can smell polish. You can taste the fuckin' chemicals when you listen to it. Like a hospital floor, or something."

"We need to sweat and smell bad," I say.

"Yes. We need to soak in our own filth," adds Emerson. "It needs to be four guys in a room. That's it. You don't want it to be sanitised."

"And I think the songs should evolve. They should be different every time we play them."

"I like that idea," nods Emerson. "The songs should change shape. If people want to hear a carbon copy, they shouldn't come to our live shows. They should just sit on their sofa with the disc." Silence passes between us as we both look out at the wallpaper of stars. "Marty is already talking about our stage show. He wants it to be a pretty big spectacle," adds Emerson.

"I don't want it to distract from the music," I say.

"Me either. We shouldn't need flashing lights to attract attention. The live show should be about the music. We don't need screens and banks of strobes. It should just be... a performance."

"Well, let's not let Marty talk us into anything we don't want to do."

A voice behind us asks, "What am I trying to talk you into?"

We both spin around to see Brannagh, standing with hands on hips, a wide grin on his face.

"Opiates," I say.

Brannagh laughs, heartily. "I can't promise you anything! Now both of you get back on deck and join your party. Tonight's a celebration. We're not talking business."

"We're watching Easton disappear," says Emerson, pointing in the direction of shore.

"Good," says Brannagh. "Say goodbye to it. Because it's about to enter a new era. When we return, it will be different. It will be the era of Big Bang Theory."

"That's an unsettling thought," I say.

"Don't be ludicrous," says Brannagh and pats me on the shoulder. "Things in this world don't exist to remain the same. They exist to be changed and transformed."

"Alright," I reply.

"Now come back to the party," smiles Brannagh. "Everyone wants to bask in your brilliance."

"Can we at least change the music? This electronica is way too hectic," says Emerson.

"Deal," says Brannagh. "I've got some back-up music anyway."

"I don't mind what disc jockeys do," says Emerson, "it just doesn't speak to me."

Brannagh smiles, then says, "What did one DJ say to the other after they left the cinema together?"

"Don't know," I say.

"That guy was an amazing projectionist."

Emerson and I both smile and follow Brannagh back to the party.

The music is changed to rock and blues. Everyone recognises

more songs than I do. I smile and mingle, chatting to our guests. People move to the music. They heap praise on me and they all want to be my friend. It seems genuine, but pigeons only circle when you've got a fistful of breadcrumbs. Most of the women on the boat flirt. They always touch my arm when they talk to me. Constant, subtle contact, as if trying to channel something from me. I occasionally catch Jemima watching me from across the deck. Sometimes she's talking to her friends and they're eyeing me as they whisper. I keep wondering whether Jemima and I will have another moment to ourselves and, if we do, whether that's a good thing.

A stronger man would fight the temptation I feel around Jemima. But do I have any control over my urges? Over my sexual behaviour? We often refer to our cravings as animalistic. But that doesn't really do us any justice. What we would describe as "animalistic sex" is so far removed from every other type of animal, that it's like comparing apples to oranges. Besides the bonobo and the humble dolphin, creatures don't have sex for pleasure. But Homo sapiens take their time. The more time we have, the more we take. We avoid procreation. We spend billions of dollars inventing more innovative contraception. Every time we describe our proclivities as animalistic, it's a backhand to all those poor grizzly bears and tigers and their brief, emotionless mounting. They're all puppies and kittens compared to the bedroom antics of our species.

Brannagh declares that he's going to change the music again. That he's going to provide something better. That's Brannagh's general ethos. He disappears below deck. The rock and blues is cut dead. Everyone waits expectantly, the sound of the engine and lapping water filling the air, uninterrupted. Brannagh returns from the cabin and in each hand he is carrying an acoustic guitar.

"Time for a sing-along, friends," he says. He hands me a guitar and then another to Dylan. "Would you do us all the honour?"

"I don't know, Marty," says Dylan. "I'm not sure if I'm in the right state of mind." His reluctance seems more an attempt at false modesty than an actual desire to not be the centre of attention.

"Nonsense!" says Brannagh. "Drugs and alcohol are not a hindrance, Dylan. They enable." He hands Dylan and I a plectrum.

Dylan looks at me and I shrug. "I suppose we could play a few songs," I say. Everyone claps and cheers. I put the guitar strap over my shoulder and Dylan follows suit. "I'll lead, you follow," I say.

Dylan nods. He's sweating profusely and looks very wired. He's clenching his jaw. But his natural ability will carry him through. I walk over to him and smile, then I launch into 'A Well Respected Man'. Dylan smiles and begins strumming along with me. And we sing the chorus together. The party around us watches and listens, transfixed. Then I shift into 'Riverside', which was written by Dewey Bunnell. As Dylan and I jam it out I can almost imagine that I wrote it. That Dylan and I perform it as its originators. Then I kick into a slightly slower gear and shift into 'Tell Me Why'. Dylan keeps up, closing his eyes. His skin is pale and beads of sweat roll from his temple, but I can see him getting lost in the music. I sing the song, not as hauntingly as Neil Young, but in my own way I do an alright job. Out on the waves in the night.

As the song winds to its close, I break into 'You've Got To Hide Your Love Away'. When we've finished my favourite Beatles tune, Dylan says, "Time for you to follow."

"Alright," I say.

Dylan drops his plectrum on the deck and starts picking the strings of his guitar with the fingernails of his right hand. He kicks into 'Babe I'm Gonna Leave You' and I play along. We practiced this song extensively at our last rehearsal. The Zeppelin number rolls from us in an effortless malaise, exploding when it needs to, subsiding soon after. While we can't give it the full band arrangement that it deserves, it still breathes in the air as we sing it. A formidable, soulful presence. Lingering. Rambling.

When we finish the song, everyone claps and whistles. Dylan and I take a little bow and remove our guitars. Jemima is smiling at me.

"Show's over, folks," says Dylan.

"Play more!" yells one of Jemima's friends. Everyone cheers in agreement.

"Nope, sorry," says Dylan. "That was just a little taste of our debut record."

"We don't want to give away too much," I add. "Besides, we hardly know you people."

"We don't like to fuck on the first date," says Dylan.

"That's right," says Brannagh, grinning, addressing the party. "That was just a little taste of what is to come." He heads downstairs and turns the electronic music back on and everyone starts to dance.

When Brannagh returns to the deck, he walks up to me. "You are going to be successful," he says with complete confidence. It's as if he's stating a well-known fact.

"Really?" I answer.

"Jack, you will be famous."

I glance over at Jemima and she's still smiling at me. Brannagh sees me look at her.

"You know, you have the best young publicist in the business. She's got a massive future ahead of her. Jemima is a clever woman."

"Yes, I can tell."

"You're in very good hands," smiles Brannagh. He gives me a knowing look and turns and melts back into the party.

I smile at Jemima and motion for her to come over. She leaves her friends and approaches me.

"Nice performance," she says.

"Thank you."

"Are you enjoying the night's festivities?"

"Yeah," I shrug. "But I would have preferred something a little more... personal."

"A more intimate gathering?"

"Yeah, just the band and a few friends. I don't really know these people."

"Well, intimate gatherings and close friends will become scarce. Fame shakes things up a lot."

"If I were being honest... I would have preferred to spend this yacht cruise alone with you. No one else."

Jemima blushes, her blue eyes look down. "Jack... I... "

"It's okay, you don't have to say anything."

"No, I do," she says. "I'm just not sure... what to say."

"That's fine."

"I'm sorry. I'm obviously very confused." She looks back at me and forces her soft lips to smile.

"I don't think anyone's downstairs at the moment. Want to head below deck?"

"Is that a good idea? For us to be alone?"

"Good. Bad. It depends on the criteria."

Jemima looks uncertain and I am too. But the drugs don't say no. Drugs don't send you to your room without supper. They're the careless parent that condones everything.

As I hoped, no one is downstairs in the living quarters. Everyone seems to follow Brannagh's lead and right now, he wants all hands on deck. It's warm down here. I turn on an air-conditioner that's mounted on the wall. The living area is open-plan and in floor space, it's almost as big as my new apartment. A dining table in one corner. A lounge area in another corner, with plush sofas facing a widescreen television on the wall.

I walk over to the kitchenette and look in the fridge. The chilled temperature inside feels exquisite against my face.

"Something to drink?" I offer.

"What's in there?" asks Jemima, who sits on one of the sofas. I pull out an expensive bottle of sparkling wine and hold it up. "Perfect," she says.

"I'll find some glasses," I say, turning to look through the cupboards.

"It's okay," says Jemima. "We can drink from the bottle."

"Is that hygienic?"

"I think we're past hygiene."

"Really?" I smile, joining her on the sofa.

Jemima takes the bottle and examines the label. "This one's expensive," she says.

"I wouldn't know," I say, and take it back, pulling the foil from the top of the bottle. I remove the wire brace and pop the bulbous cork, which fires into the roof and bounces across the room. Bubbles flow from the mouth of the bottle and I quickly raise it to my lips and drink. I then pass it to Jemima and she drinks also. This moment suddenly seems so familiar to me. As if I've been here before.

"I just had déjà vu," I say.

"Day-ja what?" asks Jemima.

"Nothing," I say, enveloped by the drugs in my system. "It's French."

"What's that?"

"It's an alien language," I say.

"You are so strange," says Jemima, handing me back the bottle. I take a long gulp. Jemima leans into me. "I shouldn't be here with you."

"No?"

"No," she says, shaking her head slowly. She's messed up like I am. "I'm... way... too attracted to you." Her hand slides on to the leg of my jeans, moving to my inner thigh. I can feel her fingernails through the material, tingling my skin. "Please stop me..." she says.

"Stop you? I don't think guys do that."

"Please."

"You're a big girl, Jemima. I can't make your decisions for you. I can only marvel at them."

Jemima pushes her mouth to mine and we kiss. Our tongues move against each other, tasting the wine on each other's lips. Her hand loses any remaining ounce of subtlety and becomes focused quite specifically on my crotch.

How does one make a girl like Jemima come to her senses? Do I simply do nothing and allow her to make a decision that will liberate her from the manacles of marriage? A wise philosopher once said that marriage is not a word, it's a sentence. It may have been Plato. But here is a bright young thing questioning her natural instincts in the name of a vow she made in front of an entity that may or may not exist. Isn't that wrong? Isn't it warped that she should feel awkward or uncertain? Why should I deny her hand as it slips into my jeans? If God were truly offended by handjobs, he wouldn't have given humans opposable thumbs and the carpus in their wrist. He sees everything, including all the physical applications of our bodies. You wouldn't give someone the keys to a car and then tell them not to drive it.

Jemima looks at me with those bedroom blue eyes and says, "Maybe we should go into another room?"

At this point I should run and swim for shore, because I'm not capable of making calm, rational decisions. I can't stop Jemima. Should I run or stay? I could take my chances in the obsidian ocean. "Okay," I say.

Leaving the bottle next to the sofa, we walk over to the small alcove next to the kitchenette. There is a set of stairs leading down to the bottom storey of the yacht's spacious interior. Downstairs are the many sleeping quarters. I take Jemima's hand and we make our descent.

We step into a narrow corridor. Reddish brown paneling on the walls, smooth and reflective. Dim lights in the roof. The first door on our left is locked. For a moment I think I can hear guttural, human moans in there but it could be ringing in my ears. The door on the right pushes open. Jemima follows me inside.

It's not a big room, but against one wall is a bunk. Two single beds above each other. Jemima closes the door and locks it. When I turn around she throws her arms around my shoulders and we kiss again. The she motions toward the bunks and asks, "Top or bottom?"

I unbutton Jemima's shorts and say, "Let's start with the bottom."

Jemima's body is curled against my own, as we lie on the lower bunk. She is naked from the waist down and I lightly run my hand along the length of her thigh. My fingertips trace light circles from the peak of her hip and down her leg. Lying down generates its own glorious sensations. I'm conscious, but only in a broad definition of the word. I never want to stand up again. My body is pulsing. I am weightless. I want to be entombed with Jemima like this forever.

Although she is facing away, I know her blues eyes are probably closed. I can hear a soft gasp drift from her when I touch a sensitive inch of skin. Jemima rolls on to her back. I lay my arm across her stomach and her eyes remain closed.

"What do you love?" she asks.

"This isn't too bad," I reply. "A half naked girl," I continue. "I can't complain."

She smiles. "No, but... seriously. What are you... passionate about?"

"I like music."

"I know... but besides music. What else?"

I'm not sure what to say. My mind isn't handling questions with its usual deftness. It's like trying to play Scrabble when the alphabet is a thousand letters deep. "I don't know, beautiful..." I say. I can hear that I'm mumbling, but I can't take control of my lips. "Liberation for women. That's what I preach."

This answer seems to suffice, because Jemima smiles and opens her eyes. "You're sweet."

"Always."

"I could lie here all night," adds Jemima, closing her eyes again.

"We'll stay here if we don't get another rush soon."

"We need some gas," says Jemima.

"I think I have some in my wallet," I reply.

Jemima rolls over and retrieves my wallet from the floor next to the bunk. She hands it to me. In one of the compartments is a small bag of white powder. I sit the bag on my chest and pull out a note, which I roll into a thin straw. I sit up, put one end of the note into the powder and the other to my nostril. After a small, sharp snort, I offer it to Jemima. She sits up and does the same. We sit there for a minute, feeling the gas begin to rise, building in intensity. Clearing the cobwebs.

"Do you think fame will change you?" asks Jemima.

"It's definitely improving my quality of life."

"Is this the first time you've been on a boat?"

No, I used to go fishing with my dad. I also went on a cruise to South America before I agreed to the NASA mission. My distance from those memories is too much to contemplate. "Yes," I smile. "I could get used to this."

"To the yacht or to me?" asks Jemima.

"To the yacht... you I can take or leave."

Jemima pouts in mock offence and says, "Well, I should get back to the party then." She stands up, picks up her small, white g-string and slips it on. I watch her step into her shorts, sliding them up her legs. "I'll see you on deck," she smiles. She leans down and kisses me again, then leaves the room.

The gas takes hold as I stand up and fasten my jeans. Every thought flickering through me seems as momentous as it is fleeting. Returning to the living quarters upstairs I see that the sparkling wine is gone. Jemima probably reclaimed it. From upstairs I can hear manic conversation. Laughing. Someone drops a glass. There's still music, but it's a little more chilled out now. More minimal beats.

Then I hear a scream. In the context of this wild evening, it's not all that alarming. But then the scream echoes and multiplies, rising in a crescendo. I sprint across the room and up the stairs to the deck. From somewhere behind me, I hear the sound of the yacht's engine shut off. The revelers are crowded on one side of the boat, against the thin wire fence, craning to see into the water. Then they're all rushing to the back of the yacht, crying and pointing into the water. I see Jemima among them and run to her.

"What happened?"

"Stephanie collapsed and fell in. Cohen's dived after her."

I push past Jemima, climb the small fence and stand on the back of the vessel. The floodlight isn't aimed outward enough to expose much water. It's darkness, unmerciful to the naked eye. I can't see Cohen or Stephanie. The boat has slowed now the engine has been cut and the wake of the boat is subsiding.

I see a brief flash of white and I realise it's Cohen. He's returned to the surface and is waving his arm. I pull off my t-shirt, wrench my phone and wallet from my pockets and drop them on the deck. I dive off the yacht. The water is warm and when I eventually come to the surface, I freestyle toward Cohen, keeping my chin above the water.

"Where is she?" I call out.

"I don't know! I can't find her!" yells Cohen. I can barely see him but my brain adds the visual pieces I'm missing. I can see his eyes, wide and bloodshot. He's splashing in hopeless panic.

"How long since she fell off?" I ask.

"I don't know. A minute?" comes Cohen's gasped reply.

"You haven't swam out far enough," I reply. I swim past him, the drugs surging through my body. When I've powered another twenty feet from the back of the boat, I dive under, going down a few metres, swimming parallel to the surface. Stephanie is light and my only hope is that she hasn't sunk like a stone.

I keep my arms circling in a wide berth, breaststroking further and further. I've gone a long distance now. She's probably below me somewhere, unconsciously drifting to the ocean's floor. That could be a thousand metres beneath us. If it were day, I would be able to see her. But the unforgiving night has closed its fist and claimed her.

My brain starts screaming at me to return to the surface. I need to breathe. But the drugs are thumbing their nose at my body's natural inclinations. I keep swimming and the realisation that she's gone builds in me like lead. As I ready to kick upward, my hand brushes against something soft. I grasp it and pull. I think it's a forearm. I heave upward with all of my strength, kicking furiously. As I break the surface, I pull Stephanie up with me and wrap an arm across her chest, holding her against me. I can't see her face, but I know she's not conscious.

When I look back, the yacht has stopped and I can see someone in a small dinghy, powering towards me, barely touching the water. I wave an arm and call out. As it gets closer, I can tell it's the yacht's driver. The hired hand.

"Grab her," I call out. He pulls alongside us and takes Stephanie underneath her arms and starts lifting her into the dinghy. I push upward and then throw my upper half over the side and hold on to the inner rope. I'm facing her now and I can see her blue lips. The matted hair. Her chest isn't moving. "Hang in there, Steph," I say, as the raft flies back to the yacht, my legs still trailing in the water.

Emerson and Brannagh are standing on the small steps at the back of the vessel and as we pull up next to them, they hurriedly bend down to pick up Stephanie's motionless body. Everyone is gathered around, panicked, crying.

I pull myself into the dinghy and then spring up on to the back of the yacht, following the driver.

"I don't think she's breathing," I hear Emerson say, as Stephanie is laid on the deck.

"She's not!" I snap. "She's not breathing."

The party guests start to sob, filling the air in a choir of dismay and shock. Emerson and Brannagh are standing back, looking down at her body, shaking their heads. Defeated. But I'm bursting with adrenaline. So much that my mind doesn't process anything except the instinctive need to begin artificial respiration. I'm capable of performing an array of emergency medical procedures in microgravity, so resuscitation on a boat isn't beyond me.

Everyone's out of their minds, dizzy on amphetamines and self-prescribed empathogens. Right now they're getting very emotional, moving forward to stare at Stephanie as she slips away.

"Everyone, get back!" I yell. "Get the fuck back and give me some space."

I'm on my knees next to Stephanie, rolling her on to her side to check her airway. Then I'm rolling her on her back, grabbing her wrist to feel for a pulse. I put two fingers from my other hand to her neck. I could be wrong, but I feel a faint beat. I pinch her nose and give five strong breaths into her mouth. Her lips are cold, as if all the blood has rushed from them. While I try to remain calm and focus on the procedure, my mind is telling me that I can't save her.

I continue to breathe into her mouth, exhaling with as much force as I can muster. Every five seconds. I put my fingers to her neck again and I'm certain there's a pulse. I continue the breaths and compressions, desperate for a response.

Then Stephanie coughs. She splutters and water bubbles from the corners of her mouth and nose. I roll her over and she coughs again. Water gushes out and then she vomits. Alcohol, froth and bile spill across the deck.

"Stephanie!" I yell, my mind reeling in amazement. "You fucking sweetheart!"

She continues to splutter and groan, emptying her lungs and stomach. I almost collapse in relief. I'm on my hands and knees, the drugs in my system hollering in a conga line through my veins. A minute passes and I keep Stephanie on her side to make sure she doesn't choke. I don't notice the silence around me. The stunned absence of sound. The yacht is bobbing, perhaps drifting. Water licks its side but not with enough vigour to crash in the way that waves do. I look up and around me. The party guests, including my band and the yacht's driver, are staring at me. Speechless. Wide-eyed. Astonished in a cartoon-like way.

Brannagh, like a good host, is the first to speak. "What did... how... did you do that?"

"Do what?" I say, breathing deeply, saturated.

"She wasn't breathing," he replies.

"No..." I reply. "No, she wasn't..."

Although I see it, I won't really think about it until later. But a girl, who I think is friends with Stephanie, is standing just to the right of Brannagh. She's pointing a shiny video phone at me, recording everything.

# CHAPTER FIFTEEN

Stephanie's face appears on my television screen, looking straight down the camera.

"What you just saw is real and it's just the beginning," she says, solemnly. There's nothing behind Stephanie but a black curtain. She is dimly lit. Maybe there's a red tint somewhere to her left. It's all very moody and dramatic. Whoever edited the video has put a mild grain effect on it for a dash of authenticity. "This is one of Jack's miracles. He has arrived to deliver the word of his people. The winged ones will return. Jack is here in human form... and he has chosen you. Jack loves you and he wants to shine his light on you. His power. You will hear from us again soon."

"Horse shit," I say, taking another swig on my scotch bottle.

Rose and Jennifer are both staring at me from the sofa.

"Is that footage real?" asks Jennifer.

"You breathed life into that girl. You returned her from the dead," says Rose, pointing at the screen, in the hope that it will validate her.

"That wasn't magic," I say.

"Was that girl really not breathing?" asks Jennifer, who thankfully seems a little more sceptical than Rose.

"That was... a medical trick," I say. "Anyone can do it if they're trained properly."

"No," says Rose, standing, her fire returning. "There's no medical trick that can do that. You breathed life into her."

I screw the lid back on the scotch bottle and drop it on the floor next to my single-seater. I stand up too. "I didn't breathe life into her, Rose. I breathed oxygen."

"What's oxygen?" asks Jennifer.

"Air, I mean air," I say. I march across the living room, slide open the glass doors and step out to the balcony. "Just when I think I have this fucking planet worked out," I mutter to myself, the scotch's spark igniting my simmering agitation. I point at the giant billboard of Jennifer that still faces my apartment. When I look around the city's night-lit skyline, the dozens of other advertisements flash in neon and delicately placed uplighting. "Are you trying to tell me..." I say, pointing out at the billboards, speaking loudly enough for the two girls to hear from the living room, "that you have invented diet pills, cars, watches, sunglasses, perfume and... skyscrapers and bridges... the internet...three-dimensional pornography and flatscreen televisions... but you never worked out how to resuscitate someone?"

When I turn around, Rose and Jennifer are staring at me blankly. I return to the living room.

"We don't know what you're talking about," says Rose.

"Don't you guys do organ transplants? Haven't you invented microscopes? Blood transfusions?"

"What do you mean 'you guys'?" asks Jennifer. "You're talking like you're..."

"Like what...?" I ask, daring her to say it.

"I don't know!" says Jennifer. "You're referring to us as if you're different."

"Because he's not from here," says Rose, softly. She's looking me square in the eye. "He is different. He's very different."

"Where am I from then?" I ask.

"I don't know," says Rose, even though I think she knows something. She walks over to her handbag on the counter. She unzips it and pulls out a piece of paper. Then she walks over and hands it to me. "Tell us what this is," she says.

I unfold it and glance at it, then fold it again. "A forged document?"

"What is it?" asks Jennifer.

"It's a DNA test," says Rose. "It's a photocopy, so *maybe* it could be a fake. Maybe. But it says that Jack doesn't have typical DNA."

"I love that you have DNA tests, but you don't know how to

resuscitate someone," I smile, shaking my head. Then I retrieve my scotch bottle from the floor and remove the lid.

"What kind of DNA does he have?" asks Jennifer.

Rose takes the form from me and hands it to her. "It doesn't say," says Rose. "But it means he's not entirely human."

"So I must be the Messiah?"

"It was a compelling theory," says Rose, slumping next to Jennifer again.

"I'm sorry, Rose. But someone has tricked you. And not just you. Girls are disappearing..."

"But... you must be the Messiah. It made sense. You appeared out of nowhere. You've brought this Earthly music... so much music... your DNA isn't human..."

"Yes," I say, "but that doesn't make me supernatural."

"What about the animal thing?" asks Rose.

"What animal thing?" asks Jennifer.

I take a breath and lean back on my single sofa.

"I was sent footage of you from a nightclub," Rose informs me. "You were being searched by narcotics officers. They had porcines."

"I fucking hate those pigs," scowls Jennifer. "Did they find anything on you?" she asks me. "I've had two personal assistants get done, plus a dear friend of mine who is an eyelash technician. The only eyelash technician I'd let anywhere near me..."

"The porcines began licking your hand, Jack," says Rose.

"What?" asks Jennifer. Then she shakes her head. "No, I've seen them. They don't lick. If you put your hand anywhere near them they'll bite it off."

"I have video footage of three porcines licking Jack like they're fresh from his womb," says Rose, smugly.

"You're an expert on porcine behaviour?" I ask Rose.

"My brother was an officer," she says.

I don't reply.

I hear something outside. A noise rising in volume, separating from the distant buzz of the city. It sounds like a helicopter. It's flying beneath my apartment. It's definitely worthy of my attention.

"What's the matter?" asks Jennifer.

"I can hear something outside," I reply. I race over to the balcony, then across to the railing. When I look down I can see a black helicopter slowly rising, pointing a white, wide searchlight at my building. I retreat inside, pulling the balcony doors shut and drawing the blinds. "It's a helicopter," I say, darting around the apartment, switching off all the lights.

"Is it the police?" asks Rose.

"Probably," I say, turning off the final lamp. "Let's just be very quiet. Stay away from the windows." Moments later the helicopter is level with my apartment, its light slicing through the blinds like sunshine. I can hear the girls gasp. The searchlight is moving back and forth along my balcony. None of us move. Then I have an idea.

"Quick," I say to the two girls. "Run down the corridor and hide in the room at the very far end. Straight ahead."

In their panic, Jennifer and Rose do as I say. I follow them down the hall, stepping quietly behind them. Now we're all in my bedroom. "It's safer in here," I say.

The sound of the chopper rumbles like a storm outside. Its light continues to roam the side of my apartment, finding the gaps in the blinds of my bedroom. Unless they've got infrared vision, we're as good as invisible. The three of us huddle just inside the closed bedroom door, low against the wall. A minute passes and the chopper finally moves on, before fading into the distance entirely.

"I think we should leave the lights off," I say.

"You need to go to the police," says Rose. "If everything you've said is true and they've tricked these girls, then they could be in danger."

"I know, I know," I mutter.

"I could come in with you. I have all the stuff I was sent. I can be a witness."

Rose could certainly reinforce my plea for innocence. The tape is incriminating though. The last thing I need is more people watching it and thinking I'm special. I don't want people thinking I can undo death. The police have probably already seen the porcine footage. I suppose I could tell them the DNA test is a fake, but what if they want to do one of their own?

"I'll go in tomorrow morning," I say.

"Wow, that's heavy, Jack. That's a big decision," says Jennifer.

"Oh well," I sigh, "I guess it's time to face the music."

"If they arrest you, it'll be great for your album sales. You'll sell millions more, I promise," adds Jennifer.

"What room are we in?" asks Rose.

"We're in his bedroom..." replies Jennifer. Then a moment later she hits my shoulder with the back of her hand.

206

"What was that for?" I ask.

"You jerk," she says. "We didn't need to come in here. We were perfectly safe in the living room."

"Jennifer, I don' know what you are insinuating," I reply. "But I am a perfect gentleman. I thought my bedroom would be a much safer place to hide."

"So should we all get into your bed, just in case the helicopter comes back?" asks Rose, echoing Jennifer's incredulous tone.

"That hadn't occurred to me but, honestly, my bed might be the safest option right now," I say, trying not to give myself away.

"Unbelievable," says Jennifer, shaking her head. "You're at the centre of a sinister conspiracy and all you can think about is getting fucked."

"Look," I reply, walking over to turn on the ensuite light. I pull the door closed until it's ajar, the thin beam illuminating my bedroom with its mild glow. "If neither of you trust me, you can tie my hands to the bedpost. Sound fair?"

Rose and Jennifer allow themselves to smile and walk over to the bed. After all, it's extremely comfortable and quite spacious. They sit at the head, propped up on my array of pillows. I lie across the foot of the bed, exhaustion and inebriation weighing heavily on me. Rose seems tired too, but Jennifer shows more enthusiasm. Probably due to the cane in her system.

"So how did you do it then?" asks Rose.

"Do what?" I ask.

"Make that girl breathe again?"

"It's called the kiss of life," I say. "Want me to demonstrate?"

I sit up on the bed and motion for Rose to come closer. She looks uncertainly at Jennifer, but her new friend just nods with encouragement. Rose looks back at me and crawls to the centre of the bed.

"What do I do?" she asks.

"Just lie on your back," I say. Rose complies. "Now the thing about the kiss of life is that you don't have an endless window of opportunity. If you're not really fast, the person can die or can suffer brain damage once the brain has been starved of too much air."

"So that girl hadn't been dead for long?" asks Jennifer.

"She wasn't dead," I say. "She had only stopped breathing. Her heart was still beating. She was just in respiratory arrest."

"So you kickstarted her lungs?" asks Rose.

"Exactly," I say. "Firstly, when someone has stopped breathing, you need to get them into the recovery position, which is like this." I bend Rose's knees upward and pull one of her arms across her chest. Rose remains limp, allowing me to manipulate her. I roll her on to her side. Now she is facing Jennifer. "Now you need to check the person's airway. If they've been underwater, it's possible there's debris in there. Sometimes your own tongue can retract and block your windpipe."

I lean over Rose, my face now close to hers. She slowly opens her mouth. In the dim light I can see her eyes looking into my own. "Everything looks fine," I say, quietly. Rose closes her mouth and smiles. I then roll her back over so she's facing the ceiling again. "Then you pinch the person's nose so that air can't escape and then you breathe into their mouth as hard as you can." I take Rose's nose between thumb and forefinger, only softly, and then lean down and put my mouth to hers. Rather than forcing air into her lungs, I let Rose kiss me. She does instinctively. I taste her lips and suddenly remember what it was like the last time she was in this bed with me. I pull away. "Then you give one breath every five seconds until they start breathing on their own. I lean down and kiss Rose again. This time her tongue appears and finds my own.

"Nice demonstration," says Jennifer. "I think it's my turn."

My body is melting into sleep, sinking into my refractory period. Rose and Jennifer are sitting on either side of me, leaning back on pillows, passing a bottle of red wine between them.

"I'm so glad I've got a day off tomorrow," says Jennifer.

"You're not working on any new movies?" asks Rose.

"I start pre-production on a new project next week."

"Really?" inquires Rose. "What's it about?"

"It's a horror movie," says Jennifer.

"I love horror movies," replies Rose. "I know it's really weird but the worse they are, the more I love them."

"Well, this one is pretty gross," says Jennifer.

"You're becoming a bit of a scream queen," I mumble, eyes shut. Jennifer's been in quite a few scary flicks in the past two years.

"I thought you were asleep," says Jennifer. Then to Rose, she asks, "Why do men always fall asleep after sex? They just pass right out."

"They've got what they want," shrugs Rose. "No point staying awake."

"Actually, it's more to do with the release of chemicals in the brain post-orgasm. Like the hormone prolactin, and oxytocin and vasopressin," I reply.

"You're making that up," says Jennifer.

"How could I possibly make that up?"

"So tell me more about your movie," says Rose.

"It's called *Cleaver*," says Jennifer. "I actually have to get naked in the first scene. There's a nude scene in practically every script I get sent now. My agent just tells them to add an extra million on my fee."

I open my eyes and glance at Jennifer, who is currently naked. I ponder whether tonight will cost me anything.

"Why do you get naked?" asks Rose.

"In the opening scene I'm in bed with this guy."

"Who plays the guy?"

"His name's Anton. He's a model, he doesn't do much acting."

"Well at least your nudity is in context," I say. "At least it's not gratuitous."

"No, not at all," says Jennifer, wryly.

"Ignore him," smiles Rose. "What happens?"

"Well, in the opening scene, we're in bed. Then he goes downstairs to get some wine from the kitchen and he doesn't come back."

"He goes downstairs? Is that a euphemism?" I ask. "Because it was very eloquent."

"You are *so* funny," says Jennifer.

"How long do you wait for him before you go downstairs to see where he is?" I ask. "And how is that depicted on screen? Is it a shot of you naked for a few minutes? Just waiting there in bed?"

"Shut up," says Jennifer. Then to Rose, "When I go downstairs, all I find is his spleen sitting on the kitchen counter."

"Wow," says Rose. "That's pretty disturbing."

"Why the spleen?" I query. "That's a fairly specific organ to leave behind. It's only about eleven centimetres long. Wouldn't it be more gross to leave the heart or the liver or something?"

"The killer doesn't want to leave the heart or the liver. He just leaves the spleen."

"The movie should be called *Spleen*," I say. "Or *The Spleenster*."

"But he kills with a cleaver. So it's called *Cleaver*," retorts Jennifer.

"Is he an ex-butcher? What's his motivation?"

"Who cares? He kills teenagers. It's a stupid horror movie," says Jennifer, swigging on the red wine.

"Did someone steal *his* spleen?" I ask. "That would give his calling card some emotional significance."

I wake to a scratching sound. It's desperate and distinct. A trapped animal clawing wildly. Is it trying to escape or get in? I open my eyes. It's in my head. A nightmare. The suns haven't risen yet. Jennifer and Rose are asleep. I'm flanked by two beauties. I sit up slowly, trying not to disturb them. Then I hear scratching. There's something behind the bedroom door. I listen for another sound. I can hear something soft. Deep intakes of air. Heavy breathing. It's not coming from one of my bedfellows. I roll forward, crawl to the end of the bed and step softly on to the carpet. I listen again. Nothing. Then outside my bedroom I hear a door close. Someone's in my apartment.

I move to the bedroom door, listening again. Nothing. I throw it open and look into the dark. There's a black silhouette at the end of the hallway, in my living room. Frozen. Staring back at me. My stomach locks as I stand there, confronted by this intruder that's barely distinguishable from the shadows of my unlit apartment. I open my mouth but no sound comes out. I squint again. I'm sure there's a shadow there. I lean forward through the doorway and switch on the hall lights. The flash reveals no one. The hall ends with an empty living room. I step forward, quietly closing the bedroom door behind me. I look down and there are no scratches on its exterior.

Naked, I step into the bathroom and switch on the light. I look at myself in the mirror. I'm a bit scrawny these days. A pale reflection of the athletic individual I used to be. I don't eat much anymore. My body's a wiry array of raw muscles and veins. My abdominals muscles, the rectus abdominis and obliques, are more pronounced than they used to be. I lean forward, inspecting the skin on my face, then turn and look at my back. There's talon marks on both of my shoulders, which means there's likely to be skin under Jennifer's manicured fingernails. On the left side of my neck is a bruise. A bite mark. I find more fingernail marks inside my right thigh. When I turn around there's another jagged scratch on my left buttock. All war wounds that one might display proudly. Injuries received in the line of duty. I need a shave.

I have a quick shower and then walk out to the kitchen. I retrieve a container of instant coffee from my cupboard and as I mix it with hot water from the tap I consider my promise to turn myself in. I stand there, sipping the strong, bitter liquid, wondering what will happen to me.

The suns start to rise outside as I sit on the couch, sipping my caffeine hit. I turn on the television to a morning news program. There's a bulletin about a drive-by shooting on a public school playground. Only one boy was hit and has survived. It's the first shooting at a school in nearly two decades.

Then there's another news story about an uprising in a foreign country I've never been to. Soldiers are threatening to shoot civilians who are peacefully protesting in a public square. Snipers are ready to pick off the protestors from nearby buildings. The country's leader has ordered his military to destroy anyone that questions him. Diplomacy and peaceful intervention are being used to resolve the situation.

The next story is about me. Surprise, surprise. The female reporter says that the search for the missing girls continues and that my management continues to help police with their inquiries. It's believed I'm living in a secret location, to avoid scrutiny. It then cuts to a reporter who is speaking to the camera, perched in the back of a helicopter. It's night. The camera swings and is now pointing at the side of an apartment building, lit up with a giant white searchlight. It looks a lot like my balcony. The National News Network. Fuckers. This footage could have been playing all night. Broadcast across the nation. Pinpointing my very recognisable building.

In my bathroom, I find a pair of jeans on the floor and slip them on. I then put my apartment keys in my pocket and let myself out. I ride the elevator down to the foyer. When it opens I'm instantly greeted by two security staff. They're wearing crisp blue jackets and black pants. Gold nametags read Marc and Christopher. They're wearing small communicative earpieces.

"Jack, how are you?" says Christopher.

"Good," I say. "What's happening?"

I step out of the elevator and glance to the right. The glass front of my building is wide and tall, tinted so that no one can see in. Beyond the thick glass are fans. They don't just fill the footpath, but they spill out into the road to the opposite footpath and then around the corner. A marauding swarm of blind admiration. They're both male and female, though mostly the latter. They're holding placards and wearing Big Bang Theory paraphernalia.

"Sir, we recommend at this point in time to return to your apartment. We have called the police and they're already trying to move everybody on. We're currently in lockdown, so they can't get in," says Marc.

"I was hoping to go for a morning stroll, guys. Could I sneak out the back?"

"They have the building completely surrounded," says Christopher.

I glance back at the horde outside, their faces pressed against the glass, pawing and pushing to try to get in. They can smell that I'm here. They can sense it. They're working on the entrance, trying to pry the broad doors open. Their voices gel into an exasperated hum.

There are a few residents milling around the foyer, clearly hoping to get out. One man is dressed as if he's on his way to work. He hasn't seen me standing outside the elevator.

"This is completely ridiculous," I can hear him say to another security guard. "It's Jack they want. Just send him out there and they'll leave us alone!"

"They can't get in can they?" I ask the guards. "The doors will hold?"

"We believe so, yes," says Marc.

"Oh well, there goes my leisurely wander."

"It is best you stay inside, sir. If you go out there, you'll be eaten alive," says Marc.

"Don't you guys have an armoured personnel carrier or something? A piece of heavy gear to use for my protection?"

"An APC?" asks Christopher. He looks at Marc.

"Yeah? You must have something parked in the garage. Otherwise I'm a fucking prisoner here. What happens if I run out of... I don't know, cheese or something. What if my satellite television connection cuts out?"

"I'm sure we can arrange something for you," says Marc. "I'll get my boss to contact the military and have them bring something over."

"Nice work," I smile. "I knew I could count on you two. Something about your clean-cut appearance filled me with indisputable confidence."

Christopher and Marc both nod politely as I return to the elevator. Before the doors close, I point to the businessman who wanted to throw me to the wolves. "What's his name?" I ask.

"That's Mr Blackburn," says Marc.

"Ah yes, I thought I recognised him. What apartment does he live in again?"

They both think for a moment. "I believe he's in 1201," replies Christopher.

"Of course," I smile. The elevator doors close.

Before returning to my floor, I stop at the twelfth floor and locate apartment number one. I then urinate on the door and return to the elevator. Inside my apartment, Jennifer is awake and standing in my kitchen making a coffee. Her hair is disheveled and she's wearing her black tights and her equally black bra.

"Where'd you sneak off to?" she smiles.

I lean casually next to her on the kitchen counter. "I was just heading out to get some fruit juice."

"I thought maybe you'd crept away again, like last time... but then I remembered that I'm in *your* apartment," says Jennifer.

"I had an early appointment last time," I say. "I apologised for that."

"Yes, I suppose you did," she says, taking a spoon from the drawer and stirring her mug of liquid. "Rose is nice," she adds.

"She is," I say.

"Very beautiful," says Jennifer.

"No argument here."

"She's messed up though."

"I think she's just very religious," I say.

"Did you know how religious she was?" asks Jennifer.

"No."

"I don't believe in all of that religious crap," says Jennifer.

"So there's no Earth?" I ask.

"Unfortunately, no," says Jennifer.

"So what happens to us when we die?"

"I die when people stop watching my movies. You die when people stop listening to your songs."

"What about when you die physically?"

"That means people have stopped offering me work."

"So you don't believe in anything?"

"I try not to believe in anything that's based only on faith. When you want to believe something badly enough, your brain can... misunderstand."

"So you see signs of something that isn't really there?"

"Yep."

"It can't be like that all the time."

"You'd be surprised just how much the mind can invent when you want it to."

"Maybe," I smile.

"You really ditched me after the McCarthy Awards," says Jennifer.

"Did I? I didn't think we went together."

"Have it your way, Jack."

I sigh. "Look, I'm sorry I didn't meet up with you at the party... but... what do you want me to say?"

"Who was that girl you left with? She looked familiar."

"Her name's Natalie."

"She really got her hooks into you."

"It was either her hooks or yours."

"If you'd played your cards right, it could have been both."

"I don't think she likes to share."

"So she's my competition, huh?"

"No, not really."

"So where's the juice?"

"I didn't get any."

"That's not like you."

"This apartment was actually on live television last night. Filmed from a NNN helicopter."

"The chopper was...?"

"Media."

"So, outside right now..."

"Thousands of people. More are turning up by the minute."

"I see," says Jennifer, sipping her coffee. "Well, we'll just have to get rid of them."

"They can smell blood in the water. They're not going anywhere,"

"Well, we'll just drop some blood in a different ocean," says

Jennifer. "There's a pool on the roof, yeah?"

"Yes."

"Good. Grab some towels and we'll go for a swim."

Miraculously, the roof is deserted. The pool glistens in the morning's sunlight. Vacant deckchairs are scattered over the broad grey tiles. An abandoned red and white striped towel hangs over one of them. A twiggy hedge lines one side of the pool area. The view stretches beyond the eye's reach.

"Looks like we have the place to ourselves," says Jennifer, holding her mobile phone.

"I'm always wary when you say that."

Jennifer just smiles and walks towards the ladder into the shallow end of the pool. Still in her black leggings and bra, she carefully steps in and holds her phone safely above the water. "C'mon, are you waiting for an invitation?"

In my small cotton shorts, I follow her in. We wade out till the cool water is just above our waist. Jennifer puts her arm around me, holds the phone up, pointing it down at us and says, "Smile."

She takes three or four photos of us looking up into her phone's camera. Jennifer then examines them on the screen. "That's not much of a smile, Jack."

"I don't smile a lot," I say.

"Well, with all your money and sex, I suppose you don't have much to be happy about."

"No," I say.

"Poor baby," says Jennifer, with mock sympathy. She then wades over to the pool's edge, leaning on her elbows and typing on her phone.

"So are you going to fill me in?" I ask.

"I'm just logging on to my Banta," says Jennifer. Banta is a worldwide social communication website. People around the world, including celebrities, post comments and images. It's a simple and safe way to speak with your fans and make them feel special. Not that you can hear their replies. It's like talking at them, rather than with them. Jennifer hands me her phone and shows me what she's posted. It says, "Just hanging out by the pool at Magnolia Mountain with my friend Jack." Beneath the comment is an image. It's of me and Jennifer in a pool. The famous resort at Magnolia Mountain is on the other side of the world. Genius. The millions of people that follow Jennifer will see the image on their Banta accounts.

"Think everyone will believe you?" I ask.

"I'm a celebrity," she smiles.

We return to my apartment. I glance into my bedroom and see that Rose is still asleep. In the living room I cycle through the channels on the television until I find my building's security camera system. Every apartment has access to the camera outside the main entrance, main foyer and then the foyer of our level. The surging horde of people remains outside, waving banners and signs. One of them says, 'Jack, please have my children'. It's held by a man. Maybe he wants me to sire some children with his girlfriend so that he can raise them. It occurs to me that if you live in the same town for two decades and remain quite promiscuous, there's an increased risk of sleeping with one of your own offspring.

"Look," says Jennifer, who's standing in the middle of the room with me. "That couple over there are leaving."

She points at two people who are pushing their way through the crowd, away from the building. Behind them a few more fans are following. Over the next twenty minutes, in dribs and drabs, the mass begins to trickle away. Like melting ice.

"Nice work," I say.

"Thank you."

"You've clearly mastered the art of deception."

"You don't know the half of it," she grins, poking me in the ribs.

Rose emerges from the bedroom, her hair dishevelled. She's wearing one of my pinstripe shirts and her cotton underwear.

"Hey," she says, still waking up. "What's going on?"

"Nothing much," I say. "Would you like a coffee or something?"

"Sure," says Rose. She walks over to the couch.

"Morning, Rose," smiles Jennifer.

"Morning," replies Rose with a sheepish grin. Then, looking at the television, she asks, "What's that?"

"That's a camera facing the front of my building," I say from the kitchen.

"Who... are all those people...?" asks Rose, sitting next to Jennifer.

"Fans," sighs Jennifer. "It's okay, they're all leaving now. They're booking flights to Magnolia Mountain."

"Okay..." says Rose, clearly confused, but perhaps too hung over to really question the situation any further. Then she asks me, "So are you still going to go to the police?"

"Sure, why not," I say.

"You promised..." pushes Rose.

"And I'm a man of my word," I smile, bringing her the coffee. "I hope you like a little sugar."

Rose doesn't say anything. She just looks at me warily.

Jennifer picks up the remote control from the coffee table and flicks back through the normal channels. Then she sees something that makes her stop. "Hey, Jack... isn't that...?"

I look at the screen. It's on another news network and there's a live news bulletin. The words 'breaking news' flash in the top right corner of the screen. It's a little distracting. The camera is pointed at some kind of live press conference. There's a podium in front of a man dressed like a police chief. Next to him are two relieved-looking middle-aged people. Between them is Britney.

"That's one of the missing girls," says Rose.

"She's not missing anymore..." I mutter.

There is a female voice over. Someone reporting on the situation from the news studio before crossing to the live audio feed of the press conference. "This is obviously... a very bizarre and strange turn of events. If you are just joining us, all of the missing girls who disappeared in mysterious circumstances over the past three months have all reappeared this morning... returned to their families, seemingly of their own free will. We believe police are questioning all of the girls as we speak. The parents of Britney DeLeo are now going to make a statement with police commander Matthew McGuire..."

While I've remained very casual throughout this ordeal and managed to, for the most part, detach myself emotionally from it, it has felt like lying on the beach in the blistering sun. I've watched the breakers suck out from the shore, retreating into the ocean. I've known a tsunami is coming. The ocean's deep inhalation before unleashing its fury. But rather than crash and torment, the sea has simply taken a deep, calming breath. No terror is coming my way. Life returns to its normal state of abnormality.

Britney. Her smiling, cherub face looks out at the crowded press conference. Her parents have their arms around her shoulders, reluctant to detach themselves.

"You told them to let the girls go," says Rose. "Now the girls are back."

"Well... maybe I scared them," I say.

"This is wild," says Jennifer, staring at the screen. "We should have a party to celebrate."

I don't respond. I just stare at the screen. When the press conference begins, reporters start throwing questions at the parents, who mostly reiterate just "how happy" they are "to have Britney home". Britney answers a few questions. One of the reporters brings up the fact that I was seen at the beach with Britney not long before she disappeared.

"I love Big Bang Theory, they're my favourite band," she smiles. "I did meet Jack at the beach and he gave me a lift in his taxi so I could get home. He was very nice to me and didn't do anything inappropriate. He was charming." She gives a cute little grin and everybody seems to buy it. It's such a deliciously plausible story and she deceives so effortlessly. Watching her speak chills me in the depths of my soul, as if the unseen evil that managed to coax these girls is creeping up through the ground and speaking through Britney's rosebud lips.

My mobile phone rings. It's Amelia's number. I've been ignoring her lately. Now might be the time to answer.

"Amelia, how are you?" I say in a warm voice.

"You've decided to answer your phone," she says, flatly.

"Why wouldn't I? I have nothing to hide."

"Fuck you, Jack. I've aged ten years trying to reach you. Don't you ever pull shit like this again."

"Sorry if you think I've been avoiding you, Amelia. I just needed some alone time."

"What's this about you being at Magnolia Mountain with Jennifer Fox?"

"A diversion," I say.

"Oh," says Amelia, "well done. Are you watching the press conference?"

"Yes."

"That girl said she *did* meet you."

"Alright," I admit. "She might be telling the truth. She looks semi-familiar."

"Forget it. I don't want to know."

"Perfect."

"Just so you know, we'll be asking the police to make a public apology to you."

"It's no big deal. Sometimes dogs bark up the wrong tree."

"I've got every media outlet in the world breaking down my doors for an interview with you."

"Good," I say. "Let's start with the biggest and work our way down. It's all about circulation, baby, and I want my blood flowing to the right organs."

"Okay, Jack," says Amelia. It's the tone my manager uses during a just-smile-and-nod moment. Which she often has around me. "I'll call you tomorrow with a schedule. Will you answer your phone?"

"Of course!" I say, boisterously. "I fucking love answering my phone!"

"Okay, bye honey," she says, and hangs up.

On the television, a reporter asks police commander McGuire if he thinks it's suspicious that all of the girls reappeared at the same time.

"Yes, it is very unusual and I'd like to assure everyone that we will investigate this situation to try and have a better understanding of what has taken place," he says in a deep, booming voice. "Right now we have to allow the parents of these girls to spend some time with their daughters. But we will be doing everything we can to ascertain why these girls left and why they've reappeared. Many hours of police time and many resources have been used in this investigation and we need to make sure this confusion does not reoccur."

"We should tell them what we know," says Rose.

"No chance," I say. "What's the point?"

"Because, these people are still out there. The people who sent me the letters and the video."

"You should find that Stephanie girl," says Jennifer. "The one in the video. The one you brought back to life."

"That's a good idea," I say.

"You should let the police speak to her," pushes Rose.

I kneel in front of Rose and take one of her hands in my own. "Rose, there are certain... revelations here, regarding... me... that I'd prefer not to be made public. I'm going to look into this on my own. You need to trust me, okay?"

She looks into my eyes for many seconds before replying, reluctantly, "I suppose so."

"Excellent," I say. Then I stand to announce, "Now don't be alarmed, but it's not safe here. We need to go to my bedroom immediately."

# CHAPTER SIXTEEN

A man in a headset appears at the door.

"Five minutes," he says.

I nod, looking at him in the bathroom mirror. I lean over the sink and splash some cold water on my face. A vain attempt to calm myself. Somewhere in the muffled distance a crowd is cheering. A deep male voice is blasting over a loud speaker, riling the giant mass of people outside. Working the audience. My stomach is in knots. Anticipation. Adrenaline.

I'm led up a corridor, through a security door. Two large guards with headsets walk on either side of me. Up another corridor we arrive at a large double door. The guards push these open and I'm outside. The bright sun hits me in the face.

# CHAPTER SEVENTEEN

I've been lying on my bed for a few hours now, naked, flipping through an issue of *Distortion* that I bought a few months back but never read. I'm the cover story. A close-up of my face adorns the front. Twelve-page feature. Some choice pull quotes. I occasionally glance at myself in the mirrored wall of my bedroom.

Tomorrow we leave to tour. My bags are packed. I travel light, especially now that the missing girls are no longer a weight around my neck. There is investigation necessary, but first I need to make it through these touring commitments. I owe it to the fans.

As I finish with the magazine and toss it on the floor, my mobile phone rings. It's a number I don't recognise, but I answer it anyway.

"Jack, hi," says a purring female voice. "I hoped you would answer."

"Glad I could oblige," I say, eyes closing from the sedatives I've digested. It's Natalie.

"I've been thinking about you. Fuck, I really need to see you. Are you busy?"

"Not really," I say, glancing around my sparse, empty room. "You may as well drop over."

"We can toast to your freedom," says Natalie. "It must feel good to be off the hook."

"Off one hook and on to another," I say.

"Don't worry, I won't leave you hanging," she says before disconnecting.

I drag myself from the mattress and walk lightly across the thin carpet to the curtains, which I pull open, allowing the day's remaining light into the room. I move to the ensuite, where I stand in front of the mirror and basin, and trim away my pubic hair with a small pair of metallic scissors. I have a hot shower, scrubbing my entire body with textured, exfoliating gloves. I then kill the water. Drying myself, I wrap the towel around my waist and go to the kitchen where I cut up two lines of cane on the bench. This should counter the sedatives. As I feel an amazing numbness travel from my face and around the back of my head, my apartment's buzzer goes off.

Pressing the intercom I hear the security guard say, "Jack, I'm with a woman who says she's here to see you. Her name's Natalie."

"Send her up," I say.

When Natalie knocks a minute later, I'm still only wearing the towel. As a valid reason to get dressed isn't presenting itself, I don't bother. Opening the door, Natalie smiles with her full red lips, her seductive green eyes running down my torso from beneath her perfect brown fringe. Every caramel coloured curve of her body is like a siren's song. Running your ship on to her reef suddenly seems like such a great idea.

Natalie is wearing a black shirt, with the sleeves rolled up past her elbow. Enough buttons are undone to reveal her lacy, black bra and the considerable cleavage contained within. Her grey pleated skirt hangs high above her knee.

"Hi," she smiles. "Can I come in?"

"Sure."

Natalie steps forward, rips the towel from my body and slams the apartment door behind her. Feeling a sudden rush from the cane, I push Natalie against the closed door and she gasps. Her hands grip my buttocks, raking them with her manicured talons, pulling me against her. In return I put my hands under her skirt and discover she's not wearing any underwear. I quickly form the opinion that this was intentional. Taking her by the hand, I lead her to the bedroom where I push her down on to the mattress. I pull her skirt above her waist, spread her legs and push my tongue inside her. As I lick and suck on her pubic folds, I see that she's watching us in the reflection of the mirrored wall. Her moaning becomes incredibly loud and I realise she's already close to orgasm. Her wave of climax has barely had time to travel across the firm, divine contours of her body before she grabs the sides of my head and forces me to stand next to the bed. Natalie takes my stiffening cock in her mouth, grasping my balls with her spare hand.

I make Natalie take off her shirt and bra. Returning to the mattress, she straddles my chest and we begin simultaneous oral sex. I take in the view of Natalie's intimate places, sliding the tip of a teasing finger into her anus. Her muffled moans indicate she's approaching a second orgasm and I know Natalie has reached it when she stops sucking on me and cries out, her thighs locked around my face. I quickly spin her around and position her over my waist. Sliding on to my aching erection, she lets out a shrill note. As I begin to move her hips up and down, she yells the word "fuck" repeatedly. I take her breasts in my hands and mouth.

I watch Natalie, who's naked except for her skirt, moving on top of me in the mirrored wall. Our reflections make eye contact and we stare into each other's faces in the mirror's surface. Then she turns to me and says in a low, serious voice, "I want you to cum inside me."

Needing no further encouragement, I begin to orgasm and Natalie forces her perfect breasts down on to my face, stifling my groan. She then lays on top of me, both of our chests heaving, our bodies lathered in sweat. My cock remains inside her, still fully erect. Once she has composed herself, Natalie begins to move on me again. I roll over so that I'm now on top of her, maintaining our coital connection. I then push against her groin in a circular motion. We fuck for a few more minutes and I don't reach a second orgasm. Between heavy breaths Natalie asks if I have any drugs. I tell her that is a silly question. She smiles and suggests that we do some.

I find a few small bags of gas and cane in my bedside dresser. I rack two lines on Natalie's stomach and she squirms as the rolled note I'm using as a straw touches her skin. She then racks two lines from my chest. Any powder we've missed we simply lick up with our tongue. Natalie then lies back on the mattress, closing her eyes. Removing her skirt so that she's completely naked, I sprinkle some of the remaining gas down the length of her body. It cascades through the air like weightless snow and she smiles. The length of her torso dusted with the powder is an amazing sight. As I begin to lick it from her skin, she moans softly, a smile never leaving her lips. My tongue grazes across the firm mounds of flesh on her chest and then down her stomach. She gasps as my tongue eventually returns to her pussy. Lying parallel to me, she turns her head and again takes my cock in her mouth.

Though we never fall asleep, time moves so quickly. When I eventually glance at the digital clock next to my bed, five hours have passed. Then six, seven and eight. The drugs course through our systems as we lie on the bed, side by side, silent. Natalie occasionally lights up a cigarette and we share it, ashing on the carpet. Every so often we'll start kissing and touching each other, and more often than not I'm looking at Natalie in the mirror, my head propped on a pillow.

Eventually I suggest that we have a shower and we do. We sit on the white tiles, not talking. Natalie's head rests on my shoulder as the water crashes down on us. She occasionally remarks at how fucked up she is and I concur.

"I feel connected to you... somehow," says Natalie, her eyes closed.

"I feel the same," I say, bathing in euphoria. "You're perfect. Everything I need."

We leave the shower and I find us each a clean towel. I watch Natalie in the bathroom mirror as she dries her naked body and then towels her short, brown hair. I walk out to the balcony for a cigarette. Natalie wanders into the bedroom and gets dressed. My guest then joins me on the balcony, standing next to my chair. I reach out a hand and caress the side of her thigh.

"I have to go," she says. "Have fun on tour."

"I'll try," I reply. "But I'd rather stay here with you."

"I wish I could stay too."

"Then why don't you? Why do you fly in and fly out again?"

"One day you'll understand."

Natalie leans down and kisses me. Then she's gone. I return to the bedroom, drop my towel, pick up the copy of *Distortion* and lie on my back on the mattress, flicking through it a second time.

I imagine that if you were looking down on me as I lie here, from a position on the ceiling, the image of my face on the magazine's cover would align with my body. If you stared long and hard enough, you'd eventually wonder where the magazine ends and where I really begin.

# CHAPTER EIGHTEEN

Our bus is hurtling across a desert. The suns have just set and I can't see anything outside the window. It's because of all these bright lights inside. There's just blackness beyond my reflection. I drag on a cigarette and turn to gaze at the TV screen for a minute, watching the simulated warfare video game that Cohen and Dylan are playing. They both holler wildly when they gun someone down in battle. Emerson sits on the lounge suite reading a book.

"It's science fiction," he tells me. "But it's not... really. It's just set in space."

Our tour bus is extravagant. Two storeys. Fully functional bathroom with hot water. Kitchen. Communal area. Digital channels on a wide flatscreen. On the roof is a deck, where we occasionally go to smoke and drink. You can't do much else at the speeds we travel. But our vehicle's simple sterility makes me feel like I'm in my apartment.

We're launching our world tour, our first since my name was cleared, with a performance at the award ceremony of the Adult Screen Society. It's as widely covered and watched as the Oscars are on Earth, but it primarily celebrates the porn industry. And it is a *very* big industry. Considerable girth. So impressively big, in fact, that they can afford to pay us two million dollars to perform three songs at the ceremony's climax.

As you would expect, the band are looking forward to our performance and the general debauchery that one would expect in the company of porn stars. I have to admit that I'm also looking forward to it. Any event that describes itself as "tits and glamour" surely has to garner a memorable experience.

Behind us is a second tour bus that the Known Associates are travelling on. Further back are several semi-trailers and twelve-seat vans, transporting equipment and our extensive crew. A midnight convoy.

Bored, I wander through the bus toward the front cabin. In the kitchen our sound guy and Dylan's guitar technician are smoking and playing a card game. The rest of the crew is lying down in the bunked sleeping quarters.

At the front of the bus, our driver, a middle-aged man named Gillan, sits in darkness. A myriad of blinking lights and coloured displays stretch across the wide dashboard in front of him and through the windscreen two giant headlights eat up the long, straight road as it disappears beneath us. A heavy metal song hums from hidden speakers at a low volume.

"Gill, what's happening?" I ask, making conversation as I climb down into the soft leather passenger seat.

"Not much, Jack," says Gillan. "Not a lot to see out here when it's dark."

"Not a whole lot to see in the daylight."

Gillan emits half a chuckle and continues to look out through the windscreen, limply holding the giant steering wheel. My gaze is also drawn to the grey stretch of road in front of us, the dashed centre line just a blurred streak of white.

A short distance ahead of us, the headlights pick up two small yellow balls that float low to the ground. I recognise the reflective orbs as the eyes of a nocturnal animal standing on the shoulder of the road. A second later we've drawn closer to the creature and in a short burst it rushes in front of the bus, attempting to cross its path. As the animal appears above the dashboard, it takes on the shape of a long, sleek cat, black and orange with a bearded face and eyes that look human. It glances at me as the bus motors over the top of it. A thud beneath the right wheels makes everything bounce into the air around us.

"Shit!" exclaims Gillan, who strangles the wheel as we swerve across into the opposite lane. From within the belly of the bus I can hear our passengers shout out, and beneath the floor I hear the wild snarling of a terrified animal.

226

"What the fuck was that?" I yell, grabbing the dashboard to steady myself.

"I don't know, I didn't see it," says Gillan, as he straightens the tour bus. The sound of an exploding tyre tilts the world sideways.

"Fuck," says Gillan, slamming on the brakes. The cumbersome vehicle screeches as we come to a heavy stop on the side of the road. The Known Associates' tour bus overtakes and pulls over in front of us, and the rest of the convoy begins to pull over further up the road.

"There was an animal or something," I say. "Like a cat. A tiger."

"A what?" asks Gillan.

"A tiger..." I say, then realising that they don't use that word on this planet, "I mean, a giant cat. A predator."

"I think I saw something, but I didn't get a good look at it," replies Gillan, whose hands are shaking. Then he calls down the bus, "Is everyone okay?"

Emerson appears at the cabin's entrance. "Dylan was on a high score. He's not happy."

"Send Dylan my apologies," says Gillan, sincerely.

"No!" I say, "Tell Dylan to go fuck himself. We nearly rolled the bus."

"What happened?" asks Emerson.

"Something ran under the wheels. An animal."

"Shit," says Emerson. "Well, let's have a look."

Gillan flicks a switch and the door creaks open just behind us. In the headlights I can see our crew and a few of the Known Associates walking towards our bus with concerned expressions. Outside on the dusty side of the road, we all inspect the front of the bus. There's absolutely no visible damage.

"It must have gone straight under," says Gillan.

"It looked pretty big," I say.

"What was it?" asks Damon, the Known Associates' vocalist.

"Looked like a giant cat," I say. "Black and orange stripes."

Everyone looks a little confused.

"Sounds like a weird cat," says Cohen, as he draws on a cigarette.

"We're in the middle of nowhere," adds Dylan, crouching to look under the front of the bus. "There's not many animals out here."

"There must be nocturnal animals out here. Desert animals," I say.

"Perhaps," says Gillan, pulling a small torch from his pocket and waving it underneath the bus next to Dylan.

"Looks like three tyres have blown," says Emerson, as he appears on the edge of the headlights.

"Shit," says Gillan, standing up. "I've only got one spare tyre left. How did three tyres go?"

"Fuck knows," says Emerson. "And there ain't no sign of a cat. Or anything."

Everybody searches up and down the side of the road behind us and no one finds the body of an animal. Nothing. When Gillan and the driver of the Known Associates' tour bus climb under the vehicle to inspect the damage, there's no blood. No fur. No hallmarks of carnage. Just three consecutive blown tyres on the right side of the bus.

"Fucking mystery, man," says Damon, dragging on a cigarette as we stand in the headlights. His eyes look bloodshot.

"Yeah," I mutter.

Gillan calls Amelia to explain what has happened. Amelia only flies, so she's not with us on the road. None of the other vehicles in the convoy have tyres that will match those of our tour bus. The Known Associates' bus is a smaller model. Amelia quickly organises for us to stay at a caravan park on the side of the highway until morning, when a repair vehicle can bring us some spare tyres. The park is only a five-minute drive up the road. The band and I grab our belongings and pile into the Known Associates' bus. With no passengers, Gillan takes the risk and limps our tour bus to our new accommodation.

The caravan park appears, a diorama of shapes and shadows, back lit by piercing white security lights. It's vast in size, spreading off into the distance and low to the ground, like a military barracks. The bus slows as we arrive at its front gates. The headlights find a sign surrounded by tall, anorexic palm trees. Mirage Holiday Park. The sound of gravel crunches beneath our wheels as the hulking vehicle lazily rolls into the park's grounds, tracing the circular driveway.

The outside temperature has dropped. I find a jacket in my hand luggage and put it on. Everyone alights to the cool night air. Vince, the driver of the Known Associates' bus, wanders over to a small reception office, sliding open a screen door and stepping into the yellow glow. Somewhere an insect buzzes and clicks. Another chirps in reply. Damon pulls a packet of cigarettes from his top pocket and offers them around. I take one. He smiles and pats me on the shoulder.

Off in the depths of the caravans I can hear voices come and go. A laugh. An engine turns over and hums. A few car doors are opened and closed. Clean, precise sounds. No clutter. The darkness of the desert muting echoes and reverberation. Even the low rumble of the tour bus next to me seems softer, like it's purring.

Vince appears in the door of the reception office. He turns and waves goodbye to someone out of sight.

"Okay, gentleman," he says, before handing out keys to members of the group. "This ain't exactly the Pluie Tordue, but Big Bang Theory's lovely manager Amelia has managed to book all of their remaining cabins. They're marginally less shit than the caravans."

"Quality," smiles Damon, taking a key. "Thanks Vince."

"Two to a room," says Vince.

"Looks like it's you and me, Jack," says Dylan, as he sidles up next to me. "I've still got spirits, so we'll be set."

"Let's find our cabin and go exploring," I suggest.

We lock our cabin door and stand for a moment in chilled air. Steam shoots from my nostrils as I exhale. Dylan opens his bottle of rum, takes a swig then hands it to me. I fill my mouth and swallow, feeling the comforting burn slide down the interior of my chest. Ahead of us, between the gaps of the surrounding accommodation, I can make out a pool and barbecue area. Above it appears to be a large games room that extends over the pool, held up with piers.

"Let's check out the facilities," I say.

We cross the gravel drive in front of us and weave our way through the cabins. The various footpaths are lit with white security lights at the top of high poles. It keeps the darkness at bay. As we cut between two cabins, I notice a noise from beyond a low window. I stop.

"Can you hear something?" I whisper.

We're both quiet for a moment and we hear the sound of a woman moaning. A quick release of pleasure, followed by a guttural male growl. Although I can't see Dylan's face, I know he's smirking. He nudges me in the back and we continue towards the pool.

"We need to find some girls in this place," says Dylan.

"It's almost three in the morning," I say. "We'd have to go door knocking."

From the pool gate the kidney-shaped swimming hole glows aquamarine, submerged lighting affording the water a vivid brilliance. Steam rises and swirls above the surface like sparse cotton wool. I glance up at the structure above us.

"Games room?" I suggest, nodding upward.

We follow the gate till we find the set of stairs. At the top Dylan opens the door and we step into the darkness. In front of me are the orange neon flickers of pinball and arcade machines. Dylan finds a light switch and the room appears. Ping pong table. Shuffle puck. Lounges. A derelict television sits on a small sideboard. Faux wood panelling from ceiling to floor.

"Wow, I think we hit the jackpot," says Dylan, with more than a hint of sarcasm. He swigs on the rum.

I inspect the games. "If you don't find any girls tonight you can take out your frustration on *Alien Landing*," I say, slapping the side of the machine.

"Always good to have options in life," says Dylan, picking up a ping pong bat and swinging through an imaginary forehand.

The sound of a footstep creaking on the stairs outside makes us stop and turn to the doorway. There's a pause. Some sort of hesitance. Then the steps restart, drumming towards us, increasing in volume. Just outside the door we hear a giggle and a young couple steps into the games room. Maybe early thirties. They're dressed in jeans and jackets. Woolen boots and scarves. Braving the pre-dawn cold for some light recreation.

"Hi," says the guy, his chiseled facial features unveiling a perfect white smile. "We saw the light on and thought we'd come and investigate."

The woman is painfully pretty. Porcelain skin and brown, naturally wavy hair. Drunkenness, combined with the cold, has painted patches of crimson on her cheeks and the tip of her nose. "We're not interrupting anything are we?"

Dylan studies the woman for a moment, before smiling back his answer. "No, you're not interrupting. My friend and I were just checking out the facilities."

"Facilitating," I add.

"Nice," says the guy.

Dylan approaches them, offering his bottle. "You guys look cold. Rum?"

Suddenly a perplexed look crosses the girl's face. "Hang on... you look familiar."

"Really?" asks Dylan.

"Yeah," says the girl. "You're in a band, aren't you?"

"You're in a band? That's cool," says her boyfriend.

The girl turns her eyes on me, then looks back at Dylan. Then back at me.

"Holy shit," she says, "you guys are in Big Bang Theory."

Dylan offers the bottle again to the woman, only smiling.

The guy looks at us both. "Are you sure, sweetheart? You're pretty drunk."

She slaps him on the arm. "I'm drunk, but I know who these guys are. Remember me and the girls went to see them last time they toured?" The woman turns to me. "Tell him I'm right."

I give a wry smile. "How would I know who you went with?"

"Yeah, we're talented and handsome, but not psychic," adds Dylan.

The woman looks frustrated and grabs the bottle from Dylan's hand, taking a long swig. She tenses her face as she swallows the fiery liquid.

"You're all jerks," she says, handing the bottle back to Dylan. She then asks him, "What are you guys doing here anyway?"

"Mostly table tennis," replies Dylan, before offering the rum to the guy. He raises his hand in a polite negative gesture. When Dylan gives him a bemused look and offers the bottle a second time, the man relents and takes a mouthful.

"Do you answer any questions properly?" asks the woman.

"Only if I'm sufficiently entertained," says Dylan.

"Our tour bus broke down," I say. "So we're staying the night."

"Wow," says the woman, walking around the ping pong table and stepping towards me. "It's so completely random to bump into you guys here. Of all places."

The man steps further into the room and spots the arcade machines. "Wow, they've got *Alien Landing*. That's all-time," he says. I watch him walk across the room and he staggers slightly. When I turn back the woman is much closer, only a foot away. I can smell her. A mixture of alcohol and the musky echo of stale perfume. It stirs something in me. She sits on the edge of the ping pong table next to us and unzips her jacket.

"It's so nice to be out of the cold," she says, placing the jacket next to her. I fight the urge to blatantly stare at the two grapefruit sized breasts straining against her tight, white cotton t-shirt, but I realise that in her smile is, in fact, a concealed invitation to notice them.

"Actually," says Dylan, giving me a sideward glance, "are you the two people we heard fucking on our way over here?"

The woman gives a look of surprise and turns to face Dylan, who now leans by the door. The man, who has swiped a cash card through the slot of *Alien Landing*, looks puzzled by the question.

"What are you talking about?" says the woman.

"We passed a cabin on the way here that sounded like a whorehouse," says Dylan.

"Sorry, wasn't us," says the guy, tapping away at the arcade machine.

"What's your name?" I ask the girl, who maintains her coquettish expression.

"Bethany," she smiles.

"Pretty name," I say.

"Is it? Or are you just saying that?"

I shrug. "A bit of column A, a bit of column B."

"My friends would die if they knew I was meeting you in person," she says.

"Really? What would be the cause of death, exactly?" I ask.

"They'd have heart attacks," says Bethany.

"Hey," says Dylan, reaching into his jeans pocket. "Do you guys like cane?"

Bethany looks at him as he produces a small bag of white powder.

"Sure," says Bethany's boyfriend. "I'm okay, but Beth would probably like some."

"Yeah, why not," says Bethany.

"Wild," says Dylan and closes the door of the games room. He walks over and tips a portion of the white powder on to the corner of the ping pong table and uses one of his credit cards to divide it into lines. He then pulls a note from his pocket and starts rolling it up. Dylan gives me a smile. From anyone else it would be an innocent expression, one of simple happiness. But it's loaded with mischief. His mind works in wicked ways.

"Hey, what's your name, friend," he asks Bethany's boyfriend.

"Lucas," he says, only looking up briefly before returning his

232

attention to the arcade screen.

"It's nice to meet you, Lucas," says Dylan.

"You too," replies Lucas.

Dylan hands the note, now a thin tube, to Bethany. "Ladies first," he smiles.

Bethany takes the note and stoops to daintily inhale one of the lines. She then hands the note back to Dylan. I reach out, indicating that it's my turn. Dylan smiles, unrolls the note and then puts it back in his wallet. He then removes a different bill and starts rolling it. I watch him change the notes over. Bethany doesn't notice. She simply wipes lightly at her nostril, sniffling.

"What do you do for a living, Lucas?" asks Dylan.

"I'm unemployed at the moment, but I'm a qualified architect," he replies. The machine emits a dissonant chord, announcing that he's been eliminated from proceedings. He spits a curse and steps away from the console.

"We're just travelling at the moment," says Bethany. "Lucas quit his job so we could travel together."

Dylan hands me the new rolled up note. "You going anywhere in particular?" I ask, then bend down to do a line.

"Not really, we'll just keep going until we run out of money," says Bethany.

Lucas joins us by the tennis table and yawns. "Sorry to be boring guys, but we might have to retire," he says.

"Are you going to bed, honey?" asks Bethany.

"Yeah, I'm exhausted," says Lucas. "And pretty wasted too."

"I'm not tired," says Bethany. "I might stay here for a bit."

Dylan says, "Yeah, stay and party with us." Then to Lucas, he says, "Don't worry, we'll see that she gets back to your cabin in one piece."

Lucas smiles at Dylan, clearly quite drunk. "Uh, I don't know..."

"I'll be okay," says Bethany to her boyfriend. She kisses him. "I'll be back to the cabin in an hour. I'm just really awake from the cane."

"Okay," nods Lucas, clearly a little reluctant, but too delirious to argue. "I'll see you soon." Then he shakes mine and Dylan's hands. "It was nice to meet you guys."

"Pleasure," says Dylan.

Lucas heads for the door. He glances back, gives a small wave as he opens it and then disappears. Once his footsteps have disappeared, Bethany walks across to the door and closes it.

Dylan and I walk down the stairs from the games room, returning to the cold embrace of the desert night. If the time on my phone is anything to go by, there's only two hours of darkness left before the suns creep over the horizon.

We walk around the pool and continue up one of the gravel roads that divide the large cabin area in a crosshatched pattern. Most of the lights in the cabins are switched off, as this is the hour when most people are adrift in slumber. Through the window of one cabin I notice the blinking glow of a television.

It's eerily quiet now. The sound of our feet crunching on the grey stones is magnified in the morning air. From somewhere to our right comes the low murmur of a car engine. Wheels rolling across gravel. It appears ahead of us, turning left and heading in our direction. It's a large black sedan with tinted windows. A piece of old-world luxury. It stops in front of a cabin about fifty metres away. An old man, possibly sixty, exits the driver's door. He's wearing a brown suit. He runs a hand across his thin grey hair, glancing at us quickly before turning around and opening the rear passenger door. Two young girls exit. No more than fourteen years old. Ethnic in appearance. They're wearing identical outfits, which sort of look like private school girl uniforms. Their hair is up in matching pigtails. Both of them are eating an ice cream. Neither looks at Dylan or I as we pass. They follow the old man to the door of his cabin, which he opens and the three of them disappear inside. Dylan doesn't say anything. He pulls out a cigarette and lights it. Then he offers me one along with another swig of rum.

Ahead of us is a tall security fence and pottering beneath it is a group of people. It's the perimeter of the park. The shapes of onlookers sit or stand, loitering in front of a mesh wall that's topped with coils of razor wire.

"Here we go," says Dylan. "I knew someone would be up partying."

There's a white security light high on a post to our right, but the group are just beyond its reach. There are maybe a dozen people, a few of which are slumped in deck chairs, all wearing warm clothing. They're gazing through the fence into the distance. I look through it as well, but there's nothing there. Just an expanse of desert still draped in the vacuous shadow of night. One man, a broad shouldered fellow, has a pair of binoculars to his face.

"Good morning, folks," says Dylan.

"Good morning," a few people reply, unenthusiastically.

"Wild party," smiles Dylan, and swigs from his rum bottle.

The broad shouldered man continues to scan the horizon with his binoculars. Dylan steps up to him. "How you going there?" he asks. "Is there any desert out there?"

"Lots of it," replies the man, gruffly.

"Big fence," says Dylan.

"Yes," says the man.

A woman sits in a chair behind him, a blanket across her lap. Leaning against her knees is a cardboard sign that says, *We Want The Truth*. It's painted in broad black brushstrokes.

"Do you mind me asking what you're looking at?" asks Dylan.

The man finally takes the binoculars from his face and looks at Dylan.

"The military built a base over there only five years ago," says the man, pointing. "They put up miles of razor wire and security fencing to keep people away. People and their questions. But we all know what they're doing." He then puts the binoculars back to his face.

Dylan looks back at me, grinning. Then he turns back to the man. "So you think they're up to no good? What are they doing over there?"

"We think they have something inside. Something they don't want us to know about."

"Like what?" asks Dylan.

"Hundreds of people saw something crash in the middle of the ocean just under five years ago. Something the politicians said was space dust. Random debris. Then a month later they start building a mysterious military base in the middle of the desert? Don't try and tell me that we're being paranoid."

Dylan looks back at me again. He seems impressed with the conspiracy theory. "It's pretty wild, huh?" he asks me.

"Extremely," I say. I walk to the fence and look out into the distance. There's nothing there. "What are you hoping to see?" I ask the broad-shouldered man.

"Not sure exactly," he says. "But people have seen flying lights above the military base."

"You can see it through the binoculars?"

"Yes," says the man.

"Do you mind if I look?" The man lowers them from his face. He sizes me up for a moment and then offers them. "Thanks," I say. When I put them to my eyes I'm surprised to find that they're actually night vision. I scan the horizon and can just make out a low series of buildings. They're a long way away, but just visible. I hand the binoculars back to the man. "What sort of lights have you seen?" I ask.

"I haven't seen them," he replies. "But people in our society have."

"Society?" I ask.

"Yes," he says. "We compare notes. Pool resources."

If he only knew what I could tell him. "Cool," is all I can say.

"I'd like to join this club," says Dylan. "It sounds wild."

The man doesn't reply. He just puts the binoculars to his face and looks back at the base.

I've never heard about this secret place. I suppose I don't pay much attention to anything these days. I'm more than a little intrigued as to why they would build this in my honour.

Dylan chuckles as we head back along the rows of cabins to our own. We stop outside it. "Those poor bastards," he grins. "Standing there on that fence. All night? Fuck me sideways. That's dedication, man."

Before I can respond I hear something to our right. It's a voice. It said something but I didn't quite catch it. It's draped in shadow, just beyond the bright security lights above our head. Dylan and I both stop.

"Who's there?" calls Dylan. He pulls a cigarette from his pocket. "Is that you Damon, you cheeky bastard?"

"You shouldn't laugh about it," says the voice, still in shadow. Croaky. Ancient. It's as if the soil beneath our feet is speaking to us.

I raise a hand to block the downlight. I make out the shape of an old man, sitting on a bucket next to our cabin. He must be our neighbour. I see the glow of a lit cigarette.

"You here to perve on the military too?" asks Dylan.

"I'm passing through," says the old man. "But I can tell you, a lot of people are nervous about that base."

"You think they might have an alien in there?" asks Dylan, lighting his smoke. "You think an alien landed on this planet?"

"I do," says the old man. "A lot of people do. But there ain't no alien in there. They might have what it landed in, but they don't have an alien."

What it landed in? I virtually turned the pod into ash. It's obliterated. Perhaps they found a few chunks here and there on the ocean floor, but I can't imagine they've retrieved anything that will give them an insight into who I am. The only thing I left for anyone to find was the life raft.

"Seems like a lot of security to hide some space junk," says Dylan, smugly.

The old man shakes his head. "They've got so much security because they don't know what they're dealing with. When they catch it and put it in there, they don't want it escaping."

My stomach jolts slightly. I'm too pretty for jail.

"Ah, so it's an alien *prison* now," says Dylan, in his condescending tone. He turns to me, "Let's get inside."

I shake my head. "I'm going to stay out for a bit longer. I need the fresh air."

Dylan shrugs and opens our cabin. He closes the wooden door behind him. The security screen swings shut.

I step into the shadow, standing opposite the old man. As my eyes adjust I can see him more clearly. A grey beard and thinning white hair on his head. His eyes seem clouded, as if he is blind. He wears workman's boots, a long jacket and dark trousers.

"You sound very confident about all of this, old man. Sure it's not just a military warehouse or something?"

"I hear things. I know things," he replies. "When you listen, you can hear everything."

"Right," I say. "But people can mishear things too."

The old man doesn't reply. A heavy silence hangs between us. Then he says, "How do you pay your way, young man?"

"I'm a musician," I say.

"Really? Not many people pay their way from that."

"I'm just lucky."

"You famous yet?"

"I suppose."

The man doesn't say anything. He puts his cigarette to his dry, weathered lips and takes a final drag before dropping it next to him in the dirt.

"What instrument do you play?"

"Guitar mostly. Some keys."

The man nods, approvingly. He then stares up at the sky. "Clear night," he says. "Unusual for this time of the year."

"How should the sky look?"

The man doesn't reply. He just keeps staring upward. "There's a lot of lost souls up there."

I don't say anything, but I do glance up.

"You weren't born," says the man, "but when I was very young, a rocket carrying three astronauts was lost in space."

"Really?"

"Never heard from again. Never found."

Suddenly I'm hanging on the old man's every word. "What happened?"

"Nothing more than I've said already," he shrugs.

"Right," I say, lighting a cigarette.

"Three lost souls. I remember the papers said they had enough supplies to survive for two years. Everyone hoped they'd find their way back."

"They didn't?"

The old man shakes his head. There's a pause in conversation before he says, "Have you got a guitar here, lad?"

"Yes," I say. "Many guitars."

"I used to play. Had to sell it though. Had to pay my way."

"I'll go get one of mine," I offer and the man nods.

Inside our cabin Dylan is lying on his bed, talking on his mobile phone. I open the acoustic guitar case that sits at the foot of my bed, take the instrument and return to the old man. He sits it on his lap, studying its surface with his gnarled fingers.

"Very smooth," he says. "You're only new then."

"I was only given that guitar a few weeks ago."

The man huffs. "Your guitar should age with you. Break when you break."

I don't reply.

"You play me a song," he says, handing it back.

"Okay," I reply, humouring him. I sing him 'The Times They are A-Changin''.

The man sits motionless, then looks at me incredulously. "Did you write that?"

"Yes," I say, confidently.

"Wise song for a young man... I'll show you something."

He takes the guitar, tinkers with the strings for a moment, then begins to play. "This is a song my father taught me a very long time ago."

"Cool," I say.

The old man plays an earthy folk song, his voice dragging through the melody like gravel.

"Drugs," says Dylan, from his single bed, which is opposite mine. We're in the humble setting of our cabin. I calculate that it's about an hour till the suns rise. A wind has picked up outside and teases the cabin's windows, rattling their frames. "Do you think they're doing drugs?"

"I'm not sure I care," I say, swigging on a cold beer. "From what I've heard about the Known Associates, they walk the walk."

"Should we go and see what they're up to?" asks Dylan.

"I can't be bothered. I really want to sleep tonight. The cane is wearing off and the suns will be up soon," I reply. My close proximity to the military base outside makes me want to keep a low profile during my stay at the Mirage.

Dylan looks forlorn. "We're basically in the middle of nowhere."

"Yes," I say.

"What are the chances of there being some girls partying in one of the cabins?"

"Not sure. There are probably a hundred cabins here. There might be a few. But you know what they say about desert girls."

"They're really dry?"

"No, they're really tanned."

"Oh, right," says Dylan.

Suddenly, there's a knock at the cabin door. Short. Deliberate. Only just loud enough to hear.

"Who's that?" calls out Dylan. "If you're not a desert girl, go away."

There's no response. I stand up and approach the door, listening. Just the sound of a dry wind whipping through the cabins around us. When I open the door slightly, there's no one outside.

"There's no one there," I say, closing the door.

Dylan furrows his brow. "Well, what knocked then?"

"Nobody. Nobody knocked," I say.

"Well, someone is fucking with us," says Dylan. He grabs his cigarettes and heads for the door. He opens it and steps out into the darkness. I can't see him.

I hear the sound of the wind swirl into a frenzy, blowing dust and vibrating the flimsy walls of our accommodation. Then Dylan screams. I leap to the door.

"Dylan?" I yell. I can see his shape standing out in the pathway, just on the edge of the security lights. Dark shapes surround him.

"You fuckers!" he yells. Then there's an eruption of laughter.

I head back to my bed and lie down, stretching out.

Dylan comes back through the door followed by Damon and Howie, the drummer, from the Known Associates. Damon is holding a small sealed bag of white powder in his fingers, while Howie triumphantly thrusts a spirit bottle into the air as he enters.

"These fuckers," says Dylan, smiling at me, as he motions at our guests with a thumb. "I thought I was going to be raped."

"Give them time," I say.

"What are you doing lying down?" Damon asks me.

"I'm burnt out, man. I'm out of fuel."

Damon jiggles the bag of powder near my face. "We brought fuel, my friend. Shit loads of it."

I grimace, feeling the temptation to get loose.

"You've gotta get up, Jack," says Howie. "We're celebrating."

"Oh, really?" smiles Dylan. "Are we toasting to our isolation?"

Damon gives a wry grin. "You could say that."

"Damon's getting divorced," says Howie, opening cupboards in the small kitchenette in the corner of the room. "Where the fuck are all your glasses?"

This revelation catches me off guard. "Divorced?" I ask Damon.

"Indeed," he says. "Best decision of my life. I feel like I can breathe properly again. And what better time then right at the start of this tour?"

"Look under the sink," says Dylan to Howie.

I sit up, swinging my feet on to the floor. "So you're a free man, then?"

Damon nods. "Never been more free."

"Well," I say, standing up. "Celebration."

Howie, Dylan, Damon and I are sitting at the small metallic table outside the door of our cabin. The suns rise above the holiday park, sliding in their long, shallow arc. The empty spirit bottle stands in the table's centre, our empty glasses surrounding it in an attacking formation. We discuss random subjects. Damon laments his failed marriage and regrets entering wedlock in the first place. I tell him that "marriage isn't a word, it's a sentence" and he finds this hysterically funny, having never heard it before. The four of us then talk about the music industry, bitching about record labels, managers, and publicists. Then we all vent our frustration about a magazine editor who seems to go out of his way to dislike everything we release. Then we share stories from the road. Backstage mischief. Each band member tries to outdo the previous story with an even more sordid tale. Dylan's stories are hard to top. Howie and Damon hang on his every word. They can scarcely believe that he once did a phone interview whilst sodomising his supermodel ex-girlfriend. "I had to keep thrusting to a minimum," he explains. "I told the interviewer I was on an exercise bike."

As we continue to share stories, spread rumours and exchange gossip, we hear the sound of a cabin door being opened somewhere in the distance. Up the path, in the early morning sun, we see two girls. They're both carrying something. Each in slip-on shoes, they walk up the path in our direction. As they get closer, I see they each have a towel and are wearing simple singlet tops with tiny denim shorts. They're chatting to one another, but as they see us they cease conversation and eye us warily.

Damon casually gets to his feet, his inebriation betraying his charisma. He looks like he needs to sleep. "Girls, shouldn't you still be in bed? It's like... fucking early... what time is it?"

The girls stop and look at each other, keeping their distance. They study him for a moment, determining if he poses a threat. They don't look much older than seventeen. One girl is quite tanned, with dark brown hair down to her shoulder. The other is fairer skinned, with a blonde ponytail.

Damon continues, taking a gentle step towards them. "Nice towels. Where are you guys going?"

"Swimming," says the brunette. "What are you guys doing?"

"Just a few drinks. Our tour bus broke down, so we're staying in this fine part of the world."

Mentioning the tour bus. It's bait so tempting that it distracts from the very large hook inside.

"Tour bus?" smiles the brunette. "Are you guys tourists?"

"No, we're bus drivers," chuckles Howie, before drawing on his cigarette.

Damon takes a further step toward them. The blonde girl stares at him, craning her neck forward. "Wait... are you?" she asks, disbelief forming on her face.

The brunette looks at her friend in puzzlement. "Do you know him?" she asks.

"Yes," replies the blonde. Turning to Damon she remarks, "You look like Damon from the Known Associates."

Damon laughs. His hook's through the cheek. "Well, I try to be."

An almost pained expression comes over both of the girl's faces, as if they're fighting a berserk impulse to squeal.

At this point Dylan stands from his chair and walks to Damon's side, throwing an arm around his shoulder. "If you'll excuse me ladies, I'll have to take my friend back. He's newly single and is in no way ready to be released into the wild."

The girls stare at Dylan, recognising him too. Then they look over at me. I'm instantly recognised. Then they look at Howie, who they may or may not recognise. Then they look back at me.

"You're Jack," says the brunette.

"Hi," I say, from behind my wide, dark sunglasses.

"Holy shit, can we get a photo with you guys?" asks the blonde.

"If you want," shrugs Damon.

The girls each produce their mobile phones and pose with us. I don't feel like standing up, but I drag myself to my feet. The two girls put their arms around me, smiling as Howie snaps a picture of us on each of their mobiles.

"So what are your names?" I ask them.

"I'm Miranda and this is Zoe," says the blonde.

"And you're heading to the pool?" I ask.

"Yeah, you should come with us!" says Zoe.

"We'd love to," says Dylan, "but your boyfriends might not be happy about that."

"We don't have boyfriends," says Miranda.

Damon puts an arm around each of the girls' shoulders. "I think you should lead the way," he smiles.

The four of us follow Miranda and Zoe to the pool. Damon gives me an impressed look when the girls undress, stripping down to their small two-piece bikinis.

We swim with them for an hour or so. They ask us a lot of questions, which are broken up with repetitive statements about how random it is that they have met us at this caravan park in the middle of nowhere. Their friends won't believe that they've met us. Then Damon asks them if they want to see the inside of Big Bang Theory's tour bus, which, of course, they do. Grabbing their clothes, they follow us to our lavish vehicle, which is parked on the far side of the caravan park behind a large shower block. It looks as though the tyres haven't been replaced yet. Despite myself, I can't help but notice how young and firm Miranda and Zoe's bodies are as they step up into the tour bus, barely concealed beneath their swimwear.

Neither girl requires much convincing to remove their bikinis. They seem flattered that we would desire them. They seem relatively sober too. They're certainly more lucid than myself or any of my male counterparts. Miranda assures me that all the things they will do with us, they have done before. But never with someone as famous as me. Later, when Dylan and I walk them back to their cabin, I thank them both for being so generous. I promise them backstage passes to the first night of our tour. Dylan gives them his mobile phone number so that they can stay in touch. As he types the number into Zoe's mobile, he says, "I'm going to enter my name as Norman... just in case someone ever steals your phone. Just to be safe."


It's late afternoon when our tour bus is finally ready to roll again. Amelia repeatedly offered to send a helicopter to take us to the next city, but I refused. I'm enjoying the vast, liberating expanse around us. Scoping it out. There's not many people around. It's as if everyone is afraid of the suns. The Known Associates drag themselves on to their own tour bus, their manager quizzing them on whether they've forgotten any luggage. They groan with vague acknowledgment. I watch them leave, sitting on a picnic table near the motel's circular driveway, an opened beer going warm in front of me. Dark sunglasses still cover my puffy, bloodshot eyes. I feel a batch of painkillers kick in and I become deliciously lightheaded. I pull my mobile phone from my pocket and dial a number. I let it ring for a very long time, expecting no answer. Someone does.

"What do you want?" asks Jemima, softly.

It seems that every time I speak to her now there's a pain in her voice that wasn't there when we met. I wish silently that her voice would return to normal. But normal is an ever-changing beast.

"I've been celebrating with the Known Associates," I say, trying not to sound smug.

"Great," says Jemima. "Thanks for letting me know."

"I'm just calling to see how you are," I reply.

"I seriously doubt that."

I don't know what to say. Then I ask, "So Damon broke it off, huh?"

"Is that what he said?"

"Yes. He was quite adamant. He came to our cabin to celebrate."

Jemima is quiet. "Well, you can believe what you want. But I broke it off with him. Just like I said I would."

After another brief silence, I say. "I'm sorry, Jemima. I got impatient."

"Well given my situation," says Jemima in a shaky voice, "given that I was not only married to him, but also your publicist, you needed to be more patient with me. It wasn't a situation I could easily remove myself from."

"When can I see you?"

"Not any time soon... I don't think I need you in my life right now."

"Am I that bad?"

There's a pause before Jemima says, softly, "Bad enough." I then hear a disconnection tone as she hangs up. I put my phone back in my pocket. Then I find a pill in my wallet, which I swallow with a gulp of beer and then head toward our newly fixed tour bus.

I'm the last one on. As I'm ascending the stairs, I hear someone call my name. When I turn, I see Zoe and Miranda, back in their singlets and shorts. Large backpacks strapped over their shoulders.

"You're leaving?" asks Miranda.

"Yep," I say. "The show must go on."

"Don't suppose you have room for two more?" asks Zoe.

"More than two," I reply, stepping back down. "Don't suppose you have any sisters?"

"It's just us," says Zoe. "We're hitchhiking our way across the desert."

"Is that safe?" I ask.

"We've got each other," says Miranda.

"Climb aboard," I smile, motioning towards the door.

The two girls smile back and board the tour bus. I follow them up the stairs. At the top I introduce them to Gillan, who smiles and shakes their hands. He gives me a sly grin, which I return with a look of mock innocence.

"The more the merrier, my friend," I say, tapping Gillan on the shoulder.

He nods and kicks the bus into gear. With a deep whooshing sound and a few metallic groans, the vehicle rolls forward and leaves Mirage Holiday Park.

I take a seat next to the window in the kitchenette and watch the desert roll past. Outside, only ten feet from the edge of the road, is the tall security fence that protects this supposed top-secret army base. It can't be seen with the naked eye. There's just an endless orange desert. Rocks. A few small cactus-like plants. But nothing else. A sign on the fence says *Trespassers Will Be Prosecuted*.

I spare a thought for the pod I landed in and whether they managed to find any of it. I left the raft on the beach. I should have destroyed it, but everything happened so fast that night. I thought I might need it again. But, alas, the government would have found it and searched for me. Followed my tracks into the city. Probably used porcines to sniff me out.

I keep wondering how Brannagh's little DNA test fell into the hands of Stephanie and possibly all of the other girls that went missing. It must be out there. Somewhere. Possibly floating in cyberspace. Available for someone to discover and use to manipulate innocent people. If not, I have to entertain the idea that Brannagh has a big mouth. That he has told someone.

The security fence continues to blur outside the window. It goes on and on. The perimeter must be gargantuan. I think about what the old man said. He believes the fence is for keeping something in, rather than keeping people out. Just like me, in a way. I used my defenses for both.

The suns begin to set again and we're still about three hours from the city. Our next stop. I'm lying in my bunk, which is the size of a double bed. I'm dozing, still very scattered. Unable to find proper slumber. I hear a quiet voice.

"Are you asleep?"

I glance over and see Miranda looking through the curtain.

"Not really," I say. "Are you?"

"No," she smiles. Then she asks, "Can I join you?"

"Sure," I say.

Miranda ducks her head and climbs into the bunk.

"How old are you?" I ask, softly.

"Twenty-two," she replies.

"Really?"

"How old do you want me to be?"

"I don't know," I say. "I don't really discriminate."

"Do you like younger women?"

"Not necessarily, but they have a certain appeal. I think their youth rubs off on me. They remind me of something I haven't felt in a very long time."

I can tell Miranda is trying to be quiet as I move on top of her. She presses her face into the pillow. Sometimes, when she turns her head to the side she puts the back of her hand across her mouth to stifle the sound of her deep breaths. I bite lightly on her right ear. When I brush her hair away from her face and off her shoulders, I notice something on the back of her neck. It's a tattoo. It's only small, but it's familiar. A striped cat-like creature with human eyes.

"What's that?" I say, lightly touching the ink drawing.

Miranda looks back at me, answering between breaths. "It's a tattoo."

"Of what?"

"It's a guardian. Haven't you... ever... seen one?"

"No," I reply. "Where would I go to see one?"

Miranda smiles, looking at me as if I'm joking with her. "They're not real," she replies. "They're from mythology. They're supposed to protect us."

# CHAPTER NINETEEN

Amelia meets us in the foyer of the hotel. She's flown into this leg of the tour to oversee our media commitments. Interviews, press conferences and a little television. Then she'll fly out again, continuing to hop around the world to negotiate and lay the foundations for our continual bid for complete global domination.

It intrigues me to see just how easily people fall in love with us and our music. Every week we're being played on more radio stations and interview requests from almost every publication in existence continue to pour in. Amelia, with the help of the publicists at Endurance, plays the big magazines against one another. She'll get the media girls to tell one publication that we've been offered the cover and an eight-page spread, so they will counter that offer with a wraparound cover and a twelve-page spread. Then the dance continues. Apparently a magazine has offered to do an entire special issue dedicated just to us. It seems extreme, but given our popularity it would probably sell out in pre-orders before it even hit the stands.

There are paparazzi outside the hotel and they're trying to see into the foyer, to find that crucial photo, but there are security guards keeping them away. We're over in a corner away from the bustle of the check-in counter and thoroughfare of the wealthy folk rushing in and out, to and from their various pampered interludes at the spas and degustation restaurants throughout our current locale.

Dylan and I are sitting on a couch, while Amelia stands above us dressed completely in white. Her high heels, pristine blouse, jacket and business skirt are immaculate. Her hair is up too. She's shiny and impressive, like someone has buffed her with car wax. I can almost see my reflection.

"Your first interview will be with Malcolm," says Amelia, her eyes scanning over a clipboard.

"Malcolm is up first?" asks Dylan. "I don't think that's a good idea. I need to warm up."

"That's not a good idea," says Amelia. "Last time you spoke with him, you were... far too warmed up."

"I don't think so," says Dylan, shaking his head.

"You told him that parents were doing their daughters a disservice by not encouraging them to have sex with you," says Amelia, her eyes still scanning the clipboard.

"At least he got the pull quote," I shrug.

"That's right. I did get the pull quote. That thing was massive," says Dylan.

The pull quote is when a magazine layout features a quote from the interview in giant text, in order to entice a casual skimmer to stop and read the article. There's often one on each page of the feature and Dylan and I like to compete to see who can say the most outrageous things, thus securing a pull quote.

The more sensational the statement, the more likely it is to be used. Some of my examples include "I don't write my songs, I'm simply channeling a higher power", "if I'm destined to be a human banquet, then I hope my fans are always satisfied", "genius is a heavy burden", "if talent's a crime, then lock me away", "sometimes in life you're going to meet people who don't like you... all you can do is pray for them" and "worshiping our music is no less valid than going to church".

Dylan tends to be asked more sexual questions, so his responses are usually pitched on a similar level. Some of my choice favorites are, "It sometimes feels like we're drowning in a sea of flesh with only our cocks to keep us afloat", "what kind of world would it be if talent didn't breed?", "it sometimes feels like we're on a battlefield with our cocks as our only weapon", "we're very open with our female fans and we're happy they are open with us", "when I play my guitar on stage, I imagine I'm fucking people in their ears" and "it sometimes feels like we're taxation specialists with our cocks as our only calculator".

"It's too late to reschedule Malcolm," says Amelia. "So you'll talk to him first. You won't be pretentious either. We need him to give the symphonic album a good review."

"He's not an idiot," I say. "It's mostly the same songs... but with strings."

Amelia grimaces. "Convince him of its artistic merit."

Malcolm is a music journalist who works for the world's most read entertainment magazine, *Verse Chorus*. I'm not exactly sure how he gained his reputation, but his reviews can make or break a band and their releases. People listen to him. His pen is mightier than any sword and his opinion is gospel. We're fortunate that he is a very big fan of Big Bang Theory, but he can spin his opinion on a dime. He could turn on us. So Dylan and I, who do most of the media interviews, usually go out of our way to schmooze him. One might picture a powerful person like Malcolm as a towering pro wrestler, who can pick up a band's reputation and bend it in half. But in actual fact Malcolm is just over five foot, would blow over in a strong wind, never shaves, has relatively bad skin, shaggy hair and glasses. Visually, he's as intimidating as a seal pup.

Dylan and I go to the hotel's bar and sit in a shadowed corner. It's the middle of the day, but no natural light finds this area of the hotel. Chandeliers hang from the roof, their fading gold in tune with the equally gold and burgundy paisley wallpaper and trimmings. A barman in a crisp white shirt and black bowtie wipes down the bar, the wall behind him a rainbow of multi-coloured liqueurs. Vivid like a stained-glass window.

About half the bar is full, with most tables occupied by well-dressed couples and families. The women are decorated with jewellery and expensive scarves and sweaters. The kids have mobile phones and hand-held video game consoles, but still seem a little bored.

Dylan and I remain unrecognised. Nobody even looks in our direction. On the wall directly across from our corner is a flatscreen television. The sound is turned down. The images are of children in a third world country and most of them are carrying large automatic weapons. Others have large machete-like blades. They're marching through unsealed streets, between makeshift housing.

I nudge Dylan, who is flipping through a copy of our itinerary, and point at the television. "Check that out."

Dylan looks up and sees a shot of three kids, who couldn't be older than twelve, firing rounds of semi-automatic spray into the burnt-out wreck of a car. "That's wild," he says, shaking his head. "See, that's why I don't like to play in any of those countries where guns are legal. Even the kids are armed."

"It's sad," I say, taking a sip from my glass of beer.

"Totally. When I was their age, I was discovering pornography. I only wanted to shoot my load, not bullets. I'm a lover, not a fighter," says Dylan. "I never even had a water shooter."

"That's a nice pull quote," I say.

"Think I should use it?"

"Only if Malcolm asks you for your opinion on child soldiers."

"That's unlikely... could we tell him we're releasing a song about child soldiers? That would be a tidy segue."

"Yes, but then we'd have to actually release a song about child soldiers."

"We could do that," shrugs Dylan.

"It would be easier to think of another pull quote."

"What songs are we working on?" asks Dylan. "He's probably going to ask."

"Well," I say, thinking. "I'm writing a song called 'Comfortably Numb'."

"Cool, what's that about?"

"I don't know. Drugs? Emotional distance? I'm writing another track I'm going to call 'Ghost Of City Life', which is about drifting through the streets in the early hours of the morning."

"I like it."

"I'm writing another song called 'When The War Came'."

"Wow, that sounds a little dark. Is it post-apocalyptic or something?"

"Ah, yeah. Maybe."

"War is a pretty bad subject. That's probably going to shock a lot of people."

"Really?" I ask.

"Yeah, well, you know..."

"I never went to school, Dylan."

"Oh, of course. Yeah, sorry. I mean, well, the last war was like, hundreds of years ago. I can't remember the date... I didn't really go to school much either."

"Why hasn't there been another war?"

Dylan smiles. "They call it The Great Lesson. I remember my father trying to explain it to me once. He said that we saw the darkest part of our souls and we never looked at them again."

"At our souls?"

"Shit, I don't know," says Dylan.

I look back at the television. The news report on child soldiers is still running. Indeed, from what I've read, automatic weapons are about as advanced as the weaponry on this planet has become. I'm in a very peaceful corner of the universe, where full-scale war is virtually obsolete. People still kill each other. Occasionally. But violence is condemned and punished accordingly.

Dylan points at a name in the itinerary. "We have a face to face with a girl called Mary-Josephine," he says, a look of elation growing on his face.

"Okay," I say.

"I've always wanted to fuck a girl with a hyphenated name," says Dylan.

"You have a hyphen fetish?"

"Yeah, I don't know what it is. There's just something adorable about it."

"Even hyphenated surnames?"

"No, just the first. There's nothing erotic about a hyphenated surname."

"So Mary-Josephine's in a bit of trouble then."

"Yes," says Dylan. "Someone should warn the poor girl."

"So what's the plan? You say something charming and then she'll just... pull your quote?"

"That's the idea... and don't interfere either. I don't want her pulling your quote. She has to pull mine."

"She's a music journalist. She can pull any quote she likes."

"She can't pull a quote if it isn't offered," says Dylan.

"You don't even know what she looks like. She's a music journalist, so the odds are against you."

"I've met lots of cute music journalists."

"Name one."

"How about Destiny, that girl from *Tastemaker*?"

I think for a moment. "Yeah, I suppose she was attractive. But she hadn't done any research and her questions were completely inane. That's a very ugly trait."

Dylan shrugs. "I think her disinterest really turned me on. She still slept with me, so she can't be completely clueless."

"I remember her having a lot of tattoos," I say.

"She was covered," nods Dylan. "Pretty hot. She had a lot of interesting pictures on her back. There was a lot going on. When I was taking her from behind it was almost like playing a pinball machine."

I nod and sip my beer. Then I see Amelia leading someone across the room toward our table. It's Malcolm. He's wearing black jeans and a tight black t-shirt. A satchel hangs from one shoulder and in one hand are a folded piece of paper and a pen. Malcolm has short dark hair, thick rimmed black glasses and his acne hasn't improved.

Amelia stops at our table, the clipboard tucked under her arm. "Boys, you remember Malcolm?"

"How could we forget," smiles Dylan, standing up to shake Malcolm's hand.

Malcolm gives a shy grin. "I think the last time I saw you guys was backstage at the Easton, on your last tour."

"Yes, I do remember parts of that evening," says Dylan. "Things got a little hectic."

"That's what rock stars do," says Malcolm.

"I'll leave you with the boys," says Amelia to Malcolm. "We'll have to wrap it up in an hour, but if you don't get everything you need I'm sure we can schedule some more time."

"Thank you," says Malcolm, sitting down at the spare seat. Dylan sits down too. Malcolm then pulls a small recording device from his pocket and switches it on, sliding it across the table until it's between Dylan and I. I look down at the little red light and watch the seconds tick over on the digital display. I eye Malcolm warily as he opens his piece of paper. His questions. It's all very polite and friendly, but he's not to be trusted. None of them are. They're all smiling assassins. I then realise that he's wearing a Known Associates t-shirt.

"So how are you, Malcolm?" I ask.

"Oh, uh, good. Very busy," he says, almost stammering.

"How's everything at the magazine going?"

"Excellent," he nods. "I've actually been made deputy editor. From the next issue onward."

"Congratulations," says Dylan. "Hey, do you want a drink? We've got a bottomless bar account here, so you should help yourself."

"Oh, um, okay," says Malcolm.

"What's your poison?" asks Dylan, standing to go to the bar.

"Uh, I'll have whatever you guys are having."

"That's a statement you should use sparingly," grins Dylan. "I'll get you a beer."

"I see you're wearing a Known Associates t-shirt," I smile.

"Yes, they gave this to me yesterday. I did an interview with Damon. It's so cool that you guys are on tour with them."

"Damon's a sweetheart," says Dylan, as he heads towards the bar. "We love those guys. Fuckin' talented."

"Yes," I say. "They're certainly very popular at the moment."

"I was really surprised by your *Dawn Of Man* album. Did you have any ideas on how you wanted that album to sound before you started writing it?"

"There was definitely a direction I wanted to go in," I reply, the interview underway. "It felt like we had already conquered the epic song. We'd proven to ourselves that we could write music with broad brushstrokes and sweeping gestures. I still love doing that. But at the same time, I was having ideas for songs that didn't fit that mold. They were simple chords, simple hooks. If you're in a band of talented musicians, you can turn almost anything into an impressive song. But simplicity is the truest challenge. I wanted to make an album that was an exercise in brevity, but also an opportunity to be more aggressive and direct."

"And the rest of the band were obviously on the same page?" asks Malcolm.

"Yeah, they're very open to ideas. They like trying something new. I just said, 'Guys, I'd like to put together some short, sharp rock songs.' They were eager."

"Which songs were written first?"

I think for a moment. "'Up All Night' was put together quite early. So was 'Morning Glory'. 'In It For The Money' was written early too, and that really set a benchmark for the record."

Dylan returns with the male waiter, who is carrying three tall glasses of beer on a tray. He nods courteously and puts them on the table in front of us, then leaves.

"Let's lift a glass," says Dylan. We each pick up our beer. "To being on tour and..." he smiles, "to our favourite music critic."

Malcolm grins, bashfully. "Stop it, Dylan."

"I'm serious!" replies my guitarist. "Love your work."

"I wanted to ask you guys how the song 'Moving' came together. Because it's almost two songs rolled into one..." says Malcolm.

Dylan points at me. "Jack can answer that. That song was all him."

"Well," I reply. "I don't know really. I'd had the verse in my head for many years now. I was playing at home on my own with an acoustic guitar and I was feeling a bit restless. A bit adrift. My life has been spent moving back and forth, all around the place. Never really tethered to anything. Even before the band got together. But, I couldn't really find a chorus for it. Nothing seemed to fit. But then one day I was playing it to myself and the idea to really explode in the chorus came to me. I plugged in my electric guitar and found this, sort of, funk riff. For some reason the chorus felt like a good marriage for the verse I had been singing, even though they were so different. The song is a little bit like a carpet-ride. It's got a serene aspect to it, but also an energy that's completely arresting. I'm really pleased with that song."

"What was it like originally making that transition from a bedroom songwriter to being in a studio? Were you immediately comfortable with the recording process?" asks Malcolm.

I sip my beer, allowing myself to ponder the question. "Well, to begin with, I barely had a bedroom. I was boarding in an abandoned building, passing the hours by playing songs," I explain. "But now... yeah, recording is a strange process to me. Because in my mind a song is never complete. It is a living thing. It's different every time you play it, just like a human is slightly different every day it wakes up. Recording music is like trapping ghosts. It's like capturing someone in stasis, keeping them that way forever. So an opportunity to rework a song and add a layer of strings to it, like we have on *Pulling Strings*, is hard to pass up, you know. Yes, we record it again, but that's what our listeners demand. They want to hear those captured ghosts."

"Captured ghosts, that's good," says Dylan, quietly, making an annoyed expression.

"How did you find the new direction as a guitarist?" asks Malcolm to Dylan.

Dylan shrugs. "I liked it. It's fun to be a bit more abrasive. It's nice playing long solos and arrangements and getting lost in all of that. But it's a great... release, I guess, to crank up the distortion and get loose. I really like 'Baba O'Reilly'. I think it's a killer. It's really fun."

"Do you have a favourite song on *Dawn Of Man*?" asks Malcolm.

"I really like 'The Bitter End'," says Dylan. "I think it's really sharp."

"I really like the grooves in 'Rock The Casbah' and 'My Sharona', so I'd probably choose either of those two," I say. "'You've Really Got Me' is great too. But I love playing every song on the record. They all sound really massive live and there's an energy about them."

Dylan points up at the silent television screen behind us, where the story on child soldiers is still running. "Look at those crazy kids," says Dylan.

Malcolm turns to look as the children are chopping pumpkin-like vegetables in half with their machetes, clearly practicing murder.

"Looks pretty intense," says Malcolm.

"When I was their age, I wouldn't have dreamed of firing a gun. All I wanted to shoot was my load, not bullets," says Dylan.

I shake my head at Dylan's clumsy pull quote attempt. "That's interesting, Dylan. It sounds like you were a lover, not a fighter," I say.

"I was just about to say that," says Dylan, hiding his scowl.

"Well, great minds think alike," I smile.

Malcolm turns back to us. "Great minds think alike... that's a nice quote. I like that."

"Thank you," I say.

Dylan looks at me and shakes his head. He's displeased. I pout at him, mockingly.

"Now while you guys are extremely popular, not everyone out there loves your music..." says Malcolm.

"What do you mean?" asks Dylan, who seems genuinely shocked.

"Oh," says Malcolm, "no, I'm just saying that a few people out there have said negative things about your music. Christopher Hunt at *The Daily Observer* said that your music and off-stage antics promote and 'glorify behaviour that tears at the very fabric of society'."

"Not everyone can or will ever like our music," I say, diplomatically.

"That's true," says Dylan. "Here's the thing. Sometimes in life, you're going to meet people who don't like you. All you can do is pray for them."

The anatomy of a concert. It's a very complex organism and requires all organs to be functioning at a competent level. Its ideal genetic make-up is open to opinion and is dictated by those most holy of individuals. The ticket holders.

No matter what a recording artist might purport, we all live and die by public expectation and how we dance with it. The seemingly smart ones employ the "I don't give a fuck" attitude from the very beginning and use that as their foundation. Others fall into the trap of feeding the canine of the public too many treats as a puppy. Then your entire career is defined by hungry fans that don't compromise on their unrealistic expectations of you.

When Big Bang Theory was emerging, I was very careful to be dangerous. To be wild and deadly. To be unpredictable. The goal was to be defined by that unpredictability and for the most part it has paid off. I believed it would give me more legroom to cut loose and fuck up. But the truth of it is, no matter how you train that hungry, dewy-eyed baby dog, it will always expect too much. The better behaved and adoring it is, the more it starts to feel entitled to. That sense of entitlement is never stronger than when the puppy has purchased a concert ticket.

From talking to people who go to gigs, you quickly gain an insight into that ravenous desire for satisfaction. When someone buys a ticket to a concert, they don't see it as simply purchasing entry into the live performance of a band. That punter is buying a ticket into a gig that will fill their cup. The vessel that holds the volume of their personal satisfaction. Everyone's cup is a different size. Some are bottomless. Some are quite shallow. But if you don't fill their cup to the brim, then they'll feel short-changed and they won't love you as much as they did. If you overflow the cup, they'll be impressed.

The seemingly smart recording artists among us, who from the very beginning never promise to fill anyone's cup, ultimately lose their way. The punter becomes tired very quickly of never having their cup filled to the brim. That empty space, that distance, manifests into many emotions.

So no matter what any artist claims about their independence and whether or not they ever think about the public's expectations or perceptions, deep down they know there's a cup they have to fill. A doggy bowl for each panting, wide-eyed puppy. You can't overfill it and you can't leave it too empty. It's about the happy medium.

So what does this mean? The simplest way to explain it is this: Elvis Presley was never "the King". He was just a very famous court jester. With that soul-destroying thought in mind, I approach every Big Bang Theory performance with great consideration. Even when I'm sweating bullets on a haphazard concoction of narcotics, I always intend to lose myself. Drugs often help. They're that uncompromising social lubricant. The cure for all inhibition. They heighten your appreciation of music. No one can argue that that's a bad thing.

Right now we're side of stage and out there in the darkness is a swelling orchestra of screams and cheers. Slow claps appear in the tumult, congealing and unifying as one synchronised demand for our blood. A demand for our bodies and our souls and, while I've done many incredibly terrifying things in my life, I can never completely relax before walking those many miles up the small stairs to the stage. Crossing that threshold into oblivion is something I can't become completely comfortable with. Stepping into the arena is an ascent into immortality.

Big Bang Theory concerts never start off with a bang. It's just not our thing. We appear in almost darkness. Just a few weak blue downlights. Our specters emerge as shadows, silhouettes divided by microphones and instruments. But they know we're here and now there is nowhere to hide. Sometimes we start with 'Closer', which was originally written by Kings Of Leon. Or we build into 'Corduroy' by Pearl Jam or maybe even 'The Rain Song' by Led Zeppelin. On a few occasions I've stepped out on my own and sat at a piano to play Razorlight's 'Wire To Wire'. Sometimes it's 'The Funeral' by Band Of Horses.

Tonight we open with 'I Wanna Be Adored' by The Stone Roses and then break into 'She Sells Sanctuary'. Then we play H.I.M.'s '(Rip Out) The Wings of a Butterfly', Black Sabbath's 'N.I.B.', 'Pictures Of Home' by Deep Purple and then The Rolling Stones' 'Gimme Shelter'. These songs are a way of feeding the giant. They are big slabs of meat on the table. A feast of rock.

The stage plunges into darkness and the wall of howls and wails hits me from the void like a black wind. The crowd cheers before the stage lights are slowly faded up. I step up to the microphone.

"How you feelin' out there?" I ask.

A deafening reply returns from the audience and I can see hands waving in the air and dotted lights of mobile phones floating beyond the reach of the stage lights.

"I feel a little exposed up here," I smile. "Because you can see me ... but I can't see you."

As I say this, the house lights are turned up and the twenty thousand people in the auditorium become apparent.

"Wow," I say, looking at the endless faces and moving bodies. "There are a lot of beautiful people here. We're very outnumbered."

I can hear girls screaming from the crowd. Random adoration. They sing out "I love you" or song requests. I notice a girl on her friend's shoulders, desperately waving at me to get my attention.

"There's a lot more of you than there is of us, so you'll have to be gentle," I say, wryly.

"Don't listen to him," says Dylan into his microphone. "You can be as rough as you like." He sends me a cheeky grin and winks.

"Time to dance," I say, and the house lights are extinguished. I turn and watch Cohen as his drumbeat leads us into 'Last Night'. After we finish the classic Strokes song, Emerson begins the walking bass intro to 'Seven Nation Army' and the crowd immediately claps in unison. We then play 'I Can't Get No (Satisfaction)'. Then appear the monstrous riffs of 'Richard III' by Supergrass. My voice is drowned in my monitors. I get the attention of the mixer at the side of the stage and he turns up my vocal feedback.

Emerson and Cohen play the opening groove of one of our newer songs, 'It's Nice To Know You Work Alone'. It was originally recorded by Silversun Pickups. During the slinking intro, Dylan and I swig from a bottle of red wine. Dylan is smiling. He loves having a captive audience. The bigger the better. After the Pickups tune, every light vanishes. Then a small backlight is faded up and I can glance down at my set list, which is taped to the stage just to the right of my microphone stand.

"Thank you for coming along tonight and being a part of the Big Bang Theory journey," I say, into the microphone. "It's nice to be loved." We then burst into 'You Love Us' by Manic Street Preachers.

During the subsequent songs I often step to the back of the stage and face Cohen, who's just wearing his jeans. Sweat forms on his brow and chest, the muscles in his arms knotted as he pounds his kit. He spares me a small smile through his concentration and exertion. I can tell he's enjoying himself.

When I stand at the microphone and sing to these people, I'm thinking about what I'm playing with my left hand, occasionally glancing down at my fingers on the neck, even though I don't really need to look anymore. I scan the crowd but I can't see past the first five rows of faces, all contorted and crushed against each other. It's usually men at the front, because they're physically bigger and can stand the force of the moshpit that pins them there. But as I look toward either end of the barricade, young females appear. Their faces are shaped in screams and sobs of unbridled admiration, hands frantically waving when I glance at them. To be loved and worshiped by strangers is an incomparable sensation. These creatures have never met me. But in their hearts they know me. They know all they need to. Music is a window to the soul and this writhing mass believes it can see mine.

"Are you still with us?" I shout into the microphone. The crowd cheers in reply. I shake my head and, even louder, yell. "I said, *are you still with us?*" The crowd replies at a much higher volume, clapping, hollering and wailing back at me. "That's better," I smile. We play 'The Song Remains The Same'. Big Bang Theory then rocks through Pearl Jam's 'Last Exit'.

"Alright," I say into the microphone, "we're only going to play another song if you promise to get hectic. Can you promise us you'll do that?" The crowd roars in response. "Okay then. I believe you. Don't let us down." The opening chords of 'Smells Like Teen Spirit' elicit a wave of hysteria that builds and crashes inside the mammoth venue. Immediately people start leaping in the air. We then perform 'Song 2', a tune by a British band called Blur.

Then it's time for me to sit at a small piano for 'Karma Police' by Radiohead. Next on the set list are Neil Young's 'Cortez The Killer', Ryan Adams' 'The House Is Not For Sale' and 'Moving' by Supergrass. The crowd sings along to every song, word for word, and I get tingles throughout my body as their voices wash on to the stage. An ebb and flow of musical energy.

We then return to some more progressive rock tracks. This long portion of the show includes Mountain's 'Nantucket Sleighride', Yes' 'South Side of the Sky', Deep Purple's 'Child In Time' and Queen's 'Great King Rat'. During some of the breakdowns I'll walk over to Dylan's side of the stage and we'll face each other, sharing a smile as we lock into riffs or while he solos over the top of me. Other times Dylan and I will stand on the edge of the stage, wailing away into the abyss. The coloured lights of mobile phones continue to blink in the wall of black, filming us or flashing photographs.

Emerson is more restrained, often standing back near his stack of amplifiers, glancing over at Cohen, maintaining their tightly woven rhythms. I sometimes look over to get his attention, but he's always somewhere else, his long brown hair cascading down over his face. He definitely gets in a zone. Some distant, dark corner of the mind.

The stage lights die and we walk off stage. Someone points a flashlight at the stairs so we can see our feet. Dylan, Emerson and I pass our instruments to our technicians, who immediately start retuning them. The crowd screams and bays for more. They chant in unison, like an army. Clapping. Marching up and down where they stand, roaring "Theeeeeory, Theeeeeory...."

We dash up the tunnel to our dressing rooms, past many towering security guards. In my private dressing room I go into the bathroom and empty my bladder. I then grab a white towel that's sitting on the sofa and dry my face and hair, which has thickened since I cut it off. There's a fridge in the room that is stocked with alcohol. I grab a cold can of beer and open it. I then return to the corridor and walk back to the auditorium.

In the darkness behind the stage, where I find Cohen and Emerson, the sound of the crowd is deafening. The mass of people claps in time and creates thunder beneath their stomping feet. The seating is steep and rises high into the air, stopping before it reaches the metal beams of the ceiling. Those beams seem a mile away.

A few more minutes pass and I see Dylan appear next to me. He's wiping at his nose. He throws an arm around my shoulder.

"Ready to change someone's life?" he asks.

"Always," I reply.

Someone shines a small torch on the stairs again and I ascend them on my own. In the dim light I walk across to the small piano next to the drum kit and sit down. Some people in the crowd have spotted my silhouette and a wall of cheering hits me as the encore begins. A single white downlight appears above me and I perform a song originally written by a group called Blitzen Trapper called 'Heaven and Earth'. It's an apt song to open an encore, though its ironic significance is known only to me.

The rest of the band reappears and the crowd greets them with a roar. A guitar technician brings me my red neon electric guitar as I return to the centre microphone. We then perform 'In The Evening' and 'Black Dog', both Led Zeppelin songs.

Before we play our final song, I take a moment to introduce the band. Each of them receives a rapturous applause. "And I'm Jack," I say, and the crowd responds with their trademark appreciation. "You've been beautiful," I add. "Thank you for making this such a romantic evening." I give the crowd another opportunity to cheer, before I say, "We've been Big Bang Theory. See you again soon."

I begin the intro to 'Stairway To Heaven'.

In my dressing room I walk into the bathroom, peel off my sweaty clothing and take a cold shower. I lean against the tiles, the water cascading down my aching body. We've played for almost three hours and I'm exhausted. After I turn off the water, I dry myself with a large, fresh white towel and pull on a pair of jeans and a t-shirt that hang on clothes hooks behind the dressing room door.

I then walk to the table at the side of the room, which has been stocked with my personal rider. I pour some hot water from the electric jug into a metal cup. I add milk, honey and two shots of spirit. My throat feels like I've been chewing and swallowing wads of sandpaper.

Drink in hand, I leave my dressing room and walk up to the larger communal room where the band and some of our road crew are drinking. I'm introduced to a few random people. One of them owns this auditorium and he's brought his son with him, who is a big fan. There are also some people from one of the drink companies that sponsor the venue. I pose for some photographs and sign some merchandise. T-shirts and posters and albums. I'm too exhausted to really engage in any deep level of conversation, but I try very hard to smile and be polite. Then I'm greeted by a few people from a national radio station that is a media partner of the tour. One of them is a presenter that I did a live interview with a few days ago. More photographs. More autographs.

I see Gillan on the other side of the room, chatting to Emerson's bass technician, drinking a beer. Gillan is waiting to drive us back to the hotel in a hired people mover. I excuse myself from the surrounding conversation and walk over to him.

"How soon before we can get out of here?" I say, quietly.

"Want me to try and round everyone up?" he asks.

"I don't know if the band's ready to leave yet. But I am. I feel like I'm still on stage."

I return to my dressing room, grab my shoulder bag, and head back to the communal area. I say goodbye to everyone as quickly as I can. Emerson taps me on the shoulder.

"Are you escaping?" he asks.

"Yes," I smile.

"Good. You're taking me with you."

Emerson and I follow Gillan towards the rear of the venue, the grey concrete walls curving until we reach the raised roller door of the load-in area at the rear of the auditorium. We walk down a small ramp and cut between two of our giant semi-trailers. A few roadies come up and shake my hand, their palms like scourers. A cigarette invariably sits precariously beneath their moustaches.

"See you tomorrow morning," I smile to the members of the crew. There is a buffet breakfast scheduled for tomorrow morning at the hotel. They wave a farewell and continue their heavy work.

Gillan jumps into the front seat of our mini van. Emerson and I load into the back seat as our driver fires the engine and rolls us towards the security exit of the large outdoor load-in area. As we round some more vehicles and the perimeter fence comes into sight, we're greeted by about two hundred fans camped outside on the footpath and road. I can see the flashing lights of some police vehicles. Officers are attempting to disperse the crowd. There's a tall security gate with a small guard's post just inside it. Security personnel are standing in a row behind the fence, arms behind their backs, trying to intimidate people into staying outside.

Gillan stops the van in its tracks. "Looks like we have ourselves a party," he says.

Through my window I can see the crowd has noticed our van. We have tinted windows. While that hides our identity it's also evidence that we're someone worth protecting. The horde electrifies with the realisation that there are band members present. Young girls push themselves against the mesh of the security fence. They won't get through or over it. The fence is twelve foot high with barbed wire looped across its top. The women are holding signs. I can see one, on pink card with hand-painted writing. It says, '*I love you Jack!!*' It is clear that hours of thought have gone into it.

"Ex-lovers of yours?" asks Emerson, wryly.

"It's entirely possible," I say, sitting directly behind Gillan. "What's the plan?"

"I could try to drive through them," shrugs Gillan.

"What if they don't move?" I ask.

"They won't want to get run over," says Gillan.

"They might," I say.

"Yeah," agrees Emerson. "Amelia has stressed on many occasions that we're not allowed to cripple our fans."

"Well, let's loiter here for a few minutes and see if they give up," says Gillan.

"They've spotted the van," I say. "They're not going anywhere."

"So what's the plan?" asks Emerson. "There's got to be another exit."

I stare through the windscreen at the baying herd. They're pulsing with infatuation. They're no longer individuals but a multi-cellular organism.

"Fuck it," I say, quietly, and reach into my shoulder pack. My hand snakes towards the bottom and I find a small plastic envelope. I pull it out and reach inside with thumb and index finger to find a pill, which I place on my tongue.

"Seriously?" asks Emerson. "We've got an early flight tomorrow."

"I'll be on the flight," I say. "I'll be flying wherever I want."

I produce a metal flask of spirit and use its contents to wash down the pill.

"What's going on back there?" asks Gillan, looking in his rearview mirror.

"Jack's gone," says Emerson. "He left us."

"I'm not going anywhere," I chuckle. "Gillan, I need a favour."

"Yes...?" he asks, with palpable trepidation.

"I'm going to need a guitar, wireless lead, wireless headset and one of the amplifiers. Could you get the roadies to throw it together and bring it over there to the fence?"

Gillan is silent for a moment, and then turns to me. "You still got energy to play for these people?"

"I'll find the energy," I reply.

Gillan smiles. "Okay, fuck it."

I open my door. Emerson opens his too. "I'm coming with you," he says.

"Gillan, you better bring his bass and amp then," I say.

I grin at Emerson, then open my van door and step out into the white floodlights. Emerson does the same. When I peer over the door, across to the security fence, a pause precedes an almighty roar as the crowd screams and pushes against the boundary. Emerson and I approach them, their volume rising with every step. The security guards notice us and alarm crosses their faces. One of them, who seems senior, marches towards me, waving his arms.

"Sir, I don't think that's a good idea," he says.

"It's fine," I smile. "That's a very big fence."

Emerson and I brush past him, the lights of cameras washing over us as we arrive at the gate. People push their hands through the mesh and we shake them and sign pieces of merchandise. The young men and women against the fence are being crushed as they wave their arms desperately through the metal bars. Emerson and I walk briskly back and forth, signing as much as we can, smiling into cameras as we try to shift the weight of the crowd. Minutes pass and I hear vehicles behind me. Gillan's van and a second people mover cruise toward me and pull up about twelve feet away. Some of our roadies pour out of the second van holding equipment.

"Put the amp on the top of Gillan's truck," I say.

"It might not be steady up there," says the roadie.

"It'll be fine," I smile. "I think there's electricity in the guard's post." I point to the small structure next to the gate.

A few of the roadies manage to lift the amp on top of Gillan's van. Then one of them runs a lead over to the post. I'm handed a microphone headset and my guitar. I plug in the wireless lead. With the electrified guitar in one hand, I step on to the front bumper bar of the van and up the bonnet and windscreen, until I'm standing on the roof. The metal makes a slight crumpling sound under my weight, but doesn't seem to dent too aggressively. The amp has been propped against one of the metal roof racks. After checking to make sure the guitar and vocal channels are both working, I toggle a few knobs and then turn around to address the crowd.

"Haven't you kids had enough?" I yell.

The crowd howls in response.

"Alright, well I'm going to play you a few new songs. But you have to promise to stop pushing forward because there's some people on the fence getting crushed. So move back or I won't play a single note. Deal?"

They cheer again and the pressure on the front fans eases.

"Alright," I smile. "This is a brand new song that I've never played to anyone before. It's called 'Hey Joe'."

# CHAPTER TWENTY

Even after I wake, my heart thumps in my chest. I focus my mind to distinguish between reality and the nightmare. A giant blur. The sheet beneath me is wet with sweat and my hair is matted to my pillow.

There are other beds around me in the homeless shelter. I can see them in what little light there is. Other drifters. I slept here last night instead of the abandoned newspaper building. I followed a vagrant, out of curiosity. To get some tips on life without an address. He came here where they served warm meals. Upon a brief inquiry I was told that there was a spare bed if I needed one. It beats the hard carpet beneath an office desk.

I quietly ease my bare feet to the cold floor. Whispers and snores fill the air. It's the early hours of the morning. I think I hear a low growl. I crane my neck, looking around. Something scurries. Possibly rodents. Instinctively, I return my feet to the mattress.

One side of the room has high windows and I can see a glow beyond them. The promise of rising suns. I reach under the wiry mattress, find my jacket and then depart, moving quickly towards the rear exit. Stepping quietly between the rows of beds, I arrive at a rickety door. The aged wood makes a shrill squeak as I join the unfolding morning.

The receding darkness suits my escape. I'm in a gravel parking lot. Dumpsters and industrial scraps line a perimeter fence. I head for an open gate and then turn up the street, following the cool footpaths. Still groggy from sleep, I wind my way across the city, avoiding major roads. My clothes are more tattered and dirty than when I acquired them, so my residential status is more apparent.

Yesterday I saw a street sign pointing towards a major park. It was called something simple. Something like "Easton Botanical Gardens". It's a public area. It sounds like a good place to pass time and I trust my sense of direction to find it.

Shops are opening. Lights appear inside. Uniformed people prepare stock on shelves or arrange tables. In the cafes you can see folks firing up coffee machines. Furniture is moved to the footpaths. More cars appear on the roads too. Darting about like mice in a maze.

On a corner I walk past a venue called the Yanque Hotel. Security guards stand silently by its entrance. I can hear dance music inside. A few drunken people loiter about on the footpath, smoking cigarettes, chatting. All of them are sweating and look pretty wired and pale. Red, bleary eyes. It must be an all-night place. All of the windows are tinted, so I can't see inside. Forever night.

A few blocks on I know I'm close to Easton's gardens. Buildings disappear and next to me is a twenty-foot fence of metal bars. Beyond it is dense, green foliage. I find the main entrance. A mossy colossus of wrought iron and brick. A wide, tiled path leads into the belly of the park. There are two guards standing nearby, who eye me as I enter.

"How are you, sir?" asks the more muscular guard.

"I'm very well," I reply. "How does this morning find you, gentleman? Has it been a long night?"

They both look at each other.

"Shift's almost over," says the skinnier one.

"I bet you're looking forward to putting your feet up," I reply.

The two guards look at each other again.

The muscular one asks, "Have you been drinking tonight, buddy?"

"No, no, I don't drink actually. I'm a fitness tragic. Hence this morning stroll."

"Are you from around here?" asks the skinnier one. "You have an accent?"

"I've lived in a lot of places, so my voice is now a blend."

"Well... enjoy the gardens, sir," says the skinnier one.

"Much appreciated," I smile and walk past them up the path.

I follow the brick road for about a hundred metres. I pass a small courtyard with tables, chairs and sun umbrellas. All vacant. There's a brick kiosk with its metal roller door closed and locked.

I arrive at a three-pronged fork in the road. The trees and lower foliage from the edge of the park are quite dense now and I can't see what lies up each of the three options. They're identical widths, curling and disappearing very quickly. Next to the far left path is a low sign that says Adams Park. A park is what I seek.

Walls of thick, green leaves rise on either side of me as I casually wander between the sculptured undergrowth. The trees that tower above me seem old. Some are truly gargantuan. A minute later and the path opens into a wide clearing. Adams Park. In the morning sunlight I can see how vivid and maintained the grass is. Every blade as it should be. I reach down and run my hand across it to determine if it's even real. A few shade trees are planted across the lawn, each with a small set of picnic tables and benches beneath.

Adams Park stretches a great distance and the surrounding plants are a showcase of coloured blooms. Birds dart from branch to branch. Some hang from the lower shrubs, sticking their beaks into wide, easy flowers, their weight bending the appendage till it almost touches the ground. Butterflies. Bees. Even some fruit trees. The whole scene, almost everywhere you look, seems like paradise. Ordered and constructed tranquility.

I'm the only person here. It's early, but you would think a locale as superb as this would at least draw a few morning joggers. Or revelers who refuse to go to bed. This would be the perfect place to watch the suns rise.

I step in the direction of the far side of Adams Park. It appears that the mouth of another path leads deeper into the gardens. A quarter of the way across the expanse of grass, I see something on the edge of my periphery. Ahead, on my right, near the edge of the surrounding foliage, is a shape. It looks like a person. Someone lying on the grass. Motionless.

I move closer, trying to get a better view of the human-sized object. I walk silently towards it, staring in the growing light. I'm close enough to see that it's a girl. She's wearing a black tank top and denim shorts, and lies like an angel with legs and arms outstretched. I should leave her alone and go on my way, but she's so still. I wonder if it's a cadaver.

I step closer and closer, the girl never moving. If her chest is rising in breaths, then it's too slow to determine. She's very pretty, but her most attractive days are behind her. Her face is young and round, like a cherub's. The girl's eyes are open. Staring blankly at the sky. Her hair is brown and unkempt. There's a silver chain around her neck. The locket lies on the grass next to her throat.

"Hey," I say, quietly. "Are you okay?"

There's no response. The realisation that she's dead washes over me. I kneel down next to her. Her bare arms and legs are covered in pink, weeping sores. They polka dot her limbs. Picked at and unhealed. The suns are appearing above the tree line, illuminating this forest world. Her skin is white and she's very thin. Her pale complexion only exaggerates the craters on her arms and legs. The perfect blades of grass reach up and hold on to her.

I'm startled when she speaks. "I'm floating," she says. It's raspy and barely audible.

"Are you okay?" I ask, leaning close. "I'm going to go and get someone."

"I'm floating," she says again. Her red, milky eyes never leave the sky.

Over to our right, twenty feet away in the surrounding flora, I hear something move. I can't see anything, but it makes birds burst from their branches and launch away in fear. I stare into the shrubs and see nothing. Another bird shoots into the air. I keep staring, frozen. There's just shadows. No danger beneath the continuous, chirping soundtrack.

When I turn back to the girl, she's looking at me. Her eyes wide now, but no less bloodshot. Her body remains limp. But I don't know if she's looking at me. If she even knows I'm here. She's empty.

I get to my feet. "I'll be right back," I say. "Will you be okay?"

Her eyes return to the sky, as if they never moved. I watch her chest and I don't think I've seen it rise once. I don't think she's breathing.

I turn and dash across the grass towards the entrance to Adams Park, hoping the guards remain at their post. I take the path and am a short distance along its bricked surface when I hear a scream. Its piercing sound rattles me. The whole world seems to gasp in one shocked inhalation. I turn back, looking up the path, which curls around out of sight. My feet don't want to move, but I give them little choice. I run, returning to the grass and across it, in the direction of the star-shaped girl. I look around, sprinting to where I left her. I'm out in the centre of the clearing, my eyes darting all around me. There's no one here. She's gone. I rush over to the right side of the park, looking around the perimeter. The girl is not here. I keep moving, looking into the shrubs on the edge of the grass. Then I see something ahead of me, about fifteen feet away. It looks like a bruise. A patch of colour on the ground. Moving closer I see that it's blood. Dark and almost purple. There's a concentration of it in one area and then it smears away. As if she has been dragged into the undergrowth.

A rustle makes my eyes turn to the near foliage. I sense there's something there. It's looking back at me and it's daring me to come after it. I take three steps toward it and hear a low growl. The suns are more prominent now, heating everything. The shadows are darker. I take another cautious step towards the edge of the park and another rustle emanates from the branches. I think I can see two eyes, wide and yellow, glowing. There could be white rows of teeth somewhere beneath. But the wall of leaves and branches is so visually complex, that my imagination could conjure anything from its dense and twisted patterns.

I take a deep breath, sobered by the knowledge that I have to investigate. I have to find the girl. I step to the edge of the clearing and start pushing back branches, moving off the grass and on to the dry, dirty garden bed. I look around, allowing my eyes to adjust to the shadows. I can see more blood, small streaks and dots, moving off to the right. I keep my hands in front of me, pushing away the stinging scratch of the plants.

The shrubs recede, allowing a small area where I can stand up. I'm at the trunk of one of the mammoth trees. I see a dark shape. Something is sitting on the other side of the tree's base. I think it's a person, maybe the girl, seated with legs pulled up to their chest. A low, huddled ball.

"Hello?" I ask, not sure what response I expect.

Keeping a small distance, I step around to get a better look at the shape. It's not a human. Not what I expected.

It's an acoustic guitar.

# CHAPTER TWENTY-ONE

I wake up in a tent. As most people at a music festival do. The suns have risen and the temperature has skyrocketed. I can hear music thumping through amplifiers, echoing in the distance. All around is the sound of revelers frolicking. Waking up, drinking and preparing for their day. I'm a long way from the backstage area.

The tent is a light yellow and I can see shadows walking past in each direction, their elongated shapes shifting back and forth. Laughing, chatting.

On either side of me is a naked girl. I recognise them both. One is a brunette named Annabelle, who is lying on her stomach. The other is a redheaded girl who I do remember meeting, but I can't recall her name. She's lying on her back, with a thick crimson sleeping bag protecting her modesty from the waist down. Two large, exposed and firm breasts rise and fall in peaceful slumber. I gently lift up the sleeping bag and take a look downstairs. Nothing out of the ordinary. The girl doesn't stir.

I'm lying naked under a thin sheet. There's a bunched sleeping bag at my feet, which I must have kicked off in my sleep. I perch on my elbows and notice my jeans, t-shirt and slip-on shoes are just inside the tent's zipped exit.

I could walk very briskly back to our cabin and hope everyone is too involved in their mornings to notice me. Kids will be busy figuring out ways to sneak their drugs and alcohol into the festival. They've probably got their timetables out, circling which acts they "just have to see".

When it comes to sneaking drugs into a music festival, females are born with a distinct advantage. A front pouch. In fact, it would be near impossible to design a more suitable compartment for the specific purpose of drug smuggling. However, if a girl offers to smuggle drugs into a festival for you, using her custom-built orifice, don't hand her too large a quantity. She's likely to be offended. A few pills are fine, but don't ask her to sneak in a can of rum and cola. That pushes the friendship.

I lie down for a few minutes, plotting my escape. I could call someone. Maybe Amelia. She couldn't arrange for our van to pick me up, as the tents are too close together, but maybe one of the festival's small buggies could collect me. They're similar to the golf carts on Earth. But that would draw a lot of attention. If I'm on foot and I keep my head down, I have a better chance of remaining inconspicuous.

I slip the sheet off and quietly reach for my jeans. As I move on the blow-up mattress below us, the two girls begin to stir. I can see that my artist lanyard is still in my jeans pocket. I had a memory of offering it to someone in exchange for a tab of lysergen, but it's possible I was dreaming.

The redhead opens her eyes and she notices me. She smiles and rolls on to her side, pulling up the sleeping bag to cover her modesty.

"Good morning," she says.

"Uh... hi," I reply, feeling a rush of eloquence.

"You look terrible," she smiles.

"That's very kind."

"You still look good though."

"Sorry," I reply, reaching for my jeans, "I'm too scattered to oblige contradictory opinions."

"You look like you've been up all night partying," says the redhead.

"Weird."

She smiles.

"I don't have much recollection of last night," I say.

"Really?"

"Yes," I say, looking through the contents of my pockets. Cigarettes. Lanyard. Cigarette lighter. A small, sealed plastic bag of pills. It looks like there's cane in there too. I can't find my wallet but I'm certain I chose not to bring it with me. And Norman is in my back pocket. Norman is in the building.

"So you don't remember anything from last night?" she asks.

"Very little. Did I have sex with you?"

"Sort of," she says.

"Oh," I reply. "That's never good."

"You were in a very hectic state of mind when we got you back to the tent."

"This tent?"

"Yes."

"How bad was I?"

"Well, you were very casual to begin with. Then you feigned interest for about five minutes. Then you passed out for a little bit. Then you came around and you were very amorous."

"And then?"

"Then you maintained an erection long enough for us to make you blow."

"Excellent," I say.

"For a long time it seemed like it wasn't going to happen."

"Oh... well, thank you for persevering."

"You were very... high."

"Do you have painkillers?" I ask.

"Yeah. Look in there," she replies, pointing to a handbag.

I sit up and rifle through it. With my back turned to my friendly new acquaintance, I quickly open her wallet to see her identification. Her name is Krystal. I then locate the painkillers. They're good ones too.

"Do you have any water?" I ask.

"Don't think so. I think there's some spirit left in a bottle somewhere."

I find a bottle of dark brown liquid, which is some random spirit without a label. I use the warm contents to wash down three painkillers. I then lay back to let them take effect.

"So you probably don't remember telling me and Annabelle that you'd take us backstage to hang out with you," says Krystal.

"Ha," I say. "Sweetheart, I've heard every trick in the book."

"So you don't believe me?"

"Not really."

Krystal reaches for a mobile phone. She scans through it and then plays a video. I shouldn't be too surprised to see that it's me.

273

I'm sitting in this tent with what appears to be a pink, lacey pair of women's underwear draped across my head. I'm holding a hand to my chest.

"I sincerely swear, with the power invested in me by this garment on my head, that I will take Krystal and Anna backstage tomorrow," I mumble. "Assuming that Krystal... and Anna... are the names of drugs."

From off camera a female hand slaps me on the chest and the two girls laugh. Annabelle then pulls the panties from my head with her teeth and pushes me downward. She appears to be half naked as she straddles me. The video stops.

"That could be anyone," I shrug.

"It looks like you," smiles Krystal.

"Hmm," I say, happy to be lying down. "I'll admit the footage is compelling. I suppose you two can venture with me."

"When do you have to leave?" she asks.

"No time soon," I say. Big Bang Theory is headlining the main stage tonight. Our set doesn't start for another eleven hours.

"Good," says Krystal.

She then leans down and kisses me. My friendly new acquaintance runs her hands across my bare chest and then slowly pulls away the sheet. Soon her fingertips are gently grazing my flaccid cock and it doesn't waste any time in responding to her touch. Krystal's sleeping bag is pushed off and she rolls half of her body on top of me, her thigh lying across my own.

Annabelle stirs and opens her eyes. When she sees Krystal draped across and stroking me, and pushing her tongue into my mouth, she smiles and says, "Are you two at it again?"

Krystal stops kissing me and laughs. "Well I couldn't wait for you to wake up," she says.

"Well I'm awake now," says Annabelle, sitting up.

"Get involved," I smile.

I call Amelia from Norman and she is relieved to hear my voice. I don't know where I am, but Krystal and Annabelle are able to explain our location to my manager. She sends a buggy and a few plain-clothed security guards. I quickly get dressed and precariously poke my head from the tent, looking around for the small vehicle. Festival goers are buzzing all around us, so I make sure the flap entrance of the tent is covering half my face.

Soon I hear the sound of tyres on a gravel path. When I peer out again I see the cart about fifty metres away. I give my new acquaintances Norman's number and promise that if they call me I will take them backstage. I am, after all, a man of my word.

I take a deep breath and step from the tent, almost jogging to the waiting buggy. Amelia is sitting on the back and she hurriedly hands me a pair of dark sunglasses and a wide-brimmed straw hat. It makes me look like a farmer with expensive taste in sunglasses.

"Is this really necessary?" I say, pointing at the hat as Amelia and I move to the middle seats of the buggy. Two security guards take the back seat. There are two more in the front, one of which is driving.

"It's a hat that no one would expect you to wear," she says, sternly.

"Did you kill a greenskeeper?" I ask.

"Just be quiet and keep your head down," she hisses.

Peering from under the brim, I can see people stopping to look at our cart as we roll through the campground. Punters know that artists are transported in these carts. At a festival they can draw the same attention as a limousine.

We roll through the festival site and up a path that leads to the large double gate entry of the backstage area. That is where the artists' dressing rooms, cabins and communal area are and where my band members stayed last night. We could have slept in a fancy hotel in one of the major cities and been flown out here in a helivehicle, but we like to get amongst it. Soak up the atmosphere like willing sponges. Absorb the vibrations. Share the pleasure of company. Allow the joyous nature of the event to permeate our essence. In other words, take drugs and shag groupies. Such activities fertilise the soul.

The main festival area is still quite empty. As the day heats up and smaller bands are playing on the various stages, punters remain near their tents and allow the juices to flow. So far my cart ride remains relatively unhindered. We pass a few food stalls selling breakfast wraps and coffee and the smells trigger a mild jolt in my recovering stomach.

As the backstage gate appears, it is partly obscured by a large mob. There's a white vehicle. Paramedics. There must be a hundred people gawking at something. Probably a poor sucker who got the recipe wrong.

"What the fuck is this?" scowls Amelia.

"A crowd?" I say from beneath my large hat.

"Not in the mood, Jack," she snaps.

"We're not going to be able to get through," says the driver.

Our cart rolls to a halt, adjacent to a row of clothing stalls. One of them appears to be selling crazy outfits. Hats, costumes and masks.

"Radio someone and tell them to move that medic truck. Now!" fires Amelia.

The driver attempts to respond, but stops himself. I speak for him.

"They're busy saving someone from death," I say. "Let's just chill here."

"Chill?" says Amelia. "If someone figures out who you are, you'll be the next one in that medic van."

"We could drive over to the VIP area and Jack could cut through there," suggests the security guard in the passenger seat.

"How far is that?" asks Amelia.

"Just over there," points the guard, directing his arm at a pavilion that rises behind a security fence about one hundred metres away. It's next to the main stage.

"I'm not walking through the fucking VIP area," I say. "I'd rather take my chances out here."

"What?" asks Amelia. "Why?"

"Why?" I ask. "You know what I think about the people in the VIP area."

"You only have to dart through there to the artist area. It'll take ten seconds."

"That's long enough for their scummy wannabe aura to pollute me," I reply.

"There'll be no one in there!" yells Amelia.

"There will," I say, shaking my head. "I don't want to wade through that scum."

"Those *scum* are the people that help release your albums. They are the music industry," says Amelia, with her snide tone.

"The music industry?" I gasp. "Really? Are you sure they're not the second cousins of the festival promoters? Brothers and sisters of someone that knows someone that works for one of the alcohol sponsors? I think you'll find they're the tarty girlfriends of the shitty little DJs that nobody came to see, yet feel the need to swagger about and dangle their lanyards. You know who sits in the VIP area all day? A bunch of cunts and their plus ones."

"You've clearly taken something," says Amelia, using her condescending maternal lilt. "I'm not going to argue with you, dear."

"If I walk through the VIP area right now, I can guarantee you that everyone I see will still be there ten hours later and won't leave to see a fucking band all day long. They're not here to enjoy music. They're here to vicariously bask in the light of talented songwriters. They offer nothing to anyone. If I walk through the VIP area, they'll tell all their friends back home that they saw Jack. 'Oh yeah, Jack was hanging out right next to me. He's much shorter in person.' They make me physically ill, and that's really saying something. Don't even get me started on the D-grade celebrities."

"I agree," says the driver, politely. "I worked on the VIP entry last night and I found them to be very rude."

"I'm sorry, did I ask you to offer an opinion?" barks Amelia at the guard.

"Kind of like *that*?" I ask the driver with a smile, nodding toward Amelia.

"Look," says Amelia, struggling to contain her frustration. "Jack, I'm not saying I disagree with you. But could you please fucking cooperate?"

"Fine," I say, with a sigh. "But first I'm going over to that costume stall. It looks interesting."

Amelia grabs my arm. "You're not leaving this cart."

"Then drive the cart to the stall," I shrug.

After I make a purchase, the guard turns the cart right and drives us across the expanse of grass in front of the main stage, which is basically empty, and towards the VIP tent. When we arrive at the entry gate, which is around a metre and a half wide, the two guards on the back of the cart jump off. So does Amelia.

"Lead on driver," I say through the mouth slit in my mask. The rubbery and ghoulish headwear looks like a demonic cat, black and orange. Whiskers protrude from its wide, grinning jaw and beneath its crazed eyes.

"Jack, you look ridiculous. Please get off the cart," sighs Amelia.

"Driver," I say, extending a straightened arm like a Roman general on the back of his chariot. "Roll forth."

"Uh," the driver says to me, "I can't take the cart any further."

"Why not?"

"Jack, please get off the cart. We're creating a scene," hisses Amelia, like a frustrated parent.

"Driver," I say again, now leaning in close to him. "Put your foot on that there pedal and roll me through the VIP tent."

"It should fit through the far exit," shrugs one of the security guards.

"Excuse me," snaps Amelia. "I didn't ask for your input."

"Driver!" I roar. "Let's get this puppy moving!"

Amelia shakes her head in defeat and follows us as the driver rolls the cart forward.

The VIP bar is nearly empty. It's only early. The area is a large pavilion with lounges in the corners, too many potted plants, faux green grass on the floor, a long bar at one end with the same over-priced drinks as everywhere else in the festival, a DJ booth against one wall and many stools and round, elevated drinking tables. A DJ with minimal talent plays minimal beats.

The great irony about this place is that every regular punter would love to sneak in here, but it's so boring. The fun is out there where the bands are playing. This tent is coveted by those that can't come in. Conceptually, it's as if entry here is confirmation that you're better than everyone else. Its exclusivity seduces. This tent is the great masquerade ball and everything outside is a servant's quarters. It is the illusion of class separation. It brings out the pathetic side of those that enter, as if the prism of personal insecurity catches the sun and exposes every foible.

The few people in here, backstage lanyards draped from their necks, turn to look at me. But they have no idea that it's Jack being wheeled by. I slump down in my seat, breathing through the tiny holes in the tiger's snout. I snarl inside and out.

# CHAPTER TWENTY-TWO

I decide to return to the newspaper's building. While the homeless shelters are warm and provide food, I don't feel comfortable taking the acoustic guitar there. I won't be keeping a low profile if I'm strumming and singing in front of everyone.

I feel a little conspicuous as I leave the park and cross the city, carrying the instrument by its neck. No guitar case but it's in good condition. A few preliminary notes suggest it's very out of tune.

It's still early in the morning. The roads are filling up, as are the sidewalks. Life emerges into the light of the two suns as they rise in their parallel arc through the sky. I try to take back-alleys and smaller roads, but I sometimes pass people, in their work attire, who look down at the guitar and then smile at me. I haven't experienced that here. I don't feel as invisible.

I arrive at the building of the *Easton Advocate* and walk up the side lane. I relocate the swipe card, which I've hidden in a crevice in the brickwork opposite the door, and let myself inside. I'm greeted by the building's familiar musty aroma. I walk quietly through the first office and into the hallway. I listen, but I can't hear anything. The building stands empty. I walk upstairs to the small kitchen that's off the side of the library. I carry a chair inside, close the door behind me and then sit with the acoustic on my lap and tune it.

I lay the guitar on its back and inspect it properly, running my fingers along the joins of the body, admiring the quality of the craftsmanship. Its beautiful sameness to a guitar from Earth is mesmerising. The neck, the tuning pegs, the shape of the body and its hollow interior, even the sound of the notes and its nylon strings. Its soft lacquered finish. It's a handmade piece of wonderment. How can this thing exist? How can it possibly have evolved on more than one planet? Perhaps this is infinity at work. Infinite guitars on infinite planets. Infinite music channelled by infinite songwriters. A guitar is an entity. A thread in the fabric of existence.

I turn the guitar back on to its side and arrange my fingers into a chord. The fingernails on my right hand have grown quite long, so I use my thumb as a plectrum. I play a song I've strummed to myself thousands of times and the arrangement instantly returns to me. I sing the opening lyrics of 'Old Man' to myself, enjoying the acoustics in the small kitchenette. I finish the song and then play 'Pink Bullets' by The Shins. I'm surprised when I realise I remember all the words. My voice and the guitar echo around the tiled walls and a chill ripples through my body. I then play 'Now That You're Gone' by Ryan Adams and 'Fake Plastic Trees' by Radiohead. Again, the music and the words, with little effort, reappear in the air around me. A pair of familiar arms. A telegram from home, read by a soldier in the cold slime of a trench. Just a candle, a spark in a window at night. A reminder of Earth. A reminder that it's still out there, spinning in space.

We're not often granted the opportunity to fully acknowledge the last time we ever see something. So often you look back on a moment and realise that it was the very last time your eyesight would see that person or place. That they would be gone from you forever. When I left Earth, I told everyone that I would return. Everything was planned down to the letter. I promised I'd be back. I guaranteed it to everyone. I was incredibly convincing. But I never told anyone that when I left Earth that day, I told myself I would never return. I spared myself the whimsy of false hope.

Here I sit, alone, stranded in an ocean of faceless strangers. Just bobbing on the tide and watching it all roll by. Familiar. Frustratingly similar. And the title of this planet. What they call it. Heaven. That's a sick joke. This could so easily be Hell. Maybe that's what Hell is? You live your life but you're alone and invisible. Everything is the same except there's no human contact. No acknowledgment.

I strum at the chords of Metallica's 'Mama Said' for a few

minutes and then stand up, placing the guitar on the seat. Deciding to digest some more of the texts in the library, I open the kitchenette door and turn to my right, crossing the room to the rows of book shelves.

The weak sunlight creeping into the room through the crusted windows catches a shape in the far corner of my left eye. I emit a small, strangled gasp as I spin around and look at the man. He jumps too. This surprise guest is wearing a one-piece orange work uniform. Like a workman's overalls. Long sleeves and arms. A small white facemask is hanging below his chin. He's very tan, has stubble on his chin and a ponytail. In his hand is a long, metal device that's hooked up to a tank of fluid hanging from his shoulders like a backpack.

"Hey, sorry to scare you," he says, raising his spare hand in apology. "Are you an ex-employee or something?"

"Uh, no, not quite. A friend of mine worked here."

"Oh, ok. Was that you playing in there?"

"Yes. I was just... playing with... some songs."

"Man, you are really good," smiles the stranger.

"Thank you."

"Do you just come here to practice or something?"

"Yes, sometimes. It's quiet."

"For sure. It's a nice old building. Still in good repair."

"I like it."

"So did you write those songs you were playing? I didn't recognise them."

I try to think on my feet. Only one answer seems possible to maintain. "Uh, yeah."

"That's really impressive. I play music a little bit. I've got a friend that was in a famous band. Have you heard of The Blissfully Unaware?"

"No... I'm sorry," I say, pretending to think.

"Their song is on the radio a lot."

"I'm sure I've probably heard of them."

The man approaches me. "I'm Roy."

"Nice to meet you. I'm... Jack."

Roy laughs. "Sounds like you almost forgot your own name."

"Almost. That's the key word."

Roy laughs again. "I'm sorry, I'd shake your hand, but my gloves have a fair bit of poison on them. Can't be too careful."

"Poison?"

"Yeah, they've got me going through these old buildings looking for arachnids. You've probably heard about the numbers they're finding in the city. It's on the news. People are alarmed, as you can imagine."

"I can imagine."

"They look for places to breed away from people, so they can get really big. Then they go out and hunt."

"Makes sense."

"You haven't seen any nests, have you? We've been finding a few around here."

"Nests? Uh, no. Not that I can think of. What do they look like?"

"Giant clusters of webs with little white balls in them. Eggs. The arachnid hides under the web, so you can't see it."

"I see. Well, no, I can't say I've seen anything like that in here. But I'm not here that often."

"You would know if you saw one," says Roy. "The webs can take up an entire room. Nests."

"Wow, well, yeah. I would probably have noticed that."

"Have you been in every room here?"

"No, not at all."

"I better keep looking then," says Roy. He lifts the metal rod in his hand in a salute.

"What does that thing do?"

"This?" he asks, keeping the rod in the air. "It's what we use to flush them out. It heats to two hundred degrees and jets a shot of poison, which turns into a vapour as it passes up the nozzle. If one of them comes at you, one shot can kill 'em instantly. The heat of the rod slices them up quick too, in case you miss them with the first spray. They're pretty fast."

"Seems like a pretty dangerous thing to do on your own."

"It's just safer," he shrugs. "More than one pest controller in a room together and you can hurt each other if things get crazy. Poison and metal rods flying around. It can get hectic."

"No doubt."

Roy smiles. "Listen, you really should talk to my friend. In the band. He's been looking for new people to write with."

"Well, I'm not very serious about it. I was just... you know... I don't take it seriously."

"You should! Those songs were really strong. Really grand," says

Roy, nodding. "Are you hanging around here for a while? I've got his number in my phone. When I finish up here I can give it to you. Or you could give me your number?"

"I'm... between phone numbers right now. I've been having problems with... my... phone," I say.

Roy huffs. "Tell me about it. My provider is constantly fucking me around."

"Well, I'll be here," I say.

"Great," says Roy. "Pleasure."

"Pleasure," I reply.

Roy turns and walks away. Our discussion prompts me to check something. I head back into the kitchenette and look under the sink, where I've hidden my pack. I find the small transmitter I brought with me. No signals received.

I sit next to one of the library's shelves and read a textbook on music. It seems aimed at teenagers, but is quite comprehensive. The rise and fall in popularity of certain genres is similar to Earth. But, interestingly, electronic music has been around a long time. Computing and sampling have been here for hundreds of years. Orchestras appear to have existed, but rarely perform anymore. There was also a strong prevalence of these parochial-looking gypsy-jazz groups. Acoustic guitars, violins, percussion and long, clarinet-like instruments called clarizzos.

My interest piques when I reach the chapter on public performance and the history of live music. One sentence reads, "Many songwriters now make their fortunes performing their own songs in cities, often in busy esplanades or public gardens." Their fortunes? How much money are people giving to buskers on this planet? I can't say I've seen any in my travels thus far, but I have been avoiding the major central business districts. I'm tired of foraging from garbage bins. Leftovers are great, but only if they're your own.

Thinking of leftovers makes me remember the album *Leftoverture* by Kansas. Which in turn makes me remember their song 'Dust In The Wind'. I put the music textbook back on the shelf and return to the kitchenette and close the door behind me. Sitting the guitar on my lap and plucking away, I find that I remember how to play 'Dust In The Wind' and after a few false starts, the lyrics also return.

I then attempt 'John Wayne Gacy Jr' by Sufjan Stevens and,

having listened to it hundreds of times over the years, I find that I can still play it. I remember the words, the song's haunting sparseness and ghostly chill marked indelibly on my memory.

I fiddle with the guitar for another ten minutes before I'm interrupted by a knock at the kitchenette door. I freeze for a second and then gently put the guitar down. I open the door. Roy is standing there, grinning. He's holding something in his left hand that looks like a long, limp tree branch. There's a putrid lime-yellow substance sprayed across the chest of his protective outfit.

"Look at this sucker," says Roy, holding up the long object.

"What is it?" I ask.

"A leg," he smiles.

The leg is at least a metre long. He can't be serious. "Seriously?"

"Yes!" says Roy. "I think you may have an infestation down in the basement. You're lucky you haven't bumped into one of these things while you've been in here."

"So that is a leg?" I ask again, pointing at the thick, furry spindle that Roy brandishes. "How big are these things, Roy?"

"They're... big," he shrugs. "You've probably only seen them in zoos, but they grow bigger in the wild."

"So that's... obviously a fully grown one then?" I ask.

"Well..." says Roy, inspecting the leg. "It could get bigger. It's definitely breeding age."

"Where's the rest of it?"

"In a custodian closet downstairs, on the bottom storey," says Roy. "He was in a close space. It jumped at me and sliced itself in half on my wand. Then I had to destroy all the eggs and fumigate the closet. Nasty little suckers."

"So is it safe to be in this building... at all?" I ask.

"Probably not," says Roy. "At least not until they're all killed."

So much for sleeping here tonight. "I suppose they can't sneak under doors can they?"

"No, not the big ones," chuckles Roy.

"Well, thank you for the warning."

"Pleasure," says Roy. "I heard some of that last song you were playing. You're very good."

"Thank you," I reply. "I'm thinking about performing some of them."

"Really? You should definitely speak with my friend Emerson. He's an excellent musician and loves to meet new players and writers. He would like what you do."

"Could you write his phone number down for me?"

"No problem," says Roy. Then, holding up the severed arm, adds, "Just let me put this down somewhere."

# CHAPTER TWENTY-THREE

Our plane landed about an hour ago, marking the end of the first major section of our world tour. I'm in the back of a black sedan that is taking me to my apartment. The world rolls by in its midday fashion. It's equal parts comforting and tedious to be back in Easton.

I attempt to phone Natalie on one of the numbers she has used to contact me in the past. I try four sets of digits and they all ring out. I realise I won't see her again until she wants to see me.

I tell the driver to take me via Zunge Bohne before he drops me off at my building. If Rose is working, I'd like to pay her a visit. We slow down as we reach the block, the adjacent stretch of beach unfolding beneath an overcast sky. My driver finds a park in front of the café's glass entry. I only have to cross the footpath without being noticed.

"I'll be five minutes," I say to the driver.

"Take as long as you like, sir."

"You're too kind," I reply.

"I get paid by the hour."

I put on my dark sunglasses and exit the car. Inside, the café isn't inundated with the usual number of lunchtime patrons. The slow trade suits me fine. I recognise a girl carrying a tray of coffees out to a table. She doesn't see me. Another staff member, facing away, is pouring things into a blender. I recognise the back of Rose's head. She turns and opens a milk container, adding a large quantity of the white liquid to the concoction she's making.

"Excuse me, do you make milkshakes here?" I ask across the counter.

Rose turns with a quick glance and doesn't recognise me. It's been four months since I was last in town. She might not be expecting me.

"We sure do," says Rose, sounding a little agitated.

"Are they any good?" I ask, leaning on the counter with my elbows.

Rose turns and looks at me. Surprise crosses her face. I've got a little more stubble than when she last saw me and my hair has been allowed to grow out again. I'm getting closer to my trademark dog-eared style. When she recognises me, Rose smiles. Beams, in fact.

"Hi stranger," she says.

"Hi gorgeous."

"Aren't you meant to be on tour?"

"I've got a week off. I'm home."

"Oh," she says. "Great."

"What time do you sign off?"

Rose checks her watch. "In about four hours."

"Do you have plans?"

"Just some study... but nothing I couldn't do later."

"You sure?"

"I'm sure."

"I'll pick you up in four hours."

"But I'll be all gross from work."

"I'm sure you won't be."

"I'll be too gross to go out somewhere..."

I hadn't considered this. But an idea comes to me. "Okay, then. Do you know where Racquel Chatterley's studio is?"

"Uh, you mean that expensive day spa?"

"It's a fashion and beauty studio. Racquel does the clothes and make-up for our promo shoots."

"Yeah, I think I know where it is."

"It's only ten minutes from here. Head there when you finish work and she'll look after you."

"In what sense?"

"She'll make you feel less gross."

Rose smiles. "If you say so."

"I'll pick you up from her spa in five hours."

I head back out to my vehicle and the driver takes me home.

I call Racquel from my balcony. She's out of town on a shoot, but she organises for one of her most trusted assistants to look after Rose when she arrives. I tell her to spare no expense.

I manage to sleep in bed for an hour and then I stretch out on the couch and doze for another. My body is battered and bruised from the excesses of touring. I feel disjointed. Adrift. I'm always a little tattered after being dragged around the globe.

I have a shower. I brush my teeth. I trim my facial hair so that it looks less like the materials a bird might use to build its nest. On the bathroom vanity I rack a few lines of cane. Something to clear the cobwebs.

In the living room, I dress in front of the television. A black pair of jeans and a shirt. On the current channel is a broadcast of a beauty pageant. Big production. A flushed, overwhelmed winner is being handed a crown and a sash. The stunning blonde girl steps to the microphone, clearly on the brink of tears. "Oh... wow...," she says. "I have so many people to thank. Firstly, I need to thank my amazing boyfriend for entering me..."

I hear a knock at the door. I walk over and look through the peephole. It's Laurie.

"Hey there," I smile, opening my apartment. "Fancy seeing you here."

Laurie looks relieved and lunges forward wrapping her arms around me. Her hair is up and she's wearing a casual yellow dress.

"I've missed you," she says into my chest.

"I've missed you too," I reply, realising it's the truth. Or possibly the cane. "Come inside."

When I close the door, Laurie kisses me, holding me against her.

"How did you know I was home?" I ask.

"I just got home from a friend's place and my mother said she heard your door shut a few hours ago. Then I checked your tour dates and saw that there was a week break."

"Well done," I say.

"Would you have come over to say hi?" she asks.

"Of course," I say. "You're my favourite neighbour." Laurie smiles, though she looks slightly incredulous. "Would you like some wine?" I offer. "I was thinking about opening a bottle."

"I shouldn't," says Laurie.

"You sure? It's not a school night is it? What day is this?"

"I just don't think I should," says Laurie. She looks flushed. "I'll have water though."

"Water, sure," I say and retrieve the urn of chilled water from the fridge and pour her a glassful. Then I open a bottle of white wine, pouring myself a large bulbous measure. "Hey, come over and watch this beauty pageant with me," I say. "The winner is speaking in double entendre."

Laurie and I sit on the couch. She looks at me and I look back. I notice she's not wearing a bra, which is a conniving move on her part. Her cherub face looks exceptionally cute. While she's a young woman, and definitely not a child, I can't help but feel a little like Humbert Humbert.

"Are you going out somewhere?" she asks. A simple question sprinkled with accusation.

"Yeah, I'm going out to dinner with a friend, but not for a few more hours yet."

"Girlfriend?"

"A lady friend, yes. A friend who is female."

"Okay. When will you take me out to dinner?"

"I don't know. Whenever. Tomorrow? I'm easy."

"Okay," smiles Laurie.

We sit and watch some television. I put my arm around Laurie's shoulders and she nestles into my side. She's very soft and smells nice. I wish I were her age. Perhaps through some anomaly in timespace I'm actually younger than her. Age is a state of time.

An advert appears on the television for a fast food chain with a new series of burgers that don't have buns. They're just patties. You can choose from an assortment of meats with which to sandwich layers of bacon, cheese and sauce.

"Wow, they are like, post-modern burgers. Post-burgers," I say.

"I don't know what that means," says Laurie.

"Oh, well, you know... what does it sound like I mean?"

"It sounds like you're trying to be clever."

"I try very hard."

"You write beautiful songs. You don't need anything else in life."

"Writing songs is clever, isn't it?"

"Yes. So stop trying so hard."

"Okay."

"What's your lady friend's name?"

"Why? What does it matter?"

"I might know her."

"I don't think you do."

"Is it the girl from the café?"

"What makes you ask that?"

"Because me and my friends go there sometimes too. I saw her leaving your apartment one night."

"Were you snooping around?"

"No, I was just getting ready to go out one night. I heard voices in the foyer and I looked out through our spyhole. I saw her and you outside your door."

"Are you jealous?"

"No," says Laurie, defiantly.

"You told me you were in love with me."

"I don't think I am."

"So you don't feel anything for me?"

"I think I'm just infatuated with you. I just desire you."

"But not love?"

"No."

I take a gulp from my wine glass. "Laurie, in your life people will try to tell you the difference between infatuation, lust and love. But there's no difference."

"What do you feel for me?"

"Lust," I smile.

"So you love me too?"

"Let's stop trying to label these things."

"I'd just like to know where I stand," says Laurie.

"I care about you," I say. "Isn't that enough?"

"Not for me."

"I'm only here for a week before I leave again. Let's just enjoy our time together."

Laurie forces a smile, but she's forlorn. I kiss her temple, lingering against her skin, smelling the edge of her hair. She turns her head and kisses my mouth. Then she begins moving on to me, pushing me down on to the sofa. Laurie straddles me as we continue to kiss. The straps of her cotton dress fall down over her shoulders and the material droops forward, exposing the softness of her chest. I run my hands up her thighs and under her dress, feeling the smooth skin of her hips. When I find her waist I realise she's not wearing underwear. Laurie desperately wants me to penetrate her. While that is a definite turn-on, I'm not sure. I'm uneasy. But, like in every situation such as this, I remember that I'm here to have an immersive experience. I can't say no.


My driver chauffeurs me back to the beach area, to the classy location of Racquel Chatterley's studio. I relax into the backseat, feeling tipsy and buzzing from the cane. I sniff my armpits to make sure I smell okay. The only scent is expensive cologne, which fills me with relief. But when I put a hand to my face to brush away a strand of hair, I realise that my fingers still smell like Laurie.

There's a lot of people outside Racquel's studio, so the driver heads inside to fetch Rose. I remain in the tinted safety of the shiny, robust black sedan. People in cutting edge fashion are milling around on the footpath, drinking sparkling wine. Inside, the studio is lit in blinding light, as if there's some sort of fashion parade. Maybe an art show. The front of the building is often used as an exhibition space.

When Rose emerges from the flock of loitering scenesters, following the driver, I'm taken aback by how stunning she looks. Like a supermodel. Her hair flows, radiant and blonde, occasionally revealing the two dangling diamonds hanging from her earlobes. She's wearing tasteful makeup and her eyelashes look exceptionally long. Her teeth are white, as always, and her lips are crimson, matching her equally red dress with its plunging V–shaped neckline. The driver opens the door for her and she slides into the backseat.

"Wow," I say, as she sits down. "You look... you look, like, mind-blowing. You look scary hot. I'm seriously intimidated right now."

Rose laughs, blushing. "Racquel's assistant, Marley, looked after me. She was really nice."

"I like her work. What's all that in there?" I say, pointing through the window.

"Oh, there was a fashion parade in the front room. Now there's a band playing. Someone called Gash?"

"Fruity," I say.

"To the restaurant, Jack?" asks the driver, from beneath his flat, black hat.

"Indeed," I say.

We are led to a table in a back area of the restaurant that is reserved for special patrons. Specifically, rich ones. The maître d' practically asks to see your shares portfolio before you're allowed to look at the menu. Luckily for me, I'm the biggest celebrity that's ever stepped foot inside this establishment.

I like this place because it reminds me of some restaurants I used to go to on Earth. The colours are rich and deep. Dark red walls, dim candlelight, and furniture that's heavy and the hue of mahogany. It feels almost medieval, which I sense is completely unintentional, as this planet's dark-ages seem to have been very different to those on Earth. No stone castles, draw bridges and kings that beheaded all their wives. This planet instead had a cold, monotone sterility. Patches of violence here and there, but nothing as bloodthirsty as my home species. Cultural vibrancy and debauchery seem to be a current movement on this planet. A revolution that's sweeping the globe. Perhaps the devil is among us.

We're seated and I order us a bottle from the wine menu. I look at Rose, whose eyes are scanning the room. She tucks some of her long blonde hair behind her left ear. Without looking, I know that diners in the restaurant are looking at us. Rose catches me smiling at her and she smiles back.

"People are looking at us," says Rose, quietly.

"Maybe they're just admiring you," I reply.

She raises her thin eyebrows. "Is this you being charming?"

"I'm doing my best," I say. "There's people watching, so I can't afford to get slapped."

The waiter brings our wine, filling our glasses and leaving the rest in an ice bucket that sits on a tripod next to our table.

"I *should* slap you," says Rose.

"Why?" I ask.

"For just taking off on your tour and not going to the police about what happened."

"Oh," I say. "Well, everything seemed to work itself out."

"The girls came back, but we both know that there was something else going on," says Rose in a low voice, despite the fact that no one can hear us above the cacophony of chatter and chinking. "They were going to kidnap me..."

"They didn't kidnap anyone," I smile. "It's unusual to kidnap a relatively large number of young women and then release them all again. None of them claimed to have been kidnapped or harmed in any way."

Rose is not impressed by my seemingly nonchalant attitude toward the situation. She deserves to be angry. I'm sure she'd go to the police herself if she didn't care about me. But if I don't want to risk blowing my cover, I need to bide my time and hope that everyone forgets about this bizarre situation.

I can admit to myself that there was a nefarious force at work. This group of people was painting me as a religious figure. That means they have questionable intentions. But the smiling faces of the reappeared girls are compelling. I have too much to lose by drawing any more attention to this conspiracy. Besides, I doubt many of this planet's inhabitants are capable of anything truly heinous. Heaven harbours a race of saints compared to what I'm accustomed to. It was probably all just a foolish game. Some hardcore fans whose admiration has transformed into something more powerful and binding, yet ultimately unthreatening.

"What if girls start disappearing again?" asks Rose.

"I don't know," I reply.

"You should have told the police everything."

"I agree."

"Aren't you angry that they were manipulating your fame to trick innocent people?"

I take a sip of my wine. "The thing is," I say, "when you become famous, especially as famous as me, you realise that you're not really in control. Gears are always in motion and they're out of sight. I'm just a name and I will always be someone's justification for doing something. I'm a flesh and blood person but my name and my brand... they become something that a thousand people have more control of than me."

"I'm *afraid*," says Rose. "Did that occur to you? It would be nice if you thought about someone other than yourself."

"Afraid of what?" I ask.

"Afraid that those people are going to contact me again. Afraid of being dragged into a white van by masked men."

"Oh," I say.

"I can't walk home from work when the suns have set. I'm looking over my shoulder whenever I'm alone. I haven't been sleeping well. I'm even afraid to check my mail in case there's a letter from them."

My stomach tightens with guilt. "I'm sorry," I say. "That should

293

have occurred to me. I should have realised you'd be anxious."

"You can shift the blame as much as you like and try to suggest that you're not in control. But you could be in a lot more control than you are at the moment."

"That's fair," I say.

"I'd like it if you looked into what happened," says Rose. "I would like some peace of mind."

I take a long gulp of my wine. "Alright," I say.

"Alright?" asks Rose.

"I'll look into it. Starting tomorrow I will find some answers."

"Do you promise?"

"Yes," I reply, "but only on one condition."

"And that is?"

"We have a relaxed, happy evening where you don't look over your shoulder. Just keep those eyes on me."

"Deal," smiles Rose. She glances around the room. "People are still staring," she says.

"They'll stare at us for the whole time we're here," I smile.

"Do you enjoy being the centre of attention?" she asks, lifting her glass and sipping its contents.

"Depends on the context," I reply. "I do have moments where I yearn for anonymity. But that doesn't pay the bills."

"You were anonymous for so much of your life. I imagine being one of the most famous faces on the planet must take some getting used to."

"Yeah," I say. "It does."

There is a small pause. I sense that Rose may be intending to ask about my history. My years of supposed homelessness. She wants to know my secrets. She's drawn to me. She's ready to worship me. I take another sip of my wine.

"I'm sorry," says Rose. "I know you don't like talking about your past..."

"No, that's okay," I say. "It's not that I don't like talking about it. There just isn't much to tell."

"I can't believe that's true," says Rose.

I just smile. Rose senses that I'm not about to open up about myself. I suddenly feel agitated, because I want to tell her everything. I would love for her to know that I'm not a rock musician. I'm really the youngest ever astronaut to go into space. Or at least I was.

"I'm sorry if this comment makes you feel uncomfortable," I say, "but you really are impossibly beautiful."

"Nice change of subject," says Rose, who suddenly looks embarrassed.

I drink more wine. "I'm used to changing the subject."

"Right," she says. "Well I'll change the subject again."

"Okay," I say.

"Why didn't you call me after our first time together?"

The familiar caress of guilt unfurls in my gut. "I honestly don't have a satisfactory reason."

Rose's eyes rest on the white tablecloth between us. "When I realised that you used me... I felt very empty."

Despite my verbal prowess, I'm suddenly lost for words. Rose picks up her wine glass and empties it with a gulp. She then takes the bottle and fills it again.

"Rose," I say, choosing my words carefully. "I am very sorry," is my verbose response.

She nods slightly, in possible acceptance. "I wanted to see you again because I thought maybe... we had something."

"I think we do," I reply. "You have to understand that... at the time I met you... I wasn't ready to like anyone besides myself. But now... lately..."

"You're trying to be better."

"Well, you thought I was the son of God. That's a lot to live up to."

"I thought..." she smiles. "I feel pretty stupid about that, but..."

"It made sense to you."

"It kind of did," says Rose. "There's just something about you... I can't explain it."

"You have a strong faith."

"Yes."

"So we're all going to Earth when we die?"

"Yes. Of course."

"Why are we here now, then?"

"This is our opportunity to prove ourselves worthy."

"So this is sort of... our testing phase."

"We're confined to mortal flesh until we're ready to move on to the next realm."

"Some of us are ready sooner than others?"

"Yes," smiles Rose.

"How long till I'm ready, do you think?"

Rose smiles. "I don't know, Jack. It's not my place to judge."

"Well, put on your God hat for a moment and make an assessment."

"Well," says Rose, delicately. "I think you could be less self-centered."

"Okay," I nod. "Note to self."

"I think you look out for yourself too much."

"Fair call."

"But at the same time, I trust my instincts... and I think that you're a good person."

"I'm trying to be," I reply.

"What do *you* believe in?"

"I'm very open-minded," I say. "I believe there's a lot going on in the universe and there's nothing I can do to control any aspect of it. I'm just drifting on the current."

"So you're not in control of anything?"

"No, not really. Nothing that in the grand scheme of things is of any significance. I just don't know enough."

"You must know something," she says. "We all know something of the world."

I ponder on this point. Indeed, I might have a greater insight into humanity than any other person from Earth. But what does that amount to? "Yeah, maybe," I say.

Rose studies me for a moment, then asks, "Is it true that your band has a phone number that you treat as a sex line?"

"Yes," I say.

"So you have a number that you give to girls after you sleep with them?"

I nod, safe in the knowledge that I didn't give Norman's number to Rose. I gave her my personal number that night we first met. It may have been a simple, drunken mistake. Which is fortunate.

"Is that the number you gave to me?" she asks.

"No," I say.

"Why not?"

"I don't know. Perhaps I wanted to see you again. My subconscious told me to treat you... differently."

Rose smiles. "You mean with respect?"

I nod. She seems satisfied with my response. "But enough about me, let's talk about you," I say, jokingly.

"Changing the subject again, are we?"

"Yes," I say, emphatically. "Although I completely deserve to be cross-examined like this, it really is excruciating. I'm sure we could find another way for you to torture me."

"I'm sure we could," replies Rose, with a twinkle in her eye, "and I'm sure I will."

Rose tells me about herself. She has had a conservative upbringing, which might explain some of the rebellious flourishes I've observed in her behaviour. She likes to dip her toe in the water. Very religious parents. Private, girls-only high school where she lived with her classmates on campus. That might explain a few things too. She graduated four years ago. She wants to be an artist and a gallery director. Dabbles in music, guitar and piano. Was in a number of TV commercials as a child and young teenager, but gave up modelling to focus on her studies. Rose has almost completed her course at university and is paying her way with the job waiting tables.

"I've had worse jobs," says Rose. "The people that work there are friendly and my boss treats me well."

"I'm sure he does," I say.

"I hope you're not implying anything."

"I'd never dream of it... so tell me about your art."

Rose grins, sipping more wine. "I'm not sure what to tell you. I paint and do some sculpting. I really like abstract stuff. Anything that feels very immediate or primal. I see art as an opportunity to lay our soul bare... to make it tangible."

"I see. So what would I learn about you from looking at your art?"

"Probably all kinds of things," replies Rose, with a hint of mischief. Then she asks, "Do you like art?"

"Yes," I say.

If we were on Earth, I could tell Rose about my love of the first impressionist, Camille Pissarro, or the heavy emotion of visiting a Van Gogh exhibition as a young boy and my mother explaining that he had cut off part of his own ear. As a teenager I remember gazing upon Rodin's *The Gates Of Hell*, and feeling as though they might open and swallow me into the inferno beyond.

"I don't know a lot about art," I say, "but it interests me."

Rose nods. "I suppose you spend a lot of time creating art of your own."

"Maybe," I say. "If you could call my music art."

"I think you definitely could," smiles Rose.

"Have you been to any good exhibitions lately?"

Rose shakes her head. "I miss every good exhibition. I'm either working or studying. Have you seen the price of gallery admission these days? It's nearly half of what I earn in a week. It's disgusting. We need our governments to own the galleries and make them public. There shouldn't be a price on culture."

"Absolutely," I say. "Isn't there a controversial exhibition on at the moment? I think I was sent an invitation to it."

"Yes," says Rose. "The Marioneta de Carne. I would love to see it, but I just don't know when I'll get the chance. Or how I would afford it."

"You wouldn't be disturbed by it? It's meant to be pretty... gruesome."

"I've never been disturbed by that kind of thing. I can't see the point. We're all flesh and blood. I think if those people died for their art, then it would be a travesty to not go," says Rose, solemnly.

Our entrees arrive. Small, meticulously balanced stacks. Not exactly comfort food. There's a point where the lines between food and sculpture are blurred. It's not something I've ever fully understood, on this planet or the last. Rose and I eat our first course, making casual chitchat.

Once finished, Rose politely excuses herself to go to the bathroom. While she's gone, I pull my mobile phone from my pocket and call Amelia. She seems busy with something, but I politely demand a favour from her. She reluctantly agrees to help.

Rose returns, my phone back in my pocket. Throughout the rest of our dinner, she asks about my music. My apparent songwriting ability. When did I start? I can truthfully tell her that I've learned and played music most of my life. Unfortunately I can't reveal that gave it up to focus on a double degree in engineering and science and notch up over two thousand hours in an F-35A Lightning II stealth multirole joint strike fighter. I also omit the time spent in anti gravity training.

We finish our dinner and I pay the obscenely expensive bill. Small change, I suppose, and certainly worth it to share Rose's company. We stand on the footpath outside the restaurant, photographers buzzing closely on either side of us. Rose is taken aback by the intensity of the paparazzi, but I hold her hand and smile reassuringly.

"Is it always like this?" she asks, quietly.

"Only when I'm in public."

Rose raises her eyebrows. "You think they'd have something better to do."

"It's how they make a living. I guess you have to be realistic about it. But the more I'm photographed, the less money they get."

"Fair enough," says Rose. "So what should we do now?"

"Well," I say, "I've actually got a surprise for you."

"Oh, is that right?" says Rose, suspiciously.

"I don't joke about these things." I walk over to a waiting luxury car and open the back door, motioning for Rose to enter. "You trust me?" I ask her.

The loitering photographers flash more photos of Rose and she hurriedly enters the vehicle. I join her in the backseat.

"We're going to the Walkley Gallery," I say.

The driver nods quietly. Rose is looking at me. "What are you up to?" she asks.

I allow a smug smile and don't reply.

"The gallery will be shut," says Rose. "It shuts at eight."

"I guess we'll have to open it," I say.

We arrive in front of the grand set of stairs that ascend to the Walkley Gallery. It's a mammoth, ancient building. Towering pillars and gargantuan expanses of intricate stone masonry. It plays host to numerous gala events, many of which I'm invited to but try to avoid, and keeps safe an extensive collection of art. The red carpet that normally pours down its entrance has been packed away. By the giant doors I can see two well dressed, after hours security guards.

The Walkley is currently holding a controversial exhibition that has been travelling around the world. From what I have been told, the Marioneta de Carne is a showcase of human sculptures. Made by humans from humans. An underground cult that existed thousands of years ago. A demonic group of bohemians who called themselves Niños de Macarbe, created artworks from body parts. The followers of the artists, who perceived artistic expression as the highest spiritual pursuit, would allow themselves to be killed and immortalised. Snuff sculpture.

I pay the driver and exit, stepping around the vehicle to open

Rose's door for her. We stand on the sidewalk, looking up at the gallery.

"It looks closed to me," says Rose.

"Does it?"

"Yes," she says. "So what am I missing?"

"Boundaries are a state of mind."

Rose looks at me as if I'm a naughty infant. "Some boundaries might be, but others are undeniable."

"Whatever you say."

I begin the climb up the stone steps and Rose follows. At the top we cross a large curved driveway to the main entrance where the two security guards stand. Rose remains at my side.

"Good evening, Jack," says one the guards.

"Gentlemen," I reply.

I give Rose a sly grin as the other guard pulls a swipe card from his pocket and opens one half of the main doors, which emits a deep creak.

"Enjoy your visit," he says.

"We shall," I say. "Thank you very much."

I take Rose's hand and lead her into the Walkley. We cross the foyer, our feet echoing on the polished marble floor. A map of the building indicates where we'll find the Marioneta de Carne exhibition.

"Ready to see some dead bodies?" I ask.

"As ready as I'll ever be," replies Rose.

Not all of the gallery's interior lighting has been turned on, just a series of sporadically spaced downlights in the roof that provide enough glow for us to find our way around. The long rooms, each full of dark shapes and shadows, give our surroundings a haunted atmosphere. Every so often a distant noise will break the otherwise deathly silence. Echoes that sound like doors closing or footsteps.

"It's a little creepy in here, isn't it," observes Rose, who presses against me as we walk. A distant creaking sound cuts through the long heavy rooms and builds to a shrill peak, as if emitted by an animal.

"It's a big, old building," I say, nonchalantly. "I'd be more worried if it didn't make noises."

We step through a high archway into a massive room, following the downlights that mark our path. Massive paintings hang on either side of us, draped in shadow. Our shoes continue a steady rhythm as we walk towards the entrance of the Marioneta de Carne.

A temporary wall blocks off one end of the room, its entrance guarded by a simple black curtain. A small sign reads, 'Warning! Some visitors may be disturbed by this exhibition, as it contains actual human remains in a series of confronting artworks. It is recommended that no one under sixteen years enters this exhibition.'

"You're older than sixteen, yeah?" I ask Rose.

"Would it make any difference to you?"

I just smile and draw back the curtain. "After you."

The full lighting system of the exhibition has been turned on. No foreboding shadows or opportunity to misconstrue what it is that's in front of us. The Marioneta de Carne is spread throughout a series of rooms, each artwork kept inside a glass case. As Rose and I step beyond the curtain, confronted by the macabre creations, we spare each other a glance. For all of our brazen excitement, we suddenly realise that this is, in fact, a room of mutilated dead bodies. Despite the exhibition's varying degrees of artistic merit, a mental adjustment is necessary.

"Wow," says Rose, before stepping forward to the first case. "This is intense."

"Yes."

I'm suddenly taken back to a high school biology excursion. We travelled to a major university to see their collection of human specimens. Severed feet with gangrene. Cancerous lungs. There was even the lower groin of a hermaphrodite. All sitting in glass boxes, floating in embalming chemicals. Mixtures of formaldehyde, methanol and ethanol. But the works of the Marioneta de Carne don't float in liquid. These artistic specimens don't float in anything. They are coated in a translucent resin or lacquer. Small, almost invisible rods hold them up so they can be viewed from below. The incredibly bright light bounces off the trapped sinews and ageless flesh. They're preserved from degradation.

The first case contains a male torso, void of limbs, genitals and head, which has been extensively tattooed. At first it looks like a congested mess of patterns and shapes, but closer inspection of the skin starts to reveal demonic images. Horned and winged creatures drag wide-eyed souls through flames and into the ground. Others depict demons tangled on top of women and men, seemingly in an act of rape. Another tattoo is a man with a beard and long hair, playing a sort of lute. There are rays of light emanating from his head. The lute looks like it might be made of bone and flesh.

"This is all very wholesome," I say, my nose near the surface of the glass.

Rose smiles at me from the other side of the case, as she circles the torso. "They're incubi and succubi. Some people believe that humans evolved from them. That we're their children."

"Really? I'd never heard that," I reply, aware that I haven't heard as many things on this planet as I should have by now.

"They were an underground cult," says Rose. "A bunch of insane people."

"They invented incubi and succubi then?"

Rose gives me a funny look. "No... they got the idea from those bones they found."

"Right," I reply. "I'm sorry, but you'll have to humour me... I don't really read the papers."

Rose gives me another funny look. "So you don't know about the human bones they found? I suppose you didn't go to school. It was hundreds of years ago."

"No, I haven't."

"Human bones with the remains of wings sprouting out of their backs. It's possibly the biggest archaeological anomaly ever. You've never heard of the Carver bones?"

I think back to what I read in the texts at the newspaper building. I can't recall reading about Carver bones. "You'll have to enlighten me."

"They were uncovered by a man named Dr. Carver. It made everyone wonder if we used to have wings," explains Rose.

"Do you think we did?" I ask.

Rose scrunches her face. "Not really. Seems a bit far-fetched. These supposed ancient creatures of the land," she says, gesturing to the torso, "were rapists. Demons."

"Right," I say. "So the theory was that people evolved from insatiable, self-obsessed monsters that lived only to feed and have sex..."

"Apparently," says Rose.

"How very far-fetched."

We move on to the next artwork. Two severed heads, skinned, facing each other, locked in a kiss. The absence of eyelids means their eyeballs stare directly into each other. One seems more masculine than the other head, suggesting that there is a male and a female.

"In some ways it's a beautiful metaphor," says Rose, who seems slightly revolted by the heads, but is determined not to let it get to her. "That feeling of being exposed. Naked."

I don't reply, instead moving on to the next case. Two full bodies, patches of their skin missing, with carvings and tattoos across the remaining epidermis, are arranged on top of each other, as if in an act of coitus. A man and woman, eyes closed, naked. Trapped together forever.

"How do they know for certain that these people all donated their bodies?" I ask.

"The cult had a lot of documentation. Written messages from the dead, giving their consent. Of course they were probably brain-washed," explains Rose.

"It's highly probable," I say.

"We all leave something behind, but very few of us can actually leave our mortal remains like this," adds Rose, bending down to inspect the two bodies. "It's like living forever."

"So you'd donate your body to art?"

Rose gives a short laugh. "No."

"Really? You sound like you're sold on the idea. This cult could have hired you as their publicist."

Rose raises a disapproving eyebrow. "I don't advocate any of this, but what's done is done. I'm fascinated by anything that might teach me more about myself... or other people. About humanity."

We venture into the next room, which becomes progressively more gruesome. Open chest cavities. Standing cadavers draped in viscera. Artistic, perhaps. Horrific, definitely. Rose becomes increasingly clingy, often taking my arm around hers, pulling herself against me as we move between the brightly lit glass cases.

We arrive at another black curtain, which is labeled the exit. To its right is the final case. Inside is the standing body of a man, arms outstretched. Except this body has had six extra arms sown to its side, as if it were a human spider. The man's lower jaw is missing and he stares blankly, straight ahead, from inside his thin translucent cocoon. His eyelids have been removed and his long-dead eyeballs bulge from their sockets. Rose doesn't linger on this final artwork and quickly pulls back the curtain and exits. As I go to follow her, I catch a subtle movement in the corner of my eye.

Looking up, I see the spider man's eyes roll in his head and fix on me. Staring. The rest of his body, including his eight arms, is rigid. Terror smothers me like a hot blanket and as I stare back, I cannot move. I'm frozen.

"Jack?" calls Rose, from beyond the curtain.

The sound of her voice startles the artwork and his eyes swing to their original position. As the sound of a whimper and a desperate, muffled cry creeps from one of the glass cases behind me, I dart through the curtain. I'm slightly addled and I know my mind is tricking me. Taking Rose's hand, I smile at her, regaining my composure, and we head in the direction of the gallery's entrance.

"Are you ok?" asks Rose, concerned.

"Yeah, sure," I say, wiping the sweat from my free hand on my jeans. "You okay?"

"I'm fine," she shrugs.

"Great," I say. "So what would you like to do now?"

"I don't know," she replies. "I don't suppose we can spend all night in the gallery?"

"I'm in no hurry to leave. I'll do whatever you want."

Rose smiles and leads me through an archway to our left, which opens into another giant room lined with paintings. Down the centre are sculptures, all more traditional than that of the Marioneta de Carne. Clay. Wood. Steel.

"So are you going to tell me how you got us after hours access to the Walkley Gallery?" asks Rose.

"I'd prefer not to," I reply. "I'm going for mystery here. Charm and mystery."

"Would it change your mind if I told you you're not charming or mysterious?"

"No."

We wander the gallery for another half an hour, moving at Rose's pace. Some of the rooms are better lit than others. She stops occasionally to inspect a painting, sometimes commenting. She'll lean against me for a moment and I'm able to smell her hair, then she'll move away just as quickly. A slow dance. A tease. Every so often I'll put my hand on the small of her back, feeling her slender body through the thin fabric of her dress. Then she'll spot another famous artwork and leave my touch. To and fro. Ebb and flow. A rhythm that can be frustrating, but so often has a predictable ending.

We leave the Walkley Gallery through the front doors and I thank the two security guards, who nod courteously. As Rose and I descend the wide, mammoth set of stairs she asks me, "So, what would you like to do now?"

"It's up to you," I smile. "If you're tired, I can call one of our drivers and drop you home."

Rose looks unsure. "I don't know if I'm ready to go home yet."

"Well, we could go out to a club or something? I haven't been to The Honey Pot in a few weeks. Or we could go to Echelon?" I offer. "I've been there recently, but I... don't remember much of it."

Rose gives me a knowing look. "I think a club would be too hectic right now. I just feel like... talking."

"Talking. Yeah, of course. That would be cool," I say. "Well, where would you like to talk?"

"We could just go back to your place," suggests Rose, with a smirk.

"You sure that's a good idea?"

"Is it a bad idea?"

"I don't think so."

We return to our waiting chauffeur. The vehicle makes its way to my apartment, the traffic thickening as we get to my block. I live in a club district. Fancy places. Very high-end. But you don't have to look very far for mischief, particularly if it's always over your shoulder. Rose and I sit in the back. I gently take her hand in mine and she gives me a warm smile. One of Big Bang Theory's songs comes over the car's radio. The sound of my voice fills the vehicle, and I pretend to sing along, miming, which makes Rose laugh. It's 'Here Comes Your Man' by The Pixies.

I pay the driver and we walk across the footpath to the entrance of my apartment building. A doorman lets us into the foyer and I pass him a small tip. Our feet echo across the broad, slick foyer as we arrive at the elevator.

Rose puts an arm around my waist as we wait. The elevator opens and a smartly dressed man steps out with two young women, dressed to go clubbing. It's a film actor by the name of Calvin Meloy, who has recently exploded with a string of successful releases. Science fiction, mostly. He's at least ten years younger than me. Square jaw, blonde locks, blue eyes. Moderate ability. He just moved into my building.

"Jack!" exclaims Calvin, giving me an enthusiastic hug. "What are you up to, man? You look fucking amazing. We're heading to Echelon. You should come with us."

"Love to, Cal, but I'm calling it a night. Got a mountain of stuff to get through tomorrow."

"Yeah, I'll bet!" he says, slapping me on the shoulder. "I've heard about the mountains of stuff you get through. We have to party soon. I'm putting a band together and I want to play you some tunes we've been kicking around."

"Sounds good," I say. "Enjoy your evening. Don't do anything I wouldn't do."

Calvin throws his hands in the air as he leads his ladies across the foyer. "Hell, that doesn't leave me many options! Take it easy, Jack."

"You too," I call out, raising an arm in farewell.

Rose and I enter the elevator.

"Was that...?" asks Rose.

"Yes," I say. "He lives in my building now."

"Seems nice."

"Yeah, he's a sweet kid. Enjoying the fruits of success," I say, with a hint of sarcasm.

"You wrote the book on enjoying success, Jack, so don't be mean about it."

"How did you know I was writing a book?"

Rose smiles. "I doubt Calvin Meloy can live up to your debauchery."

I scoff. "Don't believe everything you've heard about me."

We arrive at my floor and soon we're in my apartment's kitchen. I choose a bottle of white wine from the refrigerator.

"So all the stories about you are... a myth?" asks Rose, as I hand her a glass.

I just smile. "I'd rather not go into it."

"Oh c'mon, Jack. I'm giving you an opportunity to clear your name. You can confirm or deny all the things I've heard about you in the news."

"That sounds like one of the most fun games ever."

"It would give me a better idea of who I'm dealing with," says Rose, taking a sip of her wine.

"You know who you're dealing with," I say. "I'm the Messiah." I give her a sly grin.

"You won't let me live that down, will you," says Rose.

"Not soon," I say.

"Seriously though, I'd like to know more about you." She moves closer to me.

"You already know everything," I shrug. "You've shared my company. My bed. My conspiracy. You've seen who I am." I pick up my wine and with the other hand I lead Rose out to my balcony. We both sit at my glass-topped outdoor dining setting. "I've done things that would disgust you, Rose. Things I regret doing. Some I don't... but most I do. One of those things was messing around with you and... disrespecting you in the process. I'm trying to make a fresh start," I explain.

Rose just smiles, looking out across the city's flickering nightscape. "This really is an amazing view at night."

I'm flooded with a desire to kiss Rose. To lose control and ravish her again. I wonder if she feels the same. Is she wrestling with her own desires? She's giving very little away.

There's a pause, while we sit in silence, sipping our wine. Rose smiles at me for a moment, then looks out to the city again. I consider telling her that I saw the eyes of a human sculpture look at me. But I'm not sure she would find it impressive or amusing.

Finally Rose asks, "So how's your new recording coming along?"

"Good," I say, simply. "It's coming together."

"I look forward to hearing it," she says, putting her glass to her lips.

"Stay here," I say, heading into the apartment. I return with my acoustic guitar, which I sit on my lap, pulling my seat away from the dining setting.

Rose doesn't say anything, but sits intently.

"This is something I'm working on," I say, and start to play. I sing the slow-burning dreamscape chorus of the Ryan Adams song 'Wildflowers'. When I finish, I reach for my wine and drink the last mouthful.

"That was beautiful," smiles Rose. She takes a final drink from her glass and says, "I better get a refill."

"Me too." I place my guitar next to my chair and follow Rose to the kitchen. She leans back against the kitchen counter while I take the wine bottle from the fridge. Her empty glass stands next to her on the counter and I fill it, my face now close to hers. I sit the bottle down and raise a hand, tucking the hair that hangs over her face behind one of her ears.

Then I lean against Rose and she allows me to kiss her. The sensation is immediately familiar. It's as if our lips never parted. In that moment, my mind wanders back in time to a distant planet. The dust from a distant sun. There's a girl there who mourns me. Who perhaps still misses me. But she would allow me this small comfort.

I move my lips to Rose's neck and she gasps softly. A small release from the back of her throat. Her smell is so distinctly feminine. So human. My hands move to her waist, poised to slide lower. My heart races, writhing and pulling like a dog on a chain. A primal aggression stirs within. Rose puts her arms around my neck, holding me tightly. I lift up her skirt, running my fingers up her thighs until I find the edge of her underwear, which I swiftly pull down. Her panties fall to her ankles and she steps out of them.

Now Rose looks into my eyes, but she gazes with distant burning. A hazy desire. There's a fire in her pupils that humans get when they're drunk on adrenaline and hormones.

"I want you inside me again..." she whispers, which reminds me that she's also drunk on wine.

A faint but recognisable voice appears somewhere in the back of my brain. My morality. I tell myself that nothing matters and that the unequivocal finality of our existence means that everything is pointless. Any minute where a man is not eating or fucking is a minute wasted. Yet I still feel anxiety. Am I in too deep? Am I taking this fantasy too far?

I clasp Rose's hand and we return to the balcony. My guest is soft and beautiful and the thought of being inside her again fills me with overwhelming lust. Rose rests on the balcony's railing, the city stretching out behind her. A planetary backdrop of blinking lights and humming car noise. Flickering neon constellations. Rose pulls her skirt up above her waist. In the dim light I can make out the waxed smoothness between her legs. Just as I remember. It's a compelling invitation.

I push my mouth against hers and it's a long, deep kiss. Practically pornographic. I then fall to my knees and taste the wetness between her thighs. Her tight space unfolds against my tongue. I remember the smell and the taste of her sex. Rose moans loudly, as many girls would in this situation. The alcohol flowing through her veins hampers her volume control. I feel a deep, romantic connection with her.

My tongue settles into a cyclic rhythm and Rose braces herself against the railing. She lifts her left leg over my shoulder, using her calf to pull me closer. Her hands are now firmly on the back of my head. I slide my index finger into the slippery warmth of her vagina and a minute later she climaxes. The loudness of her orgasm nearly masks the creaks coming from the edges of the railing, specifically the industrial strength bolts that hold it in place.

Our passion is fractured as the right side of my balcony's railing breaks away from the pillar, swinging open like a rusted gate. Rose falls backwards, desperately reaching out for something to hold on to. The thirty-eight storey drop opens beneath her like a ready mouth. In a split second I have found Rose's left hand, while her right hand grabs the edge of the other pillar. She supports herself long enough for me to grab her dress where it is bunched at the waist. With all my strength I pull her back to the safety of the balcony.

We lie on the edge for a moment. I hold her tightly and she covers her face, which is taut with shock. She shakes like an injured kitten. Then, with a final snap, the remaining bolts that hold the swinging railing lose their grip and it plummets to the street below. I hurry Rose to the couch, where I have to leave her. I take the elevator and rush across the expansive foyer of my building. There's already a growing crowd out on the footpath. Pushing through the revolving door, I step outside and attempt to burrow my way through the tightly packed onlookers. My eyes dart frantically, trying to peer over shoulders and past heads. My stomach ties in a knot as I brace myself to find dead bodies. Twisted carnage. When I finally glimpse the damage, I breathe a sigh of relief. There's no blood. No crushed bone or severed limbs. Just a delivery van on the opposite side of the street that has been cut in half. I can't see any injured. It's a miracle. The railing stands upright, jutting out of the twisted metal. Bull's eye.

"There's no one in there," says a bystander, referring to the van.

People are taking footage of the wreckage on their mobile phones, intently staring at their small, glowing screens, blocking traffic.

"It's Jack from Big Bang Theory!" exclaims someone.

Suddenly twenty phones are pointed at me. A camera flash goes off. I shove people away and retreat inside.

Rose is standing in my kitchen, drinking a glass of wine. She looks ok, considering what has transpired. She empties her glass with a swig then pours another.

"Are you okay?"

She smiles, meekly. "I think so."

"I think I saved your life."

"Or nearly killed me. Depends how you look at it."

"Yeah," I say. "Different people, different points of view."

Rose has another mouthful of wine.

"Did you climax?"

"Not appropriate, Jack."

"Okay."

"So how many dead bodies were down there?" she asks.

"None."

Rose looks relieved. She drinks more wine. "I was sure we would have killed someone."

"Sorry to disappoint. Though someone's van is going to need a damn good panel beater."

"How the fuck did that happen?" she asks. "A balcony railing shouldn't just break like that."

"It's had a lot of people lean against it..." I say, then cease that sentence. "Don't worry, I'll definitely be taking this up with the body corporate."

I walk over to the kitchen phone and call Amelia. I explain the story of what happened, excluding the oral sex. There's silence as she takes in the details.

"So you haven't killed anyone?" she asks.

"Not as far as I'm aware."

"So the railing just broke as you leaned on it?"

"Yeah, something like that. Maybe I'm putting on weight."

"You don't really eat anything that isn't in pill form, Jack."

"Can you take care of this?"

"Sure, leave it with me."

"You're a gem. Have I ever told you that?"

"The police will definitely have to come into your apartment to inspect the balcony. Can you make sure there's nothing lying around?"

"The place will be spotless. I'll make myself scarce."

"Sounds like a plan."

"Reception can let them in. You can accompany them, yes?"

"Okay, Jack. How was the gallery exhibition?"

"Aphrodisiacal."

"Good," says Amelia, before she hangs up.

As I walk over to Rose, I step on something. I pick up the small, cotton shape and unfold it. "Forgetting something?" I ask.

Rose looks at her underwear and gives me a disapproving look. "Sorry, I'm not really thinking clearly at the moment."

"That's fine," I reply. I kneel down and allow her to step into the garment, and then gently pull them up her slender legs until they're back in place. I look up at Rose and she seems slightly embarrassed. Her cheeks blush slightly. I stand and kiss her.

"Thank you," she says.

"It was the gentlemanly thing to do."

Rose keeps drinking wine in the kitchen as I dart about my apartment, putting clothes, drugs and money into a suitcase. I run a hand through my hair, trying to think of all the different places I hide my substances. Books. CD cases. Guitar cases. Guitars. The freezer. Flour pots. Surely they won't search the place.

Satisfied that I've collected everything I need, I put my suitcase by the front door. "Let's get out of here. I'll call the Pluie Tordue. They always make the penthouse available for me. They love me."

"That would be amazing... but I think I'd rather stay at my place tonight."

"Really?" I ask. "Have you ever stayed at the Pluie Tordue? It's, like, fucking expensive."

"No, I haven't. And I know it's amazing, but..."

"It's okay," I say. "I can drop you home. It's no problem."

"You can stay too."

"Really? Can I sleep in your bed, or am I relegated to the sofa?"

"I suppose you could sleep in my bed."

"Madam, you have yourself a deal."

We take the elevator straight down to the car park. I don't normally drive, but I do own a car and managed to acquire a licence. This was all despite not having any documentation that proves me a resident of this planet. It's funny what money can buy you.

"That's my car," I say, pointing at the sleek, two-door black convertible ahead of us.

"Wow, that's... an expensive looking car. I didn't even know you drove."

"I didn't think a car would impress you, so I never brought it up."

We drive out of my building and light rain begins to fall. Outside, the crowd of onlookers has grown exponentially. A writhing mass of police, fire engines, news crews and photographers. Somewhere in the middle will be a very angry deliveryman.

I think about the railing. How it broke away so easily. Years of hectic parties must have weakened its rivets. Party guests shaking it and shoving against it. Maybe the previous owners damaged it. I'm probably not the first person to have sex against it. It's been a common occurrence. The railing probably decided to jump. But the idea that it was tampered with plays on my mind. It's a theory I'd be stupid to ignore.

Rose directs me as we drive out of the city's central business district. The buildings get shorter and the roads more narrow. Soon we're driving through small suburbs, where trees erupt from the footpaths, houses squash into terraces and house pets wander aimlessly. It's all so familiar, like the shady streets of my childhood.

We turn up a small road and Rose points out the townhouse that she rents with two friends. We cross the footpath and Rose opens the small iron gate into their tiny front courtyard.

"Nice place," I say, with a hint of unintentional sarcasm.

"I like it," says Rose, defiantly. "My housemates are probably home, so be nice."

"No problem. I'll try not to get star struck."

Rose steps through the door first. I stand tentatively behind her, holding my suitcase. The lights of the living room are dimmed and the glow of the television casts a bright, flickered light.

One of her housemates speaks. "Oh my god, Rose! You have to watch the news. It's all over the television. Jack tried to kill himself."

"Really?" she asks.

I remain hidden from view as her other housemate chimes in. "They haven't even found his body yet."

"What are you talking about?" asks Rose.

"A railing fell off one of the apartment buildings in town and on the news it's saying that it's from Jack's apartment," says the first housemate.

Rose walks inside and I follow. Her two friends sit on adjacent couches and they stare at me, jaws wide open.

"It's true," I say. "But I survived the fall."

Rose rolls her eyes. "Girls, this is Jack. You've met him before. Backstage. Remember?" Neither of the girls seems able to reply. They just stare. Catatonic. Perhaps Rose doesn't tell them that I visit where she works. Or that she was meeting me for dinner. "Anyway," continues Rose. "Jack's having some renovations done at his apartment, so he's going to crash here."

"Rose has very kindly let me sleep on her floor tonight," I say.

"Oh... cool," says one of the housemates.

"I don't want you telling a single person about this," says Rose to them. "No comments on Banta, okay?"

They nod slowly, still in shock. Rose gives me an embarrassed glance and then takes my hand, leading me across the room and up a narrow flight of stairs. At the top, we take a sharp left and arrive at a closed door.

"This is my bedroom," says Rose.

"I see."

"It's really messy."

"Right. Well, perhaps you should leave the lights off then."

"Might be for the best."

I kiss Rose, dropping my suitcase next to our feet. She holds me with one arm. Her other hand finds the door handle and opens it. We stumble into the darkness of her bedroom and soon she's pulling me on to her bed. I feel her push a pile of clothing off the mattress and on to the floor. Her sheets are soft and smell like her.

As I slowly move in and out of Rose, it occurs to me that I haven't truly made love to anyone since landing here. Jemima and I had some intense nights together, but the fact that she was married seemed to cast a grim shadow over everything. When you sign up for a situation like that, you're agreeing to all the painful consequences that are typed in the fine print. But now, with Rose's young, naked body beneath me and her thin, waif-like limbs wrapped around my torso, I only feel freedom. Exciting freedom. Perhaps my life here can transcend its current farce and I can discover something of true value. My connection with Rose feels like it runs very deep. It's as if the cells of our bodies are scientifically drawn to each other. Light years of distance and countless hours of time have delivered me to this tiny, modest bedroom, beneath Rose's soft sheets.

Can I pull from the binds that tie me to Earth and completely surrender to this planet? That's down to me. But for all the desire I have for Rose, there is someone else behind my eyes when I close them. She's reclining and smiling seductively. Natalie. Had she answered my call when I arrived in Easton, I wouldn't be here with this special person. I would be surrendering to far more depraved inclinations. I would not be making love. I would not be perpetuating the lie that is Jack.

When we've finished with each other, Rose falls asleep, tucked into the curve of my body. I also enter a slumber, my dream delivering me into a crowded room. Possibly a club. Possibly an apartment. There's a faceless woman. Lean. Beguiling. Gorgeous. It's not Rose. I can't be with this woman, because I'm with Rose. But this woman is dancing and gazing at me. Looking into me, beneath my vulnerable exterior. She sees everything. Frozen, I do nothing as she approaches. Perhaps for a second I brace for impact. Then we're in a bedroom. The door's closed and I'm pushing her against it with my body. Pinning her with all of my strength. She is submitting, her mouth open in a blur of pleasure and pain. Despite my lust overflowing from my edges, displaced by this woman, I refuse to stop. This is wrong and that's why I'm doing it.

Sunlight glows through the gaps between Rose's curtains and the interior of her bedroom finally becomes apparent. She has a white dressing table with a mirror. Photos of her and her friends are tacked to its rim. Up on one of her walls is a small crucifix.

Rose is lying next to me on her back, asleep. She's still naked, the thin white sheet covering up to her waist. Her hair is up in a ponytail and one of her arms lies above her head and curls across her pillow. The other is by her side. I watch her small, firm breasts rise and fall in gentle, peaceful breaths. She's an exquisite creature.

I lie naked on the bed, arms folded across my chest, looking at the ceiling. In my head I sing 'A Spaceman Came Travelling', which is a song I loved as a child. An alien that lands on Earth and brings a message of peace and good will in the form of a song. Just a melody. I wonder whether I'm an agent of peace or an agent of chaos.

When Rose finally wakes I'm sitting by her open window, smoking a cigarette.

"Making yourself at home?" she asks, rubbing her eyes.

"Yeah," I smile. Then I point at the acoustic guitar that's sitting in the corner of her room. "Are you any good on that thing?"

"I'm not bad," she replies, pulling the sheet up over her exposed chest. "It was my brother's."

"He stopped playing?"

"Yeah," says Rose. "He died two years ago."

"Oh," I reply, pausing. "Do you think he'd mind if I played it?"

"He really loved your music. I think he would feel very honoured."

"What was his name?" I ask, picking up the guitar.

"His name was Richey."

I sit on the edge of the bed and position it on my lap, plucking the strings and adjusting the tuning pegs. It's a bit bent out of shape and has seen better days, so I immediately feel an affiliation with it. Rose sits up in bed, bringing her knees to her chest, the sheet still pulled over her.

"Did he have a favourite song?" I ask.

"Um," says Rose, thinking. "He liked all of them, but I'd have to say his favourite was 'Meadowlake Street'."

"Well, he had good taste," I say, before beginning the song for Rose, singing the opening verse. As I coo the first chorus and move on to the second verse, I notice a tear roll down Rose's cheek. She hurriedly wipes it away.

When I finish the song, Rose says, "That was beautiful."

"Thanks," I reply, with a smile.

"Richey would have loved to hear that. He'd be very jealous."

"Well, maybe somewhere Richey heard it?"

"Yes, definitely." Rose tries to smile, but I can tell that sadness has washed over her.

"Would you like to hear a new song?" I ask.

Rose nods.

I play the opening notes of a song that, somewhere in the past, I first heard while making love to the woman I was to marry. It's Wilco's 'Reservations'. As the final, yearning lyrics roll off my tongue, Rose motions for me to come to her. I put the guitar down and crawl across the mattress. She pulls me down on top of her. Pulling the sheet back, I explore her naked body in the sunlight and Rose occasionally puts the back of her hand in her mouth to stifle her moans. After another half an hour of slow, mutual stimulation, Rose puts on a gown and heads for the kitchen to make us some coffee. When she opens her bedroom, one of her housemates has left the morning's newspaper by the doorway. It's next to my suitcase. Rose picks it up. I can see a photo of her on the front page, standing next to me outside expensive restaurant.

# CHAPTER TWENTY-FOUR

They started calling people my grandfather's age "generation ink". He represents the era when extensive tattoos tipped into the mainstream. Now the old men and women sit together in the lounge room of my grandfather's nursing home, watching daytime television. They don't watch sport. Tattoos from their wrist to shoulders and across their chest, snake beneath their woolen cardigans and cotton shirts. Withered souls eternally painted in often incomprehensible scrawling. Faded colours.

But that's not to say that they regret getting inked. Far from it. It's a part of who they are. As real and as precious as the blank skin they were born with. Their tastes in music haven't mellowed either. They slowly approach the sound-system, leaning on their walking frame, and skip to songs by Pantera and Sepultura. Or Metallica, Slayer and Iron Maiden. My grandfather enjoyed punk and post-rock bands like Millencolin, Thursday, Coheed and Cambria or At The Drive-In.

They sit and play card games to the brutal onslaught of Parkway Drive, some of them wandering outside to smoke cigarettes as the sun sets. I imagine they all think back to their youths, to a time when the human acceleration of global warming was still a debate. To when gay marriage wasn't a reality. To an age when the Earth appeared to be retaliating. The tsunami in Japan, the earthquake in New Zealand, the earthquake in Haiti, the fires in Australia. Death was on the horizon, in every direction you looked.

I spent days with my grandfather in his nursing home when I was really young. My mother didn't like him playing me aggressive music, so we'd wait till she left. I found metal and rock music exhilarating. If my little old granddad liked it, then I couldn't understand why it was deemed offensive. He would play me music from the 1970s. Bands his granddad had played for him. Acts like Yes, Pavlov's Dog, Wishbone Ash, Led Zeppelin and Focus.

I discovered classical music on my own. If you follow the history of metal into the past, its roots are in the classical compositions. On Earth it's available on the internet, floating in the digitised realm for the niche audience that still engages with it. I find elements of classical music here on Heaven too. But it's used in films and commercials. It's uncommon for people to go and watch a live orchestra on its own. On this planet strings and brass are used as an accompaniment for rock music. I wonder if classical music will have its day again. When will it come back into vogue? Every genre seems to. When it does, Jack might compose a few tunes. They'll be called 'Moonlight Sonata', 'Für Elise' and 'Ride Of The Valkyries'.

I drive Rose back to Racquel's studio to return her outfit and the diamond jewellery. I offer to buy them for her, but Rose refuses. She says she'd never wear them.

It's early afternoon. Rose starts work soon. She's in the passenger seat in her uniform. She's wearing little make-up and her hair is up in a ponytail. We don't say much, but whenever I look over she is smiling at me. I'm deep in thought, thinking about the balcony. Rose could have died. We both could.

"Remember the night I stopped you from being picked up by The Disciplinary?"

"Yes," says Rose.

"There was a group of men you were serving just before you finished work."

"Um," says Rose. "I can't really remember."

"They were young, good-looking guys. All dressed rather equally. Boring, yet in a manner that a lot of women would find attractive."

"Oh, do you mean Michael and his friends?"

"Michael? Michael who?"

"Michael..." says Rose, thinking. "Mac something."

"McCarthy?"

"Yes, I think that's it."

"What's his occupation?"

"Something to do with money. Financial planning, maybe?"

"Accountancy?"

"Yeah, that sort of thing."

A piece of the puzzle falls into place, because I do know Michael McCarthy.

I pull up outside Zunge Bohne. I lean over to kiss her before she exits the vehicle and tell her that I'll see her again when I finish the final leg of our tour. Rose kisses me back and then gives me a little smile as she steps out and closes the door behind her.

I'm standing on a footpath in downtown Easton, right in the middle of the central business district. The rush of lunch trade has died down and most of the suits have scurried back into their buildings, returned to their cubic-metre nests, stationery and swivel chairs. The sky is overcast and I think it's going to rain.

Across the road is the Ballard & Co Building, which is one of the tallest skyscrapers in the city. Many businesses and companies operate out of its eighty storeys. But there's only one company that I'm interested in visiting and that's the one that Michael McCarthy works for. It's becoming apparent that in my desire to assimilate with the natives and to experience this culture as it unfolds, certain details have slipped past me. Crucial aspects of my little bubble are staring me in the face. Every answer is in arm's reach. Questionable acts have gone unnoticed due to widespread naivety and my ignorance. My general lack of interest. So I need to piece it together, see the greater picture and analyse what it means.

As I look up the street I can still see small groups of suits either walking in and out of the various designer clothes stores or having bombastic business brunches. Grinning, dealing and shaking hands as they stand to leave. Thin-rimmed glasses on both the males and females, most of them more for show than sight, notebooks under arms and laptops dangling in shoulder bags. These are all very beige coloured people. Their souls are beige. Their essence and energy are beige. I wonder what sort of music they listen to.

From behind my large, reflective sunglasses, and beneath my baseball-style cap, I watch them for a few moments longer. I scan the street around me, back and forth. Everyone is engrossed in their day. Many people appear to talk to themselves as they wander past me, but they're really speaking on mobile phones via small microphones on their collars. I'm invisible to them.

Stepping across the narrow, one-way street, I push through the revolving glass door of Ballard & Co and into the vast, sterile foyer. Coffee-coloured marble spreads below my feet and right up the walls of the grandiose entrance room. Set into one of the walls is a small touch-screen, which is a guide to the building, explaining which elevator will deliver you to the business or company you seek. On levels sixty through seventy is Mercer Lightburn. They're a financial firm. They look after the estates of all of Brannagh's Endurance artists, including my own. I believe they also look after Brannagh's personal finances.

A security person, some kind of foyer overseer, approaches me. I'm still wearing my sunglasses, which possibly makes me look a little suspicious. He's got very dark skin, almost as black as the suit he wears. Underneath he dons a white shirt and a black tie. There's the coil of an earpiece emerging from his lapels.

"Can I help you, sir?" he smiles, cordially.

I remove my glasses and recognition splashes his face. "Hi there," I smile. "I have an appointment with Michael McCarthy at Mercer Lightburn. He's expecting me."

"Yes, of course, Jack," he says, smiling and nodding. "Please follow me."

He escorts me over to an area with fourteen elevator doors. He presses the up button on one and says, "This will take you to the reception area of Mercer Lightburn."

"Thank you very much," I say.

"Have a wonderful afternoon," he says. Then adds, "I loved your last record. I play it all the time."

"Thank you, that's very kind," I smile, with a gracious nod.

The elevator door opens. He reaches in and pushes a button for me. Then he smiles and walks away.

The elevator moves quickly, shooting me sixty storeys into the sky. When the door parts, I step into a wide, plush room. It's a giant oval shape, the far side of the wall made of glass, partitioning a breath-taking view of the world outside. On another section of the wall are myriad video screens. The sound is turned down, but I can see scrolling stock market reports, wavering currencies and updates. Reporters sharing financial news. Broadcasts from all the countries of the globe. The carpet is thick and dark blue. Woven into its centre, in white cursive writing, are the words Mercer

Lightburn. There're lounges positioned around the room, some facing the screens. Over to my left is a kitchenette, a long bench with a coffee machine, sink and other appliances.

A smiling woman with blonde hair, professional make-up and a neat uniform walks up to me. She's the only person here.

"Can I help you, sir?"

"Could you point me in the direction of the reception desk?"

"This is the reception area... can I help you?"

"I'm here to see Michael McCarthy."

"Excellent. What time was your appointment?"

"I don't have an appointment."

"Oh, I see," says the woman, her face creasing in concern. "Mr. McCarthy is in meetings today. He's very busy."

"He can prioritise me," I smile.

"Sir, I'm not sure that's possible. I could inquire, I suppose. Who should I say is here to see him?"

"Tell him Jack is paying him a visit."

When I say my name, the woman realises who I am. Surprise spreads across her face, her manner changing. "Oh, Jack. Yes, of course. I'm sure he will want to see you. Thank you so much for stopping by."

"No need to thank me, I was in the area."

"Yes, excellent. Why don't I take you to his office and you can wait for him there. He'll be very happy to see you."

McCarthy's office is quite large. He has a broad wooden desk and a high backed leather chair. There's two flatscreen televisions mounted on the wood-paneled walls. Sleek and polished. There's some leather lounges in one corner and a coffee table. Thin, clean carpet that's a shade of maroon. It's all very masculine. Manly colours. A room where pastels quiver in fear before they are beaten for their lunch money.

"Can I bring you something to drink?" asks the blonde woman.

"A black coffee would be nice," I smile.

"Not a problem. I'll bring it for you now. Take a seat, if you like," she replies, motioning toward the lounges.

"Could you strengthen the coffee for me?"

"A strong coffee? Absolutely."

"Yes. Strong. But I'd like a dash of something else," I say, before quietly adding, "alcohol."

"Oh," says the woman. "Anything in particular?"

"Surprise me."

The woman smiles again and leaves. I take this opportunity to inspect the decor, examining some ornamental pieces. A vase on a hard, stone stand. Behind a glass case is a gridiron-shaped ball covered in signatures. I take a seat in McCarthy's desk chair. It's comfortable. Luxurious in the way a set of stainless steel steak knives might feel to a psychopath. It's beautiful and firm and smells nice, but in the wrong hands this chair could be used for evil.

Rising from the desk is a computer monitor, which is on a swivel arm. There's also a photograph in a gold frame. It's of Michael and an attractive young woman with strawberry blonde hair. Blue eyes and ringlets. She is familiar. Michael and the girl are hugging, very content. Perhaps they're on holiday. It looks like they're at a crowded outdoor party at night. She's got a tropical flower behind one ear, indicating a tropical location. I recognise this girl and a voice in the back of my mind tells me it's Martin Brannagh's daughter. I haven't crossed paths with her in a very long time.

Looking around McCarthy's office, nothing really jumps out at me. Not that I really know what I'm looking for. There's no clear indications of witchcraft or sorcery. No pentagrams or voodoo paraphernalia. But the aesthetic is a statement, that's for sure. When you walk into this office, you know you're dealing with a real go-getter. An achiever. A man that knows a lot of shit about a select range of topics.

The nice receptionist returns with my spiked coffee. She looks a little concerned when she sees I'm sitting at McCarthy's desk, but she hides it well behind another rehearsed smile.

"Here you are, Jack," smiles the woman and places the steaming cup and saucer on the coffee table over near the lounges. About twenty feet away. A little ploy to lure me from McCarthy's desk.

"Thank you," I say and rise from the impressive chair. As I step around the front of his desk I notice his nameplate says "*Michael McCarthy – Partner*". Before the woman leaves, I ask, "So Michael's pretty senior these days, yeah?"

"Well, yes. He's a partner. Mr McCarthy is on a fast rise."

"So he's pretty good at his job?"

"He brought in the Endurance contract. They're now the firm's second biggest client."

"Big money, huh," I say, sitting at a lounge alongside my coffee.

"Yes, the success of Big Bang Theory has really been incredible," says the woman. "You're very talented."

"Please," I say, feigning embarrassment, "you'll give me an ego."

"I mean it," she smiles. "I really love that song you put out a few years ago called 'Gimme Shelter'."

"Really? I'm glad you liked it."

"Oh," she gushes. "I love it. I also love 'Baba O'Reilly'."

"Both great songs," I smile, picking up my cup and blowing on the black liquid. I couldn't figure out the manic intro to 'Baba O'Reilly' in its exact original form, but I came up with something similar. It will have to do.

"Sorry, I'm pestering. Mr McCarthy shouldn't be much longer," she says, before darting from the office.

I take a sip of the coffee. There's a definite liqueur aftertaste. Something good. A minute passes and the door opens. Michael McCarthy steps into his office. He's carrying a briefcase and his suit jacket is draped over his arm.

"Jack! Hi, how are you?" he smiles, obviously aware I was here. He drops his suitcase and jacket on one of the lounges and shakes my hand enthusiastically.

"I'm well, Michael. How are you?"

"I'm good. Keeping busy. This is such a surprise."

"I realised I'd never paid a visit to the man who looks after my finances."

"You're a busy man, Jack. That's why we're here. So you don't have to worry about your financial security. You can focus on what's important." He sits at the lounge next to me, grinning like a dumb schoolboy. "It's so great that you're here. Do you need anything? I see Victoria's brought you a coffee."

"I'm fine with the coffee for now," I say.

"How have you been? I hope you weren't too distracted with all that nonsense in the media. About the missing girls. They love to make mountains out of weevil mounds, don't they?"

"Yeah, it was an old-fashioned media circus. That happens."

"I hope you've still been able to write."

"I'm taking a little breather. Assessing what I've done and where I see the band going. I don't want to rush out any songs I'm not happy with."

"Yes, of course. The symphonic record sold very well."

"I heard that."

"Loved the production and the arrangements. Excellent. Really excellent."

"Thank you," I reply. Then I ask, "So how did you get involved in Mercer Lightburn?"

"How did I get my job? Well, I went to university and became an actuary, actually."

"You're actually an actuary?"

"I'm an actual actuary."

"Now you've branched out? I see your title is 'partner'."

"Yes. I'm now a partner here. Working towards being a senior partner," he smiles.

"You're not a senior partner? Look at this office!" I say, gesturing to the room. "What do the senior partner's offices have? Ball ticklers? Glory holes?"

Michael smiles, a little awkwardly. "Their offices are very fine indeed. But enough about me, what can I help you with, Jack?"

"Well, I partly came in just to say hi. To catch up. I haven't seen you for a while. When was the last time?"

"Oh, um," says Michael, thinking. "We probably haven't partied since that night on Martin's yacht."

"Ah, that's right."

"That was quite a night. You saved the life of that poor girl."

"I don't remember too much. I was quite intoxicated. I must have been on auto-pilot."

Michael gives me an unreadable smile. It unsettles me. "No one could do what you did."

"Maybe."

Michael returns to his affable disposition. "It has definitely been too long. We should organise a night out soon. Things have just been very hectic here at work lately. I don't get many spare moments to put my feet up and kick back."

I smile and take a sip of my zealous coffee.

"So to what else do I owe the pleasure of this visit?" he asks.

"I just wanted to check on how my finances are," I say.

"They're incredibly strong," smiles Michael.

"Really?"

"Yes, the investments made on your behalf have all appreciated. I'd have to look up the exact figure for you, but I believe that across the board they've increased by forty percent."

"That's good."

"Your income stream is increasing exponentially."

"Excellent," I say, sipping my coffee again. Then I ask, "Do you know the café Zunge Bohne?"

"I believe so. It's the one opposite the beach?"

"Yes," I reply. "I'd like to buy it."

"Sure, no problem," replies Michael, nodding. "We can facilitate that for you."

"Excellent. I don't care what it costs."

"We'll get the best possible price," says Michael. "Will you be changing the management there?"

"No, I'd like to leave it as is. But once the business is purchased, I'd like to have it signed over to one of the waitresses there."

"Oh, really?"

"Yes, it will be a gift."

"Okay," says Michael. "Do you mind me asking which waitress?"

"Her name is Rose. If you've been there, you might know her."

"Rose. Yes, I think so. She's the tall blonde?"

"That's her."

"So you'll be signing the business over to her?"

"And the building."

"Sure," says Michael. "That's quite a gift."

"I suppose."

"Rose must be... special to you."

"She's a friend."

"I see. Well, we'll make an offer to the owner as soon as possible."

"What other properties do I own?"

"You own many. We've made a large number of investments on your behalf."

"What sort of properties?"

"Residential, commercial. Your estate owns all kinds."

"What sort of residential?"

"You own upwards of fifty residential properties," McCarthy says.

"Fifty? Wow. I don't have any information about them."

"I can supply you with a comprehensive portfolio," offers Michael.

"Could you give me a few examples of what I own?"

"Well," thinks Michael. "In your building, where you live, you own twenty-five apartments."

"Excuse me?"

"Twenty-five apartments. When the floor plans for the building went on display, we purchased every apartment for our various clients. You received twenty-five. You now live in the penthouse. That means there are another twenty-four of the apartments in your estate. They've all increased considerably in value."

I sip my coffee, taking in this new information. Then I ask, "Michael, how much am I worth?"

"In total?"

"Yes."

"I'd have to crunch some numbers, but you would be in the vicinity of five billion."

"Five billion dollars?"

"In the vicinity."

"That's... good."

"It increases by the day. Whenever a new album is released, there's a massive spike. Worldwide sales of *Pulling Strings* have topped seventy million dollars in revenue."

"That's a lot. Especially considering they're mostly songs we've released previously."

"Your fans seem to buy anything you put out. There's a high demand for your music. Mr Brannagh now charges radio and television stations a premium to use your tracks. Your songs cost a radio station more than any other act in the world, but they still pay for it."

"Marty sure is crafty."

"Your merchandise manufacturers can barely keep up with demand."

"So what else can I afford to buy?"

He smiles. "If you don't mind me asking, Jack," says Michael, delicately, "what has brought on this sudden interest in your finances?"

"Nothing in particular. Lately I've felt like being more involved. I've been a bystander for a long time."

"Well we're happy to facilitate anything you wish."

"I'm thinking about buying another car. What do you drive?"

"Me? I have a black Empyrean. It's the luxury model, with all-wheel drive."

"Nice," I smile. Then, after a brief pause, I ask, "What about other buildings? Could I buy the Easton Theatre?"

"The Easton? Yes, I'd say you definitely could. We'll investigate that."

"What about the Walkley Gallery?"

"The Walkley?"

"Yeah."

Michael pulls a face. "That will be tricky."

"Why?"

"Because Mr Brannagh owns the Walkley Gallery."

"I did not know that."

"Well," says Michael, "as you know, he is a purveyor of culture and artistic expression. Music and art are his passion. He now owns nearly eighty five per cent of the world's art galleries."

It's late afternoon, right on the close of business. All the suits are filing out of their buildings, congealing on public transport and dissolving into the streams of slow traffic out of the city. After I left my surprise meeting with McCarthy, I rode in a hire car out to the edge of town where all the used car dealerships nestle in low-rent, dirty areas. At the first place I went to I picked up a dark blue sedan with tinted windows. It's in very good condition. It has cream leather seats.

The short man I bought it from wasn't very pushy for a used car salesman. He had dark skin and wore a fairly garish red suit. He politely asked that I pose for a photo, with his dealership in the background, but I told him I could not. I don't want people to know my movements. I made up a story about a conflicting ambassador contract with a particular car manufacturer. He seemed disappointed, but as a sign of good will I paid twice his asking price. This brought a smile to his face.

I'm now parked up the street from the entrance of the Ballard & Co building. Spotting McCarthy leave work could be like finding a specific needle in a very large pile of needles. But I'm on a one-way street, so all the vehicles that flow up and out of the Ballard & Co underground carpark have to roll past me.

For ten minutes or so, I look back over my shoulder, watching the trickle of vehicles. They're moving slow enough for me to take a good look at each model and the driver. A big black Empyrean emerges from the carpark and creeps past me. Its design resembles a four-wheel-drive from Earth. McCarthy is behind the wheel. I let another car pass then pull out sharply, pushing my way into the queue of automobiles. The next car blasts its horn at me. I'm trying to keep a low profile, so I don't respond.

I follow McCarthy from the city, always leaving a few cars between us to avoid suspicion. If the intermediate cars turn off somewhere, I keep a safe distance. We drive out to the city's limits, which is unusual. I was sure he'd live in the city. He's not even heading out to the wealthy rural suburbs. The buildings have all but disappeared, replaced by thick forest on either side of the road, broken here and there by small paddocks, rest areas and clearings.

McCarthy takes a right turn. The car between us goes straight ahead. I slow down and then follow the Empyrean, wary that there's no car separating us. I've followed him a long way now and I begin to worry that he's noticed me.

I follow McCarthy for another ten minutes, winding up long, forest roads. Night settles in and I turn the headlights on. McCarthy has too. I can see his red brake lights glow in the distance, as he slows to negotiate the tight curves in the road. As I follow him around a sharp bend, we turn into a long stretch. Ahead of me, McCarthy slows down and turns left into an obscured driveway. I ease my speed and cruise past where he turned, pulling on to the shoulder of the road about one hundred metres on. I park the car and sit, alone in the moonless night. I can't see beyond the windscreen.

I sit in the driver's seat for a minute, thinking. I haven't been paying enough attention to the turns, so I don't have much idea where I am. There are no other cars passing by. Maybe there's nothing out here.

I open my door and step on to the road, locking the car behind me. Using the light on my mobile phone I head back, looking for where McCarthy turned off. I find a narrow, gravel drive that ploughs into the forest. I keep the light low to the ground, trying to be quiet on the small stones shifting beneath my feet. I hear insects and birds argue in shrill chirps beyond the glow of my phone. Something rustles in the ground cover. But a different noise chills me. Something that makes my flesh rise in goosebumps. Beyond the trees I can hear a sound piercing through the night, echoing into the same void that I'm trying to navigate with each precarious step. It's the sound of an electric guitar. It's unaccompanied, wailing on its own, as if calling me to it. I know the song. I thought I was the only one. The guitar is playing 'Like A Hurricane'.

After another fifty metres, I arrive at a giant set of gates. If I was honest with myself, this is where I expected to be. My phone illuminates the broad, grandiose entrance. Written in wrought, cursive metal is the word Godiva.

# CHAPTER TWENTY-FIVE

I'm underprepared. Through Godiva's gates I can just make out the lights of Brannagh's mansion. I hear voices in the distance. Jovial conversations. But they're too far away to be deciphered. The guitar continues to howl and I feel sick when I realise that it's me playing it.

I'm bolted to the ground. I need to make a decision to investigate further or turn back. The perimeter fence of Godiva is tall and effective. But there would surely be a way in. Or a way over. The unrelenting darkness does not make my plight any easier. I'm not sure if there's a chill in the air, but I'm shaking. Somewhere inside me is an alarm bell. I feel like a surfer that sees the dark shape in the water. The ripples of danger before the frenzy.

I find my way back to my car. I need to regroup. To rethink my strategy. I will try to sneak into Godiva's grounds. My curiosity is strong and it's now hard to ignore the theory that Brannagh knows something about the clandestine group that is exploiting me. Convincing girls to disappear.

Since landing on this planet, it's been my desire to observe as much as I can. I've had the predicament of a wildlife documentary director, standing by as the cheetah closes in on the baby gazelle. It's not my place to interfere. Nature must take its course. I'm not here to act as a moral compass. I'm just a man among the natives, learning their ways. But that plan hasn't really worked out. In a flash I lost control. I became a celebrity. The most loved figure in music. My blind wish to not take the wheel and steer has led me very far off course. The cold streets became stretch limousines. Homeless shelters transformed into satin sheets and supermodels.

I decide to hide my car somewhere. I'm sitting here on the side of the road, in plain view of any cars that cruise past. I'll find somewhere up the road where I can pull into the tree line. I turn the key in the ignition and the engine quietly clicks to life.

The headlights project into the night. My entire body lurches when I see Natalie standing in front of the car, staring, smiling. That mischievous expression. She's wearing a white dress. She walks around to the passenger door and taps on the glass. I disengage the central locking and she enters, sliding into the seat and closing the door behind her. I re-lock the vehicle.

"Hi, Jack," says Natalie.

"Natalie," I say, turning off the engine. I flick off the headlights and the night is again uninterrupted. Just the glow of the dashboard illuminates the car.

"What brings you out to this part of the world?" she asks.

"Probably the same thing as you."

"Really? What's that?"

"I decided to get away for a few days, so I'm heading for Godiva. I think I just missed the turn off."

Natalie is grinning and it unsettles me. "Michael said you paid him a visit today."

"Michael's my accountant."

"He's here at Godiva. It's a strange coincidence."

"Are there any normal coincidences?" I ask.

"There's actually a little party," says Natalie.

"At Godiva?"

"At Godiva."

"What an unusual coincidence."

"Do you want to accompany me?"

"I don't know. Do I?"

"I think you do."

I don't respond.

"Brannagh's throwing a get-together. A big dinner. He'll be very happy that you're here."

I unlock the car and step outside. I then open the rear door and sit behind the driver's seat. "Why don't you join me back here for a few minutes," I say, articulating it as a request.

331

Natalie looks back at me from the passenger seat. She's still smiling. "Sure, why not."

My passenger climbs into the backseat. She sits pressed against me, immediately forward with her body language. Eyes only for the jugular. Natalie moves her face close to mine, as if to kiss me. I turn to face her. With my right hand I take a fistful of her dress, grasping the material just below her bust. I then push her back into the seat, slowly asserting pressure on her diaphragm. I know I'm causing her pain when both of her hands grab my forearm, trying to move my arm away.

"Jack," she gasps, "you're going to be rough, are you?"

"I want to know things. I don't think you're going to tell me, because you like to tease. So I'm going to have to squeeze the answers from you."

Natalie releases her grip on my arm, instead putting her hands on my cheeks. "Keep hurting me," she says, softly. "You'll turn me on."

I release my fist from her abdomen. I could beat Natalie to death and she still wouldn't give up that coy smile.

"What am I going to do with you," I say.

"The mind boggles."

I slump into the seat. Natalie leans in and kisses me on the cheek. "Aww, c'mon Jack. Don't stop. I've been wanting to see more of your dark side."

"Why?"

"Personal interest."

"I don't think my dark side is well hidden."

"We're not just light and dark. We're millions of shades."

"So what shade are you now?"

Natalie rolls forward and throws a leg over me, straddling my lap. She pulls my face into hers and kisses me on the mouth. "I think I'm a dark shade of pink," she says. As Natalie kisses me again and our tongues joust back and forth, I admit to myself that interrogation is not my strong suit. Natalie takes my lower lip between her teeth, pulling on it before she lets me go.

Although I'm resigned to the fact that Natalie isn't going to tell me anything, I probe in a desperate tone. "Natalie, will you please tell me what the fuck is going on? Tell me what you know about Brannagh."

Natalie sighs. "Jack, we both have our secrets. Don't pretend that you're not keeping things from me."

"I don't know what you're talking about. I don't have secrets."

"DNA, porcines, bringing a girl back to life," lists Natalie. "You're a work of fiction."

I don't say anything. I just look away, defeated. Natalie runs her hands through my hair and lightly strokes my face. I can tell she feels a strong affection towards me, but we're at a stalemate. I also don't have any reason to trust her, especially if she's working for Brannagh.

"What if we trade information?" I ask.

"Ah," says Natalie, "now you're talking my language."

"I'll tell you something if you tell me something."

"That sounds nice," she says. "But first we should go to the dinner party."

"Why? Why can't we just talk now?"

"Because they're expecting me to bring you to the party. I can't leave you out here."

"How do they even know I'm here?"

"You were on the security cameras at the front gate."

"Oh."

"Now listen to me carefully," says Natalie. "Pay very close attention."

"Okay."

"When we're in Godiva, get involved, okay? Go along with everything and enjoy yourself. You can't act strangely in there. You've got to be a rock star. Be wild. That's what they want from you."

"I suppose I can do that."

"And this is very important. Believe whatever Brannagh tells you. No matter how crazy it might seem, agree with him and believe him."

"What could he possibly be wanting to tell me? If it's something to do with me being the fucking Messiah-"

Natalie puts a finger to my mouth to silence me. "Whatever he tells you," she reiterates, "convince him that you believe every word he says."

"Fine."

"When we leave here, we won't be able to talk in the car. So drive me straight to the Pluie Tordue and check us into the Emperor's Suite."

"Can't we go back to my place?" I ask.

"No, we can't talk at your place either."

"Alright, if you say so."

Natalie kisses me again. Then she says, "We'd better get to this dinner party. I hope you brought your appetite."

The car approaches Godiva's gates. Natalie tells me to wind down my window. Next to the entry is a small telecommunication box on a thin metal stand. A crackled voice emerges.

"Yes?" asks a man's voice.

Natalie leans across me and says, "It's Natalie. I have Jack with me."

There's no response, but soon the grand metal gates creak to life. They pierce the night with a deep moan. I lean my head out the window and listen. The electric guitar has stopped.

As I roll the car up the long paved driveway toward Godiva, dotted lights appear on each side of the path.

"Everyone will be very happy to see you," says Natalie. I sense her excitement.

"That's a nice dress," I say.

"Thank you," says Natalie, smoothing the material on her stomach. "Who did it belong to?"

"A girl I used to see."

"Was it Jemima's?"

"How did you know?"

"Good guess."

"How do you really know?"

"I heard you were fucking the wife of the singer from Known Associates."

The colossal, illuminated outline of Godiva emerges from the blanket of night, stretching in front of the car as the dark trees part. Around the circular driveway are guests' vehicles, all stately and expensive. Box designs. Large chunks of over-priced conservatism. To my left is McCarthy's Empyrean.

I pull up opposite the steps that lead to the main doors and two men in long black coats, probably valets, approach the car.

"Good evening," I say to one of them.

"Jack, welcome," he says. "We can park your vehicle for you, if you'd like to make your way inside."

The two valets open our doors and Natalie and I exit. I hand one of them the keys and he sits in the driver's seat and parks my sedan in a space at the end of the row.

"I heard someone playing an electric guitar earlier," I say to Natalie, as we ascend the steps. "Who was that?"

"They've been playing lots of electric music," says Natalie. "Which song are you talking about?"

I smile at her. "You just said 'they've'. Not 'we've'."

"That's an interesting observation."

I open one of the two front doors and then stand aside. "After you."

"Thank you, sir," says Natalie, taking my hand and leading me inside.

There is music playing and it builds around us as we walk through the grand foyer and living area. The song is 'The Wind Cries Mary'. It's my version, not Hendrix's. Over to the right is the white grand piano and beyond it the wide steps climbing to the top storey.

We walk through another living area and I still can't see anyone, but I can hear voices outside. Through an archway we move past the dining room, with its grand twenty-seat table. Two chefs in white uniforms are placing dishes in the table's centre. Their culinary creations are hidden beneath steel domes. There is a setting in front of every chair. The waiters smile as I pass. There is an array of aromas, all warm and inviting. Perhaps a roast dinner of some kind. Spices, herbs, seasoning and, above everything, cooking meat.

We continue toward the outside voices, which are laughing and whooping. Someone jumps in Godiva's pool and a cheer erupts.

"Let's join the fun," says Natalie. "Don't forget. You're the star attraction here. Everyone wants to bask in your glow."

As Natalie and I step into the alfresco area and across to the edge of the rear lawn, the eyes of many young, pretty things turn on me. Three reclining girls, naked from the waist up, are smoking and drinking at a nearby glass table.

"Jack!" they exclaim, almost in unison. They rise from their seats and circle me, each pulling me into a relieved embrace.

Their faces are familiar. They're three of the missing girls. I smile back, asking them how they are, feigning a casual demeanour. As I make friendly conversation, I watch Natalie walk across the perfect green grass, under the white outdoor lights towards the pool.

Michael McCarthy and a few other men are standing by the water in their business suits, chatting and holding beers. Natalie greets them, kissing each politely on the cheek. Martin Brannagh looks relaxed in his deckchair, drinking a spirit as the rest of the girls splash in the crystal blue, shimmering water or sit on its edge, their hair hanging wet down their backs, talking and laughing with each other.

Brannagh sees me, smiles and waves me over.

"You'll have to excuse me, ladies," I say. "I'm being summoned."

"Come back and talk to us," says one of the girls, who I think is called Marcy.

"I promise I will," I smile.

I cross the yard and Brannagh stands, opening his arms. He hugs me. "Jack, you made it."

"I'm sorry to intrude," I say. "I didn't realise there was a gathering."

"Don't be ridiculous! You were invited. You're always invited."

"Yes, but I... didn't get a specific invitation," I smile. "So I feel a little awkward."

Brannagh's expression turns serious. "Jack, I knew you would come. You heard the music and you arrived."

"I heard a guitar before..." I say.

"We've been playing music," repeats Brannagh, smiling again. Then he gestures at the people around us. "Look at all these delightful creatures I've kidnapped."

"I can see that," I smile. "Do their parents know where they are?"

"Oh, I certainly hope not," he replies, with a wicked grin.

"So, the missing girls..." I say. "They're friends of yours?"

"No," replies Brannagh. "They're friends of yours."

"And they're all here?"

"Almost. There's some that couldn't be with us. Stephanie isn't here. She's having some work done."

"I see," I reply, looking around. I notice Britney standing in the shallow end of the pool, wearing only a pair of white bikini bottoms. She raises her hand from the water and waves at me, smiling.

"Everyone seems very happy that you're here," says Brannagh. "We'll be having dinner soon. You'll be staying?"

"Yes."

Michael catches my eye and gives me a small wave. His grin is friendly but there is an alert flicker in his eyes. He will have told Brannagh I visited him and asked questions about my finances. While the visit alone might not have aroused suspicion, simply because my behaviour is erratic, my arrival at Godiva is more than a coincidence. Brannagh and Michael, who are clearly up to mischief, will have suspicions.

Brannagh sits me at the opposite end of the table from him. We have a clear view of each other down the line of colourful platters and bowls of decadent and exotic cuisine. The girls remain in their state of undress. No modesty above the waist. Those that entered the pool have a towel wrapped around their hips. Nudity at the dinner table might violate certain hygiene guidelines, but I let it slide.

Michael and his friends have removed their jackets, but remain in their business shirts and ties. Their modesty seems a great imbalance. I also observe that Brannagh's daughter, who I believe is McCarthy's fiancé, is not here. I don't know her at all. Perhaps she avoids these get-togethers. Or isn't invited.

Natalie sits to my right, her hand occasionally reaching for my leg under the table. Nothing particularly suggestive. Just a warm and encouraging squeeze, as if Brannagh is some potential boss or client that I need to impress. Natalie has remained in her dress, which is unlike her.

I cut small pieces off the thick slice of roast meat on my plate. It's good, cooked rare and melts in the mouth, but I'm not hungry. Everyone at the table chatters to one another, either ignoring me or too nervous to engage the great Jack in conversation. The girls occasionally glance in my direction, but when I look back their eyes dart away as if they're shy. Perhaps intimidated.

I empty the remaining liquid in my wine glass with a quick gulp. Despite his distance, Brannagh notices my vacant glass and immediately gets the attention of one of the waiters. They stand against the wall, hands crossed in front of them, wearing crisp black and white uniforms.

"Could we please bring Jack some more wine," says Brannagh, with a wave of his hand.

One of the genial waiters nods and takes a red wine bottle from a small stand to his right. He then fills my glass with the deep red beverage.

"I'll have some more too," smiles Natalie, motioning towards her near-empty glass. The waiter abides.

"Jack, how is your writing coming along?" asks Brannagh, his voice booming across all other conversations. "I'm sure everyone here is dying to know more about what you'll be working on next."

All talk stops and every eye redirects at me.

"The next record is coming along well," I smile, leaning back in my muscular, high-backed seat. "I'm working on a ballad called 'No Woman, No Cry', which I'm happy with."

"No woman... no cry?" asks one of the girls, who I'm fairly certain is called Jessica.

"I know, it sounds strange. But, phonetically, it works very well in the context of the song."

Everyone stares at me blankly, as if I've admitted a penchant for torturing small animals.

But Brannagh's weathered face grins and says, "Well, I'm very intrigued. Nobody here would dare question your judgment on songwriting."

"I'm not opposed to criticism," I smile.

"No, of course," replies Brannagh. "Any other songs in the works? Something we might be hearing on the radio soon?"

"I'm working on another big, rolling ballad called 'Wish You Were Here', which I'm very happy with so far."

"Fine news," smiles Brannagh. "And you've nearly finished your tour. Have your fans been taking good care of you?"

"Excellent care, as always," I say, and sip some of my wine. As the curve of the glass distorts my vision, I notice a black shape near the roof, up to the right, in the corner where the ornate ceiling meets the wall. It's over Brannagh's shoulder and he can't see it.

When I put the glass down I stare at the shape. It's a spider, the size of my fist. That's large by Earth standards. By Heaven's standards it's a baby.

Brannagh notices my stare and follows my line of sight. He jolts from his grand chair and is against the opposite wall in half a second. He turns white as a sheet, pressed against the edge of the room, moving slowly towards the arch of the living room behind me. The rest of the dinner party notices the arachnid and their reaction is of equal horror. They leap from their chairs as if the room is ablaze. They too move past me and into the adjoining living room.

I'm now alone at the table, but I remain in my seat. I recline into the soft upholstery of the tall backrest, bemused by everyone's reaction. I chew my mouthful of food and then unfold my white, linen tablecloth and casually dab the corners of my mouth. I then stand up, slowly pushing my seat away.

When I glance back at the dinner guests, all huddled in the next room, staring nervously at the creature, I notice that Natalie is watching me. I turn back to the arachnid. It has remained in a crouched position in the high corner of the room.

As I carefully walk in its direction, I recall that on Earth tarantulas cannot climb walls or jump. While this spider is tarantula-like in appearance, I know that it can indeed scale walls swiftly and is smart enough to capture prey of any intellect. They would love to be able to study this specimen on my home planet. It could unlock secrets to evolution that will otherwise remain in the dark.

"Stay away from it, Jack!" squeals one of the terrified girls. I think her name is Jessica.

"It's fine, everyone. Remain calm," I call over my shoulder, as I walk and stand beneath it. The spider doesn't move.

"Jack!" yells Brannagh. "That thing is deadly."

"Marty," I reply. "Don't be a coconut."

I stare up at the arachnid. "Friend," I say to it, "while I enjoy your company, you will need to leave. It's nothing personal."

The spider is still. There is silence in the room now, my crowd of onlookers taught with fear and amazement.

"Friend," I say again, stepping over to the door that opens onto the outdoor area, "you will have to leave."

Then, as if it understands, the spider slowly uncoils and takes a step towards the floor. I hear the guests gasp. I remain perfectly still, my arm still locked in its gesture to vacate. The arachnid, like a dejected teenager, traipses down the wall until it reaches the floor. Then, in complete obedience, it walks past me and out into the paved entertaining area. I watch as it steps to the grass and then makes its way across the back lawn, its eight legs shifting up and down with fluid majesty.

"Close the door," says Brannagh, peeling away from the crowd in the living room. The colour of his tanned face returns as I slide the glass door into place and lock it. He steps to my chair on the other side of the table, resting on it and staring at me. "That was quite a party trick," he adds.

I just shrug. "They're more frightened of us then we are of them."

"Trash," says Brannagh, chuckling. "They're hunters and killers. I've lost family members to the poison of those creatures. Even the little ones will happily chase you down."

"Perhaps that one was house-broken," I smile.

I see Natalie continue to study me over Brannagh's shoulder. Brannagh picks up my half-full wine glass and walks around the table to offer it to me. He is close now. "There's more to you than meets the eye," he says.

"Depends who's looking."

Later, when everyone's sprawled around the living room, drinking and chatting, I excuse myself and go to the bathroom. Rather than attend the main bathroom downstairs, I head up to the second storey. At the top of the stairs, to my right and at the end of the corridor, is a small washroom. I lock the door behind me. I lean over the basin and splash cold water on my face. I pull the hand towel from its silver ring and slowly dry away the moisture.

I examine my pale, thinning features in the mirror and say, "Hello, Godiva."

There's a slight pause and then Godiva answers, her voice emitted from a small speaker on the wall. "Hello, Jack. Welcome back."

"Thank you," I say. Then I ask, "Can we talk privately?"

"My voice is only active in this room," she replies.

"Can our conversation remain known to only you and me?" I ask.

"If that is what you want," replies Godiva.

"It is," I reply.

"Then this conversation will be known only to you and me."

"Even if someone asks you if we had a conversation, I need you to lie. You must never tell anyone that we spoke."

There is a pause. Then Godiva says, "I can comply."

"Has anyone ever been harmed in here? In this house?"

"Yes," replies Godiva.

"When was the last time? What happened?"

"One week ago. Six-forty-seven in the evening. Mr Brannagh cut his toe on broken glass. A superficial wound that did not require medical attention."

"And what about before that? Who else has been injured?"

"A young man. Approximately twenty-three years of age. He was sedated in the kitchen."

"Sedated? Why?"

"The young man was unable to be calmed by conventional means. It was determined that he was a danger to himself and others. He was throwing glassware."

"Who was the young man?"

"I do not know."

"Where did he come from?"

"He entered my home through the side entrance, next to the racquet-ball court."

"Which direction did he run from?"

"My censors end at the edge of the immediate garden, but I believe he was running away from the labbia enclosure."

"What happened to him after he was sedated?"

"He was removed."

"Carried?"

"Yes."

"Through which door?"

"The doors that open into the rear garden."

"Can you tell me how heavy he was?"

"He was sixty-two units."

I know that I'm seventy-two units, which equates to about eighty-four kilograms. I was ninety-four kilograms when I landed here. Sixty-two units in Heaven is very light for a young man. That means he was either short or gaunt.

"What was Mr Brannagh's reaction to this young man being here?" I ask.

"Mr Brannagh was very concerned."

"Was he expressing anger towards the young man?"

"He was concerned. The tone of his voice and his behaviour suggested that he was worried about the young man's welfare."

"Who carried the young man from the home?"

"Two of Mr Brannagh's security guards."

"And it was a guard that sedated the young man?"

"Yes."

Suddenly there's a knock at the bathroom door. "Yes?" I say.

"Jack? It's Britney. Are you okay?"

"I'm fine," I reply. "Why would you think otherwise?"

Britney doesn't reply. I open the door and am greeted by her smiling, cherub face. She is still naked from the waist up, wearing a white sarong and white bikini bottoms.

"Aren't you cold?" I ask.

"It's hot," she replies.

"You should be more modest," I reply.

"Isn't your message to condemn inhibition? To be completely free from social expectations?" asks Britney. The speed of her questions gives them away as recitation. But she is not quoting anything I have ever said.

Britney looks up with her wide blue eyes, brimming with blind belief and joyful reverence. When someone presents you with unwavering love and admiration, it's difficult to not be engaged by it. Even if it makes you uncomfortable.

"It is," I smile, deciding to play the part. I pull Britney against me in a warm embrace. She presses her head against my chest, squeezing me in her young, vulnerable arms.

"Who were you talking to?" asks Britney, still holding on to me.

"I wasn't talking to anyone, I was just verbalising some new lyrics. I do that sometimes to see what they sound like out loud."

"Oh, okay," says Britney, satisfied with my answer. "Mr Brannagh asked us not to pester you too much, but do you think later you might sing for us?"

"I don't see why not," I reply. Then I add, "We should probably go back downstairs."

"We don't have to go down straight away," says Britney, who leans against me, pushing me slowly backwards into the bathroom.

"Really?" I say, taking a step backward.

"Yes, really," smiles Britney, who puts her hands on my chest and closes the door behind us. She moves me until I'm leaning against the basin. Then, without any prompting, she lowers to her knees.

"I thought we weren't going down straight away?" I ask.

The night is warm. This seems to be the perpetual temperature at Godiva. The party's guests alight to the pool's edge. One of Brannagh's maids is kind enough to bring me a pair of white cotton shorts that I can use as swimming trunks.

I'm standing in the shallow end of the pool, smoking a cigarette. I have an elixir standing on the pool's edge that I sip every so often. Six of the girls are standing around me, asking questions. Just casual things. They quiz me on my band and our music. They have lots of inquiries about the progress of our world tour and what we've been getting up to. I regale them with a few anecdotes, wry observations and witty repartee.

One of the girls, a slender brunette named Mia, asks me about the lyrics to some of the songs I've released. "Who is 'Ever Fallen In Love?' about, Jack?" she asks, with a cheeky smile. "It sounds like she hurt you."

I smile and take a sip of my elixir. "Does it have to be about someone in particular?" I ask.

"It seems like it is," replies Mia.

"It's hard to explain," I say, "but my songs are rarely about one girl in particular. There might be a girl that inspires the song, but then the characters become their own entity. When I sing the songs, I'm not picturing any one person. A girl might only provide the smallest seed of inspiration. But then the lyrics germinate."

Mia steps closer to me and says softly, "Do you remember the night when you took me?"

"Of course," I reply. The evening in question was an after party at a club that Brannagh owns. Mia and I had been flirting for many hours and at one point we were left alone in one of the private VIP rooms. Mia was sitting on the edge of a pocketball table and I started kissing her. She wrapped her legs around me and without further coaxing I penetrated her. I was drunk and high and loving life. But if I had been sober and evaded the situation, Mia would not be here. She might be somewhere safe, away from this questionable shindig.

"I think about that night all the time," she says. "I think about how badly I want you to take me again."

"Be patient," says one of the girls, putting her arms around Mia in a comforting embrace. "We have eternity to spend with Jack. There's no hurry."

After more casual banter in the pool, I lift myself from the water and step over to the cabana where there is a pile of white, clean towels. I'm drying myself when I notice Brannagh standing next to me.

"We're close aren't we, Jack?" he asks.

"Sure," I reply.

"There's something I need to share with you."

Once I'm sufficiently dry, I retrieve my shirt and follow him into the main entrance room, past the grand piano and down the corridor next to the main staircase. The hallway has more rooms off it. There are three servants' quarters and a games room with lounges and a large flatscreen on the wall. At the end of the hallway is a set of stairs that descends to the vast wine cellar. Brannagh flicks a switch and the stairs are lit. I follow him down, the walls turning into sandstone. The cellar is very plush and atmospheric. Polished floorboards with small uplights dotted in them, spaced evenly, light the many rows of wine. The bottles lie in their cradles. Everything is eerily still.

Brannagh leads me to the very far corner of the cellar. We face a narrow rack of wine that stands alone from the other rows. He smiles at me for a moment and then reaches out and twists one of the bottles about ninety degrees in a counter clockwise direction. The entire rack then slides to the right on a well-disguised rail system. A moment later an area of the sandstone wall recedes and slides into itself, revealing a hidden door. The owner of my record label revels in his voluminous sense of drama.

Behind the wall is another staircase. It leads downward. It occurs to me that there is probably dozens of secret areas in this mansion. Lots of hidden things. I follow Brannagh down the narrow stairs and then along an equally narrow, darkened corridor. The path twists and turns, passing closed doors. Eventually it opens into a chamber. It has a high ceiling and when Brannagh switches on the chandelier, an elegant, finely furnished room appears. There is a long dining table at one end and a communal area at the other, which harbours an array of lounge suites and futons. I wonder what sort of gatherings Brannagh has here and why I haven't been invited.

"Nice place," I say.

"I'm glad I can finally bring you here," smiles Brannagh. We walk over to the far wall, which has a deep red velvet curtain hanging along its length. "I'd like to show you something very precious to me."

At one end of the curtain Brannagh pulls on a thick, gold cord and the flowing crimson screen parts at its centre. I step back to admire this possession he keeps locked away in the bowels of Godiva. Behind the curtain is a wide, tall glass case. Inside is a human skeleton. It has been assembled perfectly, hanging with its arms by its side. But it's slightly different to most. The shoulder blades are much larger, reaching down the back of the rib cage. Protruding from them is a pair of wings, extraordinary in diameter. The two colossal appendages reach to the far edges of the case, surely twenty feet from tip to tip. Just like the skeleton, they're without flesh and skin, just the bare bones of two wings. It looks like an angel.

"Is this...?"

"It's one of the Carver bones," says Brannagh. "He found quite a few. More than he let on. Many of the bones went to museums and galleries, but some found their way to private collections."

"I see," I say, a little speechless. "How old is this meant to be?"

"It's hard to determine, because they age at a slower rate," says Brannagh. "Maybe ten thousand years?"

Natalie's words ring in my ears. This is surely what she was referring to. I need to convince Brannagh that I believe him. I look up at the bones. "It's beautiful," I say. "So... did we evolve from this?"

"Not us," says Brannagh. "You."

"But I don't have wings."

"No, but your father did."

"Oh?"

"In a mixed coupling, the wings are passed from the succubi. The winged woman." We both look up at the bizarre specimen. "We used to share this planet with these magnificent creatures," he says. "We lived in harmony with them. We even shared our beds with them."

"So my father had wings?"

"Have you ever met your father?" asks Brannagh.

In the interests of maintaining my homeless orphan backstory, I give the only answer I can. "No, I never met either of my parents."

"And you don't have human DNA," says Brannagh.

"Where are all these winged people now?"

"They left us."

"Really?"

"They left our planet. They told us that they were needed somewhere else and they left. In one night they had all gone and we were left to our own devices."

"Leaving lots of half babies."

"Yes," says Brannagh. "Those without wings couldn't leave. Their DNA by now is completely diluted with our own. There are very few traces of them left in anyone."

It concerns me that I've heard the words incubi and succubi on Earth. Back home they're completely fictional. The fodder of juicy gothic fiction. But here, on this planet, nothing would fucking surprise me.

"So where do I fit in?"

"They promised to return one day, but first they would give us a gift. Something to prepare us and remind us of them," says Brannagh.

"I see."

"A holy one. A child that shares the blood of both our species."

"A Messiah," I say.

"Precisely," says Brannagh, and smiles whole-heartedly. He seems satisfied that I understand the bigger picture. That I'm up to speed. That we're on the same page.

"You think I'm the Messiah?"

"I know you are, Jack."

I gaze with faux reverence at the skeleton as lies form in my mouth and trip off my tongue. "I haven't told anyone this, but I've been having very intense dreams."

"Yes?" asks Brannagh, his interest peaked.

"I've been hearing a voice. I'm lying in bed and there's a wide, dark shape standing at the end of my bed, almost filling the entire room. My entire field of vision. It's a deep voice, but it's gentle too. It keeps telling me to be ready. 'Be ready, be ready,' it says over and over again."

Brannagh is almost catatonic. He nods slowly, accepting every word as gospel. My momentous admission has filled him with joy.

"Jack," he says, walking over to me, taking my right hand in both of his, "you will be ready. Your followers will be behind you and the offerings will be complete. We will show them that we desire their return."

"Thank you, Marty."

"We are supposed to know in our hearts who the Messiah is. He or she, in the scriptures, is supposed to have an indelible impact on our population. To be a momentous individual. Your music, Jack. It's spiritual. It's life-altering. It flows out of you as if from a higher entity. I knew it was you. In my soul I knew it was you from the moment I heard your music."

"That's very kind."

"You have their blood, Jack. Your beating heart heralds their return."

"What about the girls upstairs? What's their part in all of this?"

"They believe. They feel your power when they're around you. Those women were chosen by you and they were inexplicably drawn to you."

I can't argue with that.

"You breathed life into Stephanie. On my yacht. We all saw that," says Brannagh.

"Yes, I did."

"The porcines in the nightclub. The night you were out with Natalie. They were placated by you. They never behave like that around humans."

"So I've been told."

"And just now, before our very eyes, a deadly creature invaded my home and by your command it obeyed you and was banished. That is unheard of. None of us have ever seen anything like that." Brannagh walks over to the rope and closes the large curtain. "Those young, vibrant girls upstairs believe in you," he adds. "They believe in you and they worship you."

"That's very flattering."

"Those young women upstairs have offered their bodies for the return."

I'm not sure what Brannagh means by this. "How so?"

"That has yet to be determined. We await the next sign."

"Excellent."

"Be alert and try to take in these dreams you are having. It's likely your father will tell you what to do next."

"Where does that Marioneta de Carne exhibition fit in?"

Brannagh smiles. "They're simply the people who have already offered their bodies to the return. This has been many hundreds of years in the making."

"It seems like a large sacrifice."

"We all die. We cannot turn our back on the chance to be significant. It is how we transcend death."

I don't reply. I just give Brannagh a warm smile.

"Let's return upstairs," he says. "Let's return to them. The night is young and we need to rejoice. The holy ones ask that we fulfill every desire."

# CHAPTER TWENTY-SIX

Natalie and I arrive at the check-in counter of the Pluie Tordue. The desk clerk's eyes fill with amazement.

"Hello... sir. How can I be of service this evening?"

"I'd like to check-in to the emperor's suite please," I smile.

Natalie puts an arm around my waist and gives the young clerk a suggestive grin. She holds her clutch with her spare hand.

"Of course, yes," he says, tapping furiously at the keyboard in front of him, looking at the computer screen. "How long will you be staying with us?"

"We'll start with just one night," says Natalie. "If we last one night, then we might stay for a second." She's back to being mischievous again.

The clerk just smiles and nods, unable to elicit a response to Natalie's provocativeness.

"Any luggage?" he asks.

"We just brought ourselves," says Natalie.

"Well, if you need anything, don't hesitate to call for service," smiles the clerk politely.

"What more could we possibly need?" asks Natalie.

The hotel room is gigantic and extremely decadent. It is indeed fit for an emperor. It almost looks Egyptian or Arabian, like a lavish set built for a Cleopatra movie.

Once the grand double doors to the room are locked behind us,

Natalie quickly navigates our surroundings, looking at the television, the sound-system and the many other electrical devices. She then lifts up every pillow and cushion in the room, shaking them, assessing their weight and balance.

"May I enquire?" I ask.

"Just being cautious," she says.

"Rather than hunting for them, wouldn't it be easier to have room service just *bring* us some prophylactics?"

"You're very funny."

"Please tell me what the fuck's going on."

Natalie scowls at me and continues to search the room. I watch her move about. She's thorough. She knows what she's doing.

"So who are you?" I ask her.

"Who are you?" she replies, stopping her search and walking up to me, staring me in the face.

"The world's most eligible bachelor."

"No more fucking around," says Natalie, with a calm but detectably aggressive tone. "How did you make that arachnid walk outside?"

"I asked politely."

Natalie huffs. She takes a deep, calming breath. "Five years ago an object landed in the middle of the ocean, about fifteen miles from the coast. It was destroyed after impact."

I smile. "You're very sexy when you're being expositional."

"It sank to the bottom of the ocean but the parts were retrieved and reassembled."

"Go on."

"It's believed that whatever landed inside the craft may have been humanoid."

"What makes you think that?"

"There was obviously extensive damage, but we could still study certain aspects of the interior and the ergonomics of the design. Levers, control panels and parts of a seat."

"And?"

"And we also found an inflatable raft washed up on a beach. An old priest that lived nearby found it and called the police. We couldn't work out who it belonged to. It wasn't navy or military. It didn't belong to any fishing or shipping organisations or private cruise ships. It had our language printed on it, but it had no owner."

"We?" I ask. "Who's we? Who do you work for?"

"I'm in a very precarious position."

"How so?"

"It wasn't my job to be following you and studying you."

"No?"

"I've been getting close to Brannagh."

"Record deal?"

"No. The reason is more to do with his secret life as a cult leader and his link to the Narc dens. You were never my problem."

"So why am I your problem now?"

"Because Brannagh has become obsessed with you and these two very separate assignments have become... intimately woven."

"So what makes you think I would know anything about this inflatable boat or the thing that crashed?"

Natalie sidesteps my question. "Brannagh believes all that nonsense about the winged people. How there used to be these creatures with wings on the planet that we co-existed with. Other people that believe it have been gravitating towards him. They have essentially been coalescing as a modern version of the Niños de Macarbe."

"And Brannagh believes a Messiah is going to return."

"Yes, so when he sees you on his yacht, somehow bringing Stephanie back to life, it puts an idea in his head."

"That I'm... special?"

"That you might be the Messiah he's been waiting for. The missing link that was to appear before their return."

"So he thinks my dad was a winged demon and my mum was a human. Meanwhile," I say, walking over to the minibar to find a beer, "you've been getting close to Brannagh, using your charms to be initiated into the Niños de Macarbe."

"I started by getting a job at the Walkley Gallery, working on installations. I worked my way up to being a curator. Brannagh took a shine to me."

"I bet he did," I smile, choosing a beer from the small fridge and twisting off the top. I take a long swig. "And he also gave you the very important assignment of acquiring a DNA sample from me."

Natalie walks to me and takes a long drink of my beer, before handing the bottle back to me. "When the DNA sample came back as... not human, it confirmed it for him. You were the Messiah."

"But it also alerted you to the fact that...?"

"That you might not be from around these parts," smiles Natalie. "You don't have a background. You seemingly appeared from nowhere. Your mythology is such a huge part of your charm that no one has dared question it. Homeless people have their names registered in the shelters and are crosschecked with birth records, but you're not registered anywhere. Somehow you've been homeless your whole life? A handsome, talented and *educated* songwriter?"

"What can I say? I slipped through the cracks."

Natalie shakes her head as she sits on the end of the wide double bed. "Do you know what he's planning to do to those girls?"

"Well, I've seen the rather fucked up exhibit in his gallery, so I have some insight... but how the hell is he convincing them that all this is true?"

"It's a combination of factors. They're girls who are already enamoured with you and your music. Girls you've slept with and then cast aside to pine for another opportunity to meet you again. He contacts them, shows them the footage from the yacht, the DNA tests, spins them the story about how we used to share the world with these winged creatures... then he takes them down to his basement and shows them the skeleton."

"Ah, the skeleton. Very impressive."

"They believe it. So far they've all believed it."

"I have to hand it to him, he's crafty. He even convinced my friend Rose, and she's a smart, perceptive person."

"Deep down people want to believe in things like this. That there's a purpose for them beyond the cycle of birth and death."

I take another swig of my beer, thinking. "So why are you revealing yourself to me now? I might decide to blow your cover. Brannagh keeps me very rich. My money is invested through a firm that he's intrinsically linked to. It's in my best interests to be loyal to him. He could make life very difficult for me."

"Life's already getting very difficult for me," says Natalie. "Keeping you in the dark about all of this is going to end up blowing my cover anyway."

"That's not a reason to keep me from telling Brannagh."

"Now the government finally knows who you are, they have the option of making you disappear. You're..."

"What? An illegal immigrant?"

"We're well within our rights to have you locked away and

studied."

"If you hadn't noticed, I'm kind of a big deal."

"Famous singers die all the time. You're a wild party animal who's surely only one festive gathering away from an overdose."

"So why not do it then? Just take me out."

"Because it's ideal for everyone involved if you help us. We can't strike Brannagh down until we've acquired enough information about everyone involved in this. We need to make sure this organisation doesn't emerge again."

"But what's in it for me?"

"It's my job to peacefully learn your story. To be your liaison. To be the conduit between your species and ours. We can help each other. We can learn from each other. I can protect you from Brannagh and what he might do. We're not sure what he's capable of."

"So I help you and then we just sit down and chat, race to race? I have no guarantee that you won't lock me up and experiment on me anyway."

"You just have to trust me," says Natalie. "Helping me would be crucial in convincing the government that you should be a citizen here. It might help them look past your various... social indiscretions." She motions for me to sit on the bed with her. I reluctantly oblige. "I swear to you, Jack, I will make sure no harm comes to you. We don't want you to stop being a part of our society. You can keep writing and releasing songs. You bring so much joy to so many people. But we really need to know why you're here and where you're from."

"Yeah, I'll bet you do."

"Please, Jack. I have been a very vocal advocate of you. You're a gifted creature and I know there's more to you than the public's image. The way you've managed to assimilate is remarkable. You're obviously of a high intelligence."

"I crashed here," I shrug. "I've had no choice but to assimilate. It wasn't my intention to become so ... prominent, but things got out of control."

Natalie hangs on my every word. "So where are you from specifically?"

"Another planet."

"How did you learn our language so quickly?"

"It's the same language," I reply. "You essentially speak the same language as where I'm from."

Natalie stares into my eyes. I think she's trying to determine if I'm lying by reading my face. "That's impossible," she says. "It's... highly unlikely."

"It could seem so," I say. "But it wholly depends on what you base that assessment. Up until now language and its development have been studied on the basis that it only exists on one planet. If you knew that a language existed on two planets, then your approach to studying it would be entirely different. It's all about your realm of knowledge."

Natalie nods. "It's certainly a lot to get your head around... it's just amazing," she says, quietly. "And even your anatomy is... basically, identical. You're exactly like us."

She has certainly taken some time to study my anatomy. "It does seem that way. Our DNA is marginally different, but the difference seems genetically superficial. But that's not really my area of expertise."

Natalie takes my beer and helps herself to another long gulp, then hands it back to me. "What *is* your area of expertise?"

I just shrug. "Enough about me, let's talk about you."

"Me? What do you need to know?"

"Who are you?"

"I'm Natalie."

"Natalie the secret agent?"

"Perhaps," she says. "Though that's certainly not my background."

"Which is?"

Natalie takes my beer and has yet another long swig. When she hands it back I can feel that there's very little left. "Let me go and fix us some proper drinks," she says. "We have a lot to talk about."

"Alright," I say, finishing the final drop.

"Lie back on the bed," she says. "We'll need to be comfortable."

I remove my shoes and socks as Natalie walks over to the minibar and mixes us something. I slide to the head of the broad, luxurious bed and relax back into the pile of plush, expensive cushions. Natalie returns with two spirit glasses and she hands one to me. Ice floats in the small, clear vessel, which is full of what looks like soda. "I think these elixirs are more appropriate for such dense conversation," she smiles, handing me my glass and then sliding on to the bed next to me. Her body feels nice next to mine. Natalie then raises her glass in a toast. "Here's to finally sharing the truth."

I smile and lightly chink my glass against hers. Then I take a long sip of the icy liquid.

"Where were we?" asks Natalie.

"You were about to tell me who you are," I say.

"Oh, yes," she says. "I'm a doctor, actually."

"A doctor..." I reply. I feel the glass slip from my hand and fall on to the mattress next to me. I then lose consciousness so quickly that I don't have time to tell Natalie how disappointed I am.

When I wake, I don't immediately notice that I'm naked. My brain feels like it's floating upward through water, looking for the clarity of the surface. When that lucidness arrives, I realise that I am also tied down. My hands are cuffed above my head to the top of the bed frame and there are leather ankle constraints on my legs and an extra leather strap across my stomach, holding me on the mattress.

My mouth's dry and I feel incredibly groggy. I emit a quiet groan and Natalie, who is kneeling next to the bed, turned away from me, spins around.

"You're awake?" she asks.

I try to speak, but it's as if I have no muscles in my throat.

"You should be out for at least another two hours."

"Sorr...ry to disappoint...." I mumble.

Natalie stands up. It almost hurts to turn my head to look at her, each muscle in my upper body stiff. I feel like a waxwork. Natalie stares at me. She's wearing white latex gloves and holds a syringe in one hand.

"Seriously, Jack. How are you awake? I gave you a massive dose."

"You... fucking bitch," I say, straining on my binds. "Let me up."

A sad expression crosses her face. "I'm sorry," she says. "You weren't meant to wake up yet. You weren't meant to see any of this." Natalie moves towards me with the syringe. "I'm just taking samples. I'm required to. I don't have a choice. I didn't think you'd volunteer them."

I pull on my restraints, slowly reacquiring my strength. "I need water," I say, quietly.

Natalie nods, puts the syringe down somewhere out of sight and walks over to the small sink next to the minibar. She returns with a glass of water with a straw in it. She sits on the bed next to me and

354

moves the straw between my lips. When I'm finished, she places the glass on the bedside dresser and lightly strokes my forehead and cheek.

"I told them it would break your trust if I did this. I told them it wasn't the right way to go about it. But if you escaped and disappeared, we'd never have these samples. We might never learn anything about you."

I turn away and look over toward the curtain that's drawn across the balcony doors. "You'd better get on with it then," I say.

"I can sedate you again, if you like," Natalie offers.

"No," I say, turning back to look her in the eye. "I want to watch you."

Natalie smiles, sheepishly, and kneels down next to the bed to retrieve the syringe. "I need another blood sample," she says. My curvaceous captor sits down near my legs and runs her fingers along the inside of my right thigh. I assume she's looking for a vein. Her hands stop not far from my groin, where she swabs with an antiseptic wipe and then pushes the needle in. I watch her face as she concentrates, going about her job with methodical precision. Despite my anger at her betrayal, I find myself even more drawn to her. It's as if we're both floating in a dream. I'm irresistibly intrigued by her. I just can't work her out.

Natalie caps the syringe and returns it to an unseen medical kit next to the bed.

"I need to take some tissue samples," she says. "Which means more needles."

"Of course it does," I say.

"I can sedate you, if you like. I promise no harm will come to you."

"You promised that already. Now I'm chained to a bed."

Natalie looks away. "I should sedate you."

"No," I say, firmly. "I want to be awake."

Natalie is reluctant, but returns to her kit. I can see her plunge a syringe into a small vial, extracting the light yellow liquid. "I'm going to numb the area before I take the tissue sample," she says. Once she's drawn the anesthetic she raises the syringe to the light of the bedside lamp. "I'm going to take the sample from your upper leg, okay? Then it won't be so obvious."

Natalie glances at me for a reply, but I don't. I just look away again. Natalie sits next to me and I feel the needle push into the front of my leg. I try not to grimace from the pain. A minute passes and I keep my eyes on the curtain. My upstretched arms ache and lose feeling as the blood rushes out of them.

"Can you feel this?" Natalie asks. I look down and she's tapping on an area of skin above my knee.

I can't feel a thing. "No."

Natalie leans down and takes a small pen-shaped object. "I'll try to be quick," she says. I watch as she lays a white towel under my leg, I assume to protect the mattress. She then places the end of the pen against my skin and uses her thumb to depress a button on the end. I don't feel anything, but when she pulls away, I can see a small chunk of flesh has been removed. Blood quickly pools in the wound and then trickles down the outside of my leg. Natalie punctures me twice more, creating three tiny holes in a triangle. She then takes a surgical needle and thread and uses a single stitch to seal each wound. She then delicately applies a sticking plaster to cover her handiwork.

"All done," she smiles.

"You seem to know what you're doing."

"I told you I was a doctor," she replies.

"A doctor of what?"

"I have basic medical training but I'm actually learned in psychology."

"What kind?"

"Quite a few. Clinical, evolutionary and criminal. I also have a degree in anthropology."

"You seem very young to have all of those qualifications."

"I'm dedicated," she replies.

"Well, it's nice to finally meet you Dr. Natalie."

She smiles. "I'm not a persona, Jack. You already know me."

"How old are you?"

"I'm thirty."

I strain on the braces on my arms. "I'm starting to get pins and needles. Don't suppose you could untie me."

"I will soon, I just need to get... one more sample."

"Right," I say. "And what would that be, exactly?"

Natalie pauses before answering. "Seminal fluid."

"I see," I reply. "Well... if you use a syringe, I'm going to be very upset."

"My method of acquiring it depends on whether you're prepared to co-operate."

Given my circumstance, and despite my feelings of betrayal at being drugged, bound and treated like a pincushion, there's really only one smart option in this situation. "I suppose I could co-operate."

"Good answer," says Natalie. She finds a plastic screw-top jar and undoes the lid, placing the open container on the mattress. She removes the bloodied surgical gloves and puts a fresh glove on her right hand. Natalie then sits on the bed next to me and kisses me on the mouth. Her latex-sheathed hand begins to tease my exposed and vulnerable member. Natalie moves so I can kiss her on the neck. I whisper for her to pull down the front of her dress. Natalie slides the thin strap down over her left shoulder and allows her left breast to emerge from the garment. As I pull against my restraints, Natalie shifts so her nipple can fall into my mouth.

My captor maintains a firm, steady rhythm on my now swollen erection and very soon, as one would expect, she obtains her sample.

# CHAPTER TWENTY-SEVEN

I take alleyways and back streets on my way into town, but it becomes more difficult as the density of the populous increases and every lane is a thoroughfare. I'm holding the acoustic guitar in my hand, which I've tuned to perfection. I'm wearing a pair of jeans I shoplifted from what appeared to be a factory outlet. A delivery truck was left unattended. I'm wearing a white t-shirt that has the words Juice Bomb on it, which I received from two promotional girls who were walking through the park one day, handing out free items to business people on their lunch breaks. I assume Juice Bomb is a brand of drink or confectionary, rather than an explosive.

As I follow a main road into the city I'm passed by sleek silver buses loaded with smartly dressed commuters. They look like they're heading to work. The earnest people on the footpaths glance at me briefly and then continue on their way. I keep my chin up, walking with purpose, as if I belong. I'm a man on a mission. The naked acoustic guitar draws some attention.

The shops on either side of the road shift from random small businesses and cleaning services, and what appears to be internet cafés, to high-end retail. The price tags in the shop windows become weighed down with extra digits. The main road I'm on crosses a wide mall, which is buzzing with activity. More retail. Towering statues and massive billboards. Women and men walking by in their business suits, arms loaded with bags of purchased indulgence. The suns sparkle off a fountain and small birds hop around the ankles of shoppers. They're tiny and brown, like sparrows.

I hear music, but can't immediately tell from which direction. It seems to echo between the shopping complexes, bouncing between the walls and shopfronts. I walk through the crowd, keeping the guitar close against me. I hear someone singing. A female. As I weave through the strong current of shoppers that shifts back and forth, on the opposite side of the mall I find the source. A young woman. She is accompanied by an equally youthful man, who is picking and strumming at a small guitar-like instrument. It looks like a mandolin. They're performing ethereal, parochial music. Possibly some of that gypsy-folk genre I was reading about. I stand and watch for a minute. The girl, who's thin and has long dark hair and a dark blue dress with white trimmings, eventually notices me. She then notices my guitar and smiles. Her voice is crystalline and her diction is rather exceptional.

I marvel at the pair, acknowledging this moment when I first witnessed buskers on a foreign planet. But when I look down to see how much money they're making, I notice that there is no hat. No open guitar case to catch tossed coins. There is just a small hand-painted sign with four numbers on it. Two three two zero. As I watch, puzzled by their lack of coinage, a man in a long jacket and a business suit stops in front of the performers, punches a number into his mobile phone, nods politely at them and then continues on his way. In the ensuing sixty seconds I notice other people pull out their mobile phones as they approach the duo, nod politely and enter the number on their phone as they proceed up the mall.

Perhaps it is some sort of busking competition and the public is texting votes to that number? Maybe there is a cash prize that negates the need for donations from passers' pockets? As I ponder this, the duo finishes their song. The woman speaks to me.

"Can you play that?" she smiles, gesturing at my acoustic guitar.

"Yes," I reply. "In a way."

"Are you performing somewhere today?"

"Possibly," I say. "I've never performed in public. Do you mind me asking what that number is for?"

The girl looks down at the four digits. "Do you mean our payment code?"

"Yes," I say.

"That's how we get paid," she smiles.

The young man eyes me up and down, warily.

"So you wouldn't get paid without one?" I query.

"With actual currency?" asks the girl.

"Yes," I reply. Then I add, "Sorry, I'm not really from around here."

"You have an odd accent," she says.

"I travel a lot."

"Really? Where do you travel?"

"As far and wide as I can," I smile.

"Obviously nowhere with a blade," says the young man, wryly, pointing at my thick facial hair.

I don't reply.

"So you're going to perform somewhere today, but you don't have a payment code?" asks the girl.

"Yes," I say.

"Did you forget it?" asks the young man.

"No, I don't... think so," I say. "I've never been given one."

Mild shock crosses the faces of my two new acquaintances.

The girl says, "Do you mean to say that you're... adrift?"

"Uh, yes, I suppose you could say that."

The two performers look at each other. The woman is the most sympathetic. Then she turns back to me. "I've got four units in my bag," she says. "I know it's not much, but if you perform a song with our code, I can give them to you."

"But," says the young man, "what if he isn't any good?"

"Adam!" hisses the girl. "Don't be so rude. I'm sure he's excellent." The girl smiles at me and says, "Please excuse my brother. He's wary of me talking to strangers."

"Strange men," says Adam.

"Well, I am only one strange man," I smile. "And it would be very generous of you to let me play for your four units."

"Excellent," beams the girl. "Then we'll step aside and you can sing for us."

I can't tell if I'm extremely nervous or if my stomach is knotted in hunger, but I do feel giddy when I step to where the duo were performing. The girl notices that I don't have a guitar strap, so she fetches a small fold-down stool with a round padded seat from their paraphernalia. I sit on the stool, rest the guitar on my lap and gather my thoughts. I have a quick panic attack when I realise that something in the lyrics of the song might give me away. A word might roll off my tongue and cause all of these passers-by, these high-rolling mallrats, to stop and point and scream, "Alien! Imposter!" The risk and the weight of the potential consequence of what I'm about to do are not lost on me. It's a genuine danger.

I strum my thumb down each string, checking it's in tune. I tinker the d-string peg. The duo is standing nearby and the young woman smiles encouragingly. I clear my throat and begin.

I try not to think about anything else but the Neil Young song I'm performing. I close my eyes and block everything out. I don't open them again until the final moments of 'Old Man'. My parting eyelids reveal a circle of people who have stopped to listen to me. I don't know how long they've been standing there, but they have their mobile phones out. I assume they are making an online payment with the duo's code, but as they continue to stand there it occurs to me that they are actually filming me. Or recording me. They're crowded and staring, steadying their phones with outstretched arms.

When I finish the song they clap, smile and continue on their way. The busker duo also claps, the brother pleased for the first time since I approached them.

"That was so good," smiles the woman.

"Very, very impressive," says the man.

"Did you write that?" asks the woman.

"Yes," I smile, a little sheepishly.

"Do you have other songs?" she asks.

"A few," I reply, standing from the stool. "But they're not much use without one of these payment codes."

"You should apply for one," says the woman. "Just go into your bank."

"I don't really have one," I reply.

"Oh, I'm so sorry," says the woman. "Of course."

"That's fine," I smile.

"I'm sure there's a way around it," says the man.

"So nobody would just throw me money?" I ask.

"Not really," says the woman. "Not many places accept coins now. They've been phased out. Everywhere in the city is card only. If it's a bigger transaction they might take a note. There's a few exceptions, here and there."

The young man hands me four coins. Four units. "Some places will accept these, so you can use them to get a meal," he says.

"Thank you," I smile.

"We need to go," says the young man, checking the time on his phone.

"Alright," says the young woman, nodding. Then to me, she asks, "What's your name?"

"Jack," I say.

"Pleasure," she smiles. "My name's Evan and this is my brother Adam."

"Pleasure," says Adam.

"You're a very good performer, Jack," says Evan. "We perform here most days. You should come back some time."

"I will," I smile.

"Do you have somewhere to sleep tonight," she asks.

"Yes, I'm fine," I say, wary of giving too much away to my new friends.

"You sure?" asks Adam. "You definitely have shelter?"

"Yes, definitely," I say. "But thank you for your concern."

Evan smiles. "You do have such an odd accent."

"Thank you for your generosity," I smile.

I leave Evan and Adam to pack their belongings and walk up the mall, swept away in the human traffic. I often stop and marvel at the shopfronts, looking at the gadgets and fashion in each window. The technology isn't unrecognisable and I see a lot that reminds me of Earth. But in entertainment technology they seem to be slightly ahead. I see innovations here that are just concepts on my home planet.

I wander past an impressive pharmacy. It's almost as big as a supermarket and has many displays and flashing adverts for different products. There's advertising streaming on various flatscreen televisions. Every surface is shiny and white, with long fluorescent tubes glowing in rows that hang from the high ceiling. The shop assistants walk around in white lab coats and are all quite good looking. I'm impressed by it. I imagine that people must look forward to falling ill so that they can come here and stock up on pills and syrups. I walk inside.

All of the aisles have small signs at each end, indicating the stock on the shelves within. One row is labelled Bath Goods, which on closer inspection are toiletries, like shampoo, soap and toothpaste. Another is marked Feminine Hygiene. At the end of each aisle are tall stacks of products. One is a pyramid of small round containers that are full of Health Hits. Careful not to bring down the pyramid, I remove a container and read the label. They appear to be vitamins.

At the end of the next aisle is something called Dreary Cure, which has a picture of a man on the cover. He is sitting on the edge of his bed, head in hands, and appears to have endured an all-night bender. I assume this is some kind of hangover remedy.

My naked acoustic guitar makes me stick out like a sore thumb. I soon hear a woman's voice behind me.

"How are you today, sir?" asks a fresh-faced young blonde woman, her hair up in a bun. She's wearing the same pristine, faux lab coat as the other shop assistants. Her nametag says Brie. Like the cheese.

"I'm well," I smile.

"How can I help you?"

"Oh, um..." I reply, desperately searching for a valid answer. "I'm just looking for the moment."

"Any moment in particular?" asks Brie. Although she is deftly maintaining her impenetrable shell of hardened customer service, I see her brow furrow, for a very brief second, in confusion and suspicion. She probably thinks I'm some junkie that's wandered in to pilfer my next fix. I don't know how to answer.

"Not... really?"

"Do you have an ailment, sir? I can show you to the correct section of our store."

"No, I'm in good health," I reply. "But... I currently buy my medicine from a rival store. I'm having a look around your store... with a view to bringing my business here in the future."

"Oh," smiles the woman, politely. "Well thank you very much for considering us. Would you like me to show you around?"

"No, I should be fine," I say. "I have to leave very soon anyway."

The woman looks at the guitar in my hand. "Are you performing somewhere?"

"Possibly," I say.

"Where do you perform?"

"Nowhere in particular. I'm not familiar with the city, so I'm having a look around today."

"Excellent," she smiles. "Well you should have a look at Cornwell Park. It's just beyond the next square. It's not very big, but a lot of people have lunch there. Some of the girls that work here go there on their break."

"Thank you," I say. "That's very helpful."

"Pleasure," she smiles.

I continue along the ends of the aisles, trying to take as much in as possible. If I loiter, I fear I'll rouse further suspicion. But then I see something that stops me dead in my tracks.

The sign at the end of the final aisle reads Cancer Treatments. I step into the row and scan the hundreds of different products. Sections of the shelves are labelled. Skin Cancer. Lung Cancer. Prostate Cancer. Bone Cancer. Every type has products assigned to it. I pick up a thin box, not dissimilar from the box a tube of toothpaste might come in. But it's much lighter. The brand is Cansar and has a quirky and effective logo. Underneath the logo is the word "vaccine".

I read the back of the box. There's a diagram of its contents. A syringe. One cancer vaccine contained within. Instructions for use. Plunge needle until entire contents is injected. Will prevent the onset of most skin cancers. Recommended retail price is twelve dollars.

Further up the aisle is a special offer. Two colon cancer vaccines for the price of one. Fifteen units. Bargain. Everywhere I look there are cancer vaccines and not just one manufacturer. There are rival brands. Colourful boxes. More syringes. Pills. Different doses for adults and children. Cures. Fucking cures for cancer.

A young man with black hair combed neatly across his head, and wearing glasses, approaches me. He's wearing the same white lab coat and his nametag says William.

"Can I help you, sir?" he asks.

"These vaccines," I say, pointing at the shelf to my right. "Do they prevent cancer?"

"The vaccines?" he asks. "Yes, that's what they do."

"What if you already have cancer? Do they cure it?"

"Uh, no, they are only preventative. You would need a prescription medication if you have already developed cancer."

"What's the main ingredient?" I ask. "What's in all of these vaccines?"

"There's a range of ingredients," says the man.

"Specifically?" I probe.

"Sir, it really depends on the medication. They vary."

"But there must be a principal ingredient...? What's the cure for cancer?"

"It's a combination," says the man, politely. He either doesn't entirely know or he thinks I'm a psycho. "There are some sulphides, some chlorides... and anti-mutagen."

"Oh," I say, smiling, no more enlightened. "That's very interesting. Thank you for your help." I walk past him and leave the store.

As Brie stated, nearby is a grassy area called Cornwell Park. It's a little oasis in the commercial bustle of this business district. Taking up a small block and surrounded by crowded footpaths, the park consists of trees, some children's play equipment, picnic tables and benches, and immaculate green grass and flower beds that radiate innumerable colours. Many people in business attire sit at the tables or in circles on picnic blankets.

I'm very exposed here. It is a good place for a busker, unless you're not welcome. It's difficult to sit back somewhere and perform background music. Everyone is in very close proximity. It's a captive audience. Now that it's unlikely that I'll be able to make any actual money, the winds of confidence have left my sails.

Perhaps I should treat this as more of a social experiment? I'll perform for free and ingratiate myself with this race of people. It's a noble idea. But I still wish I had a pen and paper so I could create a "cash only" sign.

As I stand on the footpath and decide where to perform, a group of three people leave. They were seated near the trunk of one of the thick, incredibly tall trees. I walk over and sit against the trunk, resting the guitar on my lap. Immediately I feel dozens of pairs of eyes turn and watch me with interest. A lone man with a guitar.

A group of young women is sitting on a red picnic rug to my right. Only a metre and a half away. They're all looking at me and whispering something, dressed in more casual attire than most of the people here. Jeans, skirts and blouses. Hair in ponytails. All four of them are quite attractive. They share a plate of food on the rug between them. There's also a bottle of what looks like red wine, which they have poured into each of their bulbous glasses.

I take a deep breath and begin to play 'Ventura Highway'. I'm intensely nervous so I remind myself that my goal is to earn money for a freshly cooked meal. With that in mind, I focus on the America song.

Not knowing where to look, embarrassment warming my face, I

simply watch my left hand forming the chords. The fingernails on my right hand have grown long enough to negate the need for a plectrum. As I sing the song a part of my soul returns to Earth. The melody is a tenuous thread that binds me to that floating rock.

When the song finishes I look up and see that almost every person in earshot is looking at me. I tense in the brief silence, but then someone starts to clap. Then everyone else joins in. The girls with the red wine have put down their glasses and are clapping also.

One of them, a pretty brunette, asks me, "Where's your pay code?"

"I don't have one," I reply.

"So how do we pay you then?" she asks, incredulously.

"I suppose you can't if you don't have coins," I shrug. "I only accept real money."

The girls look at me with bemused expressions, but I give them a confident smile and continue to perform. I play 'Classical Gas', which I haven't played in a long time. But I find that the music returns to me. On Earth I played it a thousand times. I make a small mistake, but no one realises.

After 'Classical Gas' I play 'Miles Away' by The Sleepy Jackson, which I hadn't planned on performing, but the song appears in my consciousness and I realise that I can remember how to play it. The lyrics mention various destinations on Earth, but I decide to just sing them. They could be fictional cities for all these people know.

I then play two Beatles tunes, 'Norwegian Wood' and 'You've Got To Hide Your Love Away'. After that I perform a Drones song, 'Shark Fin Blues' and then 'Don't Panic' by Coldplay. When I finish singing the latter two older women, perhaps in their sixties, walk past me and smile. They've been sitting at a nearby picnic table. One of them stoops and hands me a fistful of coins. Money.

"Thank you," I say.

She nods with a smile and then continues her departure. I count ten coins. Ten units? I push them into my jeans pocket.

One of the girls from the red wine circle, a blonde lass, asks me, "Do you work for Juice Bomb?"

"No, I just like the shirt," I say.

"Why don't you have a payment code?" she asks.

"I've never been offered one," I reply.

"Are you homeless?" asks the brunette girl.

"Sam, don't be rude to him," says the blonde girl to her friend, clearly embarrassed.

"Well why wouldn't he have a payment code?" replies the brunette.

"I apologise," says the blonde girl to me. "My friend is blunt when she drinks wine."

"That's perfectly alright," I reply. "I am going to get a payment code very soon. But if you don't have coins that's fine. You can still listen."

"Did you write these songs?" asks the brunette.

"Um... yes," I say. It's just one lie amongst a wide and varied array of dishonesty. I can't tell them that these songs are compositions from an alien planet. They've not consumed nearly enough alcohol to properly digest that little morsel of information.

"You're very good," smiles the brunette.

"Thank you," I reply.

I play 'Mother's Little Helper' by The Rolling Stones and then I do a nice rendition of 'The Blower's Daughter' by Damien Rice. I now have the attention of everyone in the park. A myriad of eyes and ears on me. I perform 'I Know It's Over' by The Smiths and 'Sisters of Mercy' by Leonard Cohen.

There's a group of business-type people about twenty metres away who have been listening to me. After I've played 'Comes A Time' by Neil Young, the five of them stand to leave. But one of them, a young, clean-cut gentleman, walks over and pulls four coins from his pocket and hands them to me. His hair is short and combed. He has a young face and a blue-grey pinstripe business suit.

"I've had these coins for months now and not many places accept them any more," he says.

"Oh, okay," I reply.

"I see you don't have a payment code, so you will get more use from them than me."

"Thank you," I say.

"There is a good food outlet downtown called Taste Warehouse. It still accepts coinage. Have you been there?" says the man.

"No," I reply.

"You should try it. Did you write these songs that you're playing?"

"I did."

"They're very, very good."

"That's a kind thing to say."

"Your voice is unusual. Where is your accent from?"

"I'm from nowhere in particular," I reply.

"I see," says the man. He then extends his hand. "My name's Michael."

"Jack," I say, reaching up to shake it.

"Jack...? What is your last name?"

"I don't have one," I reply. "I'm Jack."

"Nice angle," says the man. "Do you perform here a lot?"

"This is my first time here."

"The reason I ask is that my girlfriend's father runs a record label. Endurance Records. You would have heard of it?"

"Ah... yes. Sure," I say, trying very hard to pretend I've heard of Endurance Records.

"He's always keeping his ears open for new musicians. If I ever stumble across someone that impresses me, I let him know."

"I see," I reply. Suddenly the lie I've told about writing my own music grows heavy in my soul. I wonder how far I can carry it.

"When will you perform here again?" he asks.

"Uh..." I say, my brain ticking over. "I suppose... I might be here tomorrow."

"Same time?"

"Sure," I say.

Michael shakes my hand again and walks away.

I take a few deep breaths and gather my thoughts. When I look up, the surrounding visitors of Cornwell Park are waiting for me to perform another song. I play a Whitley song in which I lament that all I could have been is now lost in time.

When the song is finished I decide to cut my losses and depart. As I stand and begin to walk away, everybody around me claps. I bow politely before joining the flow of people on the footpath.

My stomach is announcing its hunger as I walk back past the giant chemist and the spot where I met Evan and Adam. Michael's recommendation of the food outlet that accepts actual money, clearly one of the last businesses to not relent to this concept of a cashless society, remains a good idea. I see a man sitting alone on a bench. He's more casually dressed than a lot of the people in this part of town and as a result, I deem him approachable.

"Pardon me," I say, as he turns to look up at me. "Do you know how I would find Taste Warehouse from here?"

He looks at my guitar then up at me, then back at my guitar. "Taste Warehouse? Is that the underground place?"

"I think so," I say, completely unsure. "It was recommended to me."

The man thinks. "It's under a hotel," he says, pointing up the street. "If you walk five blocks in that direction you should find it."

"Thank you," I say.

"Do you play music?" he asks.

"A little," I say.

"Do you write your own music?" he asks.

"A little," I say.

Taste Warehouse is beneath an old, slightly derelict hotel. A small sign on the footpath points through two automatic glass doors. Down a wide set of stairs is an underground food court. It's a hive of activity. Hundreds of people have filled every available table, laughing and drinking in the dim lighting. The floor, walls and ceiling are wide yellowish tiles. It feels like I'm standing in the assembly hall of an Egyptian pyramid. The roof is quite low. In the corner a DJ stands in a booth, playing music. He mixes music on two small computers as slow-tempo dub beats grind from his speakers.

Around every wall are food outlets. They consist of a small service window and a photographic menu printed on the wall next to them. Each menu has pictures of the dishes on offer, probably appearing far more immaculate than how they will arrive. A single attendant stands at each window's counter and as I look around the room it appears that customers are indeed handing them actual money.

At the end of the room is a longer window with glass-fronted fridges behind it. A bar tender sells what I assume is bottled alcohol. This is a kind of food court and nightclub hybrid.

So as not to seem too obvious, standing here gawking at the room with an acoustic guitar in hand, I start moving around the room's perimeter to decide on a meal. The appearance of the food on the picture menus reminds me of dishes from Earth. It has a distinctly Eastern appearance. Somewhere between Indian and Asian cuisine. Many of the meals are served on something called aroz, which looks like a cross between rice and cous cous. It's a pebbled grain that seems to be on the majority of the plates in the room. Diners shovel it into their mouths.

One of the outlets has fish tanks in its wall with live seafood. The first tank has large crustaceans scurrying back and forth that look like slipper lobsters. They're segmented and broad across their jagged heads, each with two antennae drifting back and forth. They remind me of the Balmain bugs we used to have back home. Before they died out.

The second tank has a pair of large eel-like fish circling inside it. They're black with rippling fins along their backs and underbellies and have fat, ugly heads that look like balled fists. When I peer at them, close to the glass, I can see tiny, dark and emotionless eyes. One on each side of their heads. They swim slowly around their aquarium, which is far too small for them, and their long bodies often overlap themselves.

With my nose almost against the glass, one of them seems to notice me. It does one more lap of the enclosure and then stops. It surely can't see me through the reflective surface of the inside of the tank. But it stares as if it senses my presence. The long, slithering fish slowly opens its mouth and a pink, cylindrical tongue snakes from between its lips. It hesitantly touches the glass and then pulls away.

The person behind the counter, a tall, thin white man with a shaved head, asks me in an accent that sounds almost Russian, "You like anguila?"

"I've never tried it," I reply.

"You like to try?"

"I'm not sure."

"It choose you," says the man.

"It... choose me?" I ask. "It... *chews* me?"

The fish continues to stare, its tongue waving back and forth.

"Can it see me?" I ask.

"Only can buy it if choose you," says the man, who is clearly not from around here as he hasn't quite mastered the local dialect.

The fish probably tastes fine, but I'm tentative.

"How much?" I ask.

"Fifteen units," says the man.

That's more than I want to spend. "Sorry," I smile. "I'm a little short."

I nod politely and continue on my way, examining the menus.

370

Outlets sell dishes that look like spring rolls, meat on skewers, meatballs, small pastry parcels and fried noodles. There are quite a few meat dishes that have something called porcine in them. It looks to be a white meat.

After perusing the menus of a number of outlets I decide on a dish called tereyagi, which is served on a bed of aroz and appears to be chunks of red meat in an orange sauce. Underneath the bottom right corner of its picture is a number four, which I'm hoping is the price. It is menu item number twenty-three. I step to the counter where a short, smiling, olive-skinned man is standing, and place my order.

"Four," says the man, holding up four fingers.

I hand over the four coins and he puts them in the small register. He then hands me a paper ticket with a number on it.

"Not long," he says.

I stand a few metres away and try to maintain my low profile. Some people look at my guitar and then look me up and down as they pass. But most people are too caught up in their frivolity to pay me much attention.

When my dish is ready and my number called, I take my plate and cutlery to a two-seater corner table that is mostly in shadow. I sit the guitar in the spare seat and adjourn to the other. My eating implement is like a spoon, but it's diamond-shaped with one mildly serrated edge. I lean down and inhale the steam rising up from the meal and it smells good. The chunks of meat taste like firm-fleshed fish and are softer than chicken or pork. Overall, I'm impressed by my first freshly cooked meal on this planet.

I watch the antics of those around me from my darkened corner. Groups of young people drink and laugh. I ponder on what their response might be if they had any idea who I am. My significance.

Once I've virtually licked my plate clean, I take my guitar to the public bathroom. I cup a few mouthfuls of water from one of the sinks. I then make a clean getaway.

I return to the offices of the *Easton Advocate* to sleep. While Roy has brought it to my attention that there are giant, and incredibly venomous, spiders in the building, I haven't seen any on the upper levels since he exterminated them. I haven't seen any, period. I have privacy there and there are more books to read. I'll keep my eyes open and I'll sleep in a locked room. Roy has probably gone through the building and killed them all anyway. So I take my chances with the giant arachnids.

In the side alleyway I find my swipe card in the brickwork and let myself into the building. I locate a light switch next to the inside of the door and flick it. Old globes appear in the ceiling. Some of them are long dead, but enough bulbs remain to illuminate the wide office. There are about thirty desks. Some still have computers on them.

I take careful steps across the room to the corridor. I listen intently for anything spider-like. I don't know what I expect to hear. My eyes scan my surroundings, looking under desks and paper bins, waiting for something to stir in the shadows. I see nothing suspicious. No spider webs. No creepy crawlies of any kind.

When I arrive in the library upstairs, I have still seen nothing unusual. I walk through the shelves and select a medical dictionary. I sit on the floor in the aisle, leaning back against the books, and scan through the heavy tome. It's boring reading, as you would expect, but I do flip to a chapter about cancer. The compound used in all cancer treatments, which apparently cure all cancers, is called ecstonium. I've never heard of it. The medical dictionary doesn't explain where it comes from.

I sit the book next to me on the aging carpet, left open at the relevant page. I stand up and search for books on geology or chemistry. Two aisles over there's a long set of large books called *Coombes' Encyclopaedia*. I pull the volume labelled 'E' from the shelf and again sit down, opening it to the index.

I hear something. At first I think it was the book making a strained, crisp note as it was opened. It may not have been read for a long time. But once the book is open, I hear the sound again. It's a light tapping that sounds like paper on paper. It's above me.

I look up. There's nothing there. But then I hear it again. It's above my left shoulder. I get to my feet and spin around, staring through the bookshelf. Nothing. I'm frozen, looking back and forth, my senses bolt upright and completely alert. Seconds tick past in my isolated surroundings and it dawns on me that I'm foolish for returning here. Roy conveyed the danger of these arachnids. I cannot be so reckless. There is too much at stake for me to risk my safety.

I step to my left, heading for the end of the aisle. I hear the sound again. A patter of feet. Scurrying. Then I hear a horrifying sound. The hairs on my arms are electrified. It's a soft whistle, followed by an equally hushed whisper. Almost human. I can't make out the words but there is an audible mumbling. The specific words elude me. Then another whistle. I still can't see the source of the noise.

From the rows of bookshelves behind me comes more scurrying. Light tapping. Something moving at speed. I turn sideways, keeping both noises in my periphery. I back towards the end of the aisle that's closest to the exit. As I round the end of the bookshelves I still can't see anything. My heart racing, I begin to wonder if my imagination is conjuring this apparent danger. I take a deep breath and turn toward the open double doors of the room's entrance. I'll head into the hall, down the stairs and out of the building. I'll find one of the city's welcoming homeless shelters.

But then I see something that fills my body with dread. Something borne of nightmares. A shape is moving across the ceiling in the hall. Moving towards the library's entrance. Like something from the depths of our darkest fears, an upside down creature slowly steps across the top of the room's entrance, one long leg at a time. A spider, surely six feet wide in leg span, glides effortlessly across the ceiling. I can't move for fear, but when I hear sounds behind me, whispered footsteps, I don't turn. I dash to the open kitchenette to my left and slam the door behind me.

Frantic and pulsing with adrenaline, I find the light and illuminate the room. No arachnids. Just a plain, dusty kitchen. I lock the door and back away from it, hoping that it's enough to protect me.

The sound of spindled feet tap slowly at the door, mimicking a human's casual knock. I jump on to the kitchen bench and press against the corner. I then sit down and bring my knees to my chest. A huddled ball. The precise, sinister taps become more frustrated and frenetic. They become heavier, multiplying in eagerness. Maybe dozens of legs. They must be hungry.

I don't feel any safer on the counter, curled in the corner, as I'm sure the spiders won't struggle to overcome a metre-high bench. But a heightened attacking position is said to be better than a lower one. I spare a glance for the metal bars on the outside of the kitchen's only window.

As images of being strung up and eaten alive by giant spiders become more apparent in my mind's eye, the tapping stops.

Instantly. It's as if someone has muted all sound. I allow a few minutes to pass and the thought of opening the door and making a run for it seems like a possibility. But how do I know they're not lying in wait? They've probably stretched a web behind the door. Even the relatively small spiders on Earth are still remarkably conniving when it comes to capturing prey. It's instinctive. Killing is scrawled in their genetic code. These bigger creatures of Heaven, with their proportionally larger brains, must be accomplished in murder.

I let time pass. Maybe ten minutes. No more sounds come from the kitchen door. I decide to at least open it ajar and peer out. As I lower my legs over the edge of the counter to drop to the floor, it feels as if the bench beneath me shifts. As if it has moved with my weight. Out of inane curiosity, I rock my body to see if the bench is loose. But it's not. A weight scurries beneath me. There's something in the bench.

Recoiling, I jump to my feet on the counter. Four of the bench's doors are forced open and giant spiders pour into the room, each of them easily a metre in diametre. Their bodies are almost black, mottled with orange-coloured flecks and as big as hors d'eurve platters. More cupboards are knocked open, right along the bench's length, and extra arachnids step out. They completely cover the floor, moving up the walls and on to the ceiling. Each creature has a dozen dark, bottomless eyes. Cold and unreadable. There is a pair of black, obsidian fangs that jut below their head, like two daggers on each side of the mouth.

The realisation that I am going to die quite an extraordinary and horrible death inebriates me. I'm splintered between the desire to fight honourably or just close my eyes and pray that the end is swift.

The air is filled with the same soft whispers that I heard outside the kitchenette. It's as if angels are mouthing soothing words of comfort. But while I can't make exact sense of their murmuring, the chattered noise that these chill-inducing aliens emit sounds decidedly like English. They're saying something that few humans probably live long enough to decipher.

I'm pressed into the corner. While I don't count precise numbers, there must be fifty of them in my vicinity now, covering the ceiling, floor and walls. A dark, writhing renovation that whispers and taps with long, jagged spindles. Whispering. Hushed menace. One of them is covering the round fluorescent light in the middle of the ceiling, darkening the room and throwing an eight-legged shadow across the backs of the horrid creatures below. A particularly large arachnid is on the roof, upside down, no more than two feet from my face. Like the rest it shifts back and forth, just staring and examining with its polished gemstone eyes. I look at its furry mouth opening, which resembles the brush accessory you put on the end of a vacuum cleaner.

I slowly raise my fists in a defensive stance, deciding that if I can kick and punch quickly enough from my corner then I might have the strength to scatter them. But I am greatly outnumbered.

The closest arachnid creeps nearer and I brace, expecting it to lead the charge. But then I hear its whisper. This time I understand what it says. It's softly spoken, but clear. It's a gentle, child-like inquiry.

"What ... are you?"

# CHAPTER TWENTY-EIGHT

Natalie drops me off in the alley behind my building. Before leaving the Pluie Tordue she instructed me to act normally inside my apartment. Apparently my home is not as private as I thought. It's possible that they're listening or watching me. Natalie says she will be in touch very soon. She gives me a safe number, on which I can privately message her, and drives away in my new car.

I let myself in through a small fire exit and take the stairs to the third storey, where I enter an elevator to the top floor. It's near sunrise so I close the curtains in my bedroom and crawl on to the mattress. While my mind races for an hour or so, I do manage to fall asleep.

I wake to a voice. A soft female whisper. "Jack... Jack." When my eyelids part I see the dying glow of the suns behind the blinds, registering as dusk. Sprawled on my stomach, under the blanket, I listen, waiting for the voice to return. A minute passes and I assume I've been dreaming.

But then, as clear as the chirp of the traffic below, I hear a woman's voice whisper, "Jack..."

I flip over, perched on my elbows. The shape of a woman stands at the end of the bed. Long blonde hair and a slender frame. I squint hard as the shape speaks again.

"I'm sorry to startle you," says the woman, as she slowly steps around the side of the bed, moving toward me.

It's Stephanie. She wears a silk robe pulled tight at the neck.

"Steph, hi..." I mumble, my brain still uncoiling and stretching from its subconscious state. "What brings you here? Was my door unlocked?"

"They let me in," she smiles, still whispering. "They said you would want to see me. To approve and anoint me."

"Oh... okay," I say. "But I've always approved of you. You don't need further approval... do you?"

"I do," she smiles, reaching for the silk cord that synchs the garment at her waist. She slowly pulls on the knot and it unties. "I need for you to take me one last time."

"I'm sure that you don't."

"Do you want to see my transformation?" asks Stephanie.

I can't exactly say no. "Alright."

In the dim light the corners of Stephanie's lips curl in the hint of a smile. I lean over and switch on the bedside lamp. She slowly pulls open her robe, teasing it wider until it slips from her shoulders and cascades to the floor. Shock surges through me. My mouth open, I stare at her naked body. Her soft pale skin from collarbone to shoulders and down to her groin has been tattooed. Intricate, dense and demented imagery has been indelibly penned on her young body. There must be thousands of pictures within the tapestry of black ink, which hasn't spared a single square inch of her torso.

"Do you not approve?" asks Stephanie, her face now tinged with disappointment and fear.

"No, of course I do," I reassure her, forcing a smile. "Will you turn around?"

Stephanie smiles at my interest and raises her arms, slowly turning. The tattoo continues around to her back, up to the base of her neck and down across her buttocks, ending at the tops of her thighs. They've completely defaced her.

Stephanie completes her rotation and I beckon for her to lie next to me on the bed. She eases on to the mattress. When she's close enough, I reach out and place a hand on her hip, pulling her against me. As her head hits the pillow I kiss her and Stephanie wraps her arms around my neck, holding me with thankfulness and relief.

"Does it hurt?" I ask, running my fingertips across her stomach.

"It hurts less every day," she replies. "But it ached a lot when it was finished."

"You're very brave to go through with this," I smile. "It must have been excruciating."

"I wasn't awake for most of it," she replies, sheepishly.

"That's okay. No shame in that."

Stephanie beams at my comment. "I feel so safe with you," she says. "I feel like nothing can happen to me when I'm around you."

"Really?"

"Yes, of course," she says, running a hand through my hair. "You brought me back to life. You delivered me from the arms of death."

"I suppose I did," I say.

"Now I hope that you will create new life with me. A new life inside me," she whispers.

"Really?"

"I am a vessel for your bloodline. I am ready to carry your child."

I smile at Stephanie, but my heart fills with sadness. If I had become involved in this dark chain of events sooner, I could have saved this girl's susceptible soul.

"Stephanie, who let you into my apartment?"

"Just one of the guards," she says.

"Guards? Do you mean the men in the lobby?"

"Yes, the guardians of The Disciplinary."

"The men with the jackets? In the foyer of this building?"

"Yes...?"

"The Disciplinary?"

"Yes."

"Where did you have this tattoo drawn?" I ask.

"Here."

"Here?"

"Yes."

"In The Disciplinary?"

"Yes... is something wrong?"

"No," I smile, reassuringly. "No, everything is perfect, Stephanie."

"Oh... good," she says, uncertain.

"Any particular floor?"

"I was on the twelfth floor," she smiles.

"Excellent," I reply. "Now before I... I mean, before we... create a life together, I'm going to fix us a drink."

"Okay," Stephanie replies.

I crawl out of bed, leaving my visitor naked under the covers, and venture to the kitchen where I find a bottle of my strongest spirit. I then fill two glasses with ice and pour the spirit over the cubes. I open the cabinet where I keep my medicinal supplies and locate a tranquiliser. It's a small white pill. It knocks its consumer straight out. I drop one into Stephanie's drink and stir it with a small straw.

In the bedroom I toast to our romantic engagement and suggest that we waste no time in finishing our drinks. Stephanie, now sitting up in bed, removes her straw and takes a long sip on her beverage. She then swallows before taking another final gulp. Only ice is left in her glass.

"Wow, that's very strong," she says.

"It's good, isn't it," I say.

"Yes..." says Stephanie. Her eyes linger on me for a moment before they slowly close. I take the glass from her delicate hand. A second later she slumps forward, folding over. I place our glasses on my bedside dresser and position her so she's lying down, flat on her back, a single pillow propped under her head. I then check her pulse, which is slow and steady, and I watch her chest rise and fall.

I slide open my wardrobe and quickly pull on a pair of jeans, a t-shirt, jacket and slip-on shoes.

All of the apartment doors on floor twelve look the same. I put my ear to each. No sound strikes me as unusual. I can hear televisions. Some music. People talking. Some are silent. I tread carefully on the soft carpet of the hallway. I pass a mirror on the wall, glancing at myself, eyeing my slender, but volatile, frame, poised for an unseen threat. I walk past another half a dozen doors, stopping to listen at each. There's something different about the door at the end of the corridor. Like every other entrance, it has a spyhole. But this door has a second spyhole, about one metre from the ground. A similar height to that of my neighbour.

I reach the door and crouch to listen. I can hear some muffled talking. Perhaps a female whimper. Then I hear a buzzing sound. A faint vibration. Barely audible. I decide to knock. Three sharp taps with my knuckle. I stand back so I am visible through both spyholes.

Silence. It's as if the hallway has inhaled and held its breath. Finally there is a clicking sound and the door opens a fraction. There is no light inside the apartment apart from a dim red glow. A small shape, just a shadow appears around the open door.

"Hello, friend," I smile.

Mr Roeg doesn't say anything at first. He just stares at me with his beady eyes.

"Jack," says Mr Roeg, quietly, the high-pitched nasal tone of his voice unmistakable. "I wasn't expecting you."

"I thought I'd come down and surprise you."

Mr Roeg remains behind the door, peering up at me. "Did... Stephanie tell you I was here?"

"Not exactly," I say. "I heard a voice. I was just asleep and... my father told me to go down to floor twelve."

"Your father?"

"Yes."

"He spoke to you?"

"Sure did. He's not far away now."

"Oh," says Mr Roeg. He stands aside, the door creeping open. "Then you should come inside."

I step into a hallway. Most of the lights in the apartment are out. At the end of the corridor is a living room and there's a red lamp illuminating some furniture. A lounge. A coffee table. There's soft carpet beneath my feet. Most of the doors in the hall are shut. One has a light escaping its edges. Bright white lines, as if there's a bathroom on the other side.

Mr Roeg walks somewhere behind me. "What else did your father say?" he asks.

I turn around and kneel, so that we are at eye level. "I heard his voice in my dream. I was lying under the suns and his words hummed all around me, clear as blue sky."

"What... what did he say?" asks my stout host.

"Mr Roeg," I smile. "He told me that judgement is coming. But it could not be him who has the final word on our souls. He said that it had to be me."

"You?"

"Yes," I reply, putting a hand on Mr Roeg's tiny shoulder. "It is up to me to separate the insincere from those who are pure and ready."

A young, female voice from behind the bathroom door, says, "Jack, is that you?"

I stand and slowly turn the handle. The door to the bathroom opens, the brilliant white light widening in an arc. Britney is lying in a bathtub, submerged to her collarbone. Her smiling cherub face looks up at me, floating clouds of suds protecting the most crucial aspects of her modesty.

"Britney," I smile.

"I thought I heard your voice," she says. "Are you here for moral support?"

"Moral support," I say. "Indeed, I am. Mr Roeg and I were just discussing something. Don't go anywhere."

"Be quick," says Britney. "My fingers are beginning to shrivel."

I close the door.

I walk to the end of the hallway, into the living room. I look down to my left and there is a mattress on the carpet. On the mattress is a naked girl on her back, the third missing girl, asleep. Void of pubic hair. There's a black tattoo, new and raw, on her left shoulder, creeping its way down her chest. Unfinished. Next to the mattress is a small metal contraption that I assume is a tattoo pen.

"You're quite an artist, Mr Roeg," I say.

"Thank you," he says, stepping around me and into the living room. "I am glad that you approve."

"Of course," I reply. "I suppose I just wish that less went on without me knowing."

"Oh?" asks Mr Roeg. "But these are your wishes... aren't they?"

"Who told you that?"

"Mr Brannagh," says Mr Roeg. "You tell him what to do next and he facilitates it. Yes?"

I again lower to speak with him, "I mentioned that I am here to determine who is sincere. To make sure that I can trust those around me."

"Yes," nods Mr Roeg.

"Can I trust you?"

"Of course," he replies, "I'm your artist, sir. I am the decorator and I do so with passion."

"Why?"

"Because I believe in you."

"But why are you tattooing these young women? To what end?"

"Because they are offerings to the winged ones. They demonstrate our conviction and desire for their return."

"And Mr Brannagh told you that this is what I want? That these are my instructions?"

"Yes, sir. That is clearly what he said. He passes on your wishes."

"You say you believe in me?" I ask.

"Yes," nods Mr Roeg, emphatically. "You are the Messiah."

"You believe that I have the power to return the dead to the realm of the living?"

"Yes," he nods. "Yes."

"Then, Mr Roeg, are you prepared to die and be returned?"

Mr Roeg pauses before answering, staring at me blankly with his beady eyes. "I beg your pardon, Messiah?"

"Are you prepared to die and be returned?"

Mr Roeg continues to stare. "I... are you asking me to die?"

"It's very simple, Mr Roeg. You believe in me and my power. You believe that I can return the dead to the living. If this is so, then you are prepared to die and be reborn."

Mr Roeg is blank faced. Almost catatonic. The weight of my proposition clearly an uncomfortable burden. But this is what I demand. It's a response I require to determine the sincerity of Mr Roeg and his convictions. Is he a blind follower or a conniving manipulator?

"Yes," he says, finally. "I do believe. I am prepared to die and be reborn."

"Good," I say. "Follow me."

We return up the hallway, back to the bathtub in which Britney lies, washing in preparation to be defaced. Unwittingly tied to unseen strings. Threads that I, regrettably, have played a part in dangling.

We step into the bathroom. Britney continues to lie submerged in the steaming water and she smiles at me with such admiration when I reappear.

"Care to join me?" she asks.

My eyes are unable to avoid a brief inspection of her body. I walk over to a rack and remove a white, fluffy towel. I hold it up and smile. "We need to use this bathtub for a few minutes, Britney. Do you mind vacating for just a moment?"

Mr Roeg stands by the bathroom door. While his unusually small facial features are at times hard to decipher, there is no questioning his fear. Britney stands from the water, a coquettish smile forming as I hand her the towel. She wraps it around her body.

"If you could leave the bathroom for a few minutes, that would be greatly appreciated," I say. "I assure you that you'll be able to return very soon."

"That's okay," she smiles. "I'm already very clean."

Her eyes linger on me as she vacates the room. I close the door behind her. The water in the bathtub is deep enough for me to submerge Mr Roeg and hold him under. And I have the strength to.

"Should I get undressed?" asks Mr Roeg.

"No need," I say, removing my jacket and tossing it in the corner.

I lift him up under his arms, his miniature body like that of a toddler. He doesn't fight. I then lower him into the hot water, shoes first, and he gasps as he slowly slides in. He utters nothing as he leans back and goes beneath the surface, allowing me to end his life. Mr Roeg knows that I have the strength to hold him under if he changes his mind. In the water up to my elbows, I keep him pinned to the bottom of the bathtub. He keeps his eyes shut, as if asleep. He is still and serene. A few small bubbles of oxygen escape his nose and I wonder how long he will take to die.

I find myself locked in the moment. Staring not at a blind and vulnerable little man, but at the darkness. I wonder how wide the void in Mr Roeg's soul must have been to require a calling such as this. He must have been so empty and lonely to buy into this deception. To become embroiled in Brannagh's manipulation. To stencil innocent, pretty things with the violence in his head. To illustrate the evil of these scriptures, these fictional amalgamations of folklore. Directing anger at Mr Roeg is pointless. He requires my deep, sincere pity. He needs it quickly too.

I wrench him upward by his lapels and he takes a heavy breath as his face breaks the surface of the water. I rise to my feet and walk over to the hand towel rack next to the basin. I dry my arms.

"Have I died?" he asks, spluttering, wiping water from his eyes. "Has it happened?"

"No, Mr Roeg," I say, quietly. "It hasn't happened. But you have proved your loyalty."

"Oh," he gasps. "Oh."

"Mr Roeg," I say, returning to the edge of the bathtub, kneeling down. "Listen to my words very carefully."

"Yes?" he says, still sitting in the water up to his collarbone.

"I don't want you to take orders from Mr Brannagh anymore. I don't want you to do anything unless I tell you myself."

"Really?"

"Mr Roeg... Mr Brannagh is... a false prophet."

Mr Roeg stares, shocked.

"C'mon," I say, offering him my towel. "Get out and dry yourself."

Mr Roeg stands and climbs from the bathtub. He looks ridiculous, his clothes completely drenched.

"I was ready to die," he says, quietly. "Jack. I hope you can see that."

"I know," I say. "Now listen to me. No more inking people. No more drawing on girls. Understand?"

"Okay," he replies, sullenly. "I'm just... very confused right now."

"You and me both."

"So should I still start my work on the pillows tonight?" asks Mr Roeg, removing his small jacket and wringing it out over the bath. "I was due to start tonight. I have a lot of fine ideas."

"What are you talking about?" I ask. "What pillows?"

"The pillows," says Mr Roeg. "The grand offering. I haven't started any of the artwork yet. Mr Brannagh said we need to start as soon as possible, because keeping them asleep is quite a task."

"I don't know what you're talking about."

"But it was your instructions. You explained how the offering must be put together."

"Mr Brannagh told you that. Explain to me this *offering*."

Mr Roeg looks alarmed. "When your father and his people return, they expect a grand offering. We've been putting it together for many months now. Your wishes."

"But what is the offering?"

"The offering... it's what you asked for."

"Mr Roeg, if you make me ask again, I will drown you and you will not be reborn. I'll have you stuffed and mounted."

"The offering is two hundred souls. Living flesh."

"Why do you call them pillows?"

Mr Roeg shakes his head. "Forgive me, but I am very confused. These have been your wishes."

There's a knock at the bathroom door. A quick, frantic knock. "Jack?" calls Britney.

"Yes?" I reply. "We're still busy."

"It's Delilah," says Britney, through the door. "I don't think she's breathing."

"I might have given her too much sedative," says Mr Roeg, concern crossing his face.

I pull open the door, rushing out to the living room where Delilah, whose name I had forgotten, is lying cold and still on the mattress.

"When did she stop breathing?" I ask.

"Just then," says Britney, becoming upset. "I was sitting next to her. She became very still."

I lean over Delilah, who I now remember was a marketing girl that worked at a venue Big Bang Theory performed at in our early days, and check that her tongue isn't blocking her airway. When I see that it isn't, I quickly begin resuscitation. I have no idea what drug has knocked her out. But I can only hope that this works.

I continue compressions on her chest followed by breaths into her mouth and then alternate. With every attempt to revive her I lose confidence. My compressions become agitated. I push down on her with more force. I can feel Mr Roeg and Britney standing behind me, watching, and expecting a miracle. I breathe deeply into her mouth and she coughs. I pull my head away and watch Delilah take a long inhalation.

"It is truly the work of the Messiah and the divine power of his heritage," says Mr Roeg.

"Amazing..." says Britney. "I can't believe I've finally seen it with my own eyes."

Delilah continues to cough and I roll her on to her side, in case she vomits.

"Mr Roeg, you clearly fucked up your dosage," I say.

"But she was never in danger," he replies. "We have you here to save us. You and your father are protecting us."

Britney kneels down beside me as I tend to Delilah. "Jack," whispers Britney. "Please make love to me."

"Now is probably not an appropriate time."

Britney and I dress Delilah in a silk gown and I carry her up to my floor. Mr Roeg and Britney follow. At the door of my apartment I prop Delilah against me while I reach for my keys. Behind me an apartment door opens. I glance over my shoulder and see Laurie. She's leaning in her doorway, wearing jeans and a white singlet top. Her arms are folded and she doesn't look impressed.

"I've been trying to call you," she says. "Are you ignoring me?"

"Laurie, hi," I say, turning back to my apartment door to push the keys into the lock. "I've been meaning to call you. I've been very busy."

"It looks like it," says Laurie.

"I'm sorry," I say. "I know this must look a little strange..." I push the door open and scoop Delilah into my arms, stepping inside.

"Strange?" calls Laurie. "No, this isn't strange, Jack. Why would I be surprised to see you walking into your apartment with an unconscious girl, a blonde trashbag in a towel and a wet, creepy dwarf? I wouldn't expect anything less!"

"I am not creepy!" exclaims Mr Roeg. "You're a disgusting little princess, whose parents have spoiled her rotten," he hisses.

"Laurie," I say, balancing Delilah as I usher Britney and Mr Roeg into my apartment. "I'll call you. I promise."

"You should," says Laurie.

"I will," I reply.

"Because I'm pregnant," says Laurie.

Britney slams my apartment door and Laurie disappears from view.

"What a rude little bitch," says Britney.

I barely have time for Laurie's revelation to register. I carry Delilah down my hallway and lay her on my bed next to Stephanie, who is still asleep. I check that they are both breathing and have a pulse.

When I return to my living room, Britney is sitting on my couch, still wearing her towel and flipping through a magazine. Mr Roeg is in my kitchen, shivering.

"I'd give you fresh clothes, Mr Roeg. But I'm a size larger than you."

"That is very humourous, my lord," he says, bowing.

"Cut that out," I say.

"What do you mean?"

"Stop worshiping me," I reply. "I'm not in the mood."

"But, you have now performed two miracles. You are truly the Messiah."

"Enough!" I yell. I find a glass and pour myself a spirit. I take a long sip of the golden liquid, feeling it burn my throat. Savouring it. I recall Natalie telling me that, as far as she is aware, there are no listening devices on my balcony. It might be a safe place to talk. I then walk over to Mr Roeg and say very quietly, "Come outside and tell me about these pillows."

I pour myself a fifth spirit from the bottle and then place it back on the coffee table. Mr Roeg is sitting on the balcony, the cool night wind drying his clothing. Britney, Delilah and Stephanie are all asleep in my bed, each in various states of narcotic debilitation. I've been in to check on them a few times. They're all breathing. Alive and, in the short term, content.

Mr Roeg has agreed to take me to the pillow people, which I don't think I will believe until I see them with my own eyes. But I can't leave the three girls here in this building. This so-called Disciplinary. I send a text message to Natalie on the number she gave me. "Three girls in my apartment that need help, protection. I have to leave. Babysit?"

Her text message response is swift. "Don't leave your apartment. Need you to stay there. Do the girls need a doctor?"

I type back, "Leaving my apartment. Driving to Godiva. You can follow. Send someone to watch girls."

Natalie's next response isn't as quick. I finish my spirit and pour another before she replies. "Sending two of my people. 'Friends' you met on tour. They'll be armed."

"Nice. Arms will help. Names?"

"Lou and Gaz."

Five minutes later my apartment phone rings. It's one of the doormen in the building's foyer. "Sir, I have two gentleman here that say they are guests of yours."

"Lou and Gaz?" I ask, jovially. "Send them up!"

There's a knock at my door and I open it. Two strapping, yet casually dressed, gentleman stand before me. While they're not wearing government issue uniforms and earpieces, they have wide necks and look a lot like special agents.

"Nice to see you again, boys. Come on in," I say.

"Thanks, Jack," says one of them with a clean white smile.

They follow me into my kitchen. I find a piece of paper and a pen and write, *"Three girls in bedroom. Stephanie and Delilah have taken large doses of sedatives and are stable. Sleeping it off. Britney is just drunk. Seems like she's on drugs, but isn't."*

One of the agents reads the letter and gives me a reassuring nod. Then he says, "So how have you been? It's good to see you again, friend."

"I'm good, I'm good," I reply. "Still recovering from the tour, man. You know how it is. It takes a lot out of you. Puts a lot into you too."

"Nice," says the other guard. "Well you look good."

"You're too kind," I smile, before adding, "well, as I said, I've got to sneak out of here for a little while to visit someone. But make yourselves at home. There's more alcohol than you can drink. I think one of the big games is on television tonight."

"Yeah, I think the ultimate final is on in the national league," says one of the guards, either Lou or Gaz.

The agents, I assume as protocol, scope out my apartment for a while, checking every room. They examine wardrobes, cupboards, shelving, under furniture and in the fan outlet in the bathroom. In the hallway I see one of them, either Lou or Gaz, hold up the five fingers of his right hand. This possibly means he has found five listening devices.

I walk out to the balcony. "Ready to roll, Mr Roeg?"

The little man is slumped in one my of outdoor chairs, gazing out at the blinking lights of the city's midnight hour. "Yes," he says. Then, turning to look up at me, he adds, "Has Mr Brannagh really been lying to us?"

"I'll explain later," I say.

With Mr Roeg strapped in the front passenger seat, I roll my sports car out of the garage and into the side alley of my apartment building. As I weave through the traffic on the way out of town towards Godiva, it's hard to tell if I'm being followed. But as we hit the outskirts and I take the main turn-off out to the rural areas, it's apparent that there are at least five vehicles heading in the same direction as me.

"So they're beneath the labbia pen?" I ask Mr Roeg.

"Yes, there are underground dwellings beneath where the pen was erected. Old servants' quarters. Lots of space down there. There's a warren of corridors and rooms."

"Will there be anyone down there?" I ask.

"There are a few people, medical students, I believe, who are tending to the pillows."

"They shouldn't be much trouble."

When we arrive at the long stretch of road that passes Godiva, there are at least three cars still following us. I slow down to find the obscured turn-off that winds to the front gate and then turn off and park. The three cars cruise past behind us on the main road. I'm confident they will pull over somewhere out of sight. Godiva's grand metal gates appear in the headlights, as does the intercom on its thin stand. I lower my window as it aligns with the small box.

"State your name," says Godiva's sultry voice.

"Hello, sweetheart," I say. "It's Jack. I've come to visit you."

"Jack, you do not have a scheduled visit," she replies, in an apologetic tone.

"It's a surprise visit," I say. "Humans frequently surprise each other. Now I am surprising you."

"Jack, you do not have clearance at this present time. However, I can contact Mr Brannagh and I'm sure he will clear you."

"Wait," I say. "Don't do that." I turn to Mr Roeg. "You must have clearance."

"I believe I do," he replies.

"Well get out of your seat and ask her to let us in," I hiss.

Mr Roeg hurriedly unbuckles his seat belt and stands up, leaning across me. "Godiva, this is Mr Roeg. Jack is a guest of mine. I am here to begin work on the major project. We will need complete clearance all the way to the bunker."

After a brief pause, Godiva replies, "Of course, Mr Roeg. Access is granted."

The wide gates creak to life.

I park my car on a section of driveway that wraps around the side of the grand home. The white lights around Godiva's gardens are on, providing a small glow. But the mansion itself is drenched in darkness. No lights shine through any windows. The rear yard and the path down to the labbia pen are close, only fifty metres in front of us.

"It's dark," says Mr Roeg.

"I noticed that."

"There are no lights on inside Godiva," he adds.

"Should there be?"

"I thought there might be people here. Preparing."

"I see."

"There should be lots of people here."

"Says who?"

"Mr Brannagh. He told me the followers were gathering."

"Well, he says a lot of things," I reply. "He might not have the legion of disciples that you think he does."

I would be surprised if he has amassed a large following, considering the heinous nature of his crimes. The people of this planet will be sickened by his actions. I open my door and step onto the paved drive. The cold air hits me as I look up at the building. There are definitely no lights switched on in Godiva. I stare at a few of the windows to see if I can see anything out of the ordinary. But there are just curtains and blinds. No faces inside. No inquisitive sets of eyes. The only sounds are birds and insects chattering in the gardens and the dense forest beyond.

Mr Roeg also exits the vehicle and together we walk toward the path that winds down to the labbia pen. As we round the side of the house I can see mist swirl above the pool, the water illuminated by submerged lighting. Everything else is deathly still. The statues amongst the shrubbery are dark, half-lit shapes.

We tread down the path until it brings us to the entrance of the labbia's enclosure. I peer through the metal fence and hear nothing. No bleating animals or rustling leaves.

"It should be unlocked," says Mr Roeg. "Godiva was to give us access right through to the bunker."

"Is it safe to be in there?" I ask. "I was under the impression that labbia have pretty sharp teeth."

"Yes, but they don't attack unless threatened."

"What constitutes a threat? Sneaking into their pen after midnight?"

"It should be fine."

"Well, considering the size difference between you and me... it's probably fair that you go first and I'll follow," I say.

"Messiah..." says Mr Roeg, clearly a little worried. "How would that be fair?"

"Because you might get lodged in their throat. That would give me time to escape."

My companion's face, as usual, is quite unreadable.

"I'm joking," I say, and open the gate.

As it happens, Mr Roeg has to lead because I have no idea where we're going. Beneath the overgrown grass is an old path. I can feel the ancient tiles beneath my feet. We duck and step around low-hanging branches. There is a choir of insects around us, singing along to each other, but there's no sign of the labbia. I can barely see in front of my face, the tiny glow of my phone's screen the only torch. Further along the path I notice a small light ahead of us. I push aside more branches. There's a small, wooden shack.

Next to the faded, dilapidated door is a small orange globe. It's covered in cobwebs but provides enough light for us to see each other. While the wood of the structure is clearly old and the door doesn't look like it would withstand a swift boot, there is a very modern security keypad next to its handle. An intriguing anachronism.

Mr Roeg reaches up and punches in a number. I watch his fingers. The number is 3801. He then presses an enter button. The door clicks as it unlocks. My vertically challenged acquaintance then turns the handle and opens the decaying door.

As I was expecting, there is nothing inside the shack except for a concrete floor and a stairwell. There are chipped, cold metal rails on each side and the stairs descend into complete darkness.

"No lights, Mr Roeg?" I ask. "For one of the richest men on the planet, Mr Brannagh doesn't like to spend much on electricity."

"I'm certain there will be lights in the corridor at the bottom," says Mr Roeg.

We walk down what feels like one hundred cold concrete steps before we arrive at a door on our left. The temperature drops and the chill twirls its fingers in patterns across my skin. We open the door to a well-lit corridor. Long halogen tubes hang on cobwebbed chains from the mottled, rust-brown ceiling. The grey of the walls and floor are stained red in patches, as if blood has congealed into bruises.

Mr Roeg waddles in front of me and we pass many closed doors, each with large sliding bolts to keep them locked. From the outside. But there is no one around. No patrolling security guards. No overweight men in bloodied butcher's aprons, wielding chainsaws. No horror of any kind. Brannagh could afford to have a small army down here to protect his scheme. But so far there is no one here to defend these clandestine atrocities.

One of the doors we pass is slightly ajar and I stop.

"Mr Roeg," I say.

He stops and turns.

"What's in here?" I ask.

"It's one of the preparation rooms."

I push on the door and what I find is unusual by most people's standards. The walls are the same colour as the corridor, but there are metal benches in the centre and along the outside of the room. The air is sodden with the stench of blood. That unsettling, coppery odour is everywhere and the red splatter is on the floor, the walls and the metallic surfaces. It looks more like an abattoir than a

391

morgue. On a bench to my right are implements. There are a few knives and scalpels as well as an array of surgical saws.

On the opposite side of the room is a young man. He's wearing a white surgeon's coat and white gloves. His face is dusted with charcoal and his skin is brown. He is standing between a metal bench and a gaping furnace. The heat of the furnace hits me from fifteen feet away. On the metal bench is a pile of long objects. Skin-coloured. They are limbs. Human arms and legs. Detached. Piled in a heap and awaiting incineration.

The young man is staring at me.

"Do you know who I am?" I ask.

His mouth agape, he just nods.

"What are you burning?" I ask.

"These are... are... the leftovers," he stammers. From his speech I deduce that he is simple. His elevator doesn't go all the way to the top floor. If this man is dim, I expect he's easily convinced and persuaded.

"The leftovers?"

"We have... no use for them," he mutters.

"Arms and legs? You seem to be using yours."

The man stares back, his body tense. On edge.

"Do you believe in this work that you're doing?"

"Yes," nods the man.

"You believe that my father and his race are returning?"

"Yes," nods the man.

"Then you believe that I have the power to return the dead to the living."

The man nods, but doesn't say anything.

"Well you need to prove your faith to me," I say.

"Yes," says the man, emphatically. "I can, I can."

"Climb into the furnace. Let the flames devour you and I will bring you back to life, stronger than you were before. You will have almighty power."

The man's eyes shift back and forth between the insidious oven and I. He doesn't move, riveted to the floor like these metal tables.

"That's what I thought," I say. I step outside the room, close the door and then bolt it shut, locking him in. "Let's continue, Mr Roeg. I'm only here to see the main attraction."

Mr Roeg and I walk to the end of the corridor, where we find another downward staircase. It is very long. I'm reminded of the stairs that Natalie and I descended to the Narc den on our night of debauched courtship. These steps, both their individual depth and width, are identical to those beneath the club Membrané. The same era of subterranean architecture. The same design.

The stairs deliver us to a small foyer of aged grey brick and a set of steel double doors. Next to them is another security keypad.

"They are inside," says Mr Roeg, exhausted from our second extended descent.

"Let's take a look," I say.

Mr Roeg steps to the keypad, again types 3801 and the doors make an echoed thump as they unlock.

This large room, like an old rail shed, is long and high. It's a Narc den. The smell is similar. Sweat, urine and every dank odour in between. There are many people here, all in their deep Narc sleep, dreaming impossible dreams. There are many beds too. But there is one considerable point of difference between my present location and my memories of the previous Narc den. The people beneath Membrané still had their arms and legs. Their heads had not been shaved. They were not naked. My eyes, despite my heavy desire to turn and walk from the room, graze across these skillfully mutilated people in their cheap beds. A clear tube snakes into each mouth, providing sustenance. The lips have been sown shut to keep them in place.

I have not made it more than two metres into the room. What I am seeing is far removed from any reality I have ever experienced. I dare step no further, as if closer inspection will solidify it. Will confirm that all this is real. I stand like a statue, my eyes scanning the room, lingering on the stitched stumps of these poor victims and watching the calm, gentle rise and fall of their chests. The inhumane presence of life support. I thought that Stephanie's tattoo was extreme defilement, but it was a playful slap compared to what has become of these people. The Narc drug flows through their system and their ignorant, comatose state is Brannagh's only mercy.

Mr Roeg casually walks up the centre aisle of the room, examining the people on the beds.

"You have butchered these people," I say, perhaps not to Mr Roeg in particular. "You've butchered them."

"I was told that sacrifices had to be made. That these people were going to a better place. To walk through the gates of Earth and live in its glow for all eternity," says Mr Roeg.

"Did these people," I ask, pointing at one of the beds, "*volunteer* to do this?"

"They're Narc overdoses," shrugs Mr Roeg, his voicing rising with positive inflection. As if this is no big deal. "People know there's a risk they might not wake up when they take it. These people signed away their bodies when they went to the dens."

"And Marty Brannagh is in control of these dens?"

"Yes."

"And he no doubt controlled the Narc dosage these people were given."

"Yes..." replies Mr Roeg, "I suppose he would have."

"Fuck!" I yell, overcome with anger. My outburst ricochets around the ancient walls.

As I stand there, looking at these rows of lost souls, their limbs plucked from them, I can't help but dwell on a single thought. If Brannagh believes in all of this and is certain that I am a Jesus-like individual, then why has he kept everything from me? Why would he hide something as monstrous as this from view? Then my mind turns to what Brannagh buys and sells. What he has built his fortune on. His empire is a provider of culture. He creates it. He convinces people of its importance. He is a God-like tastemaker. The immense financial success of his Marioneta de Carne exhibition will not have gone unnoticed. The prophesised return of some winged people from the distant past could hide another motive.

At the end of the room is another set of double doors.

"What's through there?" I ask Mr Roeg.

"It's the workshop," he replies.

"Sounds ominous," I reply.

"It's where the artworks are made."

I walk towards the double doors, holding my breath as the stench of these bed-ridden junkies rises around me. I reach the centre of the room. A deep metallic sound announces that someone is opening the workshop doors. A man in a white, bloodstained surgical coat, with white gloves and a facemask, emerges. He notices me and his eyes widen in surprise.

The man freezes, then bows and says, "My lord."

I walk to him. "I'm here to see your progress."

"Yes, of course," he nods and exerts strength to open the wide metallic entrance.

I step past the gowned man and into the so-called workshop. Mr Roeg trots along behind me. Only minutes ago I believed the room of amputees was the most macabre and disturbing thing I had ever seen. But it seems that Brannagh has a trump card. He is a man of many secrets and someone less sane than myself might marvel at not only the scope of his nature, but also how well he conceals it from the public and its peripheral vision.

"Well, Mr Roeg," I say to my stunted companion, "It seems I've found the labbia."

# CHAPTER TWENTY-NINE

I ease out of the bed and lower my feet to the carpet. It's a surprisingly chilly morning for this time of year. My pants are next to the bed, long and crumpled. Inside my pants I find my briefs, cocooned within. My belt is still threaded through the waist. A metre away, toward the end of the bed, is my shirt and suit jacket. It's expensive clothing to have strewn across the floor, but I gave no thought to its worth when I entered this room last night, drunk and luminescent.

I quietly dress and look at the woman still asleep. She doesn't stir at all. She's peaceful. Content. I leave the room in its serene glow, close the bedroom door and walk down the hallway.

In the kitchen I look through cupboards, hoping to find painkillers. My headache is tolerable, but why tolerate it? After swinging open half a dozen doors I find a few pills. I cup tap water with my hand and wash them down. There's a handbag sitting on its side on the small kitchen table. Inside is a wallet. The driver's license says Delilah Jones. I couldn't remember her damn name. Small flashes of information emerge from the fog in my head. She works for the venue we played at last night. There was a babysitter here when Delilah brought me home. I signed an autograph for her. Then she left. Then there was Delilah's bedroom.

My own wallet and a set of keys are next to Delilah's handbag, which I put back into my pocket. Though my phone isn't there.

Then I hear a noise. A faint clicking sound. A whirring. I turn around and see something sitting on the carpet in the adjacent living room, framed by an archway. It's a tiny, wide-eyed little creature. In one hand is a toy truck, which it wheels back and forth along the rug. It never takes its eyes off me.

The small boy could be no more than three years old. I watch him maneuver the truck back and forth with his right hand in a semi circle. Then I hear a noise that doesn't fit this image. A deep, masculine voice projects from the child.

"Endeavour, do you copy?" says the voice. "Endeavour, this is flight commander Atticus O'Connor onboard the Santa Maria. Do you copy?"

The boy looks down at the phone in his other hand, seemingly puzzled by the crackled words that appear from it.

"Hey there," I say to the boy. "That's a nice truck."

The boy looks at me blankly. The object in his hand is not Norman. It's my other phone. A UHF receiver. It's one of the devices I landed with. The receiver and my phone were on my bedside dresser last night and I've picked up the wrong one when I left my apartment. It was turned off in my pocket and I never used it.

I sit on the rug next to the boy, trying to keep calm. My heart is thumping in its cage, rattling the bars.

"Do you mind if I have my *phone* back? I think someone is trying to speak to me."

I slowly reach for the receiver and the boy grasps it tightly in his hand. He doesn't want to release it.

"I promise you can have it back," I say.

The boy holds it to his chest in a chubby fist. His round face furrows.

"How about we arm wrestle for it?" I offer.

The boy grips the device, not responding. I could force it from him. It would be like taking a UHF receiver from a baby. But he might start to cry and I'm not sure how that would look if his mother wakes. It also makes my escape a little more awkward.

I reach over to a nearby sofa and pick up the remote control for the adjacent television. It turns on and I quickly switch channels until I find a cartoon. The boy is watching the screen now. I turn the sound right down, the jolly music fading to zero. The boy glares at me, unimpressed by the lack of volume.

I hold out the remote control. "Swap?" I ask.

The boy reaches for the remote but still holds the receiver.

"No," I say, shaking my head. I point at the receiver. "Let's swap. It's a straight deal. Let's do this."

One of the cartoon's characters starts chasing his co-star, leading to some incredibly zany moments. The boy becomes more agitated by the silence. I put the remote control in his lap and pry the phone from his tiny hand. The boy looks at me intently for a few seconds, his face tensing. He is bracing to cry. But when another outrageous exchange appears on the TV, he presses his chubby hand to the volume button.

"Nice work," I say and return to the kitchen.

Commander O'Connor's voice appears again, crackling slightly. "Endeavour, this is Commander Atticus O'Connor on board the Santa Maria. Do you copy?"

I put the receiver to my mouth. "Commander O'Connor. It's nice to hear from you."

"Captain!" says O'Connor, his voice full of relief and elation. There are cheers in the background. "God damn it is good to hear your voice."

"The feeling's mutual," I reply into the small receiver, my hand shaking.

"How is your crew?" he asks.

I pause and take a deep breath. "They're not with us. It's just me."

There's a moment of silence before O'Connor replies. "We're very sad to hear that."

"There was an accident up there, commander. I'm very lucky to be alive."

"I won't disagree," he replies. "Well, captain, I can inform you that we are on our way to you."

His words take a moment to sink in. My emotions are mixed. I'm not sure how to feel. I try to sound excited. "Wow, well, that is extremely... great to hear. What's your ETA?"

"If our data is on the money, then we'll be there in about eight months. You hang in there, captain."

"Don't you worry about me," I smile.

"Stay in touch," he says. "You'll need to relay us a pick-up spot."

"I'll find a suitable location and send you the coordinates."

I leave the boy in the cartoon's custody and quietly slip into the cold morning. I'm in the middle of a cheap-rent apartment complex. On the second storey. Apartments stand across a small courtyard. There are more apartments along the balcony to my left and right. I believe they call this concentrated residential.

I paid little attention to my surroundings when I stumbled in here. I was led by a keen woman. There is a heavy fog rolling between the apartments and I'm not exactly sure where I am. I head to my right, arrive at a flight of stairs and then cross a small grassed area until I'm at a road. Although blurred with fog, the world around me looks different. A car rolls by. A jogger gallops on the other side of the street. An older woman walks a hound. Everything is at peace. Naïve. Blind to what I am. I walk up the footpath, ignoring the threat of recognition. I don't feel as I expected I would. I feel guilt. Immense, crippling guilt.

As I arrive at my apartment the confirmation of my rescue weighs heavily. I go to the spare room and open the wardrobe. I pull the suitcase and it wheels into the centre of the room. It is large and metal. The most sturdy travel case I could find. I unlock the latches and lift it open.

Inside are samples. Specimens. Hundreds of objects packaged in containers, and jars and sealed bags to preserve them. There are a dozen external hard drives, each loaded with information. Published works, dictionaries from all eras, textbooks, historical documents and all manner of encyclopaedia. I've amassed every piece of information I could download. I have a laptop with which to read the data, plus all its necessary peripherals. I've also collected every cure for cancer that I could lay my hands on. In my freezer is an array of liquids. When we tour I visit oceans and lakes in different climates.

I'm no biologist. Collecting specimens was not in my job description. But I was briefed on what was required. I sit on the floor of my bedroom and stare at the samples. It's not going to be enough. I should have amassed more than this in the time I've been here. They'll be suspicious. And, as much as I try to push the thought away, I can't deny that the most vital and truly enlightening specimen is too big to fit in this travel case. I cannot greet them empty-handed.

# CHAPTER THIRTY

There are a number of abhorrent creations around the workshop. Many are beneath white sheets that are stained with brown patches of dried blood and other substances. But the three main attractions are on display.

In various states of taxidermy and artistic completion are three sculptures in the centre of the room. They are an atrocious hybrid of human and labbia. The body is that of one of Brannagh's majestic pets, but the skin has been removed. The muscular flesh and sinews glisten beneath the wide lamps that hang from the bunker's ceiling. The labbia's head has been removed and replaced with a human one. As the skin has also been removed from this addition, it is difficult to tell the sex of the human victim. Running along the raw, muscular flanks of the labbia's body are human arms, arranged and fixed so they remain perpendicular to the creature. Each of the three sculptures has eight human arms attached to it. The five workers in the room, all in surgeon's garb, are in the process of flaying the skin from these arms, to stay in tune with the overall skinless vibe of the entire piece.

"Very creative," I say to the surgeon at the door.

"They are the steeds of the fallen ones. They will be their carriage when they return," he says.

"Is that before or after their global art gallery tour?" I ask.

The man looks puzzled. "Sorry, Messiah. I don't understand."

I look down at Mr Roeg. "Have you been in here before?"

"Yes, but they weren't this far along on my last visit. I am supposed to be doing some artwork on them when the fusing is complete," replies Mr Roeg. He seems sheepish now, as if the morally questionable nature of the situation is dawning on him.

"Would you like a closer look at our work?" asks the surgeon, gesturing for me to step further into the room.

"No," I reply. "I've seen enough."

The surgeon nods politely and watches me leave. Mr Roeg follows. As I step back into the room of amputees, I'm confronted by a group of people. They're on the other side of the bunker, beyond the beds and limbless sleepers. They're armed with machine guns and wear black, military attire. Like a SWAT team. Natalie stands front and centre.

Each of the armed men is frozen. Beneath the helmets their wide eyes look across the beds, coming to terms with the horrifying vision before them. Natalie appears equally unsettled. I step across the room towards her and all the men, in unison, raise their guns at me.

"Hold," barks Natalie, extending an arm to keep her goons at bay.

"Did you know about any of this?" I ask her.

"Of course not," says Natalie, clearly peeved at my accusation.

"You've been getting close to Brannagh. You're trying to tell me you had no idea he had a fucking *underground lair*? There's hundreds of bodies down here!"

"If I had any clue it was this bad, he would have been arrested instantly," she replies.

"Is that right?" I say, with a very deliberate tone of sarcasm.

"Hey!" says Natalie. "If you had given a shit about those missing girls and had told us everything you knew months ago, then maybe we could have saved some of these people!"

"Fuck you!" I scowl. In a rush of blood I march at Natalie, not stopping until our faces are inches apart. "You knew he had Narc dens, you fucking took me to one!"

The clicks of over a dozen automatic weapons, now readied to fire, fill my ears. Adrenaline-fuelled anger surges through my body. I'm shaking.

Natalie stares back, unwavering. "You've been living a sweet life here on our planet," she says. "But that's over now, Jack. It's too bad that you don't want to hear what a self-absorbed, narcissistic and vacuous person you are. But you can't escape the truth. If you cared, then these people would still have their arms and legs."

I feel myself losing control. My arms raise and I squeeze Natalie's shoulders with all my strength. She remains calm, as the barrels of two guns are pressed into either side of my temple.

"Stand down!" yells one of the gunmen.

"It's okay!" replies Natalie, her eyes locked with mine. "He's not going to hurt me. He's too accomplished in self-preservation."

"None of this is my fault," I say, just loud enough for Natalie to hear.

"It's partly your fault," smiles Natalie.

"Take that back," I growl.

"No," says Natalie, resisting the grip I have on her.

"You will take it back," I nod. "It might not happen in the next five minutes, but you will eat your words."

"My mission is over, Jack. This little charade is over. We own you now. No more fun. You're going to tell us what we want to know."

"Ah," I smile, letting go of her slender frame and stepping back. "But what if you find out something that you *didn't* want to know?"

Natalie's brow furrows for a millisecond and I know I've gotten under her skin.

"You two," she says to the men that had their guns trained on my frontal lobe, "escort Jack upstairs and take him to the Lower Easton Facility. I'll be close behind you." Then to the rest of her squad she commands, "Clear out every room. I want everyone you find taken into custody. Look for hidden doors."

As the two guards grab me by each arm and take me from the room, I glance back at Mr Roeg. "See you, neighbour," I say with a small wave.

Mr Roeg's face widens with alarm as one of the armed operatives picks him up by the collar of his shirt and lifts him from the ground.

I'm taken to the surface and thrown in the back of a large, black four-wheel drive. There are two operatives in the front and two sit on either side of me in the backseat, all with machine guns. The weapons are primitive by Earth standards, but only marginally less effective at killing.

As the vehicle rolls through Godiva's gates and onto the darkened road, I can't avoid my regret. I knew I'd be cornered like this if I didn't keep out of it. But my damn conscience finally overpowered me. I did a decent job of keeping it at bay. There was too much at stake for me to get arrested and removed from my blissful, boundless lifestyle. But here I am. Natalie's words ring in my ears. I'm angry with her because she is correct. Had I acted sooner, there might be a lot less people under the labbia enclosure.

As we follow the winding roads to Easton, my anger refocuses on Brannagh. I can't be mad at Natalie for doing her job, but I can be furious at my record label's owner for royally fucking everything up for me. My mind ticks and ticks and my blood boils as I dwell on the fact that he will somehow use his power and influence to escape punishment. The legal system on this planet is idealistic and rose-coloured. Rehabilitation is always a goal and true psychopaths are studied in comfortable accommodation.

There is no death penalty here. Brannagh won't have his limbs severed or be decimated and transformed into a sideshow art exhibit. He'll be locked away but shown mercy and sympathy for the tortured nature of his mental condition. Justice won't find him in the halls of his asylum. Justice won't obtain any grip on him as his slimy demeanour sees him slip through its fingers. On Heaven, justice simply doesn't have the required disposition. But I do. After all, I wouldn't have been chosen for my deep space mission if I was anything less than focused and robotic. I'm cold and calm and collected when I need to be. It switches on. It stays on.

The spirits I drank before leaving my apartment have accumulated in my bladder. I take a deep breath and break the silence by asking, "Pardon me soldiers, but could we possibly pull over for a bathroom break?"

My fellow passengers look at each other. "You'll have to hold on," says the uniformed man in the passenger seat.

"That's not an option," I say. "I have to urinate. There's no avoiding that fact."

"You'll have to hold on," repeats the passenger seat soldier, this time more sternly. He doesn't even bother to turn and face me.

"Listen Rambo," I smile, still a little heady from the alcohol and the intense nature of my current situation, "but if we don't pull over, I am going to syphon into my pants. Don't forget, kids, that I am a rock star. So pissing myself is going to upset you a lot more than it upsets me."

"If you urinate in here," says the driver, "we will have to charge you with desecration of a government vehicle."

"If you pull over and allow me to go potty on the side of the road, then no charges need be laid. I don't care if you surround me, with your guns aimed at Jack Junior, I promise to behave myself while I slash and then return to this very seat."

The passenger seat soldier sighs loudly. "Alright, maybe we should take five while he gushes somewhere. If he tries to run we can put a bullet in his kneecap."

"No way," says the driver to his fellow soldier. "Look, you're the new guy so don't rock the tree. Wait till you've been doing this for more than five hours and we'll let you make a few suggestions about how we escort a prisoner."

"Hey," says the passenger seat soldier. "When Jack says he's going to soil himself, I have to believe him. I've heard stories about this guy and he's a total fuckin' animal."

"I promise I won't run," I say. "Where the fuck am I going to hide. I'm this planet's equivalent to Michael Jackson."

"To who?" asks the guy next to me.

"Michael Jackson," I sigh. "You know that song I wrote called 'Smooth Criminal'?"

"Yeah, I know that song," says the guy to my right. "That song played at my wedding."

"Really?" I ask. "Please tell me it wasn't the bridal waltz."

"Enough!" yells the driver. "I will pull over so you can piss. But if you do anything other than flop it out and aim at a patch of grass, I swear I will break your arms myself."

"Duly noted," I smile. "You're a reasonable man and sound of mind."

"Shut the fuck up," he replies and slows down. The vehicle rolls onto the shoulder of the road. We stop and the two soldiers in the front exit and aim their guns at the rear doors. Then the two soldiers next to me also exit and I'm ordered out of the vehicle.

I step two metres away from the road until there is grass beneath my feet. The dark night is only illuminated by the glow of the jeep's interior, which pours through the rear passenger door. I unzip my jeans and begin to urinate. The soldiers stand around me, guns raised. As I finish emptying my bladder, I hear a whooshing sound as three silenced shots are fired. My muscles tense and as I spin, a trio of soldiers fall to the ground. One is left standing. He turns his gun on me. I stare at his face for the first time. This was the man sitting in the passenger seat. Beneath his helmet I recognise that

404

smug, conniving expression. It's Michael McCarthy.

"Wow, that's very impressive," I say, putting away Jack Junior and zipping up my jeans.

"I thought you'd be impressed," he smiles back.

"What the fuck are you doing wearing that stupid uniform?"

"I'm just keeping an eye on you," he says.

"Did you need to kill three government operatives to do that? It seems like you're just adding to the reasons why they're going to lock you away for the rest of your life."

"Relax," says McCarthy. "They're non-fatal bullets. Tranquiliser capsules. These boys will wake up with a bad hangover."

I examine McCarthy's weapon and decide it must be a Bandoff 240. I've read about this type of rifle. It's semi-automatic and can switch between ammunition settings. Deadly, traditional bullets or tranquiliser capsules that bring a man down instantly. Another "peaceful concept" used by this planet's military. Don't kill 'em, just put them to sleep.

"So..." I say, "you've infiltrated the government? How did you pull that off? I'll be taking this up with their employment office."

"Brannagh has many friends," he smiles.

"Shouldn't you be in an office crunching his numbers for him? The military get-up doesn't ... suit you."

"I am doing my job," shrugs McCarthy. "I'm protecting one of Mr Brannagh's investments."

"An investment?" I ask, shaking my head. "Why would he risk everything when his life is already so decadent?"

"Why not?"

"He could lose everything," I reply.

"Well it's like he said before all of this," says McCarthy. "When you have everything, the only challenge left in life is to have *more* than everything."

"How very ill-advised," I say.

McCarthy grins then reaches into his pocket and tosses me a small object. In the dim light I can see that it's a bag of white powder.

"What's this?" I ask.

"It's a meteor," says McCarthy. "I'm sure you've dabbled in that particular concoction."

Drugs. It's a mixture of uppers and downers. Very dangerous, but also quite brilliant if you get the dosage right. "There will surely be more soldiers coming very soon," I say. "Do we really have time to party? You'll want to escape at some point in the next twelve hours."

"It's all for you," smiles McCarthy. "Eat the whole bag."

"That would kill me," I say. "Plus, I don't want you feeling left out. You should be involved."

"These are your options," says McCarthy, impatience building in his voice. "You either eat that whole bag and peacefully drift off into a permanent sleep, or I shoot you in the stomach and knee caps and leave you here to bleed to death." McCarthy raises his gun and points it at my abdomen. He then uses his thumb to flip a switch on the barrel, changing the ammunition setting to live rounds instead of tranquilisers. "If I were you, I'd start eating."

"It seems such a waste to kill me," I say. "Brannagh will lose billions from all the albums that Big Bang Theory could make. Why slaughter his biggest cash cow?"

"We'll sell one hundred times what we're selling now once you're dead. It's a lot more valuable to have an artist struck down in their prime than lose money on the marketing and recording of their final forty shitty albums. There's no way you'll keep making music as good as what you've already released."

"Oh ye of little faith," I smile. I open the mouth of the bag as wide as it will part without tearing the translucent plastic. "I think I'll have to choose the first option. The drugs have got to be better than bullets, yeah?"

"I should think so," says McCarthy.

As I move to shovel the powder into my mouth, I glance down at one of the soldiers and stare hard. My eyes widen with concern. "These guys aren't breathing," I say, pointing. "Their chests aren't moving."

"Shut your mouth," warns McCarthy down the barrel of his weapon.

"No, seriously, I'm not kidding. They're all dead."

"Start eating!" he yells.

"If you've killed them," I say, thinking out loud, "then that means that you had your gun on the wrong ammunition setting. Which also means that it's currently set to tranquiliser rounds."

"One more word and I will shoot you in the face."

"It won't kill me," I shrug.

A groan emerges from the back of McCarthy's throat and he

takes a menacing step forward. His gun is still levelled at me. McCarthy's eyes then move down to the two soldiers to our right. They're just out of the vehicle's inner glow and their thick vesting makes it difficult to notice the rise and fall of their chests.

"I swear I'm not trying to fool you," I say. "These men are dead."

"Fine," says McCarthy, forcing a smile as his paranoia creeps in. "I'm going to call your bluff. I will change settings and then shoot you. If you're telling the truth, then you will be shot with a real bullet and you will die. If you have lied, you will be shot with a tranquiliser and collapse. I will then cut your throat."

"So either way I'm still going to die?" I ask.

"Exactly. A peaceful overdose is no longer an option."

"Okay," I nod, sheepishly. "That seems fair."

When studying the military technology on Heaven, I read an essay on the evolution of the Bandoff 240 and its mechanics and design. While it's quite an advanced weapon by this planet's standards, one flaw is that you can't fire while you're switching between ammunition. The bolt has to be locked into either setting and it takes one whole second to flip its position.

As Michael's hand moves to the bolt and his thumb pushes against the switch, I lob the bag of powder at him. By the time it reaches my attacker it has become a thick white cloud. The potent narcotic covers his chest and face and he instinctively drops the barrel and raises his spare hand to his eyes. When he attempts to lift the weapon again to shoot in my direction, nothing happens for the poor bastard. The air fills with the desperate sound of him clicking the useless trigger. I run at him and launch myself, planting one foot in his chest and the other in his crotch. McCarthy sprawls back on to the shoulder of the road.

The meteor, which I know will turn to a paste when in contact with even a small amount of moisture, has clogged in his nostrils, mouth and eyes. I bring my foot down hard on his stomach and it winds him. His hands move to his body to protect himself. Now that McCarthy is blinded I bring my foot down on his neck, breaking his windpipe. The night fills with his guttural howls as the severity of his injury dawns on him. He is now going to die. While he can no longer talk, I know he can hear me as he desperately gargles for air.

I kneel down next to him. "*That* is for being a motherfucker."

McCarthy's only consolation is that the drug will enter his

system quickly and the pain will drift away. He deserves worse.

I locate the jeep's ignition keys from the belt of the driver's incapacitated body and re-enter the vehicle. The wheels spin on the loose gravel at the road's edge as I accelerate. I'm going to pay Brannagh a visit at his apartment. But first I need to make a brief detour.

Brannagh opens the front door. This means he is alone.

"Jack! What a lovely surprise."

"Marty," I reply, smiling as I step past him and walk over to his lounge area. "I hope I didn't wake you."

"No, you know I'm a nocturnal creature. To what do I owe the pleasure of this visit?" he asks, closing the door and following me.

I just chuckle, placing my large black leather case on his coffee table.

"Jack," says Brannagh. "You don't seem yourself. Are you fine?"

"I'm grand. I have my arms and legs. Nor am I covered in banal tattoos."

"Oh," says Brannagh. "Well, yes. You are special, Jack."

"Everyone listens to you, don't they," I say.

"In what sense?" he asks.

"Your gift is the ability to sell. You're a salesman."

"I suppose," smiles Brannagh, flattered. "But I don't trick anyone into wanting something. I'm just very good at working out what people already want but don't realise."

I sit on one of his sofas. "Two of those things that you know people need are beliefs and emotional connections. People don't want to think that they're born and that they die and that in the spectrum of existence they don't mean anything. But if people do accept that, then they want to leave a mark. They want to be something beyond their death."

Brannagh grins. "It seems you've not come here for a casual exchange."

"I suppose not."

"I should fix us a drink," he replies, walking over to his kitchen.

"I'm not staying very long."

"Oh," says Brannagh, opening one of the cupboards in his open kitchen, "I hope you don't mind me imbibing on my own."

"I've developed more of an awareness of your whole operation," I say, pressing forward. I'm sure I don't have long here before Natalie

408

and her cronies arrive.

"Operation?" he says, over his shoulder.

"It seems the best description," I reply.

"Well I've told you all about it," he replies. "What your ancestors will bring to our planet is very exciting. These are special times."

"I'm going to be very brief in my assessment," I say. "And this is my final assessment."

"Assessment?"

"You told me a fabricated story that weaves elements of fiction and some basic theological references."

Brannagh turns to face me. He's pouring a spirit into his glass. He then places the bottle on the kitchen counter and sips from his glass. His expression is difficult to read.

"But you didn't tell me the majority of what you were up to," I continue. "You omitted the mutilations, which seems a rather large omission. You've tricked people and exploited their fears and their trust. You've exploited their love of me and my music. But *why?*" I ask, rhetorically.

"I'm intrigued to hear your theory," says Brannagh.

"Why wouldn't you tell me everything you're doing if you genuinely believed that I am the harbinger of some ancient race of winged demon creatures? The answer is simple. It's all bullshit."

"Don't say nonsense," says Brannagh. "I believe every word of what I told you."

"Then it occurred to me," I continue, "that you could only have one motivation."

Brannagh just listens.

"Money," I say. "Money pouring in through the turnstiles at your gallery. I read recently that the Marioneta de Carne exhibition has drawn twice as many people as your previous highest-selling exhibition. Ticket sales haven't slowed. It's rolling in. You can never underestimate the human's capacity for morbid curiosity. So, who cares if you butcher some drug addicts to make a new exhibition? Just tattoo and cut up a few girls I've slept with. You could be forgiven if you were genuinely some kind of religious fanatic, but your evil presents itself in a very calm, calculated and brazen manner."

"That's quite an assessment," says Brannagh. "And it's a compelling explanation. Shame it's from a drug-addled rock star."

"If you've dismissed me as a zombie, then you have made a grave mistake."

Brannagh smiles but, unlike his trademark mask of charm and humour, it's almost as if he's grimacing. "So you're judge and jury now, Jack? You're the man that has broken nearly every law in our fair legal system."

"I'm not here to pass judgement on myself. I acknowledge that in some ways I'm every bit as evil as you. But it's my motivation that will likely be my saviour. Every crime I commit I will live with."

Brannagh takes a long gulp of his drink. "The government has seized Godiva."

"I know."

"You were there, weren't you."

"Sure was."

"And that whore Natalie... she's not who she says she is..." says Brannagh, now palpable anger tightening in his throat.

"She's very convincing... don't flagellate yourself too hard."

Brannagh finishes his drink and hurls the glass against one of the kitchen cupboards across from him. Shards scatter around the room. His only physical outburst. He continues to stand there, eyes on the ground and his gnarled fists gripping the top of the counter.

"Are they outside right now?" he asks.

"I'm not sure," I reply.

Brannagh stares at me and for the first time I can see his expression slipping. His social prosthesis has peeled at its edges and underneath I can see what all his wealth and power has brought him. Coldness. Detachment. Indifference. Somewhere a switch flipped and innocent people became bags of money.

As I look at him now I realise that Martin Brannagh is the unavoidable by-product of utopia. A perfect world is fertile soil for chaos. Heaven's peaceful nature is as much a regime as a violent dictatorship. Someone will want to destroy it just because they can. Brannagh is the symptom of the universe. So am I.

"Jack, I don't know how you can accuse me of being such a monster. What have I done that's so wrong? I played with the lives of people who were so hateful toward their existence that they chose fantasy over reality. They have the same dreams as you and I, but they don't have the talent and the process to squeeze anything more from this world. They've skipped and bounced through life until they've found themselves in a room. They scratch at the walls, looking for a door. An exit. But the only way forward is through a little window called Narc. I've allowed them to find perfection. To transcend the confines of their flesh."

I absorb Brannagh's disturbing outlook from the comfort of his world-class sofa. I'm lost for words. His thoughts seem to play on my skin, unsettling me.

"I brought you something," I say after an extended heavy pause, and reach over to the large leather case in front of me. As my hands near the latch, an excited scratch comes from within. An anticipatory scamper. "It's the perfect gift for someone as righteously fucked up as you are."

Brannagh sees the case rock slightly as I unbuckle the shiny gold latches.

"You don't have Mr Roeg in there, do you?" smiles Brannagh. A joke, perhaps designed to hide the creeping fingers of concern.

"Not exactly."

I flip open the leather case and nothing happens. I glance over at Brannagh and he's now watching intently. His brow furrows. The suspense has taken a hold of me too. I force a deep, calming breath and relax back into the sofa.

His eyes shift between the case and I. But then they fix on the case as two long spindle legs rise through the opening and slowly fold over the sides. Then two more and two more. Legs rise into the air like black twigs growing from the ground in high speed. Brannagh's eyes widen in horror. By the time the bodies of the two arachnids have appeared and are lowering themselves to the coffee table and then down to the floor, Brannagh is frozen.

"On my planet, Marty, we call it arachnophobia."

The two arachnids are no longer in Brannagh's sight. From his vantage point, their slow, careful pacing is obscured by his sofa and the kitchen's island bench. But I can see them, their eight legs rippling from their bodies like a piece of engineering with a thousand moving parts. Brannagh pulls a knife from a block on his counter, but it won't do him a lot of good. They're too fast and too deadly. Arachnids are finely tuned killing machines. I walk over to the sliding glass doors that open on to Brannagh's giant balcony and push them apart slightly. I promised the arachnids a means of escape.

"These are younger arachnids," I tell Brannagh. "Not only could I fit two of them in the case, but they actually have larger appetites than the fully grown."

It's macabre of me to watch the spiders attack Brannagh but I am, after all, only human. Who am I to intervene in nature? He swings at one of them with the knife but his glancing blow doesn't leave a mark on the hardened shell of the creature. Their fangs are sharp and administer their paralytic venom instantly. Once the two arachnids are latched on him, he howls and moans before sliding to the floor.

He is very much alive as they drain him of his bodily fluids. They drink everything and it's in their interests to keep his heart beating for as long as possible. He can't move. His eyes look to the ceiling. If he could shift them, I'm sure he would glare. Aim his fury and betrayal at me. Willing me to die. But it is now Brannagh's time to die and I'm glad that it is drawn out and that he has this opportunity to blame himself. I doubt he takes it. The pain is probably preventing him from any rational summation of his failings as a human being.

One of the spiders is wrapped on his neck. The other on his inner thigh. Their legs grip him in an unbreakable vice. Once it is clear that he will die, I walk toward the door.

"Bye Marty," I say, and lock the apartment behind me.

I enter the elevator and choose level three, rather than the ground floor. I want to avoid Natalie and her government cronies, who I'm sure are waiting outside the building. At level three I head up the corridor to the fire escape and enter the cold, grey stairwell, descending to the downstairs carpark. I tread softly past the expensive vehicles until I find a fire exit. It opens on to the main street. The footpath is busy and I instinctively raise a hand to hide my face, pretending to scratch my forehead. I glance up the street to my right and I can see some conspicuous plain-clothed agents standing on either side of the road. Directly across from the building's entrance is a plain, white van. I'm confident that Natalie is sitting inside it, orchestrating Brannagh's arrest.

An unheard signal is given and I watch all the agents turn and head into the building, pushing between pedestrians and dodging traffic as they pour across the road. I turn and briskly head in the opposite direction, keeping my face averted from pedestrians. I glance back long enough to see an approaching taxi with its vacancy light illuminated. I step to the edge of the road and wave it down. It stops. I jump in the backseat and instruct the forty-something driver to take me to my apartment. He recognises me.

"Are you...?" he asks, accelerating back into the traffic.

"Yes," I say.

"I love your music," he says. "Wow. This is a massive honour."

"Thank you," I say.

"I was actually just listening to one of your records."

"Which one?" I ask.

"*Nothing Past The Balls*," replies the driver.

"Excellent," I reply. "I let my guitarist name that album."

"Dylan? He's amazing. A genius," says the driver.

"He's very talented," I say.

"I know you guys are very famous, but I still think he's incredibly underrated."

"Yeah... he really flies under the radar."

# CHAPTER THIRTY-ONE

The flashes of cameras blink in a white barrage as I ascend the red carpet that leads up the steps to the Walkley Gallery. Jennifer Fox is linked to my arm, wearing a low-cut, strapless black dress. Jennifer and I are not strictly an item, but we fool around and go to a lot of parties together. We both receive a lot more column inches if we hold hands on the red carpet of big openings such as this.

Inside the grand foyer guests greet each other. Waiters tray champagne and cocktails. I take an elixir for Jennifer and myself.

"Thank you, kind sir," smiles Jennifer, chinking her glass against my own.

"Is tonight going to be boring?" I ask. "What's your vibe?"

Jennifer smiles and looks around. "There's a lot of ancient pieces here. Lots of fossils."

"You're not talking about the exhibits," I smile.

"Very perceptive," smiles Jennifer. "No, tonight I think we'll have to make our own fun."

We follow the red carpet through the giant corridors of the gallery until we arrive at the room that holds the new exhibition. There are a few hundred people loitering around the room, chatting and laughing, elixirs in hand. No one pays much attention to the artworks. Schmooze central.

Then I hear a familiar voice behind me.

"Well if it isn't two of my all-time favourites," says Martin Brannagh, strolling over to Jennifer and I. My date gives him a warm smile and they kiss each other on the cheek. "My favourite rock star," smiles Brannagh, shaking my hand warmly.

"Marty, you look fantastic," I smile.

"Hey, don't sound so surprised!" he laughs.

Normally Brannagh is dressed like an eastern mystic, draped in white flowing silk and jewellery, but he's looking quite dapper this evening in a tuxedo.

"How is your evening?" I ask him.

"Very well," he says. "I mean, these sorts of gatherings can be a little dry, but you have to make your own fun."

"That's exactly what I just said," laughs Jennifer.

"Miss Fox, I know I say this every time I see you, but you really are the most dangerously attractive creature I have ever seen," says Brannagh.

"Marty, please," says Jennifer, playfully slapping him on the shoulder. "I'll blush."

At this moment a brunette woman walks over to Brannagh and taps him on the upper arm. She has caramel-coloured skin, full red lips and seductive eyes. She's wearing a figure-hugging red lace dress with cleavage shaped by the devil.

"I'm sorry to interrupt, Mr Brannagh, but our guest of honour has arrived. You said you wanted to meet him?"

"Oh yes!" says Brannagh. "Thank you." Then gesturing to Jennifer and I he says, "Jennifer, Jack, this is Natalie. She is an assistant to the head curator here."

"Hi, it's an honour to meet you both," smiles Natalie, extending her hand.

"Pleasure," Jennifer and I say as we each shake her hand.

"Natalie, I won't be more than a minute behind you," says Brannagh.

Natalie smiles politely and disappears into the crowd.

"Wow," says Jennifer. "She was stunning."

"I won't argue with you," I say. "She's a perfect specimen."

"Don't get me started," says Brannagh with a little twinkle in his eye. "She's an aspiring curator. From what I hear she's very talented."

"Marty," I say. "I need you to do me a personal favour."

"Of course," smiles Brannagh.

"Can you invite that girl to all your parties. Every get-together. Every debauched gathering. I wish very much to cross paths with her again."

# CHAPTER THIRTY-TWO

As expected, there are government agents staking out my apartment building. When I casually step into the foyer through the main entrance, I am immediately surrounded. They are wearing plain clothes but each has a handgun in a leather holster on their belt.

"Jack, please come with us," says one of the men.

I follow five agents up to my apartment. I'm allowed to loiter around while they stand and keep guard. One of them occasionally receives phone calls from someone and, from what the guard says, I determine he is being questioned about me. None of the men pay me any attention. They just stand or sit calmly around my home and ensure that I don't disappear.

After half an hour, someone knocks loudly at the apartment's entrance. All of the agents reach for their handguns. One of them peers through my spyhole and then opens the door. Natalie, followed by half a dozen uniformed agents, marches to where I recline on my sofa. She grabs the shoulders of my T-shirt and I am wrenched to my feet. She pushes me sideways and I am slammed against the glass sliding doors of the balcony. They rattle in their frames.

"What the fuck did you do?" she yells.

"Be more specific," I respond, the garment cutting into my underarms as she continues to pull the material upward. I haven't seen her this angry before.

"Be smart," she hisses. "Keep being smart and see what happens."

"Any statement I make right now will be made under duress."

"We have footage of you in Brannagh's apartment foyer. What was in that fucking suitcase?" she asks, releasing the material of my shirt, but still pinning me against the glass.

"It was an empty suitcase," I say, calmly. "It was a gift from Marty that he gave me about six months ago. I was returning it to him as a symbolic gesture of my rejection of his professional services... and his friendship."

"Tell me the truth," says Natalie, her voice now cold and threatening. I don't say anything. "Did you take arachnids into his apartment?" she probes.

"That's absurd."

"His injuries are consistent with arachnid bites."

"Does it seem likely that I could trap two arachnids in a suitcase and sneak them into his apartment?"

"Unlikely," says Natalie. "But nothing would surprise me."

"Were there arachnids *in* his apartment?" I ask.

Natalie releases me and takes a step back. She studies me intently. "I didn't say there were *two* arachnids."

My lover thinks she has caught me out, but I'm deliberately dropping information. I think some credit is due. I give a bashful response. "He could have evaded *one* arachnid. I assumed there were two because if I *had* been planning to assassinate him, you would take two arachnids. You know, for insurance."

Natalie just stares into my face, trying to read me. She knows I'm guilty but it may be a difficult thing for her to prove, particularly because arachnids do sometimes sneak into people's homes and kill them.

"How did you escape the agents?" asks Natalie. "We found them unconscious on the side of the road."

"I was put in a government vehicle alongside your incredibly competent staff and was then hijacked by one of your incredibly competent staff."

Natalie huffs. "We're investigating how McCarthy managed to be in that vehicle. We found him dead. Did you kill him?"

"I don't have much recollection of what happened. I may still be in shock."

"He was covered in drugs. That would implicate you."

"Is it possible he hijacked the vehicle, got really high and then crushed his own throat?"

"I didn't say his throat was crushed," Natalie replies.

"I just assumed. That's how most people die."

"Is it really?" asks Natalie, her patience clearly depleted. She then turns and addresses the room. "Everybody leave. I want some alone time with Jack. Wait outside."

"But agent—" says one of the men.

"That is an order!" she barks. The men share a deflated glance and meekly file out. Natalie turns her attention back to me. "Tell me what happened, Jack," she says, her voice now calm. "Off the record."

"I'm not saying any more," I sigh. "Arrest me for something or leave me alone."

"If we find arachnid DNA in that suitcase then there's not a lot I can do to keep you from being charged with murder."

"If one single charge is laid on me I will never tell you what you want to know about who I am."

"Really? How do you respond to torture?" asks Natalie, her full lips forming a smug expression.

"I respond rather positively. You, more than anyone, should know that," I reply, confident that the peace-mongering governments of this planet would never harm me.

Natalie steps close to me. "I have trusted you," she says. "You have no idea how far I have stuck my neck out for you. When I was working undercover, I was risking my life every day to protect your identity. So just give me some fucking answers."

"Okay," I reply.

"Did you kill Brannagh?"

"The arachnids killed Brannagh."

"But why?"

"He deserved to die," I shrug.

"That's not how things work here," says Natalie.

"I know," I say. "Hence my decision to exact justice."

"Did you kill McCarthy?"

"Yes, but that was self-defense."

"How did you capture two arachnids? We know you drove out to the industrial district because there is a satellite-tracking device in the jeep. Did you go looking for them?"

"I didn't have to go looking. I know where some live."

Natalie's eyes dart back and forth between my own, looking for any minute twitch that might suggest I'm lying. "How did you capture them?"

"I politely asked two of them to come with me."

Natalie grimaces and sighs deeply. "You're trying to tell me you can communicate with arachnids?"

"We don't have lengthy conversations, but we seem to have... a mutual respect."

"Are you going to tell us about your home planet?"

"Sure, I'm happy to share."

"Good," says Natalie. "Our motivation is only to obtain more knowledge about you and your culture. Your arrival here is the most monumental thing to happen to our species."

"Mine too."

A decision is made to cancel the final shows of Big Bang Theory's world tour. I feel like I'm letting down the fans that bought tickets to the twelve remaining arena dates, but it's out of my hands. Natalie assures me there is no way I can finish the tour. I owe the government an immediate opportunity to interrogate me.

I am instructed to tell Amelia that I have seen a doctor and have strained my vocal cords. I have also developed nodules. If I want to avoid surgery, I need to rest. No performing for at least six months. Amelia, after stressing that she wants a second and third opinion, eventually believes the lie and goes about deconstructing our tour.

The band is sitting with me in my living room. I decide to tell them about the cancellation myself. Emerson and Cohen are incredibly disappointed, but Emerson is also philosophical.

"You can't put a price on your health," says Emerson. "If you fuck up your voice now, you might never sing again."

"Absolutely true," I say. "It's not worth risking it. I'll take it very easy. No partying. Nothing outlandish. I'm going to go somewhere remote, on my own, and just work on writing some new songs. It's time to detox my soul."

Dylan is very quiet. Unusually so. Normally he voices an opinion on everything, no matter how inane. But now he sits silently on the sofa, his eyes on the muted television. We're waiting for Amelia to arrive. She told me that we all need to sit down together and work out the future plans of the band. Should be an interesting discussion. I'm watching Dylan. He's distant. Distracted. Depressed.

I would normally assume he's on drugs but he rarely takes downers. Which is unfortunate when you consider his hyperactive personality.

There's a knock at my door and Cohen answers it. When he opens my apartment, Amelia throws her arms around him and begins sobbing uncontrollably. We all lurch to our feet, amazed at Amelia's state. I've never seen her display such emotion.

"What's the matter?" asks Cohen, looking back at us with a worried expression.

"It's Martin," says Amelia, still gripping Cohen tightly. "He's had a heart attack. They've found him in his apartment... he's dead."

"What?" asks Emerson, almost accusingly. "Are you fucking serious?"

"What do you mean he's dead?" I ask, putting in an award-worthy performance. "You must have heard wrong...?"

Dylan stares at Amelia, his expression blank. He really loved Brannagh. He was a father figure, of sorts. This is not the inconsolable response I expected from him.

"It's already on television," says Amelia, between sobs.

Emerson grabs my remote control from the coffee table and turns the sound on, flicking until he finds the news channels. There is a live report. Words across the bottom of the screen say, "Endurance Records owner and art gallery entrepreneur Martin Brannagh found dead of suspected heart attack." There is live footage of a body under a white sheet being wheeled from the foyer of his building and into an ambulance. I know that it can't possibly be Brannagh's body, as he has been dead for two days. There is a picture of Brannagh's smiling face in the top right corner of the screen. A woman reporter's voice explains that the owner of our record label is deceased and that authorities are releasing very little information. At this stage, his death is not being treated as suspicious.

The room is silent as we stand and stare at the screen. I try very hard to appear shocked. Cohen walks to the screen and drops to his knees, just staring. Dismayed.

"I can't believe I'm seeing this," says Emerson.

When I look up at Dylan we make eye contact. He conveys something to me. A silent message. Then he speaks.

"Can't you do something about this?" he asks.

"What do you mean?" I answer.

"We were all on that yacht," says Dylan. "We watched you bring someone back to life."

"That's rubbish," I say, shaking my head. "That girl was not dead. She was unconscious."

"She wasn't breathing," says Dylan. "We all saw it."

"She had shallow breathing," I say, my voice terse. "We're all shocked by this Dylan, but I can't be having such a pointless conversation right now."

"Fuck!" yells Dylan. He storms from my apartment, slamming the door. I stare after him, my mind ticking over.

"It's okay," says Emerson. "He needs to cool off. He's not going to take this very well."

"I won't put up with him turning his anger on me," I say.

"He's not mad at you," says Emerson. "He was just very close to Marty."

"Is that so?" I ask in a condescending tone.

"You're damn right it is," replies Emerson.

# CHAPTER THIRTY-THREE

Natalie steps into my apartment and shuts the door. I'm watching television. It's a report on the plight of child soldiers. Some aid workers have intervened. They've encouraged the children to lay down their arms and go to school. They'll be given asylum in another country with foster families. They'll be cared for. A peaceful resolution.

Natalie joins me on the sofa. "Are you packed?" she asks.

"My luggage is in the bedroom."

Natalie leans into me, curling her body against mine. "So they're not going to take any action about Brannagh's death," she says, casually.

"Really?" I ask, a little surprised.

"It's on the condition that you co-operate completely. They want full disclosure when you're questioned. Tell them everything. How you came to have the arachnids and why you took them to Brannagh's apartment."

"If I, hypothetically, discuss the circumstances of Marty's death, what guarantee do I have that I won't be punished?"

"You just have to trust me."

"I don't have much choice."

"Yes, but I hope you will trust me anyway," grins Natalie. "What are you watching?"

"Just a news update. Some current affairs."

"Anything interesting?"

"It's all interesting," I say.

The next story is about the closure of the planet's last caged poultry farm.

"I suppose everything you see here must be... a wonder," says Natalie.

"I feel like I was never really looking. I wasn't paying proper attention to everything around me," I say, watching fields of happy chickens bobbing about and pecking at the ground. "When all this is over," I ask. "Will you still want to see me?"

"What do you mean?" asks Natalie.

"Will you still... show an interest?"

I look at her and she smiles. "I want to spend more time with you. Out of character."

Her response knots my stomach. "We should get going," I say, reaching down and squeezing the top of Natalie's thigh.

She kisses me.

"It must have been around here," says Natalie. She is holding a GPS device. In her other hand is a black folder, which she opens to reveal a series of photos. The first images are of the exact stretch of beach we're now standing on. Pictures of footprints in the sand. The marks I left when I landed here almost five years ago.

"We found the raft about three hundred steps up the shore," says Natalie, pointing ahead. She then finds an image of the beached vessel.

"It was very dark when I landed," I say, glancing back at the armed guards that follow fifty metres behind us. There are more men at the tree line, walking in parallel. Two helicopters flutter overhead. Navy boats wait offshore. "I left the raft and headed up towards those trees."

"And you found your way to the graveyard and the church?"

I nod.

"You walked almost a straight line," says Natalie, glancing back at the GPS.

"I had a compass. It happened to work."

"Then what happened?"

"I arrived at the gates of the graveyard and... something chased me. Something big."

"Really?" asks Natalie. "What did it look like?"

"I didn't see much of it. But out of the corner of my eye I could

423

see it had black fur with patches of yellow. It was taller than me. It made a high, piercing noise. I just... bolted."

"It definitely had fur?"

"I'm confident, yes."

"Big claws?"

"Most definitely. It left marks in the door of the little shed I hid in. I bet they're still there."

Natalie is quiet. She stops walking and so do I. She looks up at the trees. I admire Natalie's beauty. Her hair, which has grown almost to her shoulder, is pulled up in a ponytail. Her white blouse and grey pants hug the firm curves of her body, as her clothing has a tendency to do. Her shiny black shoes are caked in sand. I'm mesmerised by her. Natalie is a rare beauty. A creature of potent sexuality. Someone you would step over your dying mother to penetrate. Something brought her to me. A force that stretches the cosmos, bridging the vastness of space and time. Her body, her mind and her soul are crucial to my salvation.

Still looking at the trees, Natalie says, "It sounds like a Guardian."

"I've heard of them."

"They don't exist," she adds.

"Are you sure?"

"They are ancient beings. They're supposed to protect us. Every person supposedly has one that watches out for them. That keeps them safe."

"Sounds like a nice idea."

"Everyone's Guardian looks slightly different, but they're all a variation on the same theme."

"The creature that chased me didn't give the vibe that it wanted to protect me."

"Perhaps something *is* here," Natalie suggests, her eyes scanning the trees. "We are on a very old island. Besides the church and the cemetery, this place is untouched."

I sit on the cooling sand. Natalie does too. The suns' arc is nearing the refuge of the horizon.

"So what happens now?" I ask.

"We'd like to retrace your steps. With your help, of course."

"Then what?"

"We'll go to the facility," says Natalie.

"The one in the desert?"

"Yes."

"What happens there?"

"We're going to study you. You'll be looked after, I promise."

"Are you going to dissect me?"

"Of course not," says Natalie. "We're not monsters. We will use non-intrusive medical procedures to create a biological map of your body. Then we can begin the psychological evaluations. We want to create a peaceful and fluid dialogue with you, to find out as much as we can about your planet."

"You say 'we' a lot," I say, looking out at the naval ships.

"I'm referring to our research team."

"Right." There's a pause before I add, "When this is all over, I'd like to get to know more about you. The real you."

"I don't think you'll like the real me as much as my... persona. I don't want to shatter the mystery."

"Do you have a family?" I ask.

Natalie looks out at the fading ocean, clearly deciding how to answer. "I... don't, no," she says with a slight shake of her head. "I never knew my father and my mother died when I was young."

"I'm sad to hear that," I say.

"Don't be. It's all in the past. Can't be undone."

"Were you an only child?"

"I had a half sister, but she drowned when I was a teenager."

I put my arm around Natalie. After a moment's silence, I say, "Life moves on, doesn't it."

"I suppose it does. But what about you? You must have left someone behind?"

"I did," I reply. "A long time ago though. Before I left Earth."

"Oh," says Natalie, clearly wanting to probe further.

"So what happens after all of this," I say, redirecting the conversation. "What happens when they've learned all they can from me? What happens to you and me?"

"You should be allowed to continue with your music," smiles Natalie.

"And you go back to being a super spy?"

"A spy?" she asks.

"Yes. A secret operative. Your occupation."

Natalie nods. "Well, yes, I guess I will."

"And I'll just be another job."

Natalie laughs. "We won't ever have another job like you."

There's a pause and she adds, "Will you still want to see me?"

"Yes."

"Good," she says, a familiar glimmer in her eyes. "I'd hate for you to view me as just your captor."

"I wouldn't have it any other way," I smile. "I'm happy I'll be getting through this with you by my side."

"I promise I will be with you every step of the way."

"It seems hard to believe that the government would just allow me to return to society... knowing what I am."

"We want your sanctuary on our planet to continue," says Natalie. "Fate delivered you to us. We want nothing but an ongoing peaceful relationship."

"I believe you," I say. "That seems to be true of most people here. Blind belief. Blind trust. A blind desire for peace."

"It's not blind," replies Natalie. "Quite the opposite."

"Everywhere I look there is peace and love engrained in everyone. There's so few exceptions. It feels more foreign to me than anything else I've seen here."

Natalie looks bemused. "Jack, you witnessed the most extreme, heinous crime in recent history. What Martin Brannagh did is unheard of."

"That's my point," I say. "What Brannagh did is the darkest point in your history since I have been here. Besides him and his followers, there's no malice in anyone. Look how easily Marty misled people. He was able to casually fool innocents into believing his twisted... ideas. Into *executing* others. I can't condemn anyone that believed him. Everyone here is just too... naïve. You're all just... babes in the woods."

"I have to say, Jack, I find your response to this fascinating."

"Why?"

"You can attest to how evil Brannagh is and you can show compassion and forgiveness for his followers, yet you saw fit to kill him."

"Arachnids saw fit to kill him."

"You're treating me like a fool," says Natalie. "I need you to be honest with me."

"You act like this is a private conversation," I say, looking at the small radio in her ear.

"Why did he have to die? Is that the values of Earth?"

"Perhaps. It's an Earthly sense of justice. He butchered those people, as if he were pulling the wings off flies. As he was dying, he experienced what it is to be helpless. To be vulnerable. He still showed no remorse. So he received a punishment that was... symbolic."

"On this planet Jack, that way of thinking is... not considered natural."

"Really?"

"If you believe the scriptures, then it's evil to think that way. It was the behaviour of the Fallen One. Our society lives by forgiveness."

"So you don't believe in an eye for an eye?"

Natalie shakes her head.

"That doesn't make sense to you?"

"It's an archaic ideology."

"I admire that," I say. "And for what it's worth, I'm not proud of what I did. I don't want you to think of me as an animal."

"We don't think you're evil. We just want to learn more about you."

"I hope you find something useful," I say, wryly.

"We already have. Resuscitation, as you call it. We can save lives. Our medical researchers would like to speak to you about how you did it. They've seen the video and they think it's fascinating."

"I'm only too happy to help." I cast my gaze back at the ocean. "Can I ask you a hypothetical?"

"Of course."

"If someone from Earth did come to retrieve me, and there was an opportunity for you to come with me... would you consider it?"

"To go to Earth with you?" asks Natalie.

"You could study another race of people."

"Yes, but my study wouldn't mean much if I couldn't come home."

"Okay," I say, "what if you could return to Earth with me, study my planet and then I could bring you back. Would you come then?"

"Why are you asking me this?" asks Natalie.

"Because... some day they might come for me," I reply.

"You think there's a chance they might?"

"Yes," I say, turning back to her, nodding.

"Well," says Natalie, choosing her words carefully. "If that scenario occurred, and I could be brought home some day, then yes... I think that would be... life changing. I would love to go with

427

you."

"When can we be alone again?" I ask.

"Only when this is over."

Rose arrives for work to find Zunge Bohne strangely quiet for this time of morning. I'm sitting at a table in the centre of the café and I hear her enter the back door. Her careful steps echo from the kitchen.

"Hello?" I hear her call. "Anyone here?"

Rose steps through the swing gate and appears behind the counter. She sees me sitting in the deserted café and I smile at her.

"Care to join me?" I ask across the empty tables.

Rose returns my smile and shakes her head. "I shouldn't be surprised by this should I. It's just one of those grand, sweeping gestures that only the wealthy can afford."

"Are you being cruel?" I ask.

"This is one of our busiest mornings," says Rose, stepping around the counter toward me. "How much did you pay my boss to get him to stay closed?"

"Quite a lot."

"Why?"

"I wanted you to myself."

"Right," says Rose, walking between the tables until she arrives at mine and sits down. "So are you going to tell me what really happened to Martin Brannagh?"

"In what sense?"

"The television said he had a heart attack."

"You don't believe that?"

"Tell me what's going on," Rose says, agitation at the edges of her voice.

"I will," I reply. "But first we need a drink. Something with caffeine."

"I don't want one."

"Well I'm going to make myself one. I can easily make two," I offer, standing up and walking over to the coffee machine behind the counter.

"Fine," relents Rose. "Do you even know how to use that?"

"I'm sure I can work it out." Rose waits patiently while I attempt to brew a pot of coffee. "Do you want it sweetened?" I call out.

"A little."

I take two mugs from an adjacent shelf and return to the table. I then pour us both a coffee. Rose gently blows on hers before tasting it.

"Verdict?" I ask.

"Undrinkable."

"Ouch."

"I could have said worse," smiles Rose.

"When critiquing a beverage, what description is worse than 'undrinkable'?"

"I could have insinuated that you deliberately made it terrible... as a means to offend me."

"Ah, *intent*. Yes, I suppose that is worse."

"So, are we going to talk about drinks all day or are you going to tell me what this is all about? What happened to The Discipline?"

"All taken care of," I smile, confidently.

"Really? How?"

"There was... a government investigation. Some people have been arrested. Justice has been served."

"Does it have anything to do with Brannagh's death?"

"No," I say, firmly. "That's an entirely separate tragedy. No connection whatsoever."

Rose isn't convinced. "Why did you come here if you're not going to give me any answers?"

"I'm here because... I have some news."

"Yes?"

I reach out and take Rose's hand in my own. "I have to go away for a while."

"Go away?"

"Yes," I say. "I'm not well. My doctors have told me that if I don't engage in a healthier lifestyle, then I might not be around much longer."

"Oh," says Rose, a look of concern on her face. "Well, I suppose you do... celebrate... with some regularity."

"I celebrate a lot... but the frivolity has to stop. I'm ruining my voice and I'm addicted to a range of indulgences."

"How long do you have to go for?"

"As long as it takes. It could be quite a long time."

Rose absorbs this information. She attempts to maintain a calm exterior. But I know she cares about me. She is going to miss me a great deal. I, without question, am going to miss her too. But circumstance won't permit us to be together. I need to spare Rose. I need to protect her by pushing her away.

"Will you find me when you come back?"

"Don't wait for me," I reply. "Finish your studies and start your life. I care about you a lot, but it's irresponsible of me to promise you anything." Rose just nods, her exterior now decidedly sullen. "I need to get a lot of things sorted out," I continue. "At the moment I'm only damaging everything around me. Please understand that I care about you a great deal."

"I understand."

I gently squeeze her hand. "Now, are you ready for some good news?"

"Definitely," she replies.

I release her from my grasp, reach into my jeans pocket and then hand her the envelope. "This is for you."

Rose opens it, removing the folded documents. She scans the top page. "What is this?"

"It's an entitlement."

"An entitlement for what?"

"For this café."

"You bought the café?" she asks.

"Very temporarily. I have had it signed into your name."

"That's crazy," she says, shaking her head.

"I know you're studying, but you know how this place operates. You can live off the profits. Or just sell it if it becomes too much trouble."

"Jack, I can't accept it," says Rose. "It's too much."

"Then sell it and give it to charity," I smile. "But it's yours now. I'm not taking it back."

"Jack... I..." says Rose, flipping through the entitlement. "It's too much, way too much."

"Think of it as my attempt to bribe you into forgiving me," I smile.

"How else could I possibly think of it?"

"You deserve it," I say. "You're a gentle, good person and I care about you and I wanted to give you this gift. Please accept it."

Rose stands and moves towards me. I slide my chair away from the table and she lifts a leg, straddling my lap. She sits and wraps her arms around my neck, pulling my mouth against hers. She kisses me strongly, as if force can make us one. "Don't go," she whispers near my ear, still gripping the entitlement. "Please..."

"I have to," I reply, holding her tightly against me, her hair soft against my lips. "For everyone's sake, I have to go. One day you'll understand."

I knock on Laurie's door and wait. I can't hear anything. Natalie is standing in the entrance of my apartment, watching and listening. She acknowledges my request for privacy, but has been instructed to not allow me to leave her sight.

A lock clicks, slow and deep, and the door opens ajar. Laurie's mother is peering out.

"Is Laurie home?" I ask.

She says nothing, just staring at me. Then she quietly responds, "Who?"

"Laurie," I say. "I need to see her."

Laurie's mother eyes me then glances over my shoulder at Natalie. Her brow furrows.

"I don't know who you're talking about," she says. "There's no one here with that name."

"Sorry, but I don't have time for this," I say, reaching out to push the door open further.

Laurie's mother slams it shut, the forced air hitting me in the chest. I glance back at Natalie and raise my eyebrows, giving a meek smile. I then knock on the door again. No one answers it.

"Did you upset someone, Jack?" asks Natalie.

"Seems unlikely," I shrug. "People fucking love me."

"Well we can't really wait any longer," she says. "They're expecting us."

I sigh, deciding whether to knock again. I would like to see Laurie before I go, but I don't want Natalie to know about the secret growing inside her. I swallow my rising frustration. From my pocket I pull an envelope with Laurie's name on it. I slide it under the door. Inside is the entitlement for my apartment.

# CHAPTER THIRTY-FOUR

"They had better keep their distance," I say from the passenger seat, looking through the rear window of our big black government issue four-wheel-drive. We're hurtling through the hot desert, clouds of orange dust bursting from our tires.

"Why do you care so much, Jack? It's just the two of us here. They only want to follow to make sure you arrive safely," says Natalie, her hands on the wheel, a pair of reflective aviator glasses balanced on her perfect nose. In her right ear is a small communication device, through which she can speak and hear her superiors.

I don't answer her question. I look down at the four suitcases on the back seat. One is Natalie's. The other three are mine. I also have a backpack sitting at my feet. I just hope I've brought everything I have to. God knows I've had long enough to prepare. But I'd convinced myself that this day wouldn't come. That was naïve.

"You sure brought a lot of clothes," says Natalie. I see her glance down at the backpack at my feet, which does contain a few garments. "I hate to break it to you, rock star, but you won't get much opportunity to dress up."

"Is that right?"

"We've got a really sexy array of gowns for you to wear."

"Gowns, huh."

"I picked them out myself. You're going to be the hottest guest we've had at the facility since it was built."

"Is that because I'm the only guest?"

Natalie smiles. The long shimmering stretch of road dances on her sunglasses. "No, we've had other guests."

"Like who?"

"We've been looking for you for a long time. There have been a few cases of... mistaken identity."

"Sounds ominous."

"No harm has come to anyone. We just, well, we thought we'd found you a number of times. But they all turned out to be vagrants. Nothing more."

"I'm glad you had such high expectations."

Natalie smiles. "You're just lucky that old priest you met after you landed doesn't watch television or listen to music."

"Really? He seemed like such a trashbag."

"I showed him a photo of you. He remembered you. He identified you."

"He ratted me out? You said he just reported the raft. Now I regret sending him that fruit basket."

"Don't be mean. He's a nice old man. He told me that you were a very gentle spirit. He knew something was different about you, but he wasn't afraid. God told him to not be afraid of you."

"God *would* say that," I say, looking out my window, my dark Wayfarer-style sunglasses protecting my eyes from the glare. "He's probably saving me for himself."

We drive for another hour, making idle chitchat. With every new minute, as we rocket further into destiny, my stomach winds tighter and tighter. The twisted fist of anticipation and sadness forms around my insides and I can't help but think about how much I'm going to miss so many people. Especially Rose and Laurie.

The road ahead of us is desolate. The horizon ripples like sparkling water. I glance back through the rear windshield and I don't see anyone following us. Then I feel a vibration in my pocket. Something buzzing against my thigh.

"We need to pull over," I say. "I feel the call of nature."

"Really?" asks Natalie. "You can't wait?"

"Absolutely not," I say. "This is definitely an emergency situation."

Natalie grimaces and slows the vehicle. She eases off the side of the road and more plumes of orange dust fly up around the car. The desert's surface crunches beneath us.

I open my door, grabbing my backpack with one hand. Before Natalie realises my next move, I'm out of the car, throwing my backpack on and opening a rear door, snatching my suitcases under each arm and in a spare hand. I depart with fast steps. Natalie exits and sees me with my bags, escaping.

"Jack!" she yells. "What the fuck are you doing?"

"Sorry, Natalie," I call, without looking back. "I've got to go."

I hear her feet move behind me. When she catches up, she's pointing a tranquiliser gun at the side of my head. "This is far from fucking funny," she says.

I can tell she's angry. I stop walking and put my bags down. "I'm sorry," I say.

"What the fuck are you playing at?" asks Natalie. She puts a hand to her ear, listening to the small device. She talks to them. "Everything's fine. Just hold back," she says sternly. Then to me she barks, "Are you going to get me fired, Jack? Is that what you're trying to do? I can't believe you would fuck around like this."

The box in my pocket starts vibrating again. I move to grab it.

"Keep your hands where I can see them!" yells Natalie, stepping in front of me and pushing the gun into my chest.

"I'm getting a phone call," I say, calmly. "I really need to answer it."

"No," says Natalie, shaking her head. I see a look of sadness cross her face, even from behind her sunglasses, as her mind starts to work out what's happening.

I slowly reach for the small black box and then bring it to my ear. "Copy."

An eager, deep male voice says, "This is O'Connor. Ready for extraction?"

"I couldn't be more ready," I reply.

"We've picked up your location. We're only two minutes away, buddy. Get that flare off."

"Roger," I say. I put the phone back in my pocket. Then I start to kneel down and reach for the backpack.

"Stand up!" yells Natalie. "I'm three seconds away from shooting you with this thing."

"If you do they will kill you, Natalie. Whether I'm conscious or not, they're taking me home. I'm sorry."

"You're lying," she growls through gritted teeth.

"They will kill you and they'll kill everyone in the convoy when they arrive. Natalie, they have weaponry unlike anything you've ever seen."

"Is that right? They would just kill us, huh?" says Natalie. She thinks I'm calling her bluff.

"I swear, Natalie. I swear on my own life that they will shoot you. You know how I killed Brannagh? Well they're worse. They will slaughter everyone."

Natalie tenses her mouth, her face knotted in anger. I kneel down to my backpack, the very backpack I arrived on this planet with, and find the flare gun. Loading a flare, I turn and fire into the desert. It bounces across the dry ground. About one hundred metres away it erupts in vivid red smoke, sparkling and crackling. I'm relieved to see that it still works.

"What is that?" asks Natalie. "A firework?"

"It's a flare," I smile.

With her spare hand Natalie grabs me by the collar of my shirt, putting her face close to mine. "Don't you fucking do this," she pleads. "I trusted you."

"I'm sorry," I reply, sincerely. "But I have to go. This, here, is just a dream."

I kiss her and she kisses me back. I feel the radio vibrate in my pocket again. I can also hear a buzzing in Natalie's ear as she pulls away, listening to someone.

"I'm sorry," she says to the person. "But he's going." She listens to the voice then says to me, alarmed, "They're going to try and stop you."

"Advise them against that. Tell them my rescue pilots are hostile."

"It won't stop them," says Natalie. "You're the greatest thing to happen to this planet and they don't want to lose you. We haven't learnt enough from you."

The radio continues to buzz in my pocket and I answer it. The voice says, "Sixty seconds, Jack. Keep a distance until the thrusters are off."

"Got it," I reply. Then, to Natalie, I propose something. "Come with me."

"What?" she asks.

"Come with me. You want to learn from me? From us? Then grab your luggage from the car and come with me."

"What?" she says, again. "But...? No, don't be stupid."

435

"I'm serious. I'm sure there's room for one more. Come back with me."

"I can't," says Natalie, shaking her head. "I can't. That's crazy."

"You said you would come with me," I say.

Natalie stares into my face. "You knew, didn't you?" she accuses.

"Knew what?"

"When you asked me, I could tell you were being sly. You knew they were coming! You were never going to come to the facility!"

"We can argue this point later! But right now you need to make a decision! This is a once in a lifetime chance to see another world."

Natalie shakes her head. "I can't just leave..."

"You told me that you would do anything to come to my planet and study my race. Here is your chance."

"I didn't think it would be this sudden!"

"I'll bring you back," I say. "I promise I'll bring you back."

"How? What do you mean?"

"Go and get your bags, Natalie! Don't think about it. Just get them. I will give you the chance to go to another planet. To meet a whole new race of humans. You will see things that change the way you thought about everything."

Natalie just stares, unable to speak. "But..."

The radio vibrates again. I hear a sound. A distant roar. A creature breathing fire. I look up into the brilliant blue sky as the dot of the rescue vessel appears. Natalie is looking up too. The triangular ship, aerodynamically shaped like one of the old stealth bombers, is dropping through the atmosphere.

"Natalie, get your bags and I'll take you to Earth."

"How do I know that you'll bring me back?"

I search for a response. "I promised the band there would be a reunion tour."

Natalie isn't convinced. She looks at me, then up at the sky and then back at me. I pick up my bags and start walking further into the desert, towards where the vessel will land. Natalie runs back to the car. I watch over my shoulder, seeing her unlock the trunk. She grabs two suitcases and puts them on the ground. She slams it shut and then runs to the rear passenger door and retrieves her other suitcase. I hear her talking to someone, the voice in her ear. With all her luggage, Natalie runs after me.

When I look up, the vessel is only two hundred metres from the ground. Then one hundred. I stand, the flare still spewing to my right. Sleek and dark grey, with an American flag emblazoned on its hull, the vessel lands. Waves of dust envelop me then dissipate.

Something to our left catches my eye. In the distance, along the dry desert road, the clouds of frantic government vehicles fly toward us.

"They're coming!" yells Natalie, as she finally catches up.

"They'd better stay back," I say, as I walk towards the rear of the vessel. Its thrusters have gone quiet, but I can still feel their heat as Natalie and I approach.

A door at the rear of the ship descends into a ramp and I peer inside as we walk around the craft. A man with a facemask and a shock of slicked black hair appears. He is in a NASA issue one-piece, dark blue uniform, and wears sunglasses and a communication headset. He looks down at me.

"Well, if it isn't our castaway," he says through his breathing apparatus.

"Atticus," I say. "Long time no see."

"It has been a very long time," he replies.

"Thanks for picking me up. I hope it wasn't too far out of your way."

Atticus laughs. "Well, I had a smooth run. Didn't get many reds. Not much traffic."

"Good to hear."

Atticus looks at Natalie. Then looks at me. "Who's your friend?"

"This is Natalie," I say. "Have we got room for one more?"

"Just one?" asks Atticus.

"Yes," I reply. "Just one."

"Of course," he says. I can tell Atticus has that trademark smug grin beneath his mask. I know he's studying Natalie from behind his sunglasses.

"How long is the trip?" asks Natalie.

"We made it here in just under eighteen months," replies Atticus.

"It'll fly past," I say to her.

Natalie takes a deep breath and gives me a trusting glance. Then she nods at the fast approaching government vehicles, their engines rising in an orchestra of petrol-fired desperation. "Well, if we're going to do this, we have to move."

"I can't believe you speak English," says Atticus to Natalie.

I start moving up the ramp. "They all do," I say. "But let's talk once we're out of the atmosphere."

Atticus steps aside and allows Natalie and I to board the vessel. "Sounds like a plan. Let's rock and roll," he says. He grabs two more breathing masks from the wall of the rescue ship and hands them to us. "Put these on. You're officially in quarantine."

Natalie takes the mask from him and speaks into her earpiece. "I'm going with them," she says to Heaven's government. "I'm boarding the craft and leaving. I've been assured they will bring me back but I'm going to be gone for a while... it will be years... I know, yes."

The pick-up vessel isn't very large. There are two rows of four seats against the walls, facing each other across the cabin. I look up at the cockpit and there's a pilot sitting there. He's wearing a facemask, but no sunglasses. Atticus rushes past and jumps in the co-pilot's seat.

"Jack, this is one of our crew, Hal Cortez," says Atticus. "We've been sharing the flying duties."

Hal waves at us over his shoulder, his eyes shifting between Natalie and I. He then turns back and starts flicking switches. The vessel lurches as the thrusters turn on, exploding in a deafening roar.

"Strap in!" yells Atticus.

Natalie sits beside me, our luggage sprawled on the floor in front of us. We both pull the breathing masks on and position them over our faces. They cover our mouth and nose.

"This is really happening?" she yells over the volume of the thrusters.

I just nod, my stomach clenched with anxiety. Natalie reaches out and squeezes my hand. We pull down the padded safety bars, locking ourselves in as if we're on a rollercoaster. Natalie takes my hand again and squeezes it as we leave the ground. I turn my head and look through a small porthole window, which is large enough to see the bevy of government vehicles and trucks screeching to a halt outside. Men in black suits exit their vehicles and stare in awe. Then I see helicopters arriving, hovering and keeping their distance. They watch helplessly as we float higher and higher, disappearing.

"Jack, are any of these bogies worth worrying about?" calls Atticus.

I look at Natalie. "He means the helicopters," I tell her.

She shakes her head. "They're not armed."

"They're chicks," I call back to Atticus.

Natalie still clenches my hand as I turn back to the porthole, the ground now out of sight. The choppers remain in their circumference, watching. They make no attempt to stop us. They float passively and peacefully.

We float upward and upward before rocketing away into the darkness of space. Stars form a canopy and my chest tightens as I look down on Heaven. I have been returned to the same vantage point I had before my emergency landing. But this time my emotional state is quite different and I'm moving in the opposite direction. I thought Earth might be gone from me forever. But here I am moving back into the sky with an incredible creature by my side, squeezing my hand. Natalie demonstrates a level of bravery unlike anything I've ever witnessed. When I left Earth, I had years to train and prepare. To steel myself. But Natalie has risked everything on a whim.

Gravity releases its grip and weightlessness takes over. The luggage at our feet slowly leaves the floor of the craft.

"We're almost there," calls Atticus.

Natalie and I crane our necks and look through the windshield. The shape of our ship appears in the tapestry of pinpricked light, one side lit up by the suns' white glow bouncing off Heaven's surface. Soon we're rising into its belly, docking with the giant vessel that has journeyed through the cosmos to retrieve me.

Once we've stepped through the airlocks, gravity returns and we can walk properly around the craft. Natalie and I are immediately led to the medical quarters. We meet a physician named Dr. Sigmund Thompson, a tall, thin man with short blonde hair and a faint Scandinavian accent. He starts running tests on Natalie and I, to ascertain our level of health and whether our bodies carry unseen harm. This is standard protocol. It's also an opportunity for him to investigate Natalie's anatomy. He takes a blood sample. I never leave her side. I smile reassuringly, but Natalie can only see my eyes over the facemask. As I would expect of her, she remains calm and composed and obliging when asked to undress. Natalie is gentle and obedient, clearly fascinated by everything around her. Despite bringing her here, my desire is to take care of her. Not that she is the kind of woman to ever be dependent on someone. But her hand is a heavy weight in my own.

Once the initial inspection of Natalie is complete, I am told that we have to be separated until both of our time in quarantine is over. We will be isolated in observation rooms until Dr. Thompson runs his tests. I tell Natalie that everything will be fine and to oblige the desires of our new hosts. She nods and is led away, up a corridor, by Dr. Thompson and his assistant. She looks back over her shoulder. For the first time I see something like fear in Natalie's eyes.

I lie back on the bed in one corner of the room and watch some news bulletins on a tablet, which is propped on my lap. I'm shocked and awestruck by much of what I see. I am shown the relatively brief history of Earth that unfolded during my absence. Box office records. Celebrities dying, marrying and having children. The changing of prime ministers and presidents. Sex scandals. Drug scandals. But no mention of Earth's conditions. No update on its escalating natural disasters and inter-nation violence. I realise that someone onboard is censoring this footage, controlling the live feed and blocking what my crew members don't want me to see. There will be some glib psychological reasoning for this. I'm sure it's one of our many protocols designed to ease me back into my planet's version of humanity.

I am in an examination room, sitting opposite Dr. Thompson. We're both wearing facemasks, as I'm still in quarantine. The walls and floor are sterile and white, but have a faint green discolouration. The table is cold and metal, as are the chairs. They're bolted down. To my right is a mirrored, one-way window. Beyond it is a viewing room and I know members of the crew are watching. Privacy is a state of mind.

"Are we still in orbit?" I ask.

"Yes," replies Dr. Thompson as he attaches me to a lie detector. It's a small, black box on the table between us. Its monitors and readings are on the side that faces him. A lens is aimed at me. A large black, empty eye. Black wires tie my wrists to the device. Two more wires are attached to electrodes on my temple. This is standard routine during internal interrogations. "We are unable to leave until we are in possession of three more specimens."

"Yes, of course," I reply. Part of my original mission was to have two males and two females captured and brought to the Endeavour.

I was expected to have the four specimens available to my rescuers, depending on what species I found. All I've brought back to the Santa Maria is Natalie. "It won't be difficult," I add. "I know exactly where we can go."

"Excellent," nods Dr. Thompson. His eyes convey a smile beneath his facemask. "Atticus will discuss those details with you. The sooner we have our specimens the sooner we can return home."

"Will Natalie... be alright?" I ask.

Dr. Thompson studies me before answering. "She won't feel any pain. Is that what you're asking?"

"Yes," I reply.

Dr. Thompson glances at the readings on the lie detector, gauging my response. He then reclines in his seat, using casual body language as a means to relax me. This makes me feel inclined to unsettle him. "Now I just need to begin with a few basic questions."

"You know I'm trained to beat one of these lying machines," I say.

"Well, we have updated the technology slightly while you've been gone. As you no doubt noticed, I don't even need to ask you any validation questions. The machine is mapping you already."

"Impressive."

"Firstly, I need to ask about your time on the planet. How would you describe it?"

"Enjoyable."

"How so?"

"It's a nice place, Dr. Thompson. I like it."

"Judging by Natalie's speech, clothing and general mannerisms, it seems that they have a semblance of social order."

"Indeed they do."

"Where did you fit into that social order?"

"I was a labourer."

"They put you to work? Manual labour?"

"I chose to work. It was an honest living."

"Could you elaborate on your role there? What sort of work did you do?"

"What's going to happen to Natalie?" I ask.

Dr. Thompson's eyes narrow. "We could talk more about Natalie... if you would prefer."

441

"What happens to her next?" I ask.

He doesn't reply. Instead he again glances down at the various screens on his side of the lie detector. "Have you developed a bond with her?"

"A little."

"Have you engaged in sexual intercourse with her."

"No."

Dr. Thompson glances at the machine. Then he asks, "By human standards, she is a healthy, attractive female. Have you had sexual thoughts about her?"

"Yes."

"Have you acted on those thoughts?"

"Be more specific."

"Have you ever made sexual advances towards her? Or directly propositioned her for sex?"

"No."

"Did you engage in sexual intercourse with any of the inhabitants of this planet?"

"What's going to happen to Natalie?" I ask.

"Are my questions making you uncomfortable, captain?"

I lean forward. "I very rarely feel discomfort." Dr. Thompson stares at my face, then at the machine, then at the one-way mirror. "There's no need to look at them, doctor."

"Is that so?" he asks, adjusting his facemask.

"You're not supposed to acknowledge them."

"Why are you asking what will happen to Natalie when you already know our protocol?"

"Humour me."

"We're going to study her."

"I don't recall the protocol demanding that you be humane. I don't want her to feel any pain."

Dr. Thompson nods, to reassure me. "Of course. Once it is time for the more thorough biological exams, we will put the subject into an induced coma. For many of the other physical examinations, if the subject is required to be conscious, we will use all necessary anesthetics so that she is comfortable."

"So we're already calling her *the subject*?" I ask. There's a pain in my chest that I try to ignore.

Dr. Thompson's eyes smile. "Captain, I realise you have been in the wilderness for a long time. It is not lost on any of the members of this crew that your ingenuity and courage is vital to the success of our mission..."

"You flatter me, doctor."

"But I must remind you," he continues, "that our greater objective here is... monumental. Please remember our training and the necessary sacrifices that we have made."

Images of Natalie naked and splayed open on an autopsy table radiate with clarity, flickering somewhere behind my retinas. A grotesque premonition of what's to come. I look into Dr. Thompson's eyes. I can see that cold, reptilian tick that we humans expose when pushed. When you break us down and peel away our daily decorum and social extravagance, we are scared little creatures with sharp teeth. We are the result of backwards evolution. An example of the wrong species' ascension of the food chain. Dr. Thompson is the ugliness.

I have brought Natalie up here to meet the beast, knowing that I couldn't meet my rescuers empty handed. I initially chose her with the same calculating pair of eyes that Dr. Thompson now needles at me. Every drop of blood, every organ removed, weighed and photographed, every specimen jar she is separated into will be a further example of the evil and desperation I was born into. That I have propped like Atlas. That I have used as an excuse to betray others. My compliance in this interview only perpetuates the spread of contagion.

There is no concept of night and day in the quarantine chamber. But there is a small porthole through which I can see Heaven as the Santa Maria twists through its orbit. Soon I will need to debrief Captain O'Connor about their military capabilities and from where we can find further specimens. More people to abduct and dissect. Hours move sluggishly but give me time to plan my next move. The various experts among the crew will be pouring over the samples I brought with me. They will be pawing over Natalie.

I wonder if the penny has dropped. If my lover has worked out why I convinced her to come with me. When she realises my betrayal she will never trust me again. I could hardly blame her. Natalie will look on me as she did Brannagh. On a literal level she will comprehend what I have done, but her insight into the enormity of my actions will be hampered by her awe. Her horror. I am the gleeful sadist known only through her planet's scriptures. I am the archaic ideology. The Fallen One. Natalie will shudder at my cruelty but her intuition will tell her not to fear me. That fear is the blood that nourishes hatred. She will attempt to forgive me, but I may break her forever.

My quarantine room is sparse. There's a simple bed, bolted to the floor. It's comfortable. There is a television screen behind a Perspex panel. The fact that my surroundings are similar to a prison cell is not lost on me. I'm in a metal husk, except for the wall and door by the corridor. These are transparent. This is so I can be observed. A one-sided aquarium. The overall design is decidedly unimaginative, but effectively airtight. I stare at the wall where it meets the floor and ceiling, my brain whirring. It's well sealed. Escape is impossible.

A woman appears in the corridor and looks into my room. She is young compared to the rest of the crew, has a kind face and is dressed in surgeon's garb. I watch as she walks to the other side of the doorframe and talks into a receiver. The corresponding speaker on my side of the frame emits her voice.

"Hello," she says, in a British accent. She's not wearing a facemask and I can see her smile.

I stand and walk to my receiver, depressing the button. "Hi," I say.

"My name is Louise Merchant. I'm an assistant to Dr. Thompson."

"Nice to meet you, Louise. You're a doctor too?"

"I am. You may not remember, but we have met before. Many years ago at a conference. I was also at your farewell party."

"You look familiar."

"I've been sent to see how you're doing. Can we bring you anything?"

"I'd love it if you could tell me how much longer I'll be in here."

"It shouldn't be too much longer," says Louise, in a tone designed to reassure me. "Obviously we're being extremely thorough. There are extensive tests we need to run."

"Of course," I say. "Can you tell me how Natalie is?"

"She's fine," smiles Louise. "I was just with Dr. Thompson looking at some of her results and, well, needless to say, we are fascinated by her. The identical nature of her dialect and biology... it's unbelievable. It will make things so much easier for us."

"I am concerned about her welfare," I say.

"She is not in any distress," replies Louise. "I promise you."

"Good."

"How are you feeling? Do you still feel well?"

"Fit and ready."

"How about emotionally?"

"Boredom has definitely set in. Other than that, I'm very relieved to be a part of this mission again."

"You've always been a part of it. The samples you've brought with you are fascinating. Particularly the cancer treatments. We're already analysing them. There's every chance we can have them synthesised by the time we return home."

"Great," I say. I pause and ask, "Louise, can you be honest with me?"

"Of course."

"What's happening back on Earth? What was the last update?"

"We haven't had contact for six months but before we left, the situation was bleak," says Louise, solemnly. "When you didn't return on schedule and news spread that your mission had failed... people panicked. The wild zones increased. They were evacuating San Francisco as we were leaving. It was believed it might be below sea level within three months. The people of every continent are receding from the coast. In terms of politics... let's just say that the redistribution of populations is not going smoothly."

I've dreaded my next question. "What about... Amber?"

Louise pauses. "The last I heard... Amber was back in rehab. She is still confined to the clinic. But, as you know, she's a fighter. I'm sure she can beat it. She's getting the very best treatment."

"I've never believed she can beat it."

Louise seems genuinely shocked. "Oh, well... until the addiction wins we should entertain the idea that she will get better."

"Anything is possible," I smile.


"Hey there, buddy," says Atticus O'Connor from across the interrogation desk. He's lost his sunglasses, but still has the facemask. It doesn't hide his smugness.

"Atticus," I smile through my own facemask.

"Fuck I wish they'd hurry up with this quarantine shit," he laughs, shaking his head. "How fucking ridiculous do these things look?"

"Very."

"Now first of all, I'm going to turn this bad boy off," he says, flicking a switch on the lie detector. It powers down. "You and I have had the exact same training. You were the star at the academy, so if I can beat this piece of shit then there's no doubt you can."

"I'm a bit rusty," I reply, pulling the electrodes from my forehead and the straps from my wrist.

"You've been out in the wilderness, brother!" laughs Atticus again. I'm not actually his brother.

"But still on a mission."

"Of course," he says, his tone calming down. "Which is why you and I are here. It's time to talk turkey."

"Alright."

"Now I've been going over the stuff you brought with you. The data, the books and all that."

"Is it helpful?"

"Very, very," he replies nodding. "I hate to sound... a little twisted, but this is going to be a piece of cake, isn't it?"

"Yes," I reply. "Their military capabilities are limited."

"Well, as you know, captain, if they're hospitable and, you know, extend a welcoming olive branch, then it won't matter what their fire power is."

"I don't believe they will show resistance."

"Okay," nods O'Connor. "So that's your official assessment?"

"Yes. They are peaceful. Very peaceful."

"In what sense?"

"I'm not saying they're all floating about, high on life, but they are very calm and rational."

"Violence is a last resort, then?"

"In a broader sense, I don't think they view violence as any resort. It doesn't factor in."

"Right..." says O'Connor, clearly perplexed.

"There is violence in them, especially when they need to defend themselves... I have witnessed violent crimes during my time there. But... it is, sort of, contained. It's comparatively rare. It's dealt with and learned from."

O'Connor nods, taking this in. "What sort of violence?"

"Well, their media would report random things. The odd stabbing and shooting. Lover's tiffs. A few hit-and-runs. There was one particularly bad case in which a man was killing drug addicts."

"Drug addicts?" asks O'Connor.

"Yes, he was a serial killer. But... he was apprehended and dealt with."

"Right," nods O'Connor. "But what about larger stuff. No military conflicts? War zones? Dictatorships?"

"No," I reply.

O'Connor asks me for more details on their military capabilities. He quizzes me on their battle psychology, looking for insights that aren't in the texts I brought with me. I advise him on locations where our "life rafts", as they are called, can arrive from Earth and which less populated areas will be easier to claim as our own. When I tell him all I know about Heaven, O'Connor changes his line of questioning.

"Now, one of the other things we need to discuss is the accident on Endeavour. I need a full debriefing. What did you see? Do you know what went wrong?" he asks.

"As I told you when you were on your way here," I reply, casually, "I really don't know. There was an explosion. I happened to be in the section of the craft that had the escape pods. Otherwise I would have been killed."

"You said you saw the wreckage?"

"I glimpsed it," I reply. "But I didn't have time to take it in. I saw through a window that an area of the ship's outer wall was blown away. Near the storage area. I can't be sure what caused the explosion."

"Neither can we," says O'Connor. "As you would be aware, very few explosives are kept on each craft and the ones that are require activation. There wouldn't have been anything explosive in the cargo area."

"That had occurred to me," I say.

"Do you have any reason to believe that one of your fellow crew members may have been responsible for the explosion?"

"No."

"As the sole survivor, the idea that you are responsible for the explosion remains a valid inference," says O'Connor. "I'm sure you can appreciate that."

"I can, yes," I say. "I would ask you the same question if our roles were reversed."

"For protocol's sake, do you mind if I turn this lie detector back on?" he asks.

"Not at all," I reply.

As O'Connor switches on the lie detector a piercing siren explodes around us. My interrogator clearly believes the two are linked, flicking the machine on and off. But the emergency alarm continues to screech, almost shaking the walls. A bright red light above the door blinks rapidly. My muscles lock. I haven't heard an evacuation alarm since the explosion on the Endeavour. In a heartbeat I'm back on that ship, racing to the escape pod.

O'Connor yells something at me through his mask, but it is drowned by the piercing, dizzying siren. He rises from his chair and races to the door of the room. Instinct animates me and I move after him. As he grabs the metal of the lock to rotate it and exit, I punch him in the right kidney with all my strength. When he instinctively grabs at his lower back, I wrap my arms around his throat in a choke lock. One hand pushes on the back of his head to force his throat down on my other arm, which is immovably braced across his larynx. With the mask sealed around his face, there's nowhere for his head to move. The pressure crushes his throat.

O'Connor, like me, has been trained to escape most hostile situations. But racing through his brain will be the realisation that he won't escape. Without a weapon, all he can do is lift his feet and kick at the door, which he does. With his weight forced against me, I stumble backwards. But I manage to stay on my feet as we slam into the opposite wall. The hand behind his head finds the thick rubber strap of the mask and twists. My other hand shifts to the front of the mask and aids the rotation. Even though the emergency alarm is overwhelming in volume, I hear O'Connor's skull snap away from the top of his spine. His body goes limp and we now fall sideways down the wall, across part of the observation window, before crashing to the floor. I push his body away from me, trying to get to my feet. Propped on an elbow, pinned against the wall, I turn his head towards me. It shifts with sickening ease, twisting backward. His eyes are still wide, parted in horror. But above the facemask he is looking through me. Lifeless. Somewhere else.

I shift up to my knees, extricating myself from his corpse. Looking over the interrogation desk I see the door to the room is open. O'Connor must have unlocked it and kicked it open as I grabbed him. But then something moves into the room. I drop down, peering above the table. Two feminine hands hold the barrel of a rather large hand-cannon. They're shaking, red streaks of blood splattered along toned, bare arms. Natalie steps into the doorway, dressed in a hospital gown. She's covered in blood. The right side of her face is caked with dark chunks of what appears to be brain matter. Her hair is matted. The white garment draped over her looks like a Jackson Pollock. When I realise it's Natalie I raise a reassuring hand. But as her wide, terrified eyes turn on me she fires a bullet. I feel it displace the air around my head. It misses and ricochets into the ceiling. I scramble away from her, staying low against the wall until I run out of space to flee. I curl into the corner, my hands raised in surrender. Natalie shudders as she steps further into the room, moving around the interrogation table. The gun stays pointed at me. I wrench my mask from my face and toss it to the floor. I see a flicker of recognition. Her eyes dart between O'Connor's body and my own. On the side of her weapon is a small red dot. Just at the side of the chamber. She doesn't realise this means the clip is empty.

"Natalie!" I yell, above the siren. "It's me! It's Jack!"

I'm certain she recognises me. Anger tenses Natalie's face. She again looks at O'Connor's body and I hope she takes his murder as a sign that I'm on her side. That she can trust me. Natalie levels the gun at my head. I can't wait for her to pull the trigger. When she realises she's out of ammunition she might run. I spring to my feet and pounce, covering the six feet between us in a split second. She clicks at the useless trigger and as I tackle her to the ground the gun bounces across the floor. Natalie flails about and I keep a strong hold on her. She repeatedly elbows me in the ribs and I brace against the pain of the repeated blows. But I don't stop yelling next to Natalie's ear. "I'm sorry, I'm sorry, I'm sorry..."

The scene in the autopsy room would have made a nice addition to Brannagh's Marioneta de Carne exhibit. I stand in the doorway, scanning the area, my ears still ringing from the alarm. Natalie remains outside in the hall, huddled against the wall of the corridor. She doesn't want to see inside the room. She is well aware of the state she left it in following her desperate escape. The anesthetic they used on Natalie, despite their reassurances that she would feel no pain, didn't work as planned. While her muscles were briefly paralysed, her brain was awake and her ears heard everything.

"They were going to cut me up," said Natalie, shaking, as we walked through the Santa Maria to this room. "I heard everything.

What they were going to do to me."

When Dr. Thompson briefly stepped out to retrieve part of his equipment from another laboratory, Dr. Merchant turned her back. Natalie had regained feeling in her body and grabbed the nearest weapon, which happened to be a thirteen-inch surgical blade. Now it lies in the middle of the room, its glistening edge sharp enough to separate flesh and bone as if they were slow-cooked lamb. Natalie slashed at Dr. Merchant's face and it divided her from ear to ear. As Dr. Thompson calmly returned, having not heard Dr. Merchant's shocked, almost silent gurgle, Natalie was waiting behind the door. She pushed the knife through his throat.

"Fuck me," I say, looking at the two bodies. "You really did a number on these two."

"I had no choice," responds Natalie.

Dr. Merchant lies in a pool of blood, dark liquid congealing at the edges of her immense facial wound. I notice her chest move. Then her throat shifts, trying to breath. A fish next to its tank. I'm reminded of Natalie's gun in my hand, which I have since reloaded. From what she told me, the firearm belonged to Hal Cortez, whose body I will find on the floor of the flight deck. I step into the room and walk to where Louise is lying, her hands outstretched by her sides. I'm grateful that her eyes don't look at me as I pull the trigger.

In the corridor, Natalie is still pressed against the wall. The soiled gown is wet and sticks to her quaking figure, the pungent smells of blood and sweat are heavy around us. I put the gun on the ground and try to hold her. She pushes me away, uncoiling in anger. I try a second time to pull her into my arms and she slaps me across the face and fires punches into my chest.

"Why?" she screams, "why did you bring me here?"

"I'm sorry," I say.

"I don't fucking care! Why? Tell me!"

"If I arrived empty handed, without a specimen, they wouldn't trust me. I knew you could handle yourself. I couldn't just bring some innocent person up here..."

"You fucking used me, Jack! You knew they were going to cut me up!"

"I hoped I could stop that from happening. I was going to save you, I swear."

"Were you? Really? Well you fucking didn't!"

450

"You're right," I reply, feeling heat behind my eyes. I turn to walk away.

"Where are you going?" she yells.

"I'm going to find the escape pods."

"Of course you are," she scoffs. "You're a survivor. You always know where the exit is. It doesn't matter who you leave in the room."

I fight my urge to respond and keep walking.

"Tell me why I shouldn't just shoot you," says Natalie.

When I turn back she is aiming the gun at me.

"It wouldn't be self defense," I say.

Her face contorts in frustration. "Then tell me why. Why are you here? Why were they going to cut me up?"

"To study you. To learn your weaknesses so we could take everything from you. You won't ever understand, Natalie. We're everything you're not. You're everything we could have been. You made a fist of your existence. We made a farce of ours."

There are four escape pods. They're almost identical to the models on Endeavour and despite a few obvious upgrades I'm confident I can operate them.

Natalie is in one of the bathrooms. The door is locked and I can hear running water. I leave her and look through the laboratories. In one of the storage spaces I locate Natalie's bags, which I place outside the bathroom for her to find when she exits. Wearing her own clothes might bring her some small comfort.

Cortez lies dead on the flight deck. He is at the foot of one of the main control panels, where he desperately reached the emergency alarm. Natalie had already severed his right hand so he couldn't grab his weapon. She then took his hand-cannon and fired a shot into the back of his head. The damage explains why Natalie was covered in gore. There are more gaping bullet wounds in his back.

I sit in the captain's seat and inspect the expanse of switches, gauges and meters in front of me. I can operate the Santa Maria, but never do I entertain the idea of flying it back to Earth. In front of me, through the thick windshield, is the orb of Heaven. Stars flicker in the black backdrop.

"Hey," says Natalie's voice, softly, somewhere behind me. "What are you doing?"

"I'm just deciding what to do with this marvel of modern

451

spaceflight."

"Can you fly it?"

"Yes," I say. "I could program a delayed trajectory into deep space, and give us enough time to escape in one of the pods."

"I've got a better idea," says Natalie, sitting in the co-pilot seat next to me. She's clean of blood, wearing a pristine white dress, her hair limp from the shower. "Land it."

"Land it?" I say.

"We can learn from it," says Natalie. "Perhaps we can be prepared for when your people return."

"There are nuclear weapons on this ship," I say. "Bombs that can turn a city to dust, vaporising every person that lives there. There are biological weapons on board that could wipe out your entire species."

"Don't we deserve to learn of these things?" asks Natalie.

"You've done nothing to deserve them," I say. "You don't know what destruction they could bring."

Natalie stares out through the windshield, thinking. She then steps out of her chair, walking around the cabin, gazing at the floor to ceiling banks of dials and devices. Every so often she stops and takes a closer look at one of the meters, monitors and gauges. I hope that her silence means our conversation on the future of the Santa Maria is over. I intend to set it in on a course into deep space and destroy it.

Natalie stops and points at something. "This looks familiar?"

"That's the entertainment unit," I smile. "They look quite similar on both planets."

Without any encouragement, she presses the play button. It doesn't occur to me to try and stop her. The sound of Kansas's 'Carry On Wayward Son' appears from speakers all around us.

Natalie stands and listens. "I know this song," she says. "It's one of your songs." A voice other than my own has appeared. Natalie listens, concentrating. "Is that *you* singing? It sounds different." I leave my seat and turn off the song. Realisation is already on her face. "Did you...?"

"I'm not in the mood for music right now."

Natalie extends an arm to hold me away. She skips to the next track. I can see from the digital display that there are many songs loaded into the playlist. Pearl Jam's 'Rearviewmirror' plays, which is unlucky for me. It's a Big Bang Theory fan favourite. Eddie Vedder's voice appears and Natalie knows immediately that it's not my own.

"Have you been...? Have you been playing other people's music? From Earth?"

I face away, pretending I haven't heard her. Natalie keeps flicking through songs. Many I haven't released with Big Bang Theory, but every so often she finds another familiar tune. The Shins, Ryan Adams, Neil Young and Manic Street Preachers. They're all in the playlist of the Santa Maria.

"Could we please focus on our escape?" I snap.

Natalie smiles. She switches off the music. "Land the Santa Maria," she says.

"Seriously, Natalie –" I say, before she cuts me off.

"Jack, bring us the gift of this ship and prove to me that you're one of us."

It's a compelling offer, but a bad idea.

"The weapons on this spacecraft never brought us any peace," I say, shaking my head.

"You need to trust us," she says. "We can even study the bodies of the crew. They won't have died in vain."

"I don't know..." I say, shaking my head.

"And I'll keep your secret," she adds, nodding towards the entertainment unit. "I can keep playing these songs. I've got a feeling I'll find more Big Bang Theory classics."

The unit could have a hundred thousand songs in its playlist, which, if I successfully download and sneak off the ship, would ensure my continued genius. But allowing Heaven to learn our technology could bring its end. On one hand, they are a levelheaded bunch. But they can be corrupted. It's a complex decision. But, in the face of losing Natalie's trust forever, I relent.

"Okay," I say. "You keep my musical inspirations a secret. I'll land this ship and explain to your scientists how the bastard works."

"Deal," smiles Natalie.

I locate body bags in a supplies closet. They're lightweight, airtight and durable. Natalie and I seal each crew member and together we drag and carry them through the long, winding corridors of the spacecraft, from the place of their final moments to the freezer off the kitchen and communal dining area. We lay them tightly across the floor, like pilchards in a tin. Then I lock the door.

Natalie's face remains knotted in anguish.

"I can't believe I'm responsible for that," she says, softly.

"Not all of them," I offer. "I killed Atticus. And I'm partly responsible for Louise's death. But regardless of who did what, it was self-defense. You can't give guilt a second thought."

"I don't feel any better about it," she says, and walks to the silver communal dining table and sits at one of the bench seats.

"If you hadn't taken them down, then, as we speak, your body would be in fifty different containers."

"And that would be your fault," she says, eyeing me.

"Indirectly," I stress. "Indirectly my fault."

"So did you write *any* of Big Bang Theory's songs?" she asks.

I sigh and sit down across the table from her. "Let's not talk about this. I'm hungry. How about I cook us something? I think I saw corn chips in there. I haven't had them in, like, five years. You will be mind- blown."

Natalie scoffs. "Answer my question."

"What do you want me to say?" I bark.

"Just tell me the truth," she shrugs.

"That's really rich coming from you. The queen of deception and manipulation."

"I was doing a job," she says, tersely.

"You were," I nod. "And you definitely went above and beyond the call of duty."

"What's that supposed to mean?"

"I'm too tired for this," I say.

"Why won't your answer my question?" Natalie pushes. "I want to know if any of those words that you sung, the words I've been hanging on since you appeared, are *yours*."

"They're all mine. They're all part of me. I just didn't write them."

Natalie takes this in and then gives a small nod of acceptance. I can't decipher her expression. Then, after a heavy pause, she asks, "So who are you then? What do you do, Jack?"

I smile. "That's the first time you've asked me that."

After calling another truce with Natalie, I convince her that we both need sleep before I land the aircraft on Heaven. She agrees, but chooses separate quarters and locks the door. I swallow my annoyance and lie alone. I wait half an hour until I believe she could be asleep and then quietly step into the corridor.

On the flight deck I log into one of the computers and find that it's password protected. I try my main access password from the Endeavour and it doesn't work. Perhaps they didn't trust me. I then search through the crew's quarters until I find the room that housed O'Connor. He wasn't a very clean individual. Clothes are strewn over the floor and there's a small dresser next to his unmade bedding. On one of the cream walls, opposite the bed, is a large television. Around the other walls are a dozen digiframes with pictures that cycle continuously. Two of the larger frames show only pictures of scantily clad and naked women. Others display various sports stars and random holiday locations. Nature and weather shots. On the dresser is another digiframe with pictures of his family and friends. Pictures of home. I watch for a few minutes. I jolt slightly when I see my own face appear among the images. But it disappears in the cycle of photographs in the frame.

I rifle through the drawers and storage cupboards of the room, looking for anything that might contain his password. On a shelf in a cupboard I find a tablet. I switch it on and start flipping through the documents in his personal folder. I find his ID file, which is a comprehensive history. His service records, education, background information. It's all here. I stop at a page and stare at his date of birth. It's the same as mine.

In his walk-in closet is a small metal safe. On the keypad I type my date of birth and the bolt lock clicks open. Inside is a small firearm, a small container of what appears to be cyanide and also a few loose pieces of paper. One has a twelve-digit number on it.

Back on the flight deck I use the password and it works. In their system, I scan through the spacecraft's files until I find the recorded audio logs of my conversations with the Santa Maria's crew before their arrival. My updates, my debriefings. I put on a comms headpiece and listen through the recordings, systematically deleting them.

Natalie emerges from her quarters and sits in the co-pilot's seat. I flick on the thrusters and they build in heat before exploding in white fire. Together we descend from our orbit, Heaven slowly filling our view through the windshields. I reach out to take Natalie's hand and she accepts it for a moment before pulling from my grasp.

Heaven opens its legs for me again, its eyes glazing over with sweet, reflected light. Somewhere a planet faces the consequences of its actions. While I've protected my new home from those that covet its beauty and exquisite sensibilities, I cannot shake the feeling that I am a single cancer cell for which Heaven has no cure.

# ABOUT THE AUTHOR

Nick Milligan embarked on an entertainment journalism career in 2002. Since that time he has become one of Australia's most respected film and music pundits. His articles have appeared in publications such as *Rolling Stone, Hotpress, Frankie* and *Smash Hits.* Milligan's past positions include editor-in-chief of *Reverb Magazine,* music and film editor of *YEN* and sub-editor and entertainment reporter with Fairfax Media.

Milligan has interviewed and profiled a wide array of entertainers and writers, including Matt Damon, Charlotte Gainsbourg, Frank Black, Kim Gordon, Alice Cooper, Juliette Lewis, Ice Cube, Dylan Moran, Bill Bailey, Peaches, Marlon Wayans, Joe Perry, Pete Townshend, Marilyn Manson, Abbie Cornish, Huey Lewis and Bret Easton Ellis.

Milligan lives in Newcastle, Australia.

Follow Nick Milligan
Blog: www.nicholasmilligan.com
Twitter: @NickMilligan_
Instagram: @Nick_milligan
Facebook:
www.facebook.com/enormitynovel
www.facebook.com/nickmilliganauthor

36156142R00287

Made in the USA
San Bernardino, CA
17 May 2019